A Paco and Molly Murder Mystery

Hot Grudge Sunday

By Rosemary and Larry

Mild

Second in the Paco and Molly Mystery Series
Along With :
- *Locks and Cream Cheese*
and
- *Boston Scream Pie*

Magic Island Literary Works • Severna Park, MD • 2013

Second Edition 2013 Magic Island Literary Works.
     ISBN 978-0-9838597-4-1

First Edition—2004, **AmErica House** (Publish America)
     ISBN 1-4137-3945-8

Printed in the United States of America by
Magic Island Literary Works.

Interior book design by Larry Mild.
Cover design by Marilyn Drea, Mac-In-Town, Annapolis, MD.

Library of Congress Cataloging-in-Publication Data
Mild, Rosemary P. ; Mild, Larry M.

Mild, Rosemary P. ; Mild, Larry M.
ISBN 978-0-9838597-4-1

10 9 8 7 6 5 4 3 2 1

<u>**Dedication:**</u>

For our beloved grandchildren—
Alena, Craig, Ben, Leah, and Emily

For our wonderful children—
Jackie and Myrna

For our marriage—soul mates, partners, lovers

Acknowledgments

The two of us send a huge bear hug to Jessica Lopez Pearce, a United States Park ranger now working in Colorado. As a former Grand Canyon National Park Ranger, she lent us invaluable expertise so that we might get it right. We Thank her for her patience, enthusiasm, and valuable insights

We thank the following individuals for their helpful technical advice: Officer Mark Ruffennach of the Scottsdale, Arizona, Police Department; Dr. Robert F. Highsmith, Professor of Molecular and Cellular Physiology and Associate Dean and Director, Office of Research and Graduate Education, University of Cincinnati College of Medicine; and the Engineering Department and Web site of Fi-Shock Inc., Knoxville, Tennessee. We also gleaned useful information from the excellent publications issued by the National Park Service and AAA.

Many thanks to our former Maryland Writers' Association critique group and our professional writers' critique group in Honolulu, whose members gave us insightful advice and encouragement.

To Ann and John Pollack for their keen observations and suggestions. And for always cheering us on.

Disclaimer

Hot Grudge Sunday is a work of fiction. Its characters, their names, and the events in which they are embroiled are entirely the products of the authors' imaginations. Any resemblance to actual events, locales, or persons living or dead is purely coincidental.

Hot Grudge Sunday draws information from many sources. Any errors are strictly our own and, of course, unintended.

Contents

Contents

Chapter 1
GREAT ESCAPADES
Day One, Thursday, September 10, 1981

THE OUTRAGEOUS CAPER took place in suburban Denver, where a branch of the Alpine State Bank occupied a strip-mall space much like a narrow volume in library stacks. A drive-through alley passed between the bank and Mattress Heaven next door, leaving the appearance of a book borrowed. But certainly nothing was borrowed that morning.

Inside the bank, an elfin woman in her mid-thirties tapped out a personal letter on her IBM typewriter. Branch Manager Dora Ireland typed to look busy, to fill the glacially paced minutes, for no one had come through the front door in the past hour. She reached for her half-eaten sugared doughnut, took another bite, and washed it down with cold coffee from a mug bearing the bank logo.

The only other employee, a teller, accepted a check at the drive-through window. "And how would you like that, Mrs. Zales? In twenties?" asked Claire in her practiced, chatty tone.

Dora peeled the page from the typewriter to admire her letter. As she leaned back, her peripheral vision took in two newly arrived patrons waiting in the armchairs of the small lobby. A gray-haired woman with granny glasses hunched over her knitting. The needles clicked rapidly, producing a blue rectangle that grew as Dora watched. A man in army camouflage fatigues and matching peaked cap sat one chair apart from her. His upper body hid behind the Denver Post. Only his cap showed above the headlines.

Dora swiveled herself face front and called out, "Next, please."

The woman tucked her knitting into a large tapestried tote bag and slid to the edge of her seat. Leaning forward, apparently fighting seventy-plus years, she pushed down on the arms of the chair and stood up. Her flowered house dress hung loosely around her body. She shuffled toward the desk.

"Ah, Mrs. Klimple, Alice Klimple, isn't it?"

"Oh, my!" The woman lit up with a crinkled smile. "You're a good one, you are. I got trouble even remembering my own name, let alone somebody else's. And you only met me the one time."

Dora rose to greet her. "Of course, I remember you. You rented a safe deposit box."

"Got somethin' to put in it today, dearie."

"Certainly." Pressing the hidden desk lock, Dora pulled out her bottom right-hand drawer and retrieved a ring of keys. "If you'll just follow me, ma'am."

Behind Dora's desk stood an L-shaped partition decorated with branches of anodized gold and silver leaves. This divider shielded the vault entrance and its elephantine, armored door from general view. She led the patron around the divider to a wooden sign-in dais and extracted Mrs. Klimple's card from an alphabetized file.

"I'll need your signature first," she said, holding out a pen.

Alice Klimple, in white cotton gloves, wrote her name slowly in a bold, yet shaky script. She returned the pen and held out her box key. "Number 286," she said.

Dora stepped through the vault doorway to unlock and roll back the folding gate. On either side of her, the walls comprised hundreds of double-locked stainless steel doors in four sizes. A long fluorescent fixture bathed the vault in chalky light. On the rear wall of the vault, an internal door concealed similar boxes and drawers. These contained accounting records, loan contracts, legal documents, currency, and coin for the bank's own use. Bank policy required this door to be kept locked at all times. But its combination proved so difficult that the managers frequently left it unlocked, sometimes even ajar.

Dora slid a small stool into position and stepped up on tiptoe to reach number 286. Taking the key from Alice, he turned it in the lock, along with a second key from her own ring.

"Something smells . . ." Dora gasped.

A hand appeared in front of Dora. A large gauze pad clamped across her mouth and nose. A pungent sensation invaded her nostrils. She tried to steady herself against the wall of steel boxes.

"Mmph! Mumph! Ehhhhhaah!"

Dora tried to peel the fingers away from her face, but they gripped like claws, pulling her slowly backward. The stool! Feeling herself tottering on the edge of it, she struggled to regain her balance . . . to find a handhold or a place to anchor her feet. She tried to turn and face her assailant, but the strength of a woman much younger than Alice held her in place. Soon the foreign sweet odor overtook her, and the manager melted into waiting arms that eased her to the carpet.

Mrs. Klimple moved quickly, using wide duct tape to bind and gag the limp figure on the floor. Alice's long limbs stretched easily to retrieve the ring of keys from box 286. Her adrenaline surged, and she leaped over Dora's slight body in her haste to get to the rear of the vault. The large combination door stood ajar. Alice had noticed it when the bank manager first led her into the vault. She swung the door wide to reveal the larger boxes and drawers reserved for the bank's own use.

Alice felt the walls of the chamber pressing in on her like a time-driven vise as she fumbled to locate the individual drawer keys on the ring. Sweat trickled from her hairline down her neck. The vault's commanding silence shattered each time a key turned in a lock--and again when she upended drawers on the carpeted floor. In less than five minutes, the contents of a dozen drawers lay spread before her. Selecting only packets of fifties and twenties, she stuffed as many as she could into the compartments of her tote. Methodically, she arranged her two skeins of yarn over the stash with the needles protruding.

Alice emerged from the vault doorway and rounded the partition. Over her shoulder, she called out pleasantly, "I certainly will. Sorry I made such a mess of things. You have a nice day now, dearie, y' hear?" Alice resumed her bent, arthritic posture, shuffled through the bank, and continued out the double set of glass doors to the street.

The waiting man seated in the third chair glanced at his watch, folded his paper, and impatiently shook his head. He got up and left the bank, using his newspaper to push open one of the doors.

* * *

At half past eleven, shortly after the disgruntled man had left, Claire finished with her last drive-up customer and turned to speak with her manager. How odd, the desk was still empty. She decided to check on Dora. As Claire passed the divider, she saw the half-open gate, but heard no conversation, no movement. A foreboding added weight to her step as she inched toward the front of the vault.

Claire's eyes locked onto the rear wall. The inner safe door stood open. Among the rows of steel boxes she saw four gaping holes. She backed out of the doorway and stood frozen at the sign-in dais. Her shock melted into awareness only moments later, and she reached for the nearest silent panic alarm.

Still, neither signs nor sounds of life came from within. The frightful prospect of finding Dora dead kept her from entering the vault itself. But what if Dora were alive and needed her? Claire took a deep breath and slid the gate all the way back. The over-turned drawers on the floor at the rear caught her attention first. She stepped inside. Her right foot bumped up against a soft mass. Dora's body!

Screaming, Claire ran out of the vault to the lobby. Once there, common sense took charge. Recalling bank instructions to preserve the crime scene, she locked the front door and returned to the vault.

Her manager had recovered consciousness. As Claire began the painful task of pulling off the duct tape, Dora uttered frantic soprano whimpers. The adhesive left ugly red patches across her cheeks and lips, and she began sobbing in wordless spasms. The teller worked with a pair of scissors to cut the restraints from her manager's wrists and ankles--a task made more difficult by Dora's trembling.

Fists banged on the front door. The police had arrived.

* * *

Several miles from the bank, Alice Klimple hopped off a city bus and strode briskly, shoulders erect, into the side street entrance of the Mile-High Sportsmen's Inn. She paused before an easel to read its sign: WELCOME VERMILION TOURS. MEETING IN BRONCO AUDITORIUM AT 5 P.M. She smiled and headed straight to room 1010. Five minutes later, a man with a folded newspaper entered the hotel and proceeded to the same room.

Inside, they greeted one another with a warm hug and then, holding him at arm's length, she said, "Well, LeRoy, honey, we did it again."

"We shore did, Miz Milton," he replied in an exaggerated Western drawl, "we shore did." Laughing, he removed his sunglasses and cap.

Ruth Milton kicked off her sensible thick-heeled shoes and shed the white cotton gloves and print dress, then the granny glasses, the gray wig, breast padding, and support hose until she stood before him in just bra and panties. Her close-cropped hair, matted with moisture from the tightly fitted wig, looked a shade darker than her natural cocoa brown. She stood before the full-length mirror with the confidence of a woman who exercised regularly. Feeling her husband's yearning eyes upon her, she reached into his partially open shirt and lightly teased the curls on his chest.

"First things first," she whispered.

The dimple in his chin deepened as he smiled in agreement; they still had work to do. LeRoy continued to watch her as he stripped. His bushy hair had been gray since his late twenties. Now at forty-seven, his boxer shorts covered a thick middle, and his five-foot-eight frame was beginning to take on the look of an overfed terrier. He tossed his military outfit on the clothes pile.

The Miltons stuffed their disguises into a green plastic trash bag, just like the ones used by the hotel housekeeping staff. Turning the tapestried tote upside down, Ruth shook the contents out onto the bed. The packets of cash landed in thuds. She tossed the tote and the knitting into the garbage bag.

"A shame," he said.

"What's a shame?"

"Throwing all this good stuff away. And those roomy fatigues felt great."

"Gotta get rid of it all, dearie." She chuckled in her best Alice dialect. Afterward, her expression turned pensive as she thought about the Alpine State Bank. "You know, today--the exposed cash drawers? They left the same rear door open--the one we saw when we cased it last month. It's the tiny combination dials on that model of lock. The settings have to be too precise. Too annoying. Just like at the bank in Ann Arbor. Those wonderful dummies."

LeRoy unscrewed the cap on a large bottle of pancake syrup. He propped the garbage bag open and poured the maple topping in methodical swirls all over their abandoned disguises. The thick, sweet liquid seeped into the dress, the wig, the tote, the skein of blue yarn. "This'll give the yellow jackets and ants a field day," he said. "I'll bet no one will nose into this bag." He tossed the empty bottle on top of the clothes, gathered the garbage bag up into a compact bundle, and set it by the door.

Ruth sat cross-legged on the bed, stacking banded bills into piles of $1,000 each. Sixty-one piles across the bedspread: thirteen piles of fifties and the rest, twenties. Satisfied with the total, she redivided the bills into six nearly equal stacks and carefully fitted them into sturdy cardboard mailer boxes. Then she pulled off the peel--stick backings and smoothed on pre-addressed Flite-Express labels.

"What time is Flite-Ex coming?" he asked her.

"Between four and five. They told me that's as close as they can figure. If the express pickup man doesn't get here on time, you go to the five o'clock Vermilion Tours meeting. You take notes while I wait in the lobby for Flite-Ex."

"I don't want to go to the meeting alone. I'm not good at that," LeRoy whined. "You go to the meeting and I'll wait for the guy."

"If I agree to that, you'll take a nap and miss him altogether. I know you."

"So what?"

"So you want to stash the cash in your carry-on for the next fourteen days? On the whole damn bus tour?"

"Who's gonna know?"

"Stop being so smart-assed with me. We'll both wind up in jail."

"Don't you have any faith in me? What if I take my nap now?"

He lay down on the bed and tried to sleep. So many nights he'd just lain awake and fretted. That didn't help his heart condition. His doctor called it mitral valve prolapse, an unpredictable pounding of timpani drums within the breast. The doctor told him it was nothing serious, but "try to avoid stress." LeRoy wondered how the doc would rate bank heists on the stress scale. Half an hour later, the adrenaline still charged through his veins. He decided no sleep for the wicked.

"Let's go for a dip in the pool. It'll help me unwind," he said.

"You could use it, dear."

After pulling on swim trunks and T-shirt, LeRoy picked up the garbage bag he'd left by the door, carried it around to the restaurant's service area, and threw it in the dumpster, where it landed among dozens of other green plastic bags. By the time he returned to the room, she had donned a one-piece suit with high,

French-cut legs that emphasized her muscular thighs. An amazing body, he thought, for a woman of forty-six.

Ruth closed their room door, rattled the handle to be sure it locked, and they headed down the hall to the pool. She gave his fanny an affectionate squeeze.

Chapter 2
LESSER BEGINNINGS
Same Day, Thursday, September 10, 1981

MOLLY LESOTO CHUCKLED. "They must be newlyweds, too. Did you see where she had her hand?"

Grinning, Paco LeSoto swung the door open to room 1023 in the Mile-High Sportsmen's Inn. But Molly hesitated in the hall. Her eyes remained fixed on the couple in bathing suits hurrying by. When they passed out of view, she turned to her husband of only twenty-seven hours.

Paco slid one arm around Molly's waist. The other reached down behind her chubby knees to carry her across the threshold. Though Molly stood only five feet tall, her beach-ball shape posed a serious threat to his determination.

"No, Paco, no! You'll break your sacroiliback."

He loved the way she talked. Her malapropisms had delighted him from the day they met-: -Mollyprops he called them. He knew her formal learning had ended at sixth grade, but her personal education had continued in the homes of the wealthy and privileged, where she kept house and cooked gourmet feasts. She listened to conversations and stirred the words into an idiomatic stew to flavor her own sweet and sour view of life.

Molly wiggled and squirmed and squealed, but he lifted her anyway. She grabbed him tightly around the neck. The king-sized bed had been his destination, but after a few shorts steps he had to set her down. She continued to clutch him and began to giggle almost hysterically. For now, at age sixty-three, she looked at her first marriage bed.

Paco sensed her apprehension and knew she needed more

9

time. He guided her gently to the windowed wall and drew back the drapes. From behind, he slid his hands around her waist as far as they could reach.

Molly had never been out West, and their tenth floor view of downtown Denver enchanted her. On the floor below, two roof-top tennis courts butted up to the hotel. Beyond, skyscrapers jockeyed for dominance. One, sheathed in copper-colored mirrors, reflected clouds, the setting sun, and neighboring offices. A stone church, resembling a medieval fortress, stubbornly guarded its space. Farther away, mountain crests peeked through a concrete ravine.

"You're seeing the Rockies, my dear," he said.

"My first mountains."

"We're lucky today. Sometimes Denver's so overcast you wouldn't know the mountains existed at all," Paco said, undoing the top two buttons of his new striped sport shirt. Dark bushy brows arched over keen hazel eyes. A thick shock of salt-and-pepper hair fell into place as he ran his fingers through it.

Homicide Detective Paco LeSoto had retired from the Baltimore City Police Department four years ago. He'd moved to rural Black Rain Corners, Maryland, on the Chesapeake Bay only ninety minutes south of the big city to take up part-time police work. The honorary title of inspector went with the small-town job. Three years later, he met Molly Mesta, who collaborated with him on a case at her employer's home. After eleven months of dating, Paco's charm and Molly's homespun humor drew them together. A mutual interest in culinary skills and gourmet dining led to their wedding, truly a marriage made in heaven's kitchen.

Paco's lean strength resulted from a lifetime of police fitness. Molly professionally acquired her rotund expanse in layers of rich cooking for the widowed Dr. Avi Kepple. The psychoanalyst had employed her for the last twenty-four years, and there she had become a family fixture. This honeymoon trip was largely due to Dr. Avi's generosity.

Together, Paco and Molly pulled the wicker love seat in

front of the massive window, and she wriggled down into it. Before joining her, he retrieved a bottle of complimentary Mumm's champagne from a silver-plated tray on the coffee table. Paco unwrapped and popped the white plastic cork and poured bubbly into two fluted glasses. The embossed card on the tray surprised him: it wasn't from the management. He handed a glass and the card to Molly and wedged himself in beside her.

"Well, Molly, it took murder and thievery to bring the two of us together and just look how peaceful we are now."

"You were magnificent, Inspector LeSoto, great slooping."

"Molly, I couldn't have done it without you. After all, you found all the important clues in that case."

"Yeah. But, best of all, I found you and you found me. Cheers!" She clinked her glass to his, then read the note. "He's so sweet. It's good wishes from Dr. Avi."

"It's obvious he wants to hold onto his housekeeper," Paco said.

"Oh, I want to hold on, too-: -he counts on me." As she sipped, the bubbles tickled her nose. "It's gonna be strange, going home to your house after work. I never did that before. But you'll be there, won't you?"

"Of course, sweetie pie."

Molly kissed him lightly on the ear. "How much time do we have before the meeting?"

"About two hours."

"Oh, that's plenty of time." She pecked him on the lips, stood up, and crossed the room to her suitcase.

"Time for what?" he asked.

"Oh...you know." She held up a frilly, very wide pink nightie and giggled, then toddled off to the bathroom.

Paco closed the drapes, folded down the bedclothes, and put on a pair of pajamas. In front of the mirror he straightened his collar and smoothed out his sleeves. Slowly, he became aware of another face in the mirror, bearing just a hint of sadness--or was it sadness at all? Turning to Molly, he kissed her in a dozen places across her pink moon face, stroked her taffy-brown curls, and led her to the bed, tucking her in. He turned down the lights and climbed in beside her.

Paco spoke just the right words and affectionate promises, touching gently where excitement rises, leading her down tender paths toward total exhilaration. And she yielded.

* * *

Ray Symington slid the key card in the door of room 1016 and removed it as soon as the green light flashed. He pushed open the door and stepped back to let his wife enter first. Loretta slid past him, immediately sat down on the first double bed, and bounce-tested its softness. Her hard blue eyes scanned the room. "Not bad," she said. "Western decor does turn me on."

"I didn't know your taste ran to corny prints of buffaloes and Indians," he said. "Oh, of course, my dear Loretta, how could I forget? Decorated rooms turn you on. Saks Fifth Avenue and Nieman Marcus turn you on. Unfortunately, I don't. Well, at least there are two beds. Maybe now I can get a decent night's sleep."

"I could take the next plane home, you know."

"Now don't go getting drastic on me. How would that look--me leading the award-winning sales group and every one of them with a wife?"

"Oh, I'm sure you'd find some young chickie on the bus to replace little ole me fast enough. You don't need a wife. You need an ornament to hang on your arm for official functions."

"Yeah, you're decorative, all right," her husband said. "It sure costs me enough to keep you in designer duds and sparkling doodads."

He emptied his toiletry kit onto the dresser top and set out his electric razor, pre- and post-shave lotions, and assorted tooth and hair care items. He was nine years older than Loretta, and lately it had occurred to him that his looks might be fading. New folds in his neck now met his square chin. He had stabilized the color of his hair at dark brown, thanks to Adonis Touch for Men.

But he couldn't control his hairline's stubborn march backward, leaving his brow deeper and wider. He tried to make up for it by keeping his hair full on the sides and almost tickling his collar in the back.

Loretta opened her large makeup kit at the dressing room sink. She re-penciled her brows to a noticeable point and ran a comb through butterscotch blond, bouffant hair. Neither a fresh layer of frosted blue eye shadow nor eyeliner could hide the crow's feet. Adjusting a few bottles to make room for others produced a clinking sound that caught Ray's attention.

"Oh, I see you brought your chemistry set along," he said. "Are we in for any new discoveries this trip?"

"At least I'm not trying to perform any miracles." She picked up his bottle of Rogaine. "This hasn't worked yet. Maybe you should try Scott's Turf Builder."

He let it go. Silently, he admired the way his wife still fit neatly into a size eight dress. He knew she underestimated her mature appeal. She worked a helluva lot harder than necessary to conceal her forty-three years. But giving compliments wasn't his style.

She took his silence as an attack. "And don't give me that 'poor boy' routine," she said. "You're the friggin' sales vice president of Indent Machine Tool and that's not too shabby, so stop being such a tightwad."

"It wouldn't matter if I were the CEO, you'd still spend more than I make."

"And it wouldn't hurt if you were a little more sociable toward our friends and stopped trying to seduce every young bimbo who says hello to you." Loretta savored her anger, but stopped short of gusting their daily squall into a full-blown tornado. She picked up her Coach leather purse and headed for the door.

"Where're you going now?" he asked.

"To stress your bankroll, Mr. Wonderful. I'm going shopping till five." She closed the door behind her.

"Bitch!" he bellowed.

* * *

The Bronco Auditorium had comfortable seats arranged amphitheater fashion. Down front, a small table held brochures and leaflets. Forty-some tourists rifled through their papers like college kids awaiting a final exam. A lanky, freckled man of perhaps thirty-five began speaking.

"Good evening, everyone. Welcome to Vermilion Tours. My name is Glenn Haniford and I'm going to be your guide throughout our fourteen-day journey together. I'm an easy-going guy with only a bare minimum number of rules to follow." He paused and grinned broadly. "My company requires me to wear my official gold blazer tonight, but this is the first and last time you'll see me in it. We're going to relax together, and I expect us to have a great tour. This is the twenty-fifth one I've led." He waited for the fidgeting and rustling of papers to stop.

"Now--there are forty-seven in our group. One couple is from the West Coast. Four are from the South, and the remainder are from New England and the mid-Atlantic Coast. You'll get to know everyone's name before long--sooner than you think. I understand that ten of you are traveling together and several groups of four, the same. We will try to accommodate you wherever possible. Your suitcases should be outside your room door by a specified time on the days we're traveling. Tomorrow, it will be 5:45 a.m. That's 5:45," he repeated. "The restaurant opens at 6 a.m. for breakfast, and you need to be at the front of the lobby by 7:30 to board the bus."

A groan traveled through his audience.

"What time do we need to get the bags outside our room?" someone piped up.

"Five forty-five tomorrow morning," answered Glenn patiently.

"And what time does the restaurant open?"

"Let me say it again: Six o'clock, and be at the front of the lobby by 7:30 to board the bus." Glenn was accustomed to repeating himself. On every tour, there were always a few who just didn't listen the first time around.

"Now tomorrow," he said, "seating on the bus is up for grabs, so sit anywhere you like. This will be the only opportunity for any groups among you to sit together. Thereafter, you must all rotate your seats twice each day--first thing in the morning and again after lunch." He paused and scanned the faces to see if his words had sunk in. He couldn't tell. "When we rotate, you will move one row back on the door side of the bus and one row forward on the driver's side of the bus. Those of you in the last row on the door side will move over to the last row on the driver's side. The first row on the driver's side will move to the first row on the door side. Out of fairness to everyone, there are no exceptions. I'll explain it again when we get on the bus. Oh, yes, there's a seat at the front door that will be exclusively for me."

"Do we have to rotate?" a voice asked. A few others tittered.

"Yes, everyone has to rotate," Glenn answered patiently. He paused to field a number of other questions and then pointed out the small table. "These pamphlets," he went on, "will tell you about the optional side trips. A jeep ride into the mountains around Sedona to see the red rock formations. White water rafting and scenic floats down the Snake River. A Grand Canyon fly-over. The cost of each option is clearly stated. You can think about them and you'll be given opportunities to sign up later." He shuffled the wad of notes before him into a single pile as he waited for the din to fade.

In the eighth row, Molly whispered in Paco's ear. "Isn't that the couple we saw in the hall in their bathing suits? Over there in front of us."

Paco nodded.

"And now, about dinner," Glenn continued. "The Tailgate Restaurant is down the hall to the left. Excellent food. You can select any appetizer, entré, and dessert you want from the menu and sign the check with your name and room number. We'll take care of the bill. Have a good night, and we'll see you at 7:30 in the front of the lobby."

"Can we order anything we want?" a small voice chirped.

Glenn suppressed a sigh.

* * *

Inside the hotel's Quarterback Bar, Dora Ireland and her boyfriend, Porter, sat at a window table watching the tour group leave the Bronco Auditorium next door.

"Umm...great margarita," she said. "I'm glad you brought me here."

"Did the doctor at the hospital say it was okay for you to drink so soon?"

"I didn't ask him. I suppose I should've. But I do feel better being out with you," she answered.

"You've never wanted to go out on a week night before," he said.

"I know. But after what happened at the bank today, I just couldn't go home to an empty apartment."

"You've been through a helluva lot. You know, honey, I could fix that easy enough by spending the night."

"Not on your life," she responded. "You know how I feel about that. I--oh, my God!"

"What's wrong, sweetheart? You look worse than the picture on your driver's license."

"That's not funny, Porter."

"I'm not trying to be funny. But you do look like you've seen the ghost of Lizzie Borden."

"Worse...much worse."

Dora reached for her drink with a trembling hand. It slipped from her grasp and toppled over, a tequila rivulet heading straight for her lap. She pushed her chair back, and with her meager cocktail napkin, tried to blot the spilled drink from her suit skirt and panty hose. The salt-rimmed margarita glass rolled off the table onto her soggy lap as she strained to get one more glimpse of the corridor beyond the lounge.

"Dora, what's going on?" Porter asked, grabbing his own

napkin to soak up the puddle on the table. "Who did you see?"

Her entire body began to shake. "For a minute," she whispered, "I thought I recognized a face in that crowd out there."

"Whose face?"

"I--I'm not sure...from today, I think."

"Should I call the cops?"

"No--don't. I don't know what I'd tell them. Oh, God, what a mess. For a flash I was positive, now I'm not sure at all."

"Think hard, maybe it was her."

Dora's voice grew sharp. "I am thinking, for God's sake, but..." She looked furtively around to see if any other Happy Hour patrons had heard her. Apparently no one had--all deep in their drinks and small talk, lulled by the piped-in piano music.

"The robber was an older woman with gray hair and granny glasses. But just now a younger woman with that group out there--something about her struck me. The lopsided smile, the pointy nose. But maybe it's just my nerves." Dora took a deep breath. "I've got a feeling I'll be seeing that woman's face everywhere from now on. No matter who comes into the bank, I'll never feel safe again." She retrieved the empty glass from her lap, and her anxious fingers collected the dried salt.

"They're going into the restaurant," he said. "Want to get a closer look? We could even eat there."

"Porter, take me home. I need to go home. Now!"

"Sure thing, hon." He dropped two folded bills on the table.

"And Porter..."

"Yes?"

"Promise you'll stay with me tonight."

"I will, sweetheart, I will."

Chapter 3
OVER DINNER, OVERDONE
Day One, Thursday, September 10, 1981

THE HOSTESS AT THE TAILGATE RESTAURANT led the LeSotos to a table and asked the foursome already seated there, "Would you mind being joined by another couple from your tour?"

"Delighted!" The middle-aged man closest to them sprang up with the vigor of someone half his years and extended his right hand to Paco. "I'm Thom Moyer and this is my wife, Theo." As he spoke, his upper lip disappeared under a cinnamon-colored mustache. Theo smiled, showing large perfect teeth. The couple mirrored each other's friendliness.

"That's most kindly of you, Mr. Moyer. I'm Molly LeSoto and this is my husband, Paco. We're honeymooning." A sweet grin orbited its way around her face.

Paco's olive complexion turned a shade of pimento while the second man rose and extended his hand.

"We're George and Reba Hurles. And when was the big event?"

"It was a nooner yesterday," Molly replied. "A small and tasty affair in Dr. Avi's living room."

"Dr. Avi?" questioned Reba.

"Yes, I'm the doctor's housekeeper." Reba gave her a startled look. "For twenty-four years," Molly added. Then, staring straight at Reba, she asked, "And what do you do?"

George guffawed and slapped his leg. "She doesn't do a thing." Reba stuck her tongue out at her husband.

"That's my wife, master of the repartee. Just kidding, dear," George said hastily. "Actually, my wife's a bowler, and crackin' good

18

at it. I can tell you, she keeps me on ten pins and needles." He chuckled at his own joke. "I'm in sales and so is Thom. For the same company." His heavy but pleasant face turned serious as he handed a business card to Paco.

Paco read it aloud. "Indent Machine Tool Corporation, George Hurles, Regional Sales Manager."

"In fact," Thom added, "four of us regional managers and our VP boss are on this tour as a reward for a banner sales year, wives included."

"We deserve something just for putting up with you guys," Theo interjected. "It's not easy living with a super-salesman's ego." She patted her husband affectionately on the shoulder.

Thom leaned slightly forward, his expression earnest. "And what do you do, Paco?" he asked.

"I'm a retired Baltimore cop, a homicide detective. But now I..."

He didn't get to finish. A commotion had erupted on the other side of the dining room. Heads turned and ears perked. Paco saw a tall, solidly built man in a navy blue blazer standing next to a table, glaring down at the four diners seated there. Reba scowled, Theo chuckled. Their men simply smiled.

Molly asked, "What's going on?"

"Oh, nothing unusual," said George. "It's our boss, Ray Symington."

"He's refusing to sit with the Whitmans and Davies. He thinks he's too good for lowly regional sales managers--for the Messiah, even," said Reba.

"He wants his own table," noted Theo, "but the hostess is shrugging him off."

"Thom, five will get you ten, Ray gets his way. His hands are already on his hips."

"You're on, George," answered Thom.

"Is he always like that?" Molly wanted to know.

"Always!" four voices whispered in unison.

"Jeez, George, you're right!" said Thom. "They're setting up a table in the corner for him and Loretta. Damn, I should know better." He retrieved a bi-fold wallet from his hip pocket, flipped it open, and held out a $5 bill to George.

George grinned, but didn't take the money. "Never mind, Thom, you can buy us a drink later."

"Your boss seems to like things his own way," Paco remarked.

"Let's just say he's not the easiest guy in the world to work for," George offered.

"Some people in this company--I'm not telling who..." Reba murmured, "think he takes the credit for everyone else's hard work and successes, their new ideas, too, and passes them off as his own."

"Hey, guys," Thom said softly, "we'd better cool it. No tales out of school. We wouldn't want the LeSotos to think we're ungrateful for this trip, would we?"

"Yeah, Reba, cool it, he is our boss," George interjected, "and we're beholden to him for his largesse, aren't we?" Irony wove through his words.

"So, who are the people he scummed?" asked Molly, unwilling to miss some lively gossip.

Theo's gray eyes glinted with amusement. She brushed an imaginary crumb from her skirt.

Paco eyed the two men. "If your company's celebrating a banner year, I assume he must be doing something right."

"Well," said George, "he's managed to sell the CEO and board of directors on his own talents."

"And don't forget everyone he stepped on--and the wives he diddled--on his way to the top," Reba piped up.

She was one of those wives. Six years ago she'd campaigned heavily for Ray's attentions. He had exuded a dangerous, ruthless virility that excited her. And she had thought that maybe seducing him would help her passive husband get ahead. But all she'd managed was half an hour in the hay.

"Is that what they mean when they say he screwed up?"

asked Molly. Theo joined her in giggling like third graders trading secrets.

George gave his wife a puzzled look. "Okay, time out," he said. "Here comes the waiter."

The waiter approached Molly first. "May I take your order, madam?"

"Oh, yes, sir. I'll have the black-eyed fish with seizure salad and scalped potatoes."

"Very good, madam, the blackened walleyed pike, Caesar salad, and scalloped potatoes. Would you prefer the seafood bisque or the fruit cup?"

"Oh, the seafood brisk. It goes with fish food."

"Of course, madam." The waiter gestured to Reba next. His eyes wandered to her neckline and below.

With every breath, Reba's cleavage swelled bulbously from the low-cut blouse. Her gypsy earrings, large silver coins, swayed this way and that as she spoke. "I'll just have the bisque and a Caesar salad."

"Watching our weight, are we?" asked George.

"You're not complaining, are you, darling?" she said.

"What? Me complain?"

"Oh, what the heck," she said, "we're on vacation. Maybe I'll get a wicked dessert."

"Go ahead. I'm not paying for this," said her husband.

"And you, madam?" the waiter nodded to Theo. "What would you like?"

"I'll have the fruit cup and the olla podidra...no salad."

"What's an olla po...whatever?" asked George.

"It's a Latin American stew of diced sausage and veggies," declared Molly. "It's one of my especialties and it has to simper all day."

"I think the word actually means 'hodgepodge' or 'anything goes'," said Theo.

The conversation continued for another thirty minutes before the waiter returned with their entrees.

A bass voice across the room assaulted their ears. "I said medium rare. This is well done."

"I'm terribly sorry, sir," defended Symington's waiter. "I specifically..."

"You specifically what? I expect better in a restaurant of this quality. Now don't just stand there..." Not that Ray's voice was particularly loud; it was more the tone that carried: low-pitched, nasty, threatening. "Take it back and do it right this time."

The entire dining room suddenly went silent. Loretta shrank into her chair, an ostrich hiding in a hole. Ray drew a long, deliberate sip of his sparkling burgundy and came up for air with an innocent What's-all-the-excitement? expression. A crooked smile emerged across his square jaw.

The restaurant returned to its gentle din.

"He needs to be sent to his room," Molly whispered.

"You got that right, Mrs. LeSoto," said Thom.

"But it's really nothing new," Theo added. Her eyes smiled behind sophisticated glasses in black and gold frames.

"It's probably none of my business, Thom," began Paco. "But I seem to detect a personal note of dissatisfaction here."

"Is it that obvious?" Thom asked. He bent over his plate, hacking his steak into bite-sized chunks. "Paco, I've got a degree in mechanical engineering and a master's in engineering management from Wharton. Given the chance, I could double the company's sales in three years, maybe even two. But Ray thinks I'm after his job. He's seen me perform and he's afraid of me. So he bad-mouths me to the board. And I'm not the only one."

Thom raised a forkful of steak to his mouth, hesitated, and then returned it to his plate. "George, here, is Ray's top producer. Ray won't promote him or transfer him because of his age. George is only fifty-nine, but he doesn't want to pursue the age discrimination route because it's too hard to prove." George threw his friend a grateful glance.

"Why don't we change the subject now?" Theo suggested. "Say, Molly, where'd you say you hailed from?"

"I didn't...Maryland," Molly announced. "Black Rain Corners is the place."

"Population 2,100," added Paco. "I think she knows just about everyone by name, too. So where's your company located?" he asked Thom.

"Connecticut. An industrial part of East Haven, but we live in a suburb called Woodbridge--not much larger than your home town."

"Are you anywhere near Annapolis, Molly?" asked Theo. "We have friends who go there to sail. I understand most of the residents have sailboats."

"Not most," Paco countered, "but many do, yes. Everything from kit-built twelve-footers to million-dollar yachts. But my Molly and me, we're not into boating."

"The doctor has lots of money, and he doesn't have one," Molly piped up. "He's even a philanderer."

"Oh, really? How fascinating," declared Theo.

"She means he's a philanthropist," corrected Paco, "a patron of the arts, a museum trustee and extremely active in the charities."

"And a psychoanalyst," added Molly. "All his work is brainy, not briny." A loud laugh erupted around the table.

The six of them had barely started their second cup of coffee when a maniacal shriek pierced their congenial mood.

Chapter 4
ODD BAGGAGE
Same Day, Thursday, September 10, 1981

THE HIGH-PITCHED SHRIEK BOUNCED off the muraled walls of the Tailgate Restaurant. It came from the Symington table. A woman with disheveled dirty blond hair and a crazed look stood over Ray. She stopped screaming long enough to take in a fresh breath, then swung her hand, palm open, toward Ray's right cheek. He saw it coming and ducked.

Her open hand landed smack on the shoulder of the hapless busboy clearing the table. His tray went flying. Dirty plates clattered to the floor, breaking. Salad dressing slimed his shoes; cherry tomatoes rolled out of sight. The busboy fled to the kitchen.

The blonde gasped in horror. "Now look whatcha made me do."

Ray leaned back in his chair, folding his arms across his chest. "I did nothing, Joanne. I'm not the one who's out of control. Isn't it about time you went to AA?"

"You can go to hell, Ray Symington."

"Now, now, you'd better calm down--and don't you think you ought to apologize to that poor busboy? He could sue you, you know."

Joanne clenched her fists as if to make a second pass at her target, but instead she snarled, "I may have missed this time, Ray, but next time you won't get away from me."

Her sunburned husband grabbed her from behind. Gordon Whitman's grim expression revealed that this scene had been played many times before. She clawed at his bare arms, trying to wrench herself free. But he gripped her shoulders firmly and led her

24

away whimpering, babbling, no longer coherent.

The impromptu floor show had come to an end. The sounds of silverware rose as the waiters distributed desserts. At their own table, Paco and Molly learned that the wayward blonde and her interceding husband were Joanne and Gordon Whitman.

"Looks like Ms. Joanne is three sheeps to the wind," said Molly.

"You got that right," said Reba.

"So how come she gets so alleviated?" Molly asked.

"It's a long story," Theo said. "Gordon has been an outstanding salesman for IMTC," she dropped her voice to a whisper, "but he's pissed off over some kind of dispute with Ray."

Paco shook two sugar packets into his coffee and stirred. "What kind of dispute?" he asked.

"A nasty patent thing," George replied.

He went on to explain that Gordon Whitman had a long list of registered patents to his credit, many of them extremely valuable to the firm. Gordon had developed other ideas, having nothing to do with the company, on his own time. Ray had taken extreme pleasure in interpreting the company's employee patent agreement literally. He'd engineered it so Gordon's private patent royalties had to be deposited with the firm as well.

Reba relished adding a footnote. "Joanne's bitter about the patents. She thinks he's getting shafted."

"And is he?" Paco asked.

"Hey, guys, maybe the LeSotos don't want to hear about all our dirty laundry," Thom interjected.

"Oh, we're all loyal company wives," Theo said, ignoring him. "Joanne, too. We're good little girls expected to further our husband's careers. We travel, entertain, and otherwise promote the successful company image. But the message we get is, 'Don't rock the boat.' Joanne has a little problem with that."

The waiter arrived with their checks. Abruptly, all conversation stopped while the men signed them.

Reba could hardly contain herself until the waiter left.

"While you're telling tales out of school," she blurted, "why don'tcha just come out and say it--Joanne's an alcoholic and Michelle's an ex-con."

Paco's eyes narrowed.

Molly's parfait spoon clattered to her plate. She licked the lingering chocolate from her upper lip. "You mean Ms. Michelle went to prison? What did she do to preserve that?"

The Moyers and Hurles shot furtive glances at one another and rose from the table without a word.

Chapter 5
JUST A PEEK
Day Two, Friday, September 11, 1981

MOLLY, IN A BILLOWING PRINT DRESS, stepped into the breakfast buffet line. Paco, wiry and trim in his khakis and flannel shirt, followed behind her.

"Careful what you take, honey," he cautioned.

"I'm sixty-three, lover, and I sure can't change my geography now. Besides, there was this much of me when we met."

A bird-like woman inching along directly in front of Molly turned her head and chirped, "My goodness, after a dozen days of this, I'll have to let my pants out."

"I know," agreed Molly, yet she wondered why skinny people always talked like that. After a shrug, she ladled and speared from every platter in the culinary array, ending with strawberries and whipped cream on a Belgian waffle.

"I'm Molly Mesta, er--Molly LeSoto," she told the woman ahead of her. "And this is my new husband, Paco."

"Hi," answered the woman shyly. "I...I'm Bess Izaks and this is my traveling companion, Cookie Adams."

"Pleased to meetcha," said Molly. "Gosh, Cookie sure is a tasty name. Wanna sit together for breakfast?"

"Yes, that would be delightful," said Bess.

Balancing their loaded plates, they snaked a path to a booth with a view. Outside, a thousand skyscraper windows reflected the rising sun.

"Oh, the morning--so magnificent," said Cookie. "Skip would have loved it." Her dull brown eyes brightened for an instant.

"I take it there's a Mr. Adams at home then," said Paco.

"Don't I wish. I buried my Skip nine years ago last April."

"Oh, I'm so sorry," said Paco.

Cookie pushed scrambled eggs around her plate. "Still a young man--only forty-one. Didn't have to die. The insurance investigator said it was an accident. I don't believe any of it."

"What happened?" asked Paco.

"My husband had bought..." She broke off. Her body stiffened. She sensed that conversation at the table behind her had stopped.

"Paco," she whispered, "I can't really talk about it now." The voices at the other table picked up where they'd left off.

"Is this your first bus tour, Bess?" asked Molly.

"Uh, yes," she answered. "I'm a widow, too. The children paid for this trip. A present for my eightieth birthday. They had this crazy idea it would breathe new life into me. My son even talked Cookie into coming along with me."

Cookie added, "We're members of the same garden club back home in Jamestown, Rhode Island."

Bess Izaks took a final sip of her coffee, then excused herself from the table. She'd forgotten to put a toothbrush in her purse, she told them, and wanted to retrieve it before her luggage got loaded on the bus.

Bess trotted down the corridor in her little white tennies. Suitcases rested on their wheels and toes by each of the doors. Although Bess's body moved quickly enough, her mind sometimes failed to keep up. In a slightly addled state, she stopped one door short, in front of a black canvas suitcase hardly different from her own. Her palsied fingers grappled with her generic luggage key until it popped the toyish padlock.

Bess unzipped the suitcase. Her hand reached inside for a satin cosmetics bag, searching until her fingertips felt a smooth, hard package. She began to sense the strangeness, but her brain didn't fully register the alien texture. Something beyond reason compelled her to pull out the package. It resisted. She tugged and soon both hands gripped an unfamiliar cardboard mailer. The sticky end flap had pulled open, leaving Bess irreversibly drawn to examine its contents. She let out a canary-like cry. Inside the open end she saw packs of $50 bills, neatly stacked and banded. Crisp new money. Her heart began thumping in her frail chest.

Bess glanced up and down the hall and saw no one. Emboldened, she pulled the box up closer and poked through one packet of bills after another. Almost holding her breath now, she shoved the mailer back into the space it had come from. Reaching in, she remembered to re-tuck the wayward flap. This time she encountered a second and a third mailer. She withdrew her hand. Bess nervously zipped up the suitcase, snapping the little lock around and through the metal tabs.

Voices echoed down the hall, but no one had turned the corner into view. Bess saw the Vermilion Tours luggage tags: Mr. and Mrs. LeRoy Milton. Puzzled, she looked around for her own room, her own suitcase. She found them right next door. Bess moved to her own doorway and slid the key card into the lock mechanism. It flashed green, and she opened the door, jerking her own bag in behind her. The voices grew louder now, couples talking, rounding the corner, approaching. She couldn't make out what they were saying. Someone tried her door.

Cookie entered the room to find a near-hysterical Bess sitting on the bed next to her suitcase--a toothbrush clutched in her hand.

"Bess? What's wrong?" she asked, laying her newspaper down on the nightstand. "Your bag should be in the hall. The bellhops are already loading them on the bus."

Between gasps and sobs, Bess re-locked her bag and motioned to Cookie that it was ready to go. Cookie rolled it out into the hall and returned to sit next to her on the bed. Bess breathed easier now.

"Hey," Cookie joked, "I don't get a chance to play mother hen very often. Skip and I never got to have kids. If you think you're getting on that bus without telling me what's wrong, you've got another guess coming."

Bess blurted the whole story out. Cookie, in turn, grabbed the newspaper off the nightstand. She scanned the front section, her eyes landing on a half-column item with the headline "Suburban Bank Held Up Yesterday."

"Ah! There it is." She handed the folded paper, story exposed, to Bess.

"Do you suppose it's them?" asked Bess. "I mean the bank robbers--living right next door to us?"

"The article says the robber was a lone elderly lady," replied Cookie. "The description fits you, dear."

"That's not funny!"

"Well, what do our neighbors look like, then?"

"I don't know, it's a husband and wife. It might be risky, or at least embarrassing to turn them in, seeing as how we don't have any proof or anything," Bess said.

"We don't even know if it's the same money. So what should we do?" Cookie asked.

"Do?" replied Bess. "I don't want to do anything. Maybe I should just go home right now and forget the trip. I can say I'm sick."

"Not on your life, Bess, we're gonna have fun on this trip if it kills us."

"Oh, for heaven sake, don't say that!"

"Sorry, bad choice of words," said Cookie. "Look, if it'll make you feel any better--for now we do nothing. You, on the other hand, should march into the bathroom and fix your face. We're due in the lobby in fifteen minutes. We don't want to be late the first day, do we?"

"You're right," said Bess. "I'm not going to let anything spoil our trip." She stopped at the bathroom sink. Her hand trembled as she ran a comb through her short red hair, so wispy her scalp showed through.

Minutes later, Bess emerged from the bathroom in a new state of frenzy. "I can't find my purse." As Cookie rose to help her, they heard a sharp knock at the door to the hall. Cookie opened it. There stood a woman in a paisley playsuit, holding out a purse.

"We've been knocking on a few doors. Does this belong to you?" the woman asked. "We found it on the floor by our room."

"It...it's mine," Bess stammered. She inched closer and took the purse in her hands. "Thank you very much." She clutched it to her chest and quickly backed away.

"Swell," said the woman, smiling. "Glad to help. Gotta go now. See ya'll on the bus." She disappeared from the doorway, and only then could they see the man who had been standing behind her. He too moved out of view, and Cookie closed the door.

Bess's fingers flew to her forehead. "Oh, my, I dropped my purse when I unlocked their suitcase. Do you think that's her? Oh, how could it be? She's not elderly."

Cookie thought for a moment. "I suppose she could have made herself look older, but not likely."

"How can you be so sure? Oh, my God, if it's her, then she knows who's been poking around in their bags."

"Calm down Bess, you can't do anything about it now. They probably haven't a clue anyone's been in their bags. And I'll bet the bellhop took 'em before they found your purse. Besides, it's time to get on the bus. Grab your carry-on and let's go."

They know. They know it's me," persisted Bess. "I'll be murdered in my nightie."

* * *

In an alcove at the other end of the hall, two people stood next to the ice machine and argued.

"Damn it, LeRoy," said Ruth. "I can't even trust you to watch the bags for twenty minutes while I go get breakfast for the two of us." She lowered her voice by half. "Where the hell were you?"

"I had to pee, for God's sake. I couldn't wait any longer. Besides, the bellhops were already picking up the bags. What harm could there be in my going then?"

Ruth glowered at him, hands on her hips. "Sometimes I think you haven't got a brain in your head. You call yourself an engineer? A detail man, you're always telling me. Well, that's a good one. First the Flite-Ex man calls and cancels..."

"You're blaming that on me? Wait just a damn minute, Ruth. Now I'm supposed to control the screw-ups of Flite-Ex? Is it my fault they couldn't come 'til nine o'clock this morning? We'll be long gone by then."

Ruth ignored him. "And we're stuck holding the packages. Then you leave the bags out in the hall unguarded."

"Hey, look, I can't help it if we're running with a busted plan," LeRoy said peevishly. He knew he was spending more and more time in the john. Enlarged prostate, the doctor had said.

She turned away and pressed her lips together. She knew it wasn't all LeRoy's fault. Flite-Ex had called to apologize and said they'd come for the pickup at nine that morning--for sure. She'd lost her cool and shouted: "Forget it, that's too late. Two hours too late." Then she'd slammed the phone down.

"Don't worry, hon," LeRoy said. "We'll ship it out first chance we get."

Chapter 6
THE BIG BUS
Same Day, Friday, September 11, 1981

THE DRIVER, A RANGY FELLOW IN AN EISENHOWER JACKET, stood by the door, smoking a cigarette. "Hi! I'm Lew Getz, your Vermilion Tours chauffeur. Watch your step as you get on, please."

"Not much of a step for so tall a bus," commented Paco, gazing at the sleek black coach trimmed in chrome.

"No problem," said Lew. "The whole bus kneels hydraulically for loading. The 'kneel down' capability is the latest feature in our luxury liner buses."

"You mean the bus curtsies for us?" asked Molly.

"Absolutely!" replied Lew.

Climbing aboard, Molly's blue eyes lit up like headlights. "It's a posh lemonzine, Paco," she marveled.

The coach, complete with an airline-style lavatory, had been designed for comfort, safety, and sightseeing convenience. Small video screens were mounted overhead every few rows on both sides. This luxury coach would haul the forty-seven passengers for the next two weeks. Almost 2,500 miles.

Molly greeted the Whitmans and then the Moyers in the first two rows on the door side. But she preferred the shade on the other side of the bus and settled into an upholstered window seat in the tenth row just behind George and Reba. She tucked her squashy sun hat into the large seat pocket in front of her and slid her forest-green Vermilion Tours tote underneath. Paco took the aisle seat and watched as Molly tested the adjustable head and foot rests, windows shades, and reclining seat. Just sitting there primed her senses for the adventure ahead.

Within minutes, Glenn Haniford had collected a head count, and Lew coaxed the liner out onto the cosmopolitan Denver streets. It glided past promenades lined with globed lamps, period shop fronts, and designer boutiques. Then came schlock windows crammed with T-shirts and mugs, all stamped "Colorado." The golden dome of the state capitol faded out of sight. Skyscrapers and hotels gave way to suburbia. Mile-High Stadium slipped by on their left.

"Go, Broncos!" someone yelled.

The early morning haze, burned off by the sun, soon revealed the distant tablelands that lay to the north of the city. Turning northwest, the snow-covered jagged peaks of the Rocky Mountains jumped into view. Up near Boulder and more westerly on Route 36, the bus climbed higher, slower, until they reached the Beaver Meadows entrance to Rocky Mountain National Park. Inside the park the trees grew dense and the road wound sharply.

"Look out!" screamed Thom Moyer.

Lew slammed on the brakes. Forty-seven fully relaxed tourists lurched forward as the bus jerked to a violent halt. A six-point buck lumbered across the road. A doe loped gracefully behind him. Lew had braked just in time and now he slowed the bus onto the narrow shoulder. The near-miss had visibly shaken him.

Glenn moved forward and laid a hand across the driver's back. "Great reflexes, Lew. Fantastic job, man."

The passengers applauded. Glenn turned to them and said, "Every morning I rise and say my prayers. I ask God to guide me and my driver--his eyes and his hands--to keep us all safe."

"Amen!" said Molly. A murmuring of Amens followed.

They stopped for lunch in a rustic log-constructed park building with hot and cold sandwich and soup service. The tables filled up quickly. As Judge Harry Sessions and his wife, Caroline, passed the Symington table, Loretta and Ray pointedly bent their heads away to study their menus. Just as pointedly, the Sessions brushed past their table and chose to join the LeSotos in a cozy far corner.

After the four had introduced themselves Molly whispered. "Are the Symingtons so uppity they don't even want a judge at their table?"

"Not this judge," answered Harry. "However, I admit the feeling is mutual." He turned his wrist to see the time. "Hmm, I think we should all stick with the sandwiches--keep it simple and fast." He wasn't aware that he'd drummed his fingers on the table three times.

Even seated, Harry's carriage and bulk spelled power. He didn't socialize, he presided, as if the checkered tablecloth and silverware belonged to his courtroom. A carpet of wavy white hair and thick white brows dominated his face. But sagging jowls and the red-mapped whites of his eyes gave him the woeful look of a bloodhound.

"I take it the Symingtons aren't your best friends," Paco said.

"You can say that again," said Harry, his voice much louder than before. "He's a petty crook with a devious mind."

"He plays with peoples' lives," added Caroline, all too quickly. "The man is poison."

"Then this is more than a professional beef, Your Honor?" said Paco.

The judge looked pleased by Paco's show of respect. "Off the record?" he asked.

"Off the record," confirmed Paco.

"Symington tried to bribe me in a price-fixing case involving his company. I ruled for the plaintiffs, two tiny struggling firms, and cited him for contempt." He picked up his fork and tapped out his irritation on the table. "IMTC and another firm, Convex or Con-something, had conspired to force all the regional garage and basement machine shops out of business. After driving prices below cost, IMTC would own the market. The most critical piece of evidence was Symington's own interoffice memo spelling out the fix." Anger built in Harry's voice. "Actually, IMTC got off too damned light. Eighty thousand dollars in damages--peanuts these days."

"Speaking of peanuts, I could sure use some," said Molly. She studied her watch. "A half-hour already. And only two waitresses for this whole big place. I guess that's why they call 'em waitresses. We wait for them until they wait on us." Caroline and Harry managed a strained laugh.

Miraculously, a waitress chomping on gum appeared at their table. "So sorry, folks, we're short-handed today." She slowly wrote down their sandwich orders. Two ham, two turkey. It was the fixins that gave her trouble. "Mayo, hold the mayo, no chips, wheat toast, Kaiser roll..." She frowned, scratched her head, and ambled off.

Judge Sessions began to raise his voice as he told the LeSotos more of his story.

Caroline laid her hand on his arm. "Take it easy, Harry." Her right cheek twitched. Paco misinterpreted this involuntary tic, thinking she had winked at him.

Harry ignored her and barreled on. "When it became clear to Symington that the court would find for the plaintiffs, he offered me a free membership in his country club and some insider investment tips in return for imposing less stringent damages. Of course, I refused him outright, but since his attempted bribe was verbal and unwitnessed, I couldn't do anything but hold him in contempt. Fined him $1,000."

"I should think it would have ended there," said Paco.

"It didn't," Caroline said. Her cheek twitched again. "Symington was furious--he wanted revenge." A shuffle of chairs and buzz of checks being paid interrupted her. "Hey," she said, "do you believe this? We haven't even been served yet and it's time to go." Their waitress materialized once again, balancing their sandwich plates.

"Paco, honey, this is a pickle and a half. The bus is going to leave without us. Why don't I ask her for doggy bags?" said Molly.

"Forget it, we'd be here another half hour," Paco answered. "No five stars for this place!"

Molly and Caroline wrapped up the four lunches in napkins and hurried out to the bus. The two men lingered to settle up the checks.

"Your Honor," said Paco, "somehow I get the feeling there's a mite more to this story."

Harry's jowls rose to form a grim smile. "You got that right, friend." he said. "To be continued." They hastened out to the pebbled parking lot.

Molly counted the rows to the seat assigned for this afternoon--one row closer to the driver. Paco moved their totes from under this morning's seat to the overhead shelf while Molly slid in from the aisle. She reached down with both hands behind her to shift her weight out of Paco's way. In doing this her fingers crept into the crease and unexpectedly came up with a pale blue slip of folded paper. She unfolded it twice. "Sunday, 9/13, Yellowstone" had been written across it in a neat black script. An IMTC logo of dark blue meshing gears dominated the top of this three-inch by three-inch snippet of paper. Paco waited patiently for her to slide all the way over. She quickly stuffed the slip into her purse. A sudden change in scenery caused her to promptly forget the strange note.

The bus pulled onto the highest continuous road in the United States, the Trail Ridge Road, to make the fifty-mile run from Estes Park down to icy blue Grand Lake. At an elevation of over 8,000 feet, they encountered glacial rivers, crossed the Continental Divide, viewed sheer-walled canyons, and gazed up at peaks towering another 4,000 feet above them.

Glenn informed them that snow would close these roads in only a matter of weeks. "Folks, we're going to be making a rest stop in a few minutes. You're into the high altitudes now. Be sure to drink lots of water and let me know if you have any difficulty breathing."

The bus slowed and stopped in front of a small rustic outpost. The passengers not still in line at the outdoor facilities moved toward the scenic overlook.

Paco edged reluctantly toward the railing. His eyes fixed on the sheer cliff dropping 3,000 feet into a rocky gorge. A queasiness gripped his belly. An acrophobic sense of falling through liquid came over him. His head felt alarmingly light. The precipice tugged at him, and he resisted. He'd experienced vertigo many times in the past, but never quite this acutely. He wanted to turn away, but the hypnotic beauty and magnificence grabbed him and wouldn't let go.

Molly followed him to the railing. "Look, honey, there's... uh, what's wrong?"

"Just a little dizzy," he murmured. "It's the height."

"Oh. Look up there. Glenn told us we'd see some huge horny sheep in these mountains." Molly paused, trying to inhale deeply, but her lungs wouldn't cooperate. Her hand went to her chest as her labored breathing persisted. She reached for Paco and moved into his encircling arms.

Suppressing his own fears, he led her back to the bus. "It's the altitude, the lack of oxygen," he assured her, wondering whether he was convincing his wife or himself.

U.S. 34 took them past moraine-filled Lake Granby, its emerald hue shimmering in the afternoon sun. Then they drove on U.S. 40, through the dense Arapaho National Forest with its own glacial lakes and abandoned ghost towns, and on to Steamboat Springs. Just past Craig, Colorado, the bus turned northerly again and crossed the border into Wyoming.

"Oh, by the way," Glenn asked, "how do you pronounce the capital of Wyoming? Is it LAR-uh-me or La-RAH-me?" There were several guesses each way.

"Cheyenne!" he said with a chuckle.

They arrived at the Flaming Gorge National Recreation Area just as darkness covered them like a thick blanket. Lights glowed off-road ahead--a beacon welcoming them to the Wooden Nickel restaurant.

"Okay, everyone, we're here," said Glenn, standing up. "As

I've mentioned before, sides take turns disembarking. Okay, door side first." Everyone began pulling on jackets. But before the orderly procession could even begin, Ray Symington jumped up from his driver's-side seat and shoved his way to the front and off the bus.

"Hey, Ray!" Glenn called. "Let's follow the rules here."

But Ray was already trotting toward the entrance. "They may be your rules, Haniford," he called back, "but not mine."

Unruffled, Glenn recaptured the group's attention. "We'll be spending the night here in Jackalope Cabins," he said. "They're rustic but comfortable. You'll have a fabulous view of the Flaming Gorge Reservoir. It's the fishing hot spot of America, flowing ninety miles through canyons and sagebrush valleys. The cabins are right on the shore. A jackalope," he explained with a straight face, "is a cross between a jack rabbit and an antelope. They're extremely rare and sometimes they grow to be four feet tall." He paused. "Oh, I see there're some Doubting Thomases among you." He held up a photograph on the back of a postcard. "Seeing is believing, ain't it?" he twanged with a broad smile as he began doling out the cabin assignments and room keys.

LeRoy Milton slouched next to the driver and the bus, waiting for the bags to be unloaded. Ruth had already picked up the key and gone to their cabin, number two, just opposite the Wooden Nickel and the lodge office. LeRoy draped his windbreaker over one shoulder in an effort to look casual. He took a deep breath to calm his thumping heart, but a cloud of smoke plunged straight down into his unsuspecting lungs. Lew Getz just had to have that cigarette fix at every stop. LeRoy inhaled the secondary smoke like someone pinching pleasure, and he contemplated asking Lew for a smoke. But the bellhops arrived in riveted jeans and sleeveless hunter vests. They began unloading, and LeRoy had to follow their two bags to their cabin porch. As soon as the bellhop pulled them inside and left, the Miltons checked for the presence of all six mailers.

LeRoy heaved a sigh of relief. "They're all here, hon." But

Ruth kept turning one of them over and over. She looked perplexed.

"What's wrong, hon?"

"One of the tapes is coming off the end of this mailer," she replied. "It's all curled up like it's been used more than once. It doesn't make sense. Do you think someone's been inside?"

"How could they?" he asked. "It's been locked up in the bus all day."

"You abandoned the luggage altogether this morning," she reminded him.

"You're gonna go through that again? Hell, I wasn't gone that long," he said. "Maybe it just rubbed off when you stuffed the box in the suitcase."

"Wait," she said. "Remember the purse I found in the hall?"

"Yeah. You mean the old broad with the shakes? You don't actually think she'd have gone into our bags, do you?"

"How could she have? They were locked," replied Ruth. "But I'd better check inside." She carefully pulled open the flap at one end of the box. Sure enough, all the money was there. But it seemed to be not as neatly stacked as she remembered it.

"We could ask her," he offered.

"Sure, LeRoy, and how would we go about doing that?" she snapped.

"First," he said, "we've got to get rid of the money as fast as we can."

The Wooden Nickel reeked of fried fish and barbeque. Bare, wide-planked floors held sturdy round tables and captain's chairs. Piped-in country western music filled the open rafters--Patsy Cline singing "Crazy." A wagon-wheel fixture hung from the two-story ceiling. Its flame-shaped bulbs cast an amber light on paneled walls covered with antique weapons.

George and Reba settled into a table for six with the LeSotos, Cookie Adams, and Bess Izaks.

George browsed his menu. "Hey, guys, this place is for me,"

he said. "You know, this reservoir has some of the finest fishing in the world. Some day I'm going to come back out here and spend two weeks. Fly fishin' for trout, jiggin' for walleye. Anyway, I'm gonna have me the rainbow trout tonight."

"I know what a fisherman you are, big brother," said a grinning Cookie. "When we were kids you'd go out on the lake for hours. After catching absolutely nothing, you'd come home with this monster fish from Angelo's Seafood Market. Mom knew, George, but she was too nice to let you know she knew."

His beefy face broke into a smirk. "No way, Constance, I'd never do anything like that."

Cookie gave him a mock scowl and turned away to ponder the firearms mounted on the walls. "I had no idea guns could be so ornate."

"You better believe it," said Paco. "Over there, that's a Winchester sporting rifle, a real collector's item." He pointed out two pocket-sized revolvers over on the right as Colt percussion pistols, famous for their engraved silver grips. Up higher, a Hawken plains rifle, a Sharps carbine used in the Civil War, and a standard Frontier Colt .44.

During Paco's entire career, he'd never once had to fire his own weapon in the line of duty. As a detective he'd rarely even carried one.

"What's that long thin contraption at the top?" asked Cookie. "It looks like a bicycle pump."

"I believe that's a cattle prod," said Paco. "A rather persuasive device for keeping the cows in line."

"How's it work?" asked Cookie.

"From what I've seen," said George, "you pump it a few times and it builds up an electric charge that zaps the cow."

"Does it hurt them?" asked Reba.

"Suppose so," answered George. "I read somewhere the animal rights groups are trying to get them banned."

"Sounds kinda cruel t' me," said Molly. "Anyway, I don't like my steaks burnt while they're still walking."

"Do any of those guns still work?" Cookie asked.

"Highly unlikely," said Paco. "They're pretty rusty, and I'm sure the firing mechanisms have been disabled."

"Where would you get ammo for those antique babies?" George asked.

"No trouble at all," Paco answered. "There are firms that specialize in that sort of business."

Gun talk continued to shoot through their meal. After dessert Cookie announced, "My husband ran a machine shop and he liked to tinker with guns. An antique hunting rifle from his grandpa came to be his favorite. But I sold it when he died."

Paco ran a hand through his gray hair and leaned forward. "Your husband must have been quite a guy, Cookie. Skip, wasn't it? I would like to have known him."

"I think you two would have gotten along famously." Cookie glanced around the dining room. Most of the Vermilion group had already left for their cabins. "I suppose it's as good a time as any to talk about Skip."

George looked uncomfortable. "Past my bedtime, folks." He and Reba got up from the table and left.

Cookie's fingers played with the salt and pepper shakers--ceramic grizzly bears. Her dark eyes fixed on her tumbler of iced tea, the lemon slice bobbing among the ice cubes. "George gets real upset when I talk about Skip. He loved him, too. You see, my husband owned his own machine shop in Jamestown, Rhode Island. We made a nice living from it. That is, until he got killed."

"I'm so sorry," Molly said softly.

"Thanks," said Cookie. "You see, Skip went and purchased this..."

Paco wanted to hear how Cookie's husband died, but the bustle and clatter of dishes told them the waiters were setting up for breakfast. They took the hint and headed for their cabins.

On the way to their cabin, number 17, the LeSotos followed the lakeside path behind the straggling line of couples. Up ahead, Loretta and Ray Symington drifted off toward number 16.

They could be heard bickering.

"You know what I need? A hot shower," Loretta said.

"After me, my dear," insisted Ray. "You take a year and a day with that sprayed hair of yours. I bet you use enough of that stuff to lacquer a floor."

"You're just jealous, baldy," she retorted, shrugging her shoulders. "Go ahead, you need it more, but make it snappy."

Ray unlocked their door, and they stepped into stark surroundings. "If you don't mind, I'll take the bed by the window," he declared, shutting the door behind them.

"And if I did mind?" she asked.

"I'd take it anyway."

"You're all heart," she told him. "How about--you have the first shower and I have first choice of the beds?"

"No way! If you pick the one by the window, you'll keep it wide open all night and I'll freeze my buns off."

"Poor baby," she said. "Then the bed by the dresser it is. The sacrifices I make in the name of marriage."

"Don't worry, dear," Ray said as he entered the bathroom. "You'll make up for it in the gift shop tomorrow, I'm sure."

Loretta sat down on her bed and kicked off her shoes. "Maybe this is a good time to remind you of something," she said in a casual voice, but loud enough for him to hear through the door.

"What now?"

"Maynard Larchmont sent you on this trip to mend some fences."

Silence. The toilet flushed. Ray emerged from the bathroom and vigorously began washing his hands. "Damn, I hate this new trend of putting the sink outside the bathroom. What's your point, Loretta?"

"I'm just asking you to cool it, be a little nicer. That's what you're supposed to be doing, isn't it? You can't go on being so abrasive, Ray. He warned you."

"Maynard may be our CEO, but he doesn't own me. Anyway, I have been trying to be pleasant."

"You call that trying? Pushing your way off the bus before it's your turn? Refusing to sit with the Davies and Whitmans at dinner last night?"

"Can't stand Joanne. You saw the way she acted."

Loretta watched her husband undress. He'd remained handsome, sexy even, with his six-foot-two build, tight rear end, and runner's legs. But his mouth had taken on the hard set of a man who thinks he's always right, and his gray eyes had a smoky look, impossible to penetrate.

He hung his shirt and trousers on a door hook. His eyes flicked over the room: the beige walls, yellow chenille bedspreads, and Formica-top dresser. Under the single window stood an old-fashioned radiator, its paint beginning to peel.

"This place is a joke," said Ray, opening the bathroom door. "First-class accommodations, they told us. First class, my ass. I have filing cabinets bigger than this shower stall."

"We're in the woods, Ray. They don't have Hiltons in the national parks."

Before pulling off his undershirt, he hesitated, his hands crossed over his chest.

"Anything wrong?" she asked.

"I thought I heard something outside. Probably nothing, maybe a squirrel." He finished undressing and reached inside the triangular shower stall, turning both faucet handles until he achieved the desired temperature. He stepped in and reveled in the warm spray for some time before muttering, "Damn, forgot the soap." Louder then, "Loretta, get me some soap."

"Get your own soap," she tossed back.

The tiles were so slick that he had to steady himself against the shower door frame with his left hand. He opened the door and stepped out to fetch the tiny rectangle of soap in its paper packet off the sink. Upon his stepping back in, a scalding stream from the shower head assaulted his left arm. Several seconds passed before his brain registered the pain. The womb-like temperature of the water had climbed sharply.

"Aahhh!" His bellowing scream pierced the nighttime sounds of the great woods about them. An owl ceased its nocturnal call mid-hoot.

Loretta swung open the bathroom door to find her husband cowering against the stall corner, writhing in pain and shrouded in steam just outside the reach of the scorching spray.

"What's wrong, Ray, what's wrong?"

"My arm, I'm burned. I'm scalded."

She threw a doubled-over towel across her arm to protect it and, carefully reaching into the stall, turned off the two faucets. As the steam began to dissipate, she saw his left arm for the first time, blood-red and blotchy from shoulder to forearm.

"Lean on me," she said, helping him to the nearest bed. "I'll get some ice and try to find a doctor."

"Not ice, you idiot," he snarled. "Ice causes blisters. Cool water is what I need."

She settled him on the bed, then heard a pounding at the door. Loretta jerked it open and found Paco and Molly standing there. They'd heard the scream from their cabin.

"Please help me. Ray's been burned, scalded. I need a doctor and some ice. Or something," Loretta pleaded.

Paco spun sharply. "I'll get Jake Lebowitz. I think he's a doctor."

"I'll get ice," cried Molly, moving into the room. "There's a machine next to cabin 10." Loretta started to protest, but Molly had already snatched the empty ice bucket off the dresser and left.

Loretta took a washcloth from the chrome bars above the sink and held it under the tap while she turned on the cold water. A cold compress would at least remove the heat. But nothing came out of the spigot.

The still ajar cabin door swung open, and a man entered carrying a small black leather bag.

"Who the hell are you?" Ray shouted, hastily covering his naked torso with the bedspread.

"Jake Lebowitz, Ray. I'm a chiropodist, doctor of podiatry,

but--"

"Well, that's a big help. My damned arm's been scalded, not my foot," Ray said.

"Cute, Ray. My husband the diplomat," Loretta said, moving away from the bed to make room.

"I see your husband's a little meshugge. I've met crusty bagels with better manners," Jake said. He strode to the bed and set his black bag down. "Has anyone been sent for ice yet?" he asked.

Ray's large physique seemed to shrink as he sat on the bed. His voice trembled slightly. "I thought ice caused blisters."

"It will if it's applied directly to a burn, but I'm just going to make cold compresses with it. That okay with you?" Ray didn't answer. "Try it, you'll like it," Jake said. He peered down through horn-rimmed glasses set on a prominent nose. The hint of a smile lurked under the flowing gray mustache with its upswept tips.

"Yeah, sure, Doc, go ahead," Ray mumbled, refusing to look Jake in the eye. "Yeah, uh, thanks, thanks very much."

The door opened again, and Paco entered. Molly waddled after him, carrying the filled ice bucket. She set it on the nightstand.

"Mrs. Symington? I'm Paco LeSoto and this is my wife, Molly. "Sorry we're meeting under these circumstances," he said smoothly.

Loretta's constricted mouth turned into a genuine smile. "You've been so kind. Thank you for getting the doctor and the ice." She glared at Ray to prompt him.

"Hi," he said. "Yeah, sure, thanks for your help."

Jake examined the burn site and said, "You were extremely lucky. It's mostly a first-degree burn, not much swelling. Just one small place here--possibly second degree. The compresses should do wonders."

"But there's no cold water," Loretta protested. Jake, Molly, and Paco stared at her.

"How could that be?" Paco asked. He moved to the sink and turned on the tap, but nothing came out of it.

"Told you, Loretta!" Ray said. "Someone tried to scald me."

"You're paranoid," she snapped.

With Molly's help, Jake filled up two towels with ice cubes and packed Ray's arm in the compresses. He winced in pain.

"Thank you all," Loretta said. "Doctor, isn't there something more you can do for my husband?"

Jake gave Ray two pills--one for pain and the other an antibiotic to prevent infection. "I don't expect any blistering, and the swelling should be down by tomorrow," he said. "I'll check on him before breakfast. I don't see why he can't continue with the tour. He's going to be a bit uncomfortable for a few days whether he's on the tour or not." He handed Loretta a single pill. "This'll help you sleep. You've had enough tsuris for one night." He ushered Molly and Paco through the door ahead of him.

"'Night," Jake said to Ray.

"Hey, Doc, thanks a lot. I appreciate all you did," Ray said. Loretta looked pleased for the first time that day.

Outside the LeSotos' cabin, Paco patted Molly on the fanny and said, "You go on inside, sweetie pie."

"You're not coming in with me, honey?"

"Not just yet. I want to check on something first." Paco turned and started walking. Bright moonlight helped him find his way to the back of the Symingtons' cabin, number 16. Seeking the entry point for the utility connections, he located a small door at foundation level and discovered it had been left partially open.

He pulled the key chain from his pocket and lit his small penlight. The tiny beam illuminated both utility cutoff valves. The pipes coming out of the ground were heavily jacketed with insulation. Some rust had been rubbed away to the bare metal on one of the valve handles. As Paco gingerly lowered his hand to test the temperature of the valves, he noticed a long blue thread caught on the left valve. He gently lifted the thread off. Using a business card from his wallet as a spindle, he wound the thread carefully around it and tucked it into his wallet. He touched the suspected valve housing to determine the cold water cutoff. Spreading his handkerchief over the handle, he tried to rotate it clockwise, but it wouldn't turn. It had already been turned off. He reversed the handle instead and heard the rush of water.

Paco recalled that when he entered the Symingtons' cabin, Ray was sitting on the bed already soaking wet. Someone had turned off the water, either while Ray was showering or beforehand, emptying the residual cold water from the pipes before the hot water arrived.

Chapter 7
THE GIFT SHOP
Same Day, Friday, September 11, 1981

THE QUARTER MOON CAST A SILVER STREAK across the Flaming Gorge waters. On the far side of the lake, the light at the water's edge silhouetted the carcass of a drowned elk, its antlers entangled in brambles, its life snatched in the simple act of satisfying a thirst.

LeRoy and Ruth strolled hand in hand from the dining room back to their cabin, well out of earshot of the excitement at cabin 16. They picked their way along the shoreline until they caught sight of the fallen elk.

"Poor innocent thing," Ruth said. "I hope he didn't suffer."

"Dying's never pleasant. It doesn't matter whether you're innocent or guilty," LeRoy said nervously. "But it beats rotting in prison."

Ruth stopped and looked into her husband's troubled eyes. "Don't tell me you're having second thoughts?"

"I guess I'm a little scared," he replied. "Been doing too much moonlight thinking lately, but I'll get over it, babe."

"Are you sure, hon?" she asked. "We could stop now--even send the money back anonymously."

"Don't be ridiculous," he answered. "I'll be fine. Really!"

LeRoy liked her fussing over him, only he wouldn't admit it. He took her hand, and as they began walking again, allowed his mind to wander back twenty-eight years to the town of Sweetwater, Texas.

He'd walked into a barbershop and styling salon for a haircut. While waiting his turn, he chatted with the manicurist, a muscular girl with cheerleader looks sitting at a small table just inside the window. In just a few minutes, Ruth and LeRoy sensed some sort of magnetic attraction between them. She told the blond newcomer that she liked his friendly smile. Within a week the scholarship engineering student and the manicurist began dating.

A year later she followed him to the Texas Tech campus, and upon his graduation, the lovebirds married and left Sweetwater behind for Washington, D.C. An exhilarated Ruth had escaped from the commitment to her parents' salon--its lifetime trap of cutting cuticles, mucking in other women's hair, and listening to gossip.

He found employment with one of the beltway electronics firms, and she became a teller at one of the local banks. Although he made an adequate salary as an engineer, they recklessly spent more than they made. For the next twenty years, they roller-coastered through several debt-correcting, refinancing, and deprivation periods, only to find themselves back in the same hole. The bottom fell out when his company lost a major Federal Government contract. LeRoy got laid off-just about the same time his heart problems arose.

Half joking, Ruth proposed bank robbery as a way out for them. At first they laughed about it, but as the alternatives played out, the opposite side of the law seemed more viable--especially to LeRoy. He refused to end up like his pa, a Texas dirt farmer who'd toiled his whole life without reaping any rewards. Four successive years of drought, unpaid notes on new equipment, and a third mortgage had claimed the land and everything on it. Pa died face down in a wheat field furrow with a foreclosure notice in his pocket. The honesty, the backbreaking fourteen-hour days, what had they added up to?

Because the Miltons hadn't been able to have children, the risks seemed manageable. Ruth's teller experience gave her just the insider view they needed. Now they were executing their own retirement plan. In fact, after the Denver heist, they would need only two more capers to reach an investment stake of $300,000.

Bright lights ahead jarred LeRoy from his thoughts. The lighting came from two oversized log cabins: the gift shop and general store. A log-railed porch ran the length of both stores. Coarse white caulking surrounded the small windows and served as mortar between the rough-hewn logs.

LeRoy, feeling apologetic for the mood he'd imposed on his wife, offered, "Ruth, what do you say we pop in and see what's doing?"

She answered by yanking his arm toward the door. Inside, the gift shop and general store were connected by an arched doorway. One wall displayed art works of stylized figures and symbols. They heard a sales clerk interpreting them for Cookie Adams.

"The Navajos made these intricate sand paintings on the floors of their hogans. Created them as ceremonial icons to drive out illness--or an evil deed committed by a member of their tribe."

LeRoy shivered and moved away. He stopped at a tall postcard carousel, scenes of Native Americans in tribal regalia. He stepped to a second carousel and tried to spin it, but it wouldn't budge. He pushed harder.

"Ooh!" chirped a small voice. LeRoy poked his head between the two carousels and discovered a sparrow-like lady cowering behind scenes of Rocky Mountains, wolves, and eagles.

"Well, I'll be darned, if it isn't Bess Izaks," said LeRoy.

"Oh, dear, I didn't know you knew my name," she said, her voice quavering. She hastily plucked a foldout packet from the rack. "Don't you think this is a nice one for my grandniece?" she asked no one in particular. Her hand began to shake and the packet sprang loose--the postcards cascading to the floor, accordion fashion. "Oh, dear! Oh, no!" She let the entire packet fall to her feet, reached over to the next carousel, and grabbed a single postcard without even looking at it.

Ruth sprang to her side, retrieved the packet from the floor, and tucked it back in its wire rack. "Hellooooo, Bess," she cooed. "Are you all right?" Bess didn't answer. Ruth boldly took her hand and led her out to a bench beside the door.

"Just a smidgen close back there," Bess whispered. She fanned herself with the card she'd selected.

"Can't imagine why you'd go behind there at all," said Le-Roy. "The carousel stands spin completely around for you."

"It was stuck?" Bess tried, her voice rising like a question at the end.

"Well, now, Bess," said Ruth quietly. "You wouldn't happen to be hiding from us, would you? We all know that's terribly impolite, don't we?"

"Ye...yes."

"You wouldn't, by any chance, have gone through our suitcases the other day, would you?" Ruth asked.

Bess gasped, her cheeks flushed. "Oh, no, I wouldn't dream of..."

LeRoy sidled close to her, his voice gentle. "Bess, dear, there's a perfectly good reason for what you may have found," he said. "It's a trifle difficult for us to explain now, but I can assure you it's quite legitimate. I do hope you'll trust us." He leaned over the flushed sparrow and planted a respectful peck on her unsuspecting cheek. Bess looked confused.

"Oh, Bess, there you are," called Cookie, who had decided not to buy a sand painting after all. "I wondered what happened to you." By now, Bess looked worn out and asked Cookie to take her back to their cabin. Her postcard lay on the bench.

LeRoy picked it up and guffawed. "Do you suppose this is what Bess had in mind for her grandniece?" he asked. The picture showed a Pocahontas look-alike, full-breasted and naked, astride a paint pony.

But Ruth had turned her attention to a suede jacket lined in sheepskin. She slipped it on and felt the toasty warmth of the lining. She felt LeRoy staring at her oddly as she took the jacket off.

"No...wait," he said.

He picked up the hem of the coat and pulled the sheepskin liner away from the hide. Ah, a space between--more than adequate to stash all the money, he thought.

Ruth read his mind and shook her head. "Forget it, the shipping box would be too big for our rental post box," she said in a low voice.

"You can buy the jacket if you want it, hon."

"You kidding? It's 260 bucks!" said Ruth. "But thanks, Le-Roy, you're sweet. How about buying some prints? Maybe Georgia O'Keeffe, Thomas Moran, and sending them home in one of those big mailing tubes?"

"Same problem: too big for the rental box," he said. "I've got a better idea. See those bubble mailer bags on the shelf? They'd be perfect. We'll rewrap our stuff and add new labels."

"Let's do it," she said. "But where's the nearest post office?"

"Don't have one," said the clerk in a gingham dress. "But there's a mailbox outside. Big 'nuff fer packages, too. You hafta pay for the packing stuff and postage, natcherly. Better make it snappy, gotta weigh 'em, and we close at nine."

The Miltons purchased six bubble bags, clear packing tape, and labels and ambled out the door as casually as they could, then broke into a run for their cabin. They furiously repacked the $61,000 and hustled back to the store. LeRoy's chest heaved as he tried to catch his breath from all the rushing. He leaned on the counter as the clerk solemnly weighed each of the packages on the postal scale.

"Mail gets picked up 'round 6 a.m. Monday," the clerk said.

"Monday!" they both echoed.

She eyed them through her store-bought spectacles. "Post office don't work no Sundays here neither."

"Uh, right, of course," LeRoy said. He hastily paid for the postage, a $5 stamp for each package and gathered them up. "Thanks. Goodnight now," he said. Ruth followed him outdoors to the blue U.S. mailbox standing out front.

"Do you think the bags will be safe in there?" she asked.

"No, Ruth," he said wearily, "a coyote's going to climb inside and chew 'em up. What the hell do you want from me? It's Saturday night. Sure, we can hang on to 'em. You expecting to find a post office on the Snake River?" He pulled down on the large handle. The mailbox gaped open like a hungry mouth. "Speak now or it's a done deal."

"Done," she said. And away went each of the bubble bags.

"Done," LeRoy repeated, letting go of the handle. He brushed off his hands and took her arm. "Ruth, do you think Bess knows anything?"

"I think Bess might have seen at least a part of the money the way she reacted. But she's so confused now, I don't think she'll be a problem. That kiss was a stroke of genius, LeRoy. You were precious with her."

He felt his thumping heart slow to a comfortable beat at last.

Hilda Vickers tried to prop her pillow up against the headboard, but it was too thin to stay put. A hairnet capped her white waves, and a pink flannel nightgown blanketed her. Even in this getup, Hilda carried her eighty-three years with grace. She had all her own teeth and wore glasses only for reading. Michener's Centennial lay open on her lap.

Now widowed, Hilda had come from old money in Providence, Rhode Island. During her fifty-one-year marriage to Admiral Bradford Vickers, she'd developed a spirited independence. When her niece, Tina Barton--her sister's daughter--could manage it, the two of them traveled together. Tina had surprised her this time, initiating the travel plans on her own. The trip had turned into a family affair. Hilda's brother, Judge Harold Sessions, and his wife were also on board. They'd come at Hilda's insistence.

A key rattled in the door, and her niece strode into the cabin. Tina's auburn pageboy fell freely around her shoulders. She wore no makeup and didn't need any.

"Hi, Auntie. Book any good?"

"Interminable. But what was all that excitement out there?" she asked, tossing her head in the direction of the higher-numbered cabins.

"Remember Ray Symington who pushed his way off the bus ahead of everyone?"

"You mean that boorish fellow?" said Hilda.

"Yes. I heard someone say he scalded his arm in the shower. Serves him right, that lowlife."

"Aren't you overreacting a bit?" questioned Hilda. "You hardly know the man. Or do you?"

"I'd never met him before this trip," said Tina. "But I've had reason to dislike him long before this--and so do you."

"We do?"

"Yes, Auntie. He's the man responsible for all your brother's troubles."

"Harry's?"

"Uh-huh!"

Tina sat down on a corner of Hilda's bed. She weighed no more than 120 pounds, but the corner immediately dropped down at least two inches. "Whoa!" she said. The two of them began to laugh.

On her hands and knees, Tina discovered a caster missing from the bed frame. On her feet again, she fished around in the night table drawer, pulled out the Gideon Bible, and wedged it in place. "Perfect!" she said. "You can always depend on the Bible."

Tina was no less irreverent in her pursuit of business. She'd freely admit selling her soul for a lucrative deal--excelled at it, in fact. With an MBA from Harvard, she wrote for Fortune, peddled business advice, and taught corporate finance at American University. Tina did everything well. But the one thing she couldn't do was con her aunt.

"Young lady, you're in this for more than the Grand Canyon and chaperoning me about," Hilda declared. "You wouldn't try to bull this old gal now, would you?" She reached for Tina's hands.

"Auntie!" Tina pulled back.

"Don't 'Auntie' me," Hilda commanded. "Tell me what's going on here."

"I can't right now," Tina replied. "You'll just have to trust me."

Chapter 8
WHERE BUFFALO ROAM AND PEOPLE PLAY
Day Three, Saturday, September 12, 1981

GLINTS OF FIRST SUNLIGHT DANCED OVER THE LAKE. Saturday's dawn came unannounced to the travelers cocooned in their cabins. The thirty-six-degree chill penetrated Molly's comfort. She rolled out of bed and padded barefoot out the door to the tiny wooden balcony. The cold air bit her face, but she didn't mind. "Paco, wake up, we're in Wy-homing!" The fragrance of ponderosa pine blended with distant aromas of bacon and fresh bread.

A half-hour later Molly and Paco waited in the dining room to be seated. The husky young hostess saw them to a table already occupied by two women from the tour. "These here ladies said they won't mind sharing their table with you."

"Please do," said the elder of the two women. "I'm Hilda Vickers and this is my niece, Tina Barton."

"We're the LeSotos, Molly and Paco, we are. I'm always glad to meet someone new. I find other people so auxillirating."

A whitecap of silver curls washed over Hilda's forehead. Her delicate ears locked onto Molly's words, unsure whether a friendly witticism had been cast or merely an unintended misresponse had landed. "How delightful," Hilda said. "Tina's an assistant professor of business at the American University when she's not my traveling companion."

Tina grinned. "I'm sure they're not interested in what I do, Aunt Hilda." Tina seemed more amused than embarrassed.

"Actually, your university is not too far from us," said Paco, quite taken with her unaffected fresh looks. "Molly and I live in southern Maryland, Black Rain Corners. It's near--"

"Oh, we've been there, Mr. LeSoto," interrupted Hilda. "We toured the Marche House mansion. What a fine old museum. Tina, bless her, she took me there last April--exquisite Victorian pieces. At my advanced age I don't go anywhere without my niece."

"I should think the word advanced is a little exaggerated, ma'am," said Paco.

"Ah, you're much too gallant, young man," said Hilda. "Either that or you're blind. But I seem to be detaining you. Go get in line. I'm stuck with these bloody Eggbeaters. What I wouldn't give for some of that bacon."

"I'll just have to have it for you," Tina said. "And some sausage, too."

By the time the LeSotos returned to the table, Hilda sat alone sipping the last of her Earl Grey's breakfast tea.

"Your niece is a mighty pretty lady," Molly commented. "I didn't notice a wedding band."

"No," said Hilda. "She's neither married nor attached nor even dating, and that has me quite concerned."

"Can't see why it should," said Molly. "She's quite a knock-up."

"I'd have thought a lovely university professor would be in great demand," offered Paco. "I assume there are still some eligible males left with a brain in their head."

"That's just it," said Hilda. "One date and she frightens them off--they don't want the competition. She's too good for most men and not desperate enough to go get what she really wants." Hilda poured herself another cup of tea. "Women are different now, they're driven by career ambitions. Why, by the time I was twenty-four, I knew what I wanted and how to get it. My husband, the admiral, never knew what hit him. He's gone now, poor man."

"I'm sorry," said Paco. He couldn't help but admire this spunky old gal.

"Oh, that was a long time ago," she said. "My Brad used to say it was the only engagement he ever lost. But my niece, she's another story."

Suddenly her niece appeared behind her with a heaping plate. "Auntie, I can't get away for five minutes without you discussing my social condition. Shame on you. Just for that, I'll take seconds on the bacon."

An hour later, the bus knelt dutifully for its passengers. Molly squeezed her way down the aisle and paused at the third row of driver's-side seats.

"How's the arm this morning?"

"I guess it could be worse," Ray mumbled. The blotchy redness had started to fade. His left sleeve was cut up to the shoulder. "Ruined a ninety-dollar Armani shirt, though."

"Oh, he'll survive nicely," said Loretta, "in spite of himself."

Ray straightened up in his seat as if he had suddenly remembered something important. "Thanks for asking, and for your help last night, Mrs. LeSoto. And thank your husband, too," he said.

"You're more than welcoming," said Molly, as she continued to her seat two rows behind.

Ray smoothed his silk shirt as if he'd just accomplished a task. The gesture wasn't lost on Loretta. He'd remembered his assignment from Maynard: to be nice. Now if he'd only do the same with his IMTC people.

The bus eased away from the cabins and rumbled along, high above the eastern lake shore. The 200,000-acre lake fed by the Green River came alive in the Flaming Gorge Reservoir and Firehole Canyon, where the low early morning sun shimmered its hot vibrant colors in the "painted" rock formations along the canyon walls. Turning north, the bus headed into coal mining country that traced its ancestry to the miners of England and Wales. They sped through Rock Springs over the Continental Divide once more to nearby Sinks Canyon State Park.

"The park's known for its flowing river going underground, disappearing mysteriously, and reappearing again farther down-canyon," Glenn Haniford told them. "Also, the gravesite of Sacajawea is only a few miles north of here. She was the Shoshone interpreter for the Lewis and Clark expedition in the early 1800's."

The bus rolled to a stop for an early lunch in Thermopolis, Wyoming. "Okay, folks," Glenn called out. "This is one of the nicest gift shops on our tour. Great bargains. The restaurant's got the best beef stew and hottest chili in Wyoming. Have fun. Be back on the bus at 12:30."

The group converged like stampeding bison on the Hot Springs gift shop. One person hung back at the rear of the bus, drinking ice water from a Styrofoam cup. After finishing it, the woman refilled the cup with ice from the cooler on the floor at the back of the bus. With a smile she shook the cup's contents into the crease of the seat where Ray would sit after lunch. From her new fifth row vantage point directly across the aisle from him, she would enjoy the fun. She hurried off the bus.

The most athletic among them always made it to the ladies room line first, the hungriest to the lunch line, but the longest lines snaked to the gift shop registers.

Reba Hurles had her eye on a fringed suede jacket studded with beads. She flipped open her purse and trolled for a credit card. "You know, Molly," she confided, "I never met a gift shop I didn't like."

Hand-wrought earrings of sterling silver and amber caught Molly's attention, and in a moment of impulse, Paco easily consented. Hardly any of the excited tourists could pass up adding one more T-shirt or trinket to their collection. Theo purchased six bookmarks made of bark.

Monte and Michelle Davies handled nearly every piece of Native American pottery before deciding not to buy. Suddenly, a crash. Pottery pieces scrambled Humpty-Dumpty fashion across the floor. Bess Izaks stood amid the rubble, hands on her cheeks.

"Congratulations, ma'am," said the sales clerk. "You have just purchased an object of many pieces. The price is $51. How do you wish to pay for it?"

As a trembling Bess produced her credit card, Cookie appeared and put an arm around her roomie. "Honey, you've got to pull yourself together."

Annoyed with the frenetic shopping, Ray ate quickly and returned to the bus early. He settled into his seat with the current copy of Fortune. Little by little, more of the group returned. Loretta was the last to climb aboard. She hesitated just before taking the seat next to her husband.

"What's wrong, Ray?" she asked. "You have the strangest look on your face."

He closed his magazine and shoved it into the seat pocket in front of him. His right hand felt for his wallet pocket, then lower to the seat beneath him. "Damn! Damn it to hell," he yelled. He raised himself up, scooped out a large handful of half-melted ice cubes, and pushed Loretta aside in an effort to get to the aisle. "Whose sick idea of a prank is this?"

A male voice he didn't recognize yelled back, "Couldn't hold it, could ya, Ray?" Another said, "Hey, I think they sell diapers inside." The entire seat of Ray's pants was soaked.

Glenn opened the bench seat at the rear of the bus and handed a blanket to Loretta. Amid continuous tittering and comments, Ray struggled out of his sopping trousers in the narrow on-board lavatory. While he cowered on a rear seat of the bus, bundled in the Indian blanket, Loretta took his trousers into the restaurant ladies' room and air-dried them on the hand blower there. The hilarity of the interlude soured when the passengers realized they would be delayed another half-hour.

The bus left at one o'clock for Cody, Wyoming, with the Symingtons in self-imposed exile in rear seats. Shortly after three, they pulled up at the Buffalo Bill Cody Historical Center. Though it normally took days to properly relish this cultural feast, they had to make do with two hours. The center comprised Buffalo Bill Cody's house and a museum of his memorabilia, the Remington Firearms Collection, the Plains Indians exhibition, and the Whitney Gallery of Western Art.

Thom and Theo Moyer spent their first hour in the gallery, almost swept away by the grandeur of the Thomas Moran landscapes. She read aloud from the brochure: "Thomas Moran's paintings of the West so captivated Congress that they designated Yellowstone the world's first national park."

A large glassed-in room dedicated to Frederic Remington housed bronze sculptures of charging stallions and Native American warriors.

Theo placed her hand in her husband's. "Darling, this is unbelievable. Collections of such major works--yet so far from any population center."

"How about a cold drink to wash down all this culture?" he asked. They headed for the coffee shop.

She draped her purse over the back of a chair and sat with her knees under a Formica-topped table while Thom fetched two Diet Cokes. She noticed a short teenage lad in dirty blue jeans leaning against the wall, but gave him no further thought.

Just as Thom returned with the drinks, the Miltons stopped by to chat on their way to their own table. This distraction lasted long enough for the lone teenager to lift the bag from Theo's chair and dart toward the front door.

"That boy, he's got a handbag. Is it yours?" Ruth cried.

Theo swung around, looked behind her, and knew immediately. "Stop him," she yelled. "He's got my purse."

Thom jumped to his feet and joined LeRoy in pursuit of the thief. Two security guards near the front door moved to cut off the lad's escape, so he ran deeper into the complex--toward the Remington Firearms museum. Molly and Paco just happened to be standing in the museum doorway, in the boy's intended path. They saw him clutching a woman's purse and heard the guards shouting.

While most of the stunned crowd recoiled from the ruckus, Paco stepped in front of Molly and assumed a blocking stance. The thief jerked to a stop and looked over his shoulder. Cut off in both directions, he threw the purse straight at Paco and dove for the fire doors behind him. The doors flew open. The alarm blared, children screamed, and the two guards took off in hot pursuit.

Paco bent over the open purse on the floor and tucked a few articles back inside. Theo rushed forward, her hands out to pick it up.

"If you intend to press charges," warned Paco, "I wouldn't touch the leather handle just yet. I don't think he had time to go through it, so I assume all the contents are still intact. However, I seriously doubt they'll catch the sneak. He had youth and agility on his side."

Indeed, the guards returned empty handed, exhausted, and apologetic--their first responsibility must be the museum complex.

"Everything's here," Theo said. She wanted to end the ugly incident quickly.

Paco watched the Moyers hurry away, wondering why Theo had reacted so out of character. She'd shown fear and anger upon retrieving the purse. In fact, she'd snatched it from the floor. He'd have thought she'd be grateful--but not even a thanks. He shrugged and started back toward where he'd left Molly, when he noticed a pencil stub and a folded blue slip of paper lying on the granite floor. Torn between calling after them and ignoring it totally, he stooped over and retrieved the folded paper. Opening it, he found today's hand-written date and their present Cody location. He slipped it into his jacket pocket.

"Why were you so anxious to end the conversation back there? They were only trying to help us," whispered Thom as the Moyers settled into their seats on the bus.

"Can't you imagine what's in my purse?"

"No, what?"

"Well," she started, "all our traveler's checks and..."

"Replaceable!" he interrupted.

"And the renegade copy of Maynard's memo to Ray," she murmured, her lips brushing his ear.

"Good grief, Theo," he whispered. "I wouldn't want the wrong person to get their hands on that. If the Symingtons even suspect we've gotten hold of the memo, we'll have to table the plan."

"I agree. Should I destroy it?"

"Not just yet," he replied. "But I'd keep it in a less conspicuous place in the meantime."

The bus had reached its cruising speed. Outside, the uninterrupted expanse flew by. No telephone poles, no roadside trees, no fences or hedgerows; only rolling hills and staggered stands of yellow quaking aspen on the high ground. Now, only a short distance to Yellowstone through the Shoshone National Forest.

Molly commented, "Are we going to see the wonerful wizard or isn't the Yellowstone road like the yellow brick road?" That comment earned her a hug from Paco.

"Oh, look," cried Ruth Milton, seated on the door side of the bus. "Buffalo--on the hillside to the right."

"There are thousands of them up there," said George Hurles. "A whole herd even. I've only seen buffalo on the tail side of a nickel before."

"More accurately, folks, they're called bison. And they're the Wyoming state animal," said Glenn. But somehow he knew that nobody would remember to call them bison.

"Let the chips fall where they may," quipped Molly. "Hey, there's more on the left." Her eyes widened. "And they're headed for the road!"

The bus eased to a stop. A single file of the stately animals meandered across a major U.S. highway.

"This is open range country," Glenn reminded everyone. "The bison have the right of way. We're the guests here. In this unspoiled land we take away only the experience and leave only our footprints."

The huge beasts moved with surprising grace. A hush settled over the travelers, a sense of awe, a sense of being transported back hundreds of years. Nearly fifteen minutes later, forty bison had lumbered across the road before the bus found a gap large enough to move through.

Chapter 9
NOT A LEG TO STAND ON
Same Day, Saturday, September 12, 1981

THE ROADWAY DARKENED UPON ENTERING A TUNNEL of lodge-pole pines, each thin tree in the thick forest reaching and struggling for its piece of the sky. At the end of the dense green cover, the landscape brightened once more. A pelican, its wings spread like a giant kite, zoomed over the wind-swept waters of Yellowstone Lake.

"I thought pelicans were only on the Gulf coast," Paco said.

"Think again," Glenn told him. "These pelicans live here and migrate to southern California in the winter."

They had just entered Yellowstone National Park from the east, and at Fishing Bridge, followed the shore of this hundred-mile-long alpine lake. Two hours later the bus rolled to a stop, and Lew opened the door. Icy air whooshed in. From ninety degrees in Denver to twenty-eight here in northwest Wyoming. Hands grabbed for jackets, hats, and hoods. Outside, a flurry of snow-flakes swirled in ghostlike shapes.

"Snow!" squealed Reba. "And the sun is shining!"

"What's that noise?" Paco asked.

"What noise?" Loretta wanted to know.

"Off that way, in the distance." He pointed north. "It doesn't sound like thunder. Or an animal, either." Then they all heard it: an eerie rumbling and roaring.

"Ladies and gentlemen," Glenn announced, his voice almost reverential, "you're hearing the Lower Falls in the Grand Canyon of the Yellowstone River. It's 308 feet high. Twice as high as

Niagara Falls."

Everyone jumped up, ready to plunge off the bus.

"Door side out first," Glenn reminded. "But folks, I have to warn you--there are three sets of stairs to get to the Tripping Rock Overlook. Sixty steps each." A handful of older travelers sank, dejected, back down in their seats. Loretta stood patiently waiting for her turn to leave. They were on the driver's side. But Ray bolted forward, cradling his tender left arm, elbowing twice as hard with his right.

"For God's sake, man, don't you ever learn?" LeRoy grumbled.

"Apparently not," Cookie Adams replied. But Ray was already out the door, hurrying to the first set of overlook stairs. His new Minolta dangled from a plaid strap around his neck.

The snow flurries stopped as abruptly as they had begun. The sun caressed their chilled faces. Molly waddled to the first landing and planted her feet firmly at the rail.

"It's already gorgeous here, Paco. Look at all those golden yellow colors on the canyon walls. It's magnificent, but we don't hafta go to the edge. I know you got an antiphobia 'bout heights." Paco remained with his bride and put his arm around her.

"I know just what you mean, Molly," said Loretta. "I don't like heights either." She approached on the other side, trying to catch up to her husband. "You go ahead, Ray. I'll meet you down there in a few minutes."

"Yeah," he said. "Go find a gift shop or something." He hurried down the steps.

The Lower Falls thundered and roared. Foam frothed and mist rose a hundred feet. For millions of years, the Yellowstone River had been carving its way through twenty-four miles of granite and limestone canyons. The travelers stood spellbound in the face of nature's power.

Just short of the overlook, Symington pushed and bullied his way through the crowd. He stepped over the eighteen-inch-high safety chain, determined to get closer to the edge for more extraordinary pictures. What was the point of owning a Minolta otherwise? But the crowd didn't give a hoot about Ray's photography--they shoved back.

A park ranger called out from the upper landing: "Sir! Back behind the chain, please! And stay back!" When he saw that Ray was ignoring him, the ranger bellowed, "Hey, sir, get back! Get away from the edge!"

Ray pretended not to hear and leaned forward to photograph the rushing river below. He thought he felt a nudge at his back. He stumbled to his knees. He slid. His 190 pounds carried him forward. The new camera flew over the edge. Sunlight bounced off the chrome and glass as the Minolta plunged to its destruction. Ray's right arm lunged for the strap, missing it altogether. He slid some more. His foot caught. He flailed about, looking for something to grip. His large body lurched forward, and he fell flat on his stomach, sliding head-first toward the edge of the precipice. By all rights, gravity should have had its way with him. But a thickly gnarled tree root had snagged his right foot in its tapered loop--the only thing between him and a 300-foot drop.

"Help! My leg, my leg!" he screamed. "It's broken. Help me. I'm going over. I'm gonna die. Help, help!"

The crisp air echoed with gasps and shouts above the roar of the Lower Falls. Glenn Haniford ran to the guard chain and climbed over it. At the edge he dropped to his knees and wrapped his arms around Ray's legs to keep him from sliding farther.

"I need some more muscle here," he shouted to no one in particular.

"It's on the way," answered a deep voice.

The ranger raced down the remaining steps from his parked truck at road level and broke through the crowd carrying a coil of rope. He tied one end around the nearest concrete chain stanchion. Wrapping it once around his own body, he maneuvered closer to Ray's prone figure. Grasping the line tightly, he reached out and grabbed hold of Ray's waistband. With strong hands and biceps straining, the ranger yanked backward. The tension on Ray's leg slackened, allowing Glenn to untangle the twisted foot from the tree root. Glenn then joined the ranger in grabbing Ray's waistband. As they eased the victim back toward the guardrail, Ray began to slip from both his trousers and undershorts until the whiteness of his bare bottom punctuated his predicament. Before he lost them altogether, Glenn and the ranger inched a sprawling Ray back from the ledge and hefted him onto a nearby bench.

The crowd looked on, smirking and strangely silent, like the audience at a bad play. Ray orchestrated a counterpoint to the silence. His caterwauling pierced through the roar of the Lower Falls.

"My ankle, it's probably broken, for crissake. My burned arm. Do you have to be so damned rough?"

"Maybe I should get into some other line of work," the ranger muttered.

Ray raised himself to a sitting position, and without missing a beat, continued to complain.

"Sir," the ranger interrupted. "I'm an Emergency Medical Technician. If you don't want me to help you, just say so. Otherwise, I'm going to need you to calm down so I can look at your foot."

Glenn suppressed a smile.

"Try to wiggle your foot," the ranger told Ray.

"But what if it's broken?" Ray whined. "It sure hurts enough."

"Then we'll need a stretcher to carry you up," interrupted Dr. Jake Lebowitz, arriving on the scene. "Meanwhile, it wouldn't hurt for you to listen to the man. Okay, boychick, wiggle it so we can determine if it's broken." Ray complied, stretching his facial muscles in dramatic agony. Then the ranger palpated the entire leg with his fingers, slowly, carefully, before making his diagnosis.

"Okay now, sit up. Can you put some weight on it?"

With a grimace of pain, Ray pressed down on the foot. He leaned on Jake and tried to stand. He took a few steps, but then collapsed back onto the bench.

Jake volunteered to accompany the patient when the ranger transported Ray to the nearest first aid station less than a mile away. They'd catch up with the tour again that night.

"He'll be fine," Jake told Glenn. "Go on now. There's only a little daylight left and there's so much to see. You can tell Mrs. Symington what happened on the way up. Go on, we're okay."

The tour bus left for the Upper Falls with its hundred feet of cascading river--less dramatic, but nevertheless, another splendid view. The brilliant sun slid quickly behind the evergreen mountains, draping the canyon below in its nightshirt.

Following check-in at the Sagebrush Inn, the dining room filled with hungry travelers. The waiters were still serving dessert when Ray hobbled in on crutches. An elastic brace stretched around his right ankle. Jake and Loretta entered the dining room behind him. Jake's wife, Abby, had reserved a table for them. Molly and Paco sat with her.

"So what's the verdict?" Abby asked. "You've been gone over two hours."

"They said he's got a badly sprained ankle," said Jake.

"You should be as good as old in a few days," said Molly. "Congratulations, Mr. Symington."

"For what? For being a cripple?"

"Oh, so we're going to be grumpy are we?" commented Loretta. "Admit it, you did something stupid and you were fortunate enough that there were some quick-thinking souls around to save your skin. You should thank God and those who saved you instead of moping around in a stupor."

"Bull! I lost an $800 camera."

"Maybe, my darling husband, you'd be better off if you'd gone over the cliff after all."

"Loretta, that's a terrible thing to say," said Molly.

"Oh, she means it," Ray groused. "That way she'd get everything."

Loretta rammed her elbow into Ray's ribs when she saw Haniford approaching their table. Ray reacted quickly and reached out to grab Glenn's arm. "You did something wonderful and brave this afternoon. Despite how I acted, I do want to thank you from the bottom of my heart."

The immediate world went silent and Glenn's mouth fell open. He forced a smile and then moved away from the table.

Then Ray looked over at Paco. "I understand you're some kind of cop. That so?"

"I'm a semi-retired police detective."

"Well," continued Ray, "what if I told you it was no accident? Someone pushed me over the edge."

"Now," said Loretta, "you're not only making a mountain out of a molehill, you're making an ass of yourself."

"You weren't there," said Ray. "Or were you?"

"She was with us," Molly declared.

"How can you be so certain you were pushed?" asked Paco.

"Why would anyone want to kill you?" asked Abby.

"Oh, there are plenty of reasons why," said Loretta. "And plenty of people lining for the privilege. The real question is: which one?"

Chapter 10
FOUNTAINS OF AWE
Day Four, Sunday, September 13, 1981

AT THE SAGEBRUSH INN, SIX EXECUTIVE SUITES monopolized the mezzanine level. A brass-railed staircase and small elevator descended from the executive hallway to a comfortable lobby filled with overstuffed furniture. The east wall led into the Brass Rail Restaurant.

On Sunday morning at 8:15, only an eagle eye would have noticed the large hand holding the door to room 203 slightly ajar. It would have taken an even closer look to know that someone inside was spying on room 202 across the hall. Thom and Theo Moyer emerged from their room, 205, and hastened down the short carpeted staircase that led to the lobby.

Seeing the hall clear, a man in khaki pants and corduroy shirt slipped out of room 203, stole across, and listened at the door of 202. Ray Symington's bass voice carried as he talked on the phone.

"Yes, Maynard...I understand, Maynard...Yes, of course I will...I have your memo right with me...Yes, I use it as a reminder... Yes, Maynard...It's been an inspiration for me...Oh, that, a minor mishap...Yeah, I'll be fine. Oh, yes, lots of scenery. Yesterday, in the morning we..."

The eavesdropper surmised both ends of that conversation and concluded it would last at least ten minutes. Darting over to the elevator, he taped an OUT OF ORDER sign on the left-side door.

At the top of the stairs, he paused to listen and look. The lobby appeared empty except for the registration clerk, whose back

71

faced the desk as she tapped on a computer. Jovial voices and the clinking of silverware on plates drifted up from the restaurant.

Still on the mezzanine landing, the man in khakis sat down on the top stair next to the railing on his right. He pulled a key ring out of a deep pocket and detached a three-inch Crescent wrench from it. Sliding the key ring back into his pocket, he used the wrench to unscrew the two bolts that secured the brass railing to its newel post. Next, he crept down several steps and stopped to remove the two bolts at the mid-flight post. Finally, at the bottom post, he unscrewed only one bolt. Gingerly he tested the railing; it remained upright and looked perfectly stable.

Just as he had completed his task, a woman came through the glass door of the restaurant--her eyes fixed across the lobby as she beelined toward the restroom. If she had bothered to glance over at the stairs, she would have seen only a nondescript man seated on the bottom step, head down, retying his shoes. The man stood, dropped the wrench into his pants pocket, and strolled toward the restaurant. When he saw Thom Moyer emerging through the glass door and heading in his direction, the man in khakis retreated, unseen, into a telephone alcove.

Thom, in pursuit of his glasses, flew up the steps two at a time and disappeared from view. The man in the alcove moved into the restaurant, blending with the other diners.

Molly gobbled up French toast topped with cinnamon and sugar. Paco polished off his Spanish omelet. They chatted with the Whitmans and Theo while they sipped their coffee.

"You sure are in love with that blue cap, Gordon," said Molly. "Do you wear it to bed?"

"Only on weekends," said Gordon with a broad grin.

"Oh, my Gordo's a relentless New York Giants football nut," said Joanne. "He's afraid they'll lose if he doesn't wear it." She scowled. "The least you can do is take it off for meals."

Reluctantly he pulled the well-worn cap from his curly head and laid it upside down on the empty chair between Paco and himself.

Joanne continued to nag. "It could use a good washing, too—red dirt all over the inside. Yuck."

"If they lose today," said Gordon, "it'll be on your head."

"At least it won't be on yours," she said. "You don't even know what time they're playing."

"Hey," said Gordon, cocking his head, eager to stop Joanne's needling. "Hear that? Somebody must have dropped a load of dishes."

A few minutes later, the hostess who'd seated them appeared and whispered in Theo's ear. Theo's coffee cup rattled in the saucer as she set it down; she left immediately. The hostess then leaned over Paco's shoulder and whispered some words for his ears only. He pushed his chair back and said, "Excuse me. There's been an accident and Symington has asked to see me in the west lobby."

"It seems to me that guy is an accident prune," declared Molly. "Excuse me, too." The Whitmans remained.

As Paco and Molly came out of the restaurant, they were startled to see Ray just beyond the door, his body ramrod straight even as he leaned on his crutches.

"Well, Ray, what a nice surprise," Paco said. "I expected to find you flat on your backside."

"Cut the comedy, Inspector. See that?" Ray pointed to a sectional sofa across the lobby. "That was intended for me."

Paco's attention fixed on Thom Moyer stretched out on the sofa--ashen and shaking--surrounded by a group of rubberneckers. The staircase banister lay on the floral carpet next to the sectional, with brass balusters scattered about. Theo knelt beside her husband. When Paco approached, the bystanders drifted off. Only Loretta and Ray remained.

"What happened here?" asked Paco.

"You tell him, Lor," said Ray. "I can't get it together yet."

"We were late coming down for breakfast. Ray had a phone call," Loretta began. "Well, when we came out of our room to use the elevator, we found an OUT OF ORDER sign on it. So we headed for the stairs. Just then Thom came out of his room."

Loretta described how Thom had charged down the stairs ahead of them. "When he grabbed the right-hand railing, it collapsed under his weight and carried him over the side." She looked up at the staircase. "You know, this is really dangerous. There's no wall supporting the railing."

Loretta explained to Paco that, after Thom fell, they were nervous about going down. Finding the left-hand banister secure, she took Ray's crutches, and he held onto that railing as he came downstairs.

"You've got to help me, Inspector," cried Ray. "Someone's trying to kill me. I need protection."

Thom struggled to an upright position on the sofa and tried to gather his wits about him. He had landed miraculously on the overstuffed cushions. He stared at Ray in disbelief. "May I point out that I'm the one who went over the edge here?" he said.

"But it was intended for me," Ray insisted.

"How the hell would you know that?" Thom challenged.

"Read my lips, Thom," Ray snarled.

"Ray, if you feel that strongly, I think it's time you called the police," Paco said.

"And tell them what? That I'm a paranoid maniac?"

"I'm afraid I don't see any logic in this," Paco replied.

Ray drew Paco aside and said, "Look, I have my reasons. All I can say is, my job depends on my completing this tour. This is supposed to be a goodwill trip, me making nice to my staff. Those are my marching orders."

Paco's right eyebrow shot up as he eyed Ray without a word.

"Yeah, I admit I'm not so hot at that," Ray said. "But no way do I have time to involve the police. Are you going to help me or not?"

"I can't make any promises," said Paco. "But I'll look around and see what I can find." He turned back to Thom. "Do you need a doctor?"

"I'm pretty shook up, but I don't think I'm hurt. Just a little bruised. Besides, I've got Theo to help me."

"Yes, thank God for these cushions," Theo said.

Thom tested his legs and hobbled off to breakfast with his wife.

A concerned assistant manager with lawsuit on his mind ran dutifully after them. "I'm so sorry. The management wishes to express its most sincere apologies. We will, of course, pay any medical bills. I can't understand how this could have happened. I've already called maintenance to make the repairs."

The lobby emptied out. Molly swiveled her beach-ball body right and left, scanning the floral carpet. "Here's the screw that nailed 'im, Paco," she said.

"Thanks, baby, but it's not a screw. Screws are tapered, this is a bolt." Paco turned it over in his palm. "A quarter-twenty by one-inch hex head bolt, quite common."

He looked up at the mezzanine landing, thinking, a fall of ten or fifteen feet. A long way down, but unlikely to kill someone. More likely to maim. But if it wasn't an accident, then maybe someone wanted him out of the way. Off the bus? Off the tour? Out of the company? And who was the intended victim--Moyer or Symington?

Paco walked up the stairs, testing the right-side railing. Sturdy. In the mezzanine hall, he discovered the OUT OF OR-DER sign, affixed to the elevator door with masking tape. At the head of the stairs, six bolts--larger and heavier than the other hex heads--secured the uppermost wrought iron newel post to the floor. The post could not be wiggled or moved in any direction. At the top edge of each side of the post, he found two empty quarter-inch threaded holes, where the banister brackets should have been attached. The threads definitely had not been stripped, nor worn from use. A few steps below, at midpost, he discovered two more holes from missing hex head bolts. By the time he reached the lobby level, Molly had found several of the missing bolts and handed them to her husband. At the bottom newel post, Paco saw that the banister bracket remained attached, but severely twisted. "There's still one bolt missing," he said after counting them.

"I think I know where to look," Molly said. She began probing behind the plump sectional cushions. "I got it!" Triumphantly, she handed it to Paco, who slowly turned each of the bolts over in his palm.

He noticed a mark just to the right of each hex head corner--a striation, probably made by the wrench used to loosen each one. He determined that those marks couldn't have been made by the wrench that was used to tighten them down when the railing was first installed. Because, in that case, the marks would be located counterclockwise from the corners, not clockwise like these. Not likely an accident: the same wrench was used to loosen all the bolts, and two of them still had their split-ring lock washers on.

"Symington may be right," said Paco.

"But we still don't know if he's the intended fall guy," quipped Molly.

Paco wanted to spend more time analyzing the scene, but two burly maintenance men in overalls entered the lobby to clean up the mess. Paco casually slipped the bolts into his pocket, took Molly's arm, and led her back to their room.

Staring out the window of their ground-floor room, Paco hardly noticed the two red foxes darting through the brush, their fur coats glistening with dew in the sunlight of the crisp morning. The inspector had shifted his thoughts to earlier events--too many incidents to be entirely random. Joanne's attempt to slug Ray; his scalding; the shove, if there actually was a shove, at the Lower Falls; and this morning's railing disaster. Were they all meant for Symington? But then again they all were so amateurish, perhaps intended to look like botched jobs. In a way, Ray's excuse for refusing to bring in the police just didn't make sense.

Paco felt a soft nuzzle on his neck, and Molly's arms enfolded him. Ray's problems could wait.

"I hope he's got the heat on," a shivering Bess said. Cookie gave her a helpful little boost up the bus steps.

"Sure do, ma'am," Lew Getz answered. At eleven o'clock

that Sunday morning the temperature had only reached the mid-thirties. The Vermilion tourists settled into their seats and a national park ranger boarded the bus as their local Yellowstone guide. Approaching the Grand Loop road, he warned them about feeding any of the animals, especially the larger, more dangerous ones like bear, deer, and elk.

"You wouldn't believe how some folks just refuse to understand our rules," he said. "A few weeks ago a lady fed a deer while she was standing right next to a sign saying 'Do Not Feed the Animals.' "

Everyone groaned.

"The problem is," the ranger continued, "the wildlife become accustomed to the handouts, dependent even. Then in the off-season, many die of starvation. Another thing, folks, please don't litter. Sometimes the deer find Styrofoam containers and eat 'em. The animals get filled up and die of malnutrition."

"Aww, how terrible," Bess said.

Rumbling along the 140-mile Grand Loop road they spotted mule deer, antelope, and elk. "We've also got wolves, coyotes, bighorn sheep, marmots, beaver, squirrels--and they have more than 3,400 square miles of park to roam in," the ranger said proudly. "Fabulous birds too. Bald eagles, spotted ravens, ducks, geese, swans, and pelicans."

They stopped at one of the long wooden walkways that bordered the paint pots, colorful pools of boiling mineral water. "Stay on the walkways, folks. There are more than 10,000 thermal features in the park boundaries," said the ranger. "You can even see thermal bubbling out in Yellowstone Lake, behind us. And this deep blue pool over here? It's about 170 degrees."

"What if some animal wants to take a drink here?" asked George.

"He'll only do it once," replied the ranger. "In fact, there have been incidences of both a moose and a bear falling right into one of the pools. Very sad."

"Poor things!" Bess said, her voice trembling. The silence

that followed punctuated the image of that terrible fate in the minds of all who stood there.

Aboard the bus again, scrawny, sparse woods passed before their eyes, charred remnants of land devastated by fire.

"We're hit by forest fires every year," explained the ranger. "Those caused by careless or mean-spirited men, we fight with every means available. Those that occur naturally are sometimes allowed to burn under strict control. It's nature's way of starting over--note the green seedlings sprouting among the ashes."

Shortly before noon, Lew pulled into a spacious parking lot near a massive yet inviting log structure, Old Faithful Inn.

But no one paid much attention, because Glenn was pointing toward a circular area about fifty feet in front of the lodge. "Almost show time, ladies and gentlemen," he said. "As you can see, we're in the middle of a field of geysers. Old Faithful, right out here, will do its spouting thing in about thirty minutes, as it has done every seventy-eight minutes for the last hundred years."

In the distance a panorama of small geysers randomly spouted. Up close, a semicircle of stone benches--room for hundreds of spectators--formed a ring around Old Faithful. In the sharp chill the Vermilion group huddled together on the benches, pulling hoods over their heads and zipping up jackets.

A billowing accumulation of sulfurous deposits formed a spout. For many minutes now the hole in the spout had been frothing, boiling, and spitting irregular rushes of hissing steam and yellowish liquid into the air. Never stopping altogether; rising, then retracting, only hesitating to begin all over again. Each new sequence foretelling, announcing the momentous eruption to come, holding the onlookers in suspenseful attention; for this might be the one.

As the time grew nearer, Old Faithful became noisier and more active, hypnotizing the viewers. At last, in a great rush and roar, the geyser leapt taller and stronger and burst into a column towering nearly 200 feet. The gusting wind carried away the steaming, falling top, forming it into a question mark. The majestic column sustained itself for several minutes and then, in a series of syncopated thrusts, began to recede to its former self, a bubbling, gurgling fountain.

"It's like a humongous coffeepot," declared Molly. "Populating the water with coffee just before it's done."

"Well put," said Paco.

Glenn smiled with satisfaction as if he personally had staged the performance. "Okay, everyone, listen up. We're spending the night here in the lodge," he said. "So you'll have the rest of the day to explore this area of the park. I must warn you, though: stay on the designated walkways. It can be pretty hazardous around here."

"Oh, Ray!" cried Loretta. "I wish you hadn't been so clumsy and lost our good camera over the canyon. There's a buffalo or bison or whatever up by the cafeteria."

Glenn overheard. "You can get a cardboard throw-away camera in the gift shop--both panoramic and regular," he said. "And folks--that bison? Yes, he's the resident bison, but he's still not to be trifled with."

Ray leaned heavily on his crutches and glared at his wife. "Well, what are you waiting for, woman? I sure as hell can't stand in line with these damn things." He studied the animal's huge bulk. "That big ball of fuzz and horn isn't going anywhere soon. I'll wait for you here." Loretta trotted off to the gift shop, grumbling all the way.

"You'd be surprised, Ray," interjected Glenn. "When a bison gets up to speed, he can outrun a racehorse. They can reach thirty-five miles an hour in ten seconds. I'd suggest you give him plenty of berth, fifty feet at least."

"You gotta be kiddin' me," George protested.

"That's laying it on pretty thick, isn't it?" asked Ray. He sat down on a nearby bench. Glenn merely shrugged, smiled, and wandered off to answer other questions.

Michelle and Monte Davies had climbed atop a stone bench to take their pictures; then Monte sat down next to the LeSotos while Michelle faced them on the bench in the front row.

Bored now that the show was over, Michelle toyed with a small black spider as it crawled toward the edge of the bench. She used a finger to impede its way, forcing it to veer to a new direction. Whenever it got too close to the edge of the bench, she transported it to the middle once more. At one point she allowed the creature to climb onto her hand. Then, noting her husband's annoyance, she flicked it to obscurity with her thumb and middle finger.

"Guess I'll get something to drink," she said. "Anybody want one?" She'd already started toward the cafeteria.

"No thanks," Monte responded, sitting, arms folded, with his long legs stretched out.

"Interesting shoes you've got on there, Monte," said Paco.

"They're not exactly shoes, Paco, they're calf-high Wellingtons. Finest English leather. Hand-tooled, custom-made for me," he said.

"Are they that comfortable?" asked Molly. "I mean to go to all that trouble and expense."

"Oh, yes," replied Monte. "I wear 'em all the time. Nothing else. Even to work. Get a new pair from my man in London every year. Get my suits that way, too."

"Aren't they a little out of place in your plant?" Paco asked.

"Not at all," he replied. "They're quite popular, especially among corporate executives."

Now that Old Faithful had rung its curtain down, the crowd began to disperse. Ray felt a hand on his shoulder. Loretta looked down at him. "I'm going to take a few shots of the bison," she said.

Ray watched from his bench as his wife clicked away at a cautious distance. "Loretta, if you're going to be such a sissy..." he called. He hobbled over to her, grabbed the throw-away camera out of her hands, and manipulated the crutches to within fifteen feet of the animal. It raised its head in curiosity, stopped, then went on grazing the clumps of tasty grass. Ray leaned down on the crutches with both arms and used two hands to take several close-ups. Proud of himself, he started to turn away, when he saw

Michelle returning from the cafeteria. She had blown up a good-sized brown paper bag. Clutching it at the top, she impishly waved the bag, rounded and full of air, so Ray could see it.

He knew what was coming next and cried out: "Michelle, don't do it. He'll stampede! Please!"

Michelle tilted her head and smiled back at him like a little kid. Then she slammed the bottom of the bag with her free hand. The loud bang as it burst retorted about eight feet from the bewildered bison. Ray began hobbling on his crutches in awkward strides to get away. The lumbering beast moved forward to overtake him. As Ray reached the circle of benches, the bison appeared to lose interest, for it had found another patch of sweet grasses.

Michelle and Monte hurried away, with Michelle chuckling as they headed for the gift shop.

Ray swore. "Damn bitch, she knew the beast would take off after me."

"You're crazy, Ray," scolded Loretta. "It was your own stupidity to get that close. And who are you talking about, anyway?"

"That bitch Michelle," he answered. "She tried to kill me... Maybe she's tried before. She's the one who's nuts. She's an ex-con. Killed her first husband, didn't she?"

"That was only a rumor!" Loretta said hotly. "I have no idea why she went to prison. Do you always have to think the worst of people? She's really very nice."

"Don't give me that crap. She's a killer, she knows how to kill." Ray pivoted on one crutch and took off after the Davies. Loretta followed close behind.

Paco and Molly had witnessed the entire scene. "Seemed to me more like a practical joke," said Paco, "but not a very smart one, I suppose. Michelle couldn't be certain the animal wouldn't take off after him."

The LeSotos began the large semicircular trek around Old Faithful to the field of lesser geysers that lay beyond. "The thing that bothers me so much, honey," said Paco, "it's never clear-cut whether all these attempts are malicious, just to frighten him. Or accidental. Or, worst case, attempts to maim him."

"A little birdy tells me you don't really believe they're accidents," said Molly.

"Hang onto your little birdy friend," said Paco. "I don't think we've seen the last of this mess yet."

As the sun fell behind the trees, the members of the tour drifted into the lodge, weary from the long sightseeing treks and hungry, too. Most had skipped lunch in an effort to see it all. As Paco and Molly picked up their room key, they encountered a small group gathered around one of the park rangers.

"Each piece of wood used in construction of the lodge came from within the park's boundaries," he explained.

And indeed, when the LeSotos looked about them, they found every last frame, post, support, and baluster was constructed from naturally curved or gnarled branches. The three-story great room that served as a lobby astonished them with its display of utilitarian rustic beauty and Native American craftsmanship. On the second and third floors, a balcony, rather than a closed-in corridor, overlooked the lobby.

"Hey, Paco, there's the dining room. Let's eat. I'm starved."

"Sure, hon," agreed Paco. "Our showers can wait." They walked arm in arm toward the archway trimmed in elk antlers. While they waited for the hostess to seat them, the Whitmans approached.

"Those poor dears," said Molly, surveying the archway. "It seems so cruel to kill so many just to make a doorway."

"No, ma'am," said Gordon. "The elk naturally molt them--every two years, I think."

"Mold them?"

"Uh, yes, shed them," Gordon replied, still uncertain of what he'd just heard. "Then the elk grow another set. So you see, there's no need to kill the animal."

"Ah, thank you, Gordon," acknowledged Paco.

"Table for four?" interrupted the hostess.

"Molly and eh...Paco, is it?" asked Joanne. "Would you like

to share a table with us?"

"We'd be delighted," said Paco. They were led to a cozy table before a great stone fireplace and handed typewritten menus.

"I know what I want," declared Molly. "I'll have some of those tortelonelys with the Al and Freddie sauce."

"I'll have the blackened bass over linguini," said Paco. "And a Coors Light."

"That sounds great," said Gordon. "I'll also have the bass and a beer. But a Lowenbrau instead."

"The waitress nodded. "And you, ma'am?"

"I'll have the fresh salmon salad," replied Joanne, "on homemade pita bread, and make that two beers for me."

"Oh, I love pitaful bread," said Molly. "It's made from the middle yeast, isn't it?"

Joanne looked puzzled.

As they waited for their entrees, Paco observed Gordon fiddling with some object on the end of his key chain--rotating a worm screw between his thumb and index finger.

"That's an interesting little doodad you have there," noted Paco. "Looks like a miniature Crescent wrench, I'd say."

"And you'd be absolutely right," Gordon said. "It's an advertising gimmick I came up with about four years ago. We gave them away to all our customers." He unhooked the chain from his belt and handed the little wrench to Paco. "You can see the IMTC logo on the side."

"Ah, yes," acknowledged Paco. "You must be with that group of salespeople from Indent Tool." He turned the wrench over, examining the sliding jaws with particular interest. Smooth and unmarked, he noted.

"Right again," said Gordon. "That little baby'll handle up to a half-inch head, and it's strong, too. Almost everyone in the plant has managed to sidetrack one for themselves."

"Then it's more than likely that there are half a dozen or so of these on tour with us?" proposed Paco, handing the wrench back.

"I suppose so," admitted Gordon as he reattached it to his key chain. "But why the interest in how many?"

"Oh, nothing in particular," replied Paco. "I suppose it's the ex-cop in me."

"Are you acting in an official capacity, then?" asked Joanne.

"Oh, no. I have no jurisdiction here. But Ray Symington did ask me to find explanations for some of the incidents he's been experiencing."

"Do I take that to mean the members of the IMTC sales force are all suspects?" asked Gordon.

"I'm not even sure yet that any crime has been committed," replied Paco. "And if criminal acts have been attempted, I'm afraid the list of suspects would be much longer. Let's just say that--like the buffalo--I'm allowing my curiosity to roam freely."

Chapter 11
THE HOLE
Day Five, Monday, September 14, 1981

A RASPY VOICE CUT THROUGH THE CLATTER OF BREAKFAST. "Psst...psst...over here, Paco!"

The LeSotos stood in the doorway of the lodge's cheerful coffee shop. Paco's sharp eyes scanned the customers, seeking to match the raspy voice to the face. Joanne Whitman, waving frantically, motioned for them to join her, her husband, and the Miltons. Paco and Molly wove their way across the small room filled with rough-hewn bentwood furniture.

"Dr. Avi would say that woman has shpilkas," whispered Molly. "Look at how she's jumping and squirming in her seat."

"She does seem rather anxious," said Paco.

The waitress hovered at their table, having just taken the others' breakfast orders. "Coffee regular?" she asked.

"Do you have any diet coffee?" Molly asked.

"Diet coffee?" questioned the waitress. "You mean decaf?"

"Uh-huh, and a cheese Danish, please," replied Molly. "I just love that foreign pastry. Bake it all the time myself."

Paco glanced at the menu as the waitress poured the coffee. "I'll have one egg, over easy, and light toast with fruit jelly--no grape."

"You sound like a man who knows exactly what he wants," noted Joanne. "I also heard that you always get your man."

Ruth Milton's eyes narrowed as she slowly sipped her orange juice.

"Damn it, Joanne," Gordon burst out. "Quit beating around the bush and tell the inspector what you saw."

"Okay, okay. On Saturday, at the Lower Falls...Remember when Ray Symington almost stumbled into the canyon from the lookout?" began Joanne. "Well, let me tell you, that was no accident. He got pushed, and I know who did the pushing, too. I saw the tattoo on his arm, the one with the spider."

"Who?" Paco and Molly chorused as Joanne basked in the suspense she had created.

"Why, Mr. LeeeeeeRoy Milton here," she said, drawing out his name so it sounded like a sneer. She eyed her prey across the round table. "I saw his arm reach out from the crowd and push Ray."

LeRoy's head jerked up. The sugar packet he had just torn open plopped, paper and all, into his black coffee. "That's a lie! I most certainly did not push him," he snapped. "The guy had already fallen before I could get over there. I tried to grab for his arm, but I missed him entirely. Why would I want to hurt him, especially in front of a crowd? Besides which I don't even know the guy. It was a ridiculous accident brought on by a stupid, foolhardy man." LeRoy pushed his chair back. "I've heard all I can take of this."

The waitress arrived and began unloading her crowded tray.

"Miss," LeRoy said sharply, "my wife and I need to move to another table."

Ruth stood and glared down at her husband's accuser. "You set this up, Joanne. Planned it so you could accuse my LeRoy in front of the inspector. You, my dear, are the malicious one. I think you're trying to cover up for your own crimes and cast suspicion elsewhere. Everyone saw you pop that bag close to the buffalo yesterday. And God only knows what else you've done." She addressed Paco and Molly. "You'll excuse us, of course. Under the circumstances, we can't stay at this table any longer."

As the Miltons followed the waitress and their breakfasts to a table across the room, Joanne couldn't resist one more stab. "There goes Ruth and ruthless," she said.

Molly sensed an evil taint to Joanne's attempted humor, so she tried to remember where both LeRoy and Joanne were standing when Ray fell. It seemed to her that Monte stood closer to Ray than LeRoy did. Molly chewed her Danish thoughtfully until she saw Paco place his napkin on the table. Taking it as a signal, she munched one last bite and declared, "Paco, it's time. The bus leaves in thirty minutes."

"You'll excuse us, please," Paco said.

"Of course," repeated Gordon, with a sour expression intended for his wife.

They pulled away from the lodge and took one last look at Yellowstone as the bus groaned into high gear and turned swiftly southward onto route 89, past Jackson Lake and Grand Teton National Park. The sharp peaks of the snow-covered mountains loomed huge: Mount Moran and the majestic Grand Teton itself stood well over 12,000 feet. The bus raced on through wide farm and ranch lands. And then the mountains drew tightly around them like a sleeping bag as they entered the valley known as Jackson Hole: fifty miles long, twelve miles wide, and bisected by the Snake River. Ski resorts nestled tightly under the slopes and lifts. Even without the white velvet cover of winter, the ski resorts flourished year round, along with other enticements and attractions: horseback riding, hunting, fishing, swimming, golf, tennis, and the most profitable of them all, shopping.

"Be back here in exactly three hours, folks," Glenn called to the tour group flooding out of the bus. "Four o'clock, not one minute later."

The giant bus had pulled alongside a triangular-shaped park in downtown Jackson, a park surrounded by picturesque Western boutiques, booteries, galleries, and eateries. The park had three entrances, each arched with hundreds of mule deer antlers uniquely stacked and woven to provide impressive gateways. After half a minute spent admiring them sand snapping pictures, the group fanned out to the main drag.

Only Ray dawdled in the little park. He laid his crutches

against the back of a bench and tried his weight on the sore ankle. Slowly he ventured a step or two away, then another and another, until he convinced himself he really could make it without the miserable things. He'd carry them along just in case. A soreness lingered, but no pain, no reason to cling any longer. Beginning with caution and gaining a measure of confidence, he soon added his familiar swagger, so he continued to the corner and crossed the narrow street.

Ray poked his head through the open double doorway of an antique shop. Inside, he recognized Paco holding up an elaborately engraved revolver to the overhead light, sighting along its lengthy barrel. "Planning on shooting somebody?" he yelled into the store.

Paco grinned, lowered the Colt Peacemaker to his side, and faced him. "Only if I catch 'em messin' with my herd, pardner." Turning back to the shopkeeper, he observed, "Beautiful workmanship, but sorely neglected."

"Ain't nothing a little elbow grease can't fix. Make her look like new. Besides, she's still in great shooting order. There's ammo for her, too. Got a whole lot of history to her, that piece."

"Hondle with him, honey. Make him come down some," encouraged Molly.

The shopkeeper understood. "Tell you what...I'll knock off another ten percent."

"Done!" said Paco as he reached for his wallet.

Ray took another few steps into the store. "I hope you're not going to shoot that thing."

"Of course not. It's the latest addition to my antique gun collection at home."

While Paco and Molly waited for their package and receipt, Ray left the store and continued down the main street. By now, he'd been on his feet for some time. He stopped to peek in the window of an art gallery displaying oil paintings of Old Faithful and a jewelry shop flaunting turquoise and silver. For sure, his wife would be in one of them. But no. As he roamed from shop to shop looking for her, the ankle began to tire and ache. He staggered a few times and even stumbled into a passerby.

"A little early to be drinking, eh, cowboy?" The stranger jumped aside to get away.

The remark stunned Ray and revealed how his stumbling must have looked. He suddenly felt a stab of dejection as he stood uncertainly in the bright sunlight, surrounded by seemingly joyful crowds. Taking a few more steps, he decided to rely on the crutches once again. Later, in a main street trinket shop he asked for a restroom, expecting it to be in the back of the store. Instead, the clerk said, "Around the corner, two blocks on the right. Public bathroom, green doors, you can't miss it."

The two blocks on crutches seemed like a mile. He felt horrible, the ankle throbbed. The dingy restroom lay in near darkness. A single fluorescent tube cast its sallow light on the cinder block walls. Ray leaned his crutches beside the only sink and enthroned himself in the tidier of two tiny stalls.

Shortly after, the restroom door squeaked open. He heard leather shoes on the concrete floor. A shadow darted past the thin vertical crack in the stall door. He heard peeing into the urinal. Then water running in the sink. Then what sounded like two pieces of wood clacking together. Ray saw the bottoms of his crutches and leather, pointed-toe cowboy boots pass the space below his stall door.

"Hey, you!" Ray shouted. "Stop! Those are my crutches." The green door squeaked open once more. Outside light flooded the room and faded again.

Ray hurriedly zipped his pants up. But in his haste he failed to notice his wallet topple from his hip pocket. He struggled out of the public restroom, down the alley, and into the street, where he stopped a young man in faded jeans.

"You see somebody running with a pair of crutches?" Ray asked.

"What are you, some kind of nut?" the man asked.

"He wore cowboy boots," Ray added innocently.

"So do half the people in Jackson Hole." Laughing, the young man continued down the street.

Ray approached an elderly woman coming from the other direction.

"You see somebody running with a pair of wooden crutches?" he asked her.

"Sure did, sonny," she said, giggling. "I believe you'll find him next door."

Ray looked beyond her to the tobacconist shop. A larger-than-life wooden Indian stood out front, offering a fistful of wooden stogies to all who passed him. Its feathered headdress framed a painted face, its expression stern and forbidding. A crutch had been wedged beneath each armpit, a perfect fit. Only a prank. Ray's rigid square jaw softened slightly and a half-smile escaped.

Retrieving his crutches, he stepped inside the shop, intending to get change for the soda vending machine in the doorway. But as he reached for his wallet, he felt only his flat hip pocket. The bottom dropped out of his stomach and acid immediately sizzled there. He felt like vomiting. Almost in a panic now, he retraced his steps all the way back to the restroom and searched, but the wallet was gone. Leaning against the wall beside the green doors outside, his knees buckled, and the crutches clattered to the sidewalk. Ray collapsed into his shoes as his whole world faded to black.

Only a few minutes elapsed after Ray blacked out. When he came to, the first voice he heard almost made him want to black out again.

"You idiot," Loretta said. "What possessed you to wander so far on crutches? You must have passed out from exhaustion."

"Don't idiot me, you automaton of the fashion world," Ray blurted. "All you can do is ridicule me." He saw a look of surprise on her face, and for the first time, he noticed a crowd gathering on his behalf. A thought struck him and he reached for his left rear pocket only to confirm it empty. The soured expression he bore melted into a grin with the realization of a second thought. He began to chuckle.

"What do you find so amusing, may I ask?"

"Well, my dear wife, there's good news and bad."

"I'll take the bad news first," she decided.

"First of all, my wallet has been stolen," he said. "ID's, credit cards, and cash."

"Nothing to worry about," she replied. "I still have all my gold credit cards."

"Ah, my dear, aren't you the naive one," he continued. "Don't you realize that your cards have the same account numbers as mine? We have to cancel every one of them. That's the good news. There's no way the new ones will catch up with us on this trip. Sorry, dear, I hate to put such a crimp in your style."

"You bastard," she shouted. "You're enjoying this." Bolts of lightning leapt from her eyes. She spun on her toes and tore down the street away from where he sat. He held out his hand, and a stranger in blue jeans and a red and gray plaid shirt extended his hand to yank Ray to his feet. As if by the natural order of things, someone else handed him his crutches. Ray did not ponder the why of it.

Loretta locked herself up in her own head. She saw and heard nothing while rushing past buildings and people. The fast pace carried her a good distance, and she soon found herself at the edge of town. She found a rock wall and plopped down on it while she pulled off the left shoe and rubbed her toes.

She should have worn more comfortable shoes. Couldn't anything ever go right on this trip? Ray had touched a nerve and gotten to her. He'd been there before, but never had it hurt so much. Worst of all, he'd enjoyed doing this to her. Maybe their marriage would have been different if she and Ray had chosen to have children.

But Loretta had had quite enough of parenting while growing up in the Cobble Hill section of Brooklyn. She virtually raised her three younger siblings. Her mama worked at Alexander's Department Store and her daddy at the Navy shipyards. The more overtime they worked, the more mothering they required of their teenage daughter. The little mother became authoritarian and resentful.

On the other hand, Loretta didn't lack either talent or brains. On a scholarship to the Philadelphia College of Art she had pursued interior decorating. In her freshman year she met Ray on a blind date. He'd been a graduate student at Wharton. Somehow, during the courtship, Ray had managed to hide his devious and onerous nature.

As Loretta wiggled back into her shoe, her simmering temper chilled with introspection. She wasn't a bad wife. Even he would admit that. She liked playing the role of corporate VP spouse, and the perks were great.

Spotting a cab half a block away, she moved to the curb, hailed the driver, and got in.

The group began to congregate at the triangular park where the bus had left them off hours earlier. The LeSotos sat on a bench while others perched on the hefty rail fence or milled about the area. Gordon Whitman, standing in front of them, pulled a handkerchief from his trouser pocket and a small square of blue followed it to the ground next to his heels.

"You dropped something there, Gordon," said Paco.

"Huh?" Gordon glanced down at the folded piece of paper, poked at it with his toe, and shook his head. "Nope, nothing of mine." He strolled deeper into the crowd, ignoring his litter.

Paco stood up with every intention of tossing the litter into a nearby trash receptacle, but the folded blue paper looked familiar. After picking it up, he sat down once more next to Molly. Unfolding it, he discovered another cryptic memo: "Friday, 9/11, Flaming Gorge." He'd nearly forgotten the other slip of paper in his jacket pocket. Slowly, he drew it out and laid it on his lap next to the one Gordon had just dropped. They were obviously written on the same pad, in the same careful script, and with the same logo: two meshing gears with the letters IMTC across the top of each slip.

By now he'd captured Molly's attention. Without any prompting from Paco, she began rummaging through her purse for the blue slip she'd deposited there earlier. She handed it to him in silence just as their chariot, the ribbed mass of stainless steel and dark tinted glass, hissed to a stop in front of them and opened its doors. Paco shoved all three slips into his pocket and they climbed aboard.

The group arrived at the Mountain King resort with only an hour to settle into their rooms and get ready for the evening's festivities. "Wear jeans and warm jackets, folks," Glenn said before they filed off the bus, "we're roughing it tonight."

Ninety minutes later, Lew Getz deposited the Vermilion group in a corral at the Thousand-Acre Ponderosa Ranch. The pungent, macho smell of horses, hay, and leather pierced the crisp alpine air. Harness teams of work horses and saddled quarterhorses awaited their assignments at one end of the split-rail fence. At least twenty Conestoga wagons, lined up side by side, were being hitched, one at a time, to their respective teams. An attractive teenage cowgirl astride a palomino--a splendid tan horse with flaxen mane and tail--directed the flow of tourists from bus to assigned wagons. "Watch your footing!" she warned every few minutes.

"Eek squealed Bess, clinging to Cookie to avoid slipping in the slick surface of mud and manure.

The LeSotos and most of the others stepped carefully. But Joanne Whitman, already several drinks into her nightly routine, danced the dance and paid the price. With all four limbs flailing, she landed, splat, on her backside. She sat there and wailed, staring at the thick mud mixture squishing through her hands. Two strong cowboys gallantly lifted her up and brought out brooms to unmuck her jeans. Gordon somehow managed to locate himself elsewhere in the corral.

Paco boosted Molly up via the tailgate and followed her forward to one of the long benches lining the wagon until she sat directly behind the driver. George and Reba climbed in next, followed by Thom and Theo, the Miltons, sand Loretta. A ranch hand latched the tailgate, and the four-horse team hauled the wagon out of the sloppy corral onto the hard-surfaced access road, clopping hooves loudly and joining the noisy rhythm of the teams up ahead. At the end of the access road a broad trail climbed into steep, shadowy foothills above them. The four-horse team struggled, slipping and regripping against the rocks, bumps, and stumps.

"I'll bet this is where they got the idea of four-wheel drive," said Molly.

"Excellent observation," admitted Paco. "But it sure is hard on my bony rump."

"I guess there's an advantage to having a cushy tushy," Molly quipped.

"Makes you wonder about the strength, endurance, and determination of the pioneers crossing our country," said Theo.

"Yeah, you sure gotta give 'em credit," said George. "They were tough."

"I can't imagine going cross country without springs, shocks, and cruise control," offered LeRoy.

"I prefer an airplane," said Loretta. "First class, of course. How much longer is this trial by spinal torture going to last, anyway?"

"Sorry, ma'am," answered the driver. "Should be thar shortly--mebbe twenty minutes or so." He wore a black Stetson, heavy boots, and a gray long-coat, and sat sideways on the same bench as his passengers. "Time'll pass quicker ifen ya jist enjoy the sunset out back of the wagon. The moon'll be up soon, too." It struck Paco that the driver had perfected his cowboy drawl to add flavor for the tourists.

The wheels squeaked, and the stout board construction of the wagon strained with their progress. Suddenly, a thud sounded against the side of the wagon, and an inhuman screech pierced the serene evening. More thuds on the outside of the wagon, and the driver reached around the side and pulled in an arrow, holding it above his head for all to see. Now the woods filled with screams of an old-fashioned Indian attack.

"Take cover, folks. We'll git ya outta this mess yet," the driver yelled, as he cracked and snapped his whip well over the heads of his team. The horses charged headlong into the black woods, avoiding the wrath of the staged attack, while all the wagonloads applauded.

"You should have brought your new gun, Paco," laughed Molly. You could have scared all them Indians off."

"You got a gun, Paco? You brought a gun on the tour?" asked George. "I thought you didn't carry a piece."

"I don't," replied Paco. "It's just a gun I picked up in an antique store today."

The horses led them into a lantern-lit clearing, where they disembarked and made their way to a huge open-sided wooden shelter, filled with long picnic tables that would seat at least a hundred. At one end of the structure, steam curled from mammoth pots. Smoke rose from barbecue pits, saturating the ponderosa pine forest with aromas of ranch and trailside foods.

When the last wagon had dispatched its cargo, they formed a chow line for the steaks, ribs, corn on the cob, baked beans, and salads.

"Loretta, hon," asked Theo, "where's your lord and master this evening?"

"Some lord and master," she responded. "He's wimping it back at the Mountain King. Seems he overdid it this afternoon. He'll never learn, although he's probably eating better than we are and more comfortable, too."

"I understand they took his wallet," said Theo. "Did they get anything else?"

"Nothing else worth anything," replied Loretta. "They should have taken him and left the wallet."

"Oh, aren't we nasty tonight," laughed Theo. "Your husband is like that Al Capp character in Li'l Abner who walks around with the little black cloud over his head. Trouble always seems to find him."

"Theo!" scolded Thom.

"Sorry, hon," said Theo. "There I go again, foot-in-mouth-disease."

"At least I've managed to keep my thirteen-5E's out of my chops," Thom bragged.

"Wow!" said Molly. "Do they really make shoes that big?"

"Yup," said Theo, getting even. "That's my husband--a regular Yeti, a Bigfoot even." She got a mean look for her remark.

"The bus was only two-thirds full coming over here," said Loretta, trying to change the subject.

"I heard that Hilda Vickers felt a little under the weather, so she decided to make an early night of it," Reba piped up.

"What about her niece?" Loretta asked, her voice ultra-casual.

"Tina? She chose not to come either."

A three-piece band, led by a female fiddler in boots and embroidered jacket, picked up a foot-stomping, hand-clapping beat to open the show. But Loretta, frowning and deep in thought, noticed none of it.

Chapter 12
OFFHAND
Same Day, Monday, September 14, 1981

THE MOUNTAIN KING RESORT IN JACKSON overlooked a grass-covered ski slope and chair lift. A pretty view, but less dramatic in September than it would be under snow in a month or two. At five-thirty, in the near-empty dining room, the maitre d' had deserted his post to flirt with the red-headed salad chef in the kitchen. Three early diners lingered over their coffee.

Ray Symington patted his left hip pocket to feel the newly returned wallet. The bulge there reassured him. The Jackson police had told him that a Good Samaritan had turned it in intact--nothing missing. He'd always thought that a Good Samaritan was a fictional character. He'd just picked the wallet up at the hotel desk.

He scanned the room and spotted a young woman eating alone at a window table. He thought her business suit looked rather out of place in this earthy setting, where Pueblo rugs and feathered dream catchers decorated the walls.

Ray swung his crutches in tight arcs as he approached her table. "Would a farthing buy your thoughts, young lady?"

"I'm afraid you'd feel cheated if I accepted, Mr. Symington," answered Tina Barton.

"Since I haven't the foggiest what a farthing is worth, I don't see how that's possible," he said. "But I am glad you remembered my name, my dear Miss Barton." He laid his crutches against the back of the third chair at the table. "However, I would much prefer that you call me Ray." Seating himself opposite her, he added, "I hope I'm not imposing on you. I just hate dining alone."

"Of course, not Mr. Syming...Ray. I'd be delighted. It's

rather quiet here tonight. You might have trouble getting served, though. I haven't even seen a waiter for the last half-hour."

"I believe I can get that situation in hand." Ray picked up his fork and tined it against the crystal water glass--softly at first, then louder, until the swinging doors to the kitchen sprang open.

The maitre d' burst through in time to see the threesome in the center of the room abandon their table. He picked up the small tray that held their tip and bowed slightly. "Ah, thank you. Have a pleasant evening." Now he acknowledged the incessant clinking on the far side of the room. "Good evening, sir," he said. "One moment, please."

Ray smiled stiffly, flipped his fork over, and drew parallel creases in the white tablecloth until the maitre d' finally dispatched a waiter to their table. "I'd like a three-egg western omelet done easy. Pre-sauté the peppers and onions to make sure that they're well done."

"Yes, sir. Will there be anything else?"

"Coffee, decaf, with cream," answered Ray. "Hmm. On second thought, bring me a double Cutty Sark with soda--one cube." Upon seeing Tina's steady gaze, he added, "I'll have another with my meal."

"Can I get something for madam?"

"I'm fine, really," she responded. When the waiter left, she said, "I'm not sure I like being called madam."

"Somehow it fits," he whispered and stared at the same time. "There's a mature loveliness about you--classic features, finely chiseled, and you carry yourself with a unique kind of self-assurance."

"Ray...Mr. Symington," she said, her voice heavy with emphasis, "I'm afraid you've gone and underestimated me. Surely I can detect a pass when I hear one. You're about to proposition me--you, a married man."

"Oh, my dear, Tina, you misunderstand me." His hand glided across the table to touch hers.

"Now you're going to give me the my-wife-doesn't-understand-me routine."

"You're very astute," he said. "But this time you're wrong. Loretta spends a great deal of time trying to understand me. I, however, have never even tried. We have this agreement: I make the money, she spends it. We simply share a household. What we do with our individual time is our own business."

"You've got the wrong girl," Tina said. "I'm nobody's one-night stand or mattress. Good grief! I meant mistress."

"I'm sorry I gave you that impression, Tina, dear. I merely wanted to pay you a most deserving compliment. Lighten up, Little Miss Muffet, I'm harmless. I'm the one on crutches."

She looked searchingly for something in his expression, and unsure of what she found there, gave her attention to the blackened trout on her plate.

He quietly watched her consume several morsels of fish. A mellow mood enveloped him as he sipped and swirled his Scotch. His food came, and they ate in silence--their eyes meeting frequently, each reconsidering whether the other had been unfairly judged. Eventually, the conversation resumed with gusto, acknowledging a truce.

Outdoors, floodlights suddenly blinked on, illuminating a parquet deck that encompassed a large swimming pool and two Jacuzzis. For some time they observed a tall European blonde in a bikini watching over her two tow-headed charges. As the mother stretched unselfconsciously, the golden body hair on her legs and underarms seemed to glow in the light. The children cavorted in the water, dunking and dodging each other so spontaneously that Tina had to comment.

"Mmm, that seems like a lot of fun, to loll in the frothing waters."

"You're serious," he said. "You'd like to be out there, too. I suppose it would be good for my ankle." He glanced over at her, inviting an answer.

"I can serve you coffee or an aperitif poolside, sir," said the eavesdropping waiter as he removed their dinner plates.

Tina bit her lip and then said, "Let's do it!"

"You like hazelnuts?" Ray asked.

"Nuts about 'em."

"Cancel my second scotch and bring us two Frangelicas," he told the waiter. "Give us fifteen minutes to change." He laid a number of bills down on the table. "That should cover everything."

"Yes, sir, thank you very much. Fifteen minutes, then."

Ray got to his feet and grabbed the crutches. "See you in ten."

"In ten," she repeated.

Twelve minutes later Ray hobbled out to the deck just in time to catch a pale peach Lycra suit glide down the steps and disappear into the white churning waters of the hot tub. He shed his T-shirt and carefully followed her down the steps from the chilly night air into 100-degree water. The blonde mother and her kids had gone, leaving him and Tina alone. He settled onto the fiberglass bench opposite her, allowing his toes to intermingle briefly with hers on the tub floor. Heavy lids induced by heat covered her eyes, and full, parted lips shaped a sensual smile of contentment over even rows of very white teeth.

"How is it I find you alone this evening?" asked Ray, eager to jump-start their conversation. "I would have thought you'd prefer the horsey set and hoe-down entertainment."

"Ordinarily, I would," she replied. "But my Aunt Hilda wasn't feeling very chipper. I stayed behind in case she needed me, but she chose to go to bed early."

"Nothing serious, I hope?"

"No, just tired, I assume. This trip's pretty rigorous, although at eighty-three she still leads a more active life than most of her contemporaries. She's a professor emeritus at Radcliffe with a distinguished career there."

"And what about you?"

"I teach seminars on corporate finance and business decisions at American U. Plus a little consulting."

"Barton, Tina Barton. Your name sounds familiar, and I'm

not handing you a line. Honest. I've seen it in print somewhere recently."

"Perhaps you have. I've done some interviews for Fortune."

"Ah! That's where. The new issue, the interview with Gil Bates."

She looked pleased and not a little surprised. "You've read it."

"Of course. Quite well done, I must say."

She smiled and Ray knew he'd scored points with her. "I suppose it's not likely that you've heard of Indent Machine Tool Corporation." Seeing her blank expression, he continued. "We're in the design and manufacture of specialty plastic, steel, and aluminum equipment for industry. As vice president of sales, I'm proud to tell you we do over eight million a year in revenue."

"Is your company on the Big Board?" she asked.

"No, we're privately held: two million shares worth about $12.50 apiece."

"Mind if I ask who the major shareholders are?" she asked.

Ray's slate-gray eyes narrowed as he pondered her question, then decided there was no harm in giving her the information. "The CEO, has about 400K; his family maybe another 400 to 450K. The rest is distributed among the corporate officers and senior employees, with the two vice presidents holding the lion's share, myself included. Now you'll have to excuse me."

Twice, Ray submerged his whole body, face and all, and allowed himself to sink to the floor of the hot tub.

When his head emerged for the second time, she asked, "What, pray tell, are you doing?"

"I dunk my whole self because it feels so good when I come up into the night air afterward." Actually, the alcohol had begun to take effect, and he wanted to shake it off.

"Does it work?" she asked. Her eyes fixed on a sign beside the hot tub, a list of Jacuzzi Do's and Don'ts. "Maybe you'd better take it easy. That sign says alcohol and hot tubs don't mix."

"Never mind the mothering bit," he said, "I'm fine. But

thanks for caring."

The waiter appeared with their aperitifs over ice in tall glasses, set them on a small table on the deck, and left.

"Does your wife like hot tubs?" Tina said.

"My wife's whooping it up at the hoedown thing tonight. But to answer your question, no. All she wants to do is shop and read and shop some more."

"I'm sure you underestimate her. Most corporate wives are spenders. They're required to entertain and keep up appearances. But for the most part, they're a neglected breed."

"That's fiction," he retorted. "My wife wanted a summer house in the Hamptons. You wouldn't believe the price of real estate there. I had to use all my company stock as collateral to finance that palace. If you can call five bedrooms on the beach a palace. And it's all for show. Now I ask you, is that reasonable?"

"I couldn't say," Tina answered. Her slender fingers played with bubbles floating on the water.

"And the way that woman bounces checks, it's not easy to get credit, either."

Tina suppressed a grin as she processed the additional tidbit. "I don't believe that for a minute."

The churning water grew quiet as the hot tub timer played out its fifteen minutes, leaving only the sizzling sound of froth decomposing. "I'll get it," Tina said, and lazily climbed the steps.

Ray's eyes feasted on the flesh-colored suit, which clung so tightly that it almost melted into her body. He wouldn't have called her figure "girlish" exactly. Rather, it looked toned and tempting for her age--thirtyish, he guessed. He adjusted his bathing trunks.

Froth bubbled again as Tina reset the timer. The moonlight backlit her body as she lowered herself into the whirling tub. Handing him his Frangelica, she sat much closer to him this time. Ray set the drink aside on the deck. He placed an arm on the tiles above and behind her and allowed it to slowly drift downward until he cradled her shoulders. Tina anchored her feet on the opposite bench and slid lower in the water until her head rested on his arm.

Her eyelids drooped as she sank up to her chin and surrendered to the womb-like water once more.

Ray could contain himself no longer. Below the bubbling surface, he extended his reach and brushed her breast casually with his fingertips, a move that elicited no response. Taking it as an invitation to continue, his fingers touched the top of her breast and his hand slid over it.

Her body reflexed from limp to tense. Jerking her head toward him, she delivered an evil-eye warning. But he chose not to heed it. This time she pushed his hand away and sat straight up. He restrained himself for all of five minutes before making another attempt, a grip on her thigh.

"Okay, buster, you've had it, " cried Tina. Reaching into the water, she grabbed the tender area just beneath his hardness and squeezed for all she was worth. "How do you like that?"

Doubling over in pain, Ray forced himself to sit up and pry her hand loose.

"Ooh...Aah...God, that hurts." He sucked in a deep breath. "You led me on, lady, don't pretend you didn't. Maybe you'd better grow up before you try to sit at the grownups' table."

Tina ignored the challenge. "Thanks for dinner. Treat's mine next time." She grabbed her towel and terry robe and disappeared into the hallway.

Ray struggled out of the tub and collapsed onto a lounge chair. He could move no farther until the pain level in his groin subsided a little. At that point he stood with a great deal of effort, collected his crutches, and hobbled through the doors to the soda and ice room before trudging back to his room.

Knowing that Loretta would return soon, he dressed in his pajamas, lay back on the bed, and picked up the Ken Follett novel he'd brought, trying to ignore the groin pain that refused to go away.

What could he tell his wife? What would she believe?

It wasn't long before a key slid in the door. Loretta entered the room and saw him lying there in misery. "What the devil happened to you this time?" she asked, tossing her jacket on the chair and heading for the bathroom.

"I tripped over my shoes. When I fell, I caught my shorts on the footboard post. Slammed my balls. Stupid, I know. But it hurts like hell."

"Are you sure that's how it happened?" she asked through the bathroom door. "I see wet trunks and damp towels on the floor."

"Yeah," he said. "I went down after dinner to soak my ankle in the hot tub."

She baited him. "And that's where you fell?"

"Yeah," he replied. "Like I said, I fell over my shoes."

"Why do you even bother to lie to me?" she called. "I always catch you anyway." She came back into the room.

"Huh?"

"You can't even keep your stories straight," she retorted. "Or did you fall in both places?" She sat down on the edge of the bed. Her elbow pressed against his crotch, stirring a tinge of new pain.

"Aw, take it easy there," he protested.

"If you think I'm going to kiss it and make it better, think again. You don't have enough accidents--you have to go looking for them? Who was it this time, a waitress? No, let me guess...the young looker from Maryland. What's her name? Barton, I bet."

"Uh-huh, Tina Barton," he admitted.

"You let your pants do your talking for you again, and she let you have it in the brains."

"We shared dinner and a hot tub, and I paid her a compliment. Trouble is, she took it the wrong way."

"Yup, got you into hot water," Loretta said. "Must have been quite a pass for her to react that much. I've got to admit she gets right to the crotch of the matter. I admire her style."

"The fact is," Ray pouted, "she started the whole thing. She was looking for some action."

Loretta's crystal blue eyes flickered with disgust. Her shoulders slumped in dejection.

* * *

"**I** don't care if it *is* almost midnight back there," Tina shouted into the phone next to her bed. "I want to know who's holding the paper on that bastard."

Aunt Hilda scowled. "Please, Tina, keep it down or everyone will know what your doing."

Tina nodded at her aunt, and placed her hand over the receiver as she listened intently to the terms being spelled out for her. Then, taking her hand away, she said, "All right, first thing in the morning. Try for one under. Remember, I'll go a half-percent over, but no more. And no later than three days.... Yes! Mrs. Bradford will wire the transfer authorization in the morning. Okay! Thanks. Good-bye."

Tina set the phone in its cradle and took a deep breath. "I guess I've done all I can for tonight. I want to squeeze his finances the way I crushed his nuts tonight. I just know he's in arrears already. Uncle Harry will be proud of me. He'll have his sweet revenge, too."

"Whoa, young lady," Hilda cautioned. "You don't have Symington's note yet."

"Oh, but I will, Auntie."

"My dear," Hilda began. "When I handed over the management of your Uncle Brad's estate to you, it was to a cool, calculating head with astute business judgment. What I see now is an overexcited woman driven by her emotions. What do you even know about this man? Or his company, for that matter?"

"Don't worry, Auntie. The Admiral Bradford Vickers Trust is still in capable hands. Don't let my excessive enthusiasm perplex you. There's very little risk involved. I've done my homework quite thoroughly, tracking Symington and his company ever since he worked Uncle Harry over. I never knew how to get back at him until tonight. I just can't believe my good luck in picking up this new information."

"What you call excessive enthusiasm I call inappropriate anger. Just be careful, Tina."

"I will, Auntie. I will."

Chapter 13
PERILS OF THE SNAKE
Day Six, Tuesday, September 15, 1981

"**I** HOPE EVERYONE'S DRESSED FOR RAFTING on the Snake River this morning," Glenn said, gulping down his last bite of breakfast sausage. "For those of you who chose the scenic river float--that's the first stretch--the ride should be quite tame. On a white water scale of one to six, the rapids should be a one or two. All you need do is sit back and enjoy. You probably won't even get your feet wet."

"It's for wimps," someone shouted.

Chuckling, Glenn continued. "Listen up, folks. For those of you who opted for the second stretch, the white water could reach a four or five. Be prepared to get your feet wet. Each group has a separate bus to take you to the river and pick you up again. They'll be marked. Any questions? Okay, then. Out front in half an hour." As they all scattered, Glenn gazed up at the dappled blue and white sky. The morning sun blasted over the jagged eastern peaks, casting streaks of blinding brightness on the floor-to-ceiling restaurant windows. But turning to the west, he noticed an army of dark cloud formations bivouacked ominously.

The scenic float bunch disembarked in a riverside parking lot about ten miles from the resort. Here the Snake River ran southerly, smooth, steady, and just deep enough to cover the rocky bed. Eventually, the river would make a U-turn across Idaho and head northwest through Oregon before joining the Columbia on its journey to the Pacific Ocean.

Several raft guides passed out hooded slickers and orange life vests from the back of a stake truck and barked instructions for loading the rubber rafts beached at river's edge. A wooden frame to pivot the huge oars sat across each raft. To make it easy for passengers to board, a river guide continuously oared his awaiting craft against the rocky shoreline.

"Are you sure you want to do this?" Loretta asked Ray.

"Yeah," he said. "What can happen on a scenic float?"

"To everyone else, nothing. But for you, Ray, that's asking for trouble," Reba butted in.

"You bet," answered Loretta. "Tempting trouble is standard operating procedure for my husband."

"Bull," Ray said, as he took his time getting aboard. He'd been told to leave his crutches on the bus, so George helped him to a bench. Loretta followed, and Cookie Adams boarded next.

Their collective weight beached the massive rubber raft, so the guide stepped off and with help from ashore, lifted the front end of the raft off the rocky incline, waded knee deep into the river, and pushed it off. They then spun the raft 180 degrees for the guide to hop into the stern. Their guide, Zack, remained standing in the stern and, using a reversed stroke, powered the raft out into the moving current.

"What do you do the rest of the year, Zack?" asked Loretta, admiring the broad shoulders and easy strength with which he used the long oars.

"I'm a student. I study art at the Rocky Mountain School of Design."

"Why rafting?"

"I learned to navigate rivers in Alaska, ma'am. Pays my tuition."

"Make a lot of money at it, young fellow?" asked George.

"Depends on the tips," answered Zack with an innocent grin. "It's not what you'd call a living, and the raft rides are shut down in the winter. But it's what I love—being outside under the big sky. Besides, it gives me time for my art."

"What sort of art?" asked Loretta.

"Oil painting," he said. "Mostly animals and mountain

scapes."

She started to ask him something else, but he interrupted. "Look to your left, everyone, about two hundred yards, at the top of that cluster of trees. An eagle's nest, an aerie."

"Wow, it's huge!" Reba cupped her hand over her eyes in the sharp sunlight.

"You bet," said Zack. "It can weigh 2,000 pounds or more. One fell down recently, took the whole tree down with it."

Zack maneuvered the raft around a clutter of branches and logs. "Folks? Know why all these trees are floating down the river? We had 168 inches of snow last winter and when it melted, we had major flooding. Tore trees right out of the earth." Zack guided the raft over the first set of mild rapids on the winding Snake River, then poled smoothly toward the other bank, where a second set rolled them gently forward. The group's excitement ebbed into disappointment as Zack's expert navigating dominated the eddies. No one needed to hang onto the rope tethers fastened to the raft.

Theo trained her camera on the shoreline. "Look at that huge dead tree lying there," she said.

"Yes, ma'am," Zack replied. "See the base of it, folks? Chewed away by beavers."

Theo snapped her picture. "Amazing," she said.

"Them damn beavers," George joked.

His sister, Cookie, swayed back and forth to the rhythm of the raft, her eyes half closed. "Like a rocking chair," she said. "So smooth."

Zack kept looking skyward at regular intervals and then at the rafts ahead and behind him. The casual speed of the scenic float quickened, the river grew deeper and slightly choppy. The sky stubbornly remained light, but a rain-filled darkness moved south, marching up behind them. Suddenly, the distant mountain forests ahead disappeared into the mist. High up, the black clouds from the west drew closed like a curtain. Lightning danced in the canyon crevices--too far off for sound, but a smoking tree could be seen. A hush fell over the jovial group.

"Don't worry, folks," said Zack. "Just a little activity way up in the higher canyon. Not likely to bother us down here."

Suddenly, colliding layers of clouds exchanged greetings. Several quick bolts of lightning streaked down the canyons. Then sharp cracks of thunder. Precipitation fell--not rain, but pea-sized white pellets.

"Hey!" cried Cookie. "This stuff is hail. I love it!"

"It melts in your hand," yelled Reba. "Can't take it home, so no one will ever believe it happened."

"It's turning to rain now," complained Ray. "And I'm getting wet."

"Oh, goodie," said Loretta. "Maybe you'll melt."

The rain beat down, puddling the raft's rubber floor. Water sloshed over sneakers. Drawn in by swirling eddies, the raft took on a waltzing motion. But intermittently, the bow rose high out of the water and then slapped flat and hard on the river surface.

White knuckles gripped the tethers now as a sense of fear stirred among the passengers. Zack wisely chose the more timid rapids whenever he could, but even the meekest of them brought white water crashing over the bow.

Not everyone was scared. Theo's eyes gleamed with excitement. "Go over there, Zack, let's get some real white water." She pointed to roiling turbulence near the opposite shore.

"Yeah, Zack, do it!" Reba shouted.

Ruth Milton tucked her arm into LeRoy's as they huddled together, transfixed, fascinated. And cold.

A wave sloshed over the gunwales, and Theo leaned forward to snap another picture. Thom grabbed her arm. "Better put the camera away before the rain ruins it."

"Okay, but just one more." Theo focused and clicked. "You'll be glad when we show the pictures to the kids," she said, finally tucking the camera inside her slicker pocket.

The chilling rain sloshed onto the rubber raft seats, soaking pants through to calves, knees, thighs, and fannies. Now nearly everyone sat in puddles. Ray would have none of it. He half-stood, intending to move out of his port-side seat in the bow to what he thought would be a dryer spot.

Zack yelled, "Keep your seat, please, and hang on! We're completely safe as long as you don't move around. It's only water."

But Ray would not be deterred from his goal. He wanted a different place to sit before they ran the next set of rapids. He started toward an empty seat on the starboard side, between Reba and Thom--a pointless move, the entire bench was already soaked. Lunging forward, Ray slipped on the slick rubber floor just as the raft pitched forward, slapping hard into a wave.

Like a trained seal, he belly-flopped over the starboard gunwale into the turbulent river.

"Oh, for crissake!" Reba shouted. She reached out and grabbed his pants leg just as he went over. She held tight and tugged, but didn't have the strength to pull him back.

Loretta's scream cut through the beating rain. Zack back-paddled with all his strength to reverse the raft's motion and prevent it from moving downstream, away from Ray. LeRoy pulled himself from his wife's grasp and grabbed the bottom edge of Ray's slicker. He shouted to Reba, "Let go of his leg! Let go, so his head can come up!" George sprang forward and peeled Reba's fingers off Ray's pants leg. Her face wore a strange, stunned look.

Now that his leg was freed, Ray's head emerged from the frothing river and LeRoy took a higher grip, this time on the strap of his life vest. Ray spat water and bellowed, "Help!" His arms flailed and his legs treaded water. Only LeRoy's grip prevented the rushing current from carrying the raft downstream away from Ray.

George and Thom, without consulting each other, dropped to their knees to steady themselves, reached down, and hauled Ray aboard. They had to fight the pitch of the raft as it hit the next set of rapids, a jolting three on the white water scale.

They lowered him face down, on the raft floor and turned his head to one side. He coughed up water for the next few minutes. Still choking, he tried to sit up. But George placed his left foot firmly in the small of Ray's back.

"Let me up! Are you trying to kill me?"

"Stay where you are," Loretta threatened. "It's safer for all of us that way."

When Ray's mouth no longer spit out water, George reluctantly removed his foot. Ray struggled to his knees and hoisted himself onto the starboard bench. Everyone inched away as he oozed river water like a squeezed sponge.

Loretta glowered at her husband. "You could at least say thank you."

"Thanks, guys," Ray mumbled, too humiliated to elaborate.

LeRoy, breathless, his chest heaving under the thick life vest, lowered himself with a thud back on the bench. Ruth hugged him, not letting him see the worried look on her face.

Zack reminded them in a loud voice, "That's what happens when you don't follow directions. Now everyone stay put!" No one dared move. Not even Ray.

Zack guided them through five more rapids, each a single point higher than the usual white water "float" rating, and then steered center stream for a mile or two until he saw the beach. Up on the hill, the yellow and black school buses awaited them. He reverse-paddled furiously to bring about a softer beaching. The rubber bottom made a loud scrunching sound as it plowed to a stop on the pebbled shore.

Once they landed on solid ground, a jubilant chatter broke the tension. They would talk about the ride for years to come.

Within minutes of the return to the Mountain King Resort, each of the four guest laundry dryers went into action. The corridors echoed with Nikes, New Balances, and Reeboks thumping round and round in the dryer bellies. In the hall, Molly and Paco stopped to talk to Cookie. They had just returned from town.

"What's that terrible noise in there?" said Molly. "It sounds like two alley cats fighting in an empty garbage can."

"You're close--it's six pairs of wet sneakers," replied Cookie.

"We all got our feet wet even on the scenic float."

"You mean you got sunk?" asked Molly. "I knew that Snakey River was up to no good."

"Oh, no, Molly, mostly rain and a little splashing, that's all. You really missed a fun day."

"No way. Boats and me have this agreement," she said. "I won't rock them if they don't mess with me."

"What happened?" asked Paco. Cookie related the day's events, including Ray's disaster.

"Is he upset?" Molly stepped closer to savor the response.

"He's hopping around madder than a wet Rhode Island Red, claiming his wife tried to drown him," laughed Cookie. "Funny part is, it wasn't Loretta. Reba grabbed his leg--she was the closest to him."

"Even so, that's prephosferous," said Molly. "Nobody commits murder with an audience around."

"Unless it's in the heat of passion," Paco corrected. "Were they arguing at the time?"

"Nope, not this time," answered Cookie. "But, with Ray's face under water, Reba did hang onto his leg a little too long, I thought. George had to pry her loose."

"You got to admit," said Molly, "after what that man's been through, it would take a bunch more 'n that to kill him."

"That is, if someone did want to kill him," reminded Paco.

Ray and Loretta ate alone that evening, at the very table he'd shared with Tina the night before. The Symingtons would have preferred the company of others--to shield themselves from each other, but their own aloofness had its price. Loretta picked at her medallions of beef, pushing them from one side of the plate to the other as she dwelt in some far-off world. He stared at her for some time, hoping to make eye contact. She didn't allow it to happen, so his eyes began to roam the dining room.

Ray searched for nothing in particular, and, for the most part, nothing caught his attention. Then he felt the weight of two eyes upon him. He quickly looked away, thinking it a coincidental collision of sight paths. As he buttered a roll, his curiosity got the best of him. He needed another look. Would the weighty gaze still be there? Not wanting to be trapped in his own game of spying, he casually forked a piece of rainbow trout, nearly missing his mouth as he glanced about. Yes, her seductive eyes remained upon him, along with a teasing half-smile. But before he could respond, an elderly woman at the same table leaned forward and obscured his vision.

"Damn!" Ray said.

"What's that?" asked Loretta, looking straight at him for the first time that evening. "You spoke to me?"

"Nothing, dear," he replied. "Just trying to identify someone at another table."

Loretta fixed on the direction he'd indicated. "You mean the woman in the floral print dress over there?"

"Yes," he lied.

"Oh, that's Hilda Vickers. She's the one mothering that Barton dish who attacked you last night. They're traveling companions--aunt and niece."

"Oh, yeah?" he mumbled, not really listening.

"Maybe you should try your luck with her. I don't think she can hit back quite as hard or fast as her niece."

"Oh, yeah?" he mumbled a second time.

The strangeness of his response caused Loretta to take a closer look. Just as she did, Hilda leaned back in her chair, fully exposing the smiling face next to her. It wasn't Tina Barton. Cookie Adams had been flirting with Ray all this time.

"Raymond Symington, you're despicable. I suppose now you've got a thing going with Cookie."

"Now wait one cotton-pickin' minute," he started. "I'm sitting here minding my own business. Some broad takes a fancy to me and I'm guilty?"

"Don't you Mr. Innocence me," Loretta whispered with controlled fury. "The day you stop flirting will be the day you're dead." Tucking her clutch purse under her arm, she slid her chair back and stood, then spun about and headed for the door. Ray scowled, wondering who had witnessed this little scene. He signaled to the waiter for the check. Quickly signing it, he followed his wife out of the dining room. But he couldn't resist looking over his shoulder. Cookie flashed him a teasing grin and cutesy wave.

Her smile sent a flash of recognition through him. But who was she? Could he be that forgetful of an old lover? From the distance of a few tables, she looked attractive, around forty, a few auburn streaks lighting up her dark hair.

Ray caught up with Loretta at the elevator, but she ducked in and jammed her finger on the button. The doors closed. Morosely, he sat down on a sofa in the lobby to brood and give his wife time to cool down.

Molly waited her turn at the cash register of the Mountain King gift shop, a Wilderness Post clamped under one heavy arm. From there her eyes followed Reba, who crossed the small lobby, settled into a wing chair, and opened a book. Reba had been two customers ahead in the gift shop, and Molly had spotted her bookmark. It looked similar to the other blue slips of paper the LeSotos had collected. Molly watched Reba remove it from her book and set it on the chair's wide upholstered arm.

The register ka-chinged. Molly's turn next. On impulse, she plucked a fancy feathered bookmark from its display rack and laid it on the counter with the newspaper and a $5 bill. The register rang again, and a few coins of change fell into her pudgy palm. She turned down the offer of a small bag and silently approached the back of the wing chair where Reba sat engrossed in her romance novel.

"Surprise, Mrs. Hurles! I thought you might enjoy one of these." Molly laid the feathered bookmark on the chair's right arm and slid the blue paper out from under it. Pocketing the filched slip, she nonchalantly lumbered toward the elevator.

Reba called after her, "Thank you, Molly, that's so sweet. But what's the occasion?"

Then Reba noticed. "Hey!" She jumped up, checked the

floor around the chair, and rushed to the elevator. With her gold hoop earrings still dancing, she said, "Hey, Molly, nice of you to give me this." She held up the bookmark. "But I had a little piece of paper on the arm of the chair and now it's gone."

Molly looked blank. "Piece of paper? Don't know what you mean. Maybe you snuck it in your book."

"Well, uh, sorry." A baffled Reba walked away. It had all happened so fast.

In their third floor room, Paco waited in his striped pajamas for his wife to return. Her soft knock brought a smile to his lips. Settled deep under the covers, he needed a little extra time to reach the door.

Molly's determined mood caught him by surprise. She didn't even kiss him. "Get your tuchus in gear, Paco, I got somethin' to show you."

She charged past him and laid her newly acquired blue slip of paper flat on the desk next to the other three. Paco sat down at the desk. Molly, hanging over him, reached around and arranged each slip by date.

Each slip came from a three-by-three-inch pad. The top of each blue slip bore the IMTC logo with its two interlocking gears.

"The notes are obviously from the same pad," Paco said. "Why would anybody fold each slip twice?" he asked rhetorically.

"To throw it away?"

"No, no," he said. "Most people would crumble it into a wad to toss it."

"Then why?"

"Perhaps so no one would see what was written on it."

"You mean like passing notes in class?" she offered.

"Something like that, only in this case we have four notes. More like a blind lottery, I'd say. And all in the same handwriting." Paco reached for the first one. "Friday, 9/11, Flaming Gorge," he announced.

Molly read the second one aloud: "Saturday, 9/12, Cody."

"Sunday, 9/13, Yellowstone," said Paco, studying number

three.

"And Monday, 9/14, Jackson," Molly finished. "That's yesterday. Maybe all we have here is an obituary."

"I should hope not," he said. "But if you mean itinerary, I quite agree. It may also be some harmless scheme of keeping tabs on the tour dates and locations. We shouldn't jump to any conclusions."

"But honey, how does a detective know when to jump on his confusions?"

Paco turned in his chair and dangled one leg over the armrest. "That's a tough one, Mol. I guess you try 'em all on, and if a clue fits one of the missing pieces, you fill it in. When it starts to make sense, you jump on it. The blue slips are clues, all right. It's just that we don't recognize their meaning or importance. We don't see the whole picture yet."

A dawning look suddenly crossed Paco's face. He rose from the desk chair, turned to his bride, and cupped his hands around her moon face. "Sweetie pie...That new note you just brought me. Exactly where did you get it?"

She gazed into his penetrating eyes with a look of surprise. "Nice 'jammies, Paco honey. Very sexy."

"Don't change the subject, sweetie."

"You don't wanna know." She pursed her lips and gave him a soft kiss.

Chapter 14
DESPERATE OVERTURES
Day Seven, Wednesday, September 16, 1981

THE INCESSANT THUMPING IN THE DRYERS ceased just before breakfast. Sneakers, damp or dry, needed to be packed for bus loading. Reba stumbled over the threshold on her way to the breakfast buffet as the toe of her sneaker separated from the sole.

George guffawed. "You had to be different, babe. Glenn told you not to use the hair dryer on your shoes. Too much heat melted the glue on those cheapies. You got what you deserved for not listening."

"Don't rub it in," she sulked.

The Symingtons stepped out of their places in the buffet line and fell in behind Paco and Molly. The LeSotos turned around and exchanged morning greetings.

Paco noticed a look of urgency in Ray's expression. "Is there something I can do?"

"Maybe." Ray stepped closer. Towering over the detective, his deep-set gray eyes met Paco's squarely and demanded attention. "May I ask you a personal question?"

"I suppose so," Paco said, trying inconspicuously to step backward from so much intensity. "It depends."

"Do you carry a piece?" asked Ray. "And I don't mean that piece of junk you bought in Jackson Hole."

"Not now. And rarely did I ever find the need to carry one."

"You're a policeman, aren't you? I thought cops always carried guns."

"Beat officers do. But many criminal investigators prefer to

118

carry only when making an arrest. Why do you ask?"

"I'm certain someone is trying to kill me."

"You suspected as much the other day," said Paco. "What makes you so sure now?"

"I know they look like accidents," Ray began in a near-whisper. "But there've been too many to be coincidental. The scalding in the shower, for openers. My going over the railing at the Lower Falls. And remember when Thom Moyer fell down the stairs at the Mountain King? That was meant for me. And yesterday on the raft trip, someone held me under water longer than necessary. Or didn't you hear about that?"

"I heard," Paco answered. "And just who do you think your assailant is?"

"I'd rather not say until I have proof. I don't even know if it's just one person. But one thing I do know, Paco: I need your help. I'm willing to pay for it--say, $300 a day for the rest of the tour. All you have to do is keep me alive and healthy."

"That's all?" Paco asked wryly. "I'm terribly sorry, Ray, I can't do that. Maybe you should contact the local police. I haven't got the resources here, and knowing you, I wouldn't be able to restrict your movements anyway. But most of all, I'm on my honeymoon and I owe all my loving attention to my bride here. Right, Mol?"

"You got that right," she said. "But why don't you and your wife watch each other's backside?"

"He doesn't even trust me," Loretta said. Her fuchsia mouth smiled, but her eyes radiated anger. Ray just shrugged.

Molly took two trays and handed one to Paco, nudging him forward. She wanted her husband away from these people. Besides, the eggs Benedict looked delicious. She scooped up two and garnished them with bacon strips, a wedge of Monterey Jack, and a buttery croissant.

Paco glanced at her plate. Both his eyebrows shot up. "Take it easy, sweetie pie, we're only halfway through the trip."

With lips pursed in a mock pout, Molly deciphered the

code his expressive eyebrows conveyed. Right one up: surprise; left one: amusement; both: disbelief. "Honeybunch," she teased, "you knew I'd never be skimpy when you married me." With her loaded tray, she looked for an empty table. Paco poured his coffee and joined her.

"Over here," Thom called to them from a corner of the room.

Molly transferred their plates to the table, set the trays on a nearby stand, and they settled into the two empty chairs.

"Good morning, everyone. Thanks for letting us join you all." Paco nodded to the Moyers and the Miltons. Then he turned to Thom. "There's something I'd like to ask you."

"What's that, Inspector? Something official?"

"Oh no," answered Paco. "It's that little Crescent wrench you fellows all seem to be carrying on your key chains. I'm fascinated by it. Does it actually work?"

"It sure does. Hey, it's no toy. Here, let me show you." Thom unhooked the wrench from the end of his key chain and handed it to Paco.

"How 'bout that!" remarked Paco as he rolled the tiny adjustment wheel between his thumb and index finger, sliding the small jaws to their maximum open position. "Smooth job of machining, not a mark on it." He handed it back with a smile of appreciation.

Thom and Theo excused themselves, leaving Molly and Paco to finish breakfast with LeRoy and Ruth.

"Paco, honey," said Molly suddenly. "I spilled holidaze sauce on my blouse. I have to get back to the room and put a new one on before they take away the luggage."

"You haven't much time," said Paco. "I think I see them bringing out bags now."

"Don't worry, honeybunch," she assured him. "I'm a reg'lar quick-change artist." As she pulled her size twenty-two sweater around her sloped shoulders, she thought she saw Ruth give LeRoy a nervous glance. Molly toddled off.

They met at the bus ten minutes later, in time to see their second bag disappear into the hold. Wearing a fresh blouse, Molly stood in line to board just behind Gordon Whitman. He pulled off his Giants baseball cap, and something dropped onto his shirt.

"Oh, Gordon," she said. "There's a little speck of dreck on your clean white T-shirt. Here, let me get it for you." She carefully lifted it off his shoulder and showed it to him.

"Hey, thanks, Molly." He gave it only a cursory look, climbed aboard, and took his seat on the door side of the bus.

But Paco took a greater interest in the rust-colored fleck. He lifted it from Molly's index finger, folded it into the gift shop receipt for his newspaper, and tucked it into his zippered jacket pocket. He helped Molly up the steps, and they took the first door-side seat, directly in front of the Hurles. Another couple climbed on. Lew Getz stood and counted heads: only one person missing. Glenn scowled and studied his watch. Loretta fumed. Finally, ten minutes after the scheduled departure, Ray came around the corner carrying a cold bottle of Evian. When Lew opened the folding doors for him, the entire busload booed and hissed. Even the bus doors hissed as they closed behind him, announcing their own displeasure.

When the jeering continued from the Davies, seated two rows behind the Symingtons, Ray lashed out at them. "That's what I'd expect from the likes of you two, a couple of jailbirds."

The jailbird remark cut Monte deeply, but his boss owned his soul now in the form of a signed confession. Three years earlier, Ray had caught Monte using the company credit card for private luxuries. A review of his expense accounts had turned up heavily padded items and many irregularities--entertaining fictitious customers and bogus travel. Taking into consideration Monte's sales expertise and quota record, Ray offered him immunity in return for restitution and a signed confession. Monte knew it was blackmail, and even tried to leave the firm last year, but Ray had waved the confession in front of his face and that ended Monte's attempted defection.

Lew urged the long vehicle away from the lodge and slowly geared up to cruising speed for their 270-mile journey south. The Bridger-Teton National Forest gradually faded into the distance. They crossed westward into Idaho for less than fifty miles, then south again.

Glenn started down the aisle toward the rear of the bus, stopping with his hand resting on the back of the Miltons' seat.

"This is Idaho, folks--near Montpelier, where Butch Cassidy robbed a bank of $7,000 in the 1890's. Doesn't sound like much today, but then it was quite a take." He patted the seat and continued down the aisle.

Skirting the far shore of Bear Lake, they left Idaho for Utah and followed a string of small towns, nestling against the Wasatch Mountain Range. In a nearby meadow a herd of pronghorn antelope grazed peacefully, ignoring the roaring engine of the bus.

"Look!" squealed Bess as a flock of long-tailed birds--black, white, and aqua--flew in and out of tall pines. "What are they?"

"Magpies," Glenn told her.

Lew left the superhighway at the next cloverleaf and made a right turn past sprawling one-story buildings, one after another--warehouses and factories. Off in the brown hills, excavating and copper mining equipment roamed the tremendous mounds like so many ants at work.

A murky gray body of water appeared on their right, stretching for miles and miles. The bus pulled up before an elaborately decorated music hall and parked.

"Folks, we're at the Great Salt Lake," Glenn began as they grabbed for their cameras. "Except for the Dead Sea, this is the saltiest body of water on earth."

Everyone walked down to the closest shoreline, eager to examine the lake's content. Molly tried to bend over and touch the water, but her roly-poly form just refused to cooperate. Taking care not to get his jeans wet, Paco approached the edge, knelt down, and scooped up two palmfuls. He held them out to Molly.

She worked the water between her fingers. "Yuck, it's

slimy."

"Yep," Glenn said. "It's filled with millions of microscopic shrimp."

"You'd have to be dippy in the head to take a dip in this," Molly said.

Glenn laughed "Oh, you'd be surprised. Over there on Antelope Island there are beaches, and people swim in the lake all the time. But you're safe, Molly, our schedule doesn't allow for it."

"Is there a Great Pepper Lake?" George joked.

"George," Reba scolded, "you're probably the millionth person to ask that." Her husband looked deflated.

When finally reloaded, the bus zoomed past mountains rich in the ores men want and need.

For the next two nights the Vermilion tour abandoned the rustic flavor of the region and embraced the pampered manner of Salt Lake City's Grand Regency Hotel. Plumped pillows on king-sized beds, marble bathrooms with gold fixtures. Not a difficult transition.

In the circular penthouse dining room, lights winked as the expansive view of city and brown mountains melted into darkness. At one of the larger arc-shaped tables along the perimeter, the LeSotos joined a group of six who were already sipping glasses of Chardonnay and White Zinfandel.

Abby Lebowitz turned to Harry, seated next to her, and asked, "I wondered if you were related to Maestro Warren Sessions, the renowned pianist. You look something like him."

"Oh, no," the judge replied. "I do play for pleasure and enlightenment, but certainly not for fame and profit."

"I saw Warren Sessions in San Francisco last year. He was magnificent," Abby said.

"Do you play at all?" Harry asked her.

"Yes...if you can call it that. I have no talent whatsoever."

"I see," Harry said, wondering how to get around this conversation stopper.

"But Jake sings opera with a local company in New Jersey."

"Just in the chorus when they're desperate," Jake said. "I'm forced to rely on my practice as a chiropodist for my living."

Molly, wanting so much to be a part of this conversation, asked, "You mean you play footsy with opera?"

Jake laughed. "Oy vey, I guess I'd be disappointed if nobody played games with my profession."

Molly grinned, pleased with herself. "I went to the opera once. Doctor Avi, my employer--well, his lady friend was indeposed for the evening, so he took me instead."

"What did you see?" Jake asked.

"Hansel and Gristle!" she replied. "It was so cute with that gingerboard house. Dr Avi even lent me his libido so I'd know the story." Everybody chuckled.

"Perhaps you'll consent to play something for us, Maestro Harry?" said Hilda, eager to change the subject back to her brother's piano playing.

"He'd love to," Caroline answered for him. "He does give recitals for friends in our living room. But I doubt that there's an instrument of quality here in the hotel." Harry smiled apologetically and gestured with both palms up.

"Now wait a minute," Jake said. "On the second floor there's a ballroom with a concert grand and a marvelous view. I got off at the wrong floor and was pleasantly surprised to find it."

"Uncle Harry, it would be my pleasure to make the arrangements with the hotel for tomorrow night," offered Tina. "That is, if you would consent to a private recital for our tour group."

"I'd be delighted. Tomorrow evening, say 6:30?"

"Hotel willing," said Tina.

"How did you like your salmon, Mrs. Sessions?" asked Molly.

"Delicious," she replied. "And your meal?"

"My lobster toreador was a mite picky-yoon," complained Molly. "All sauce and no seafood."

"Maybe," said Jake, "the good judge here will file a writ of habeas corpus for you, compelling the management to fork over

the missing crustacean."
Judge Sessions harrumphed. "I'm on vacation."

Chapter 15
MUSICAL OVERTURES
Day Eight, Thursday, September 17, 1981

EARLY THE NEXT MORNING Tina Barton stepped out of the hotel manager's office. She'd been able to pull it off. The ballroom and concert grand would be available at six o'clock following a noon wedding reception. The $1,200 rental fee was waived when the manager heard the judge's last name--he'd assumed it was the maestro. Fifty folding chairs would be set up for them.

She found Harry in the lobby reading the Salt Lake Tribune and gave him the good word before returning to her room to pick up Hilda.

Judge Harry felt appreciated, too excited to read. He folded his paper and left it on the upholstered chair as he started across the lobby. But his pleasant expression turned dark when he nearly collided with Ray Symington. "I didn't know they let slime into such a fine hotel," Harry snapped.

"Apparently they also make exceptions for fallen judges caught with dirty hands," Ray retorted.

"Symington, you lying cheat. You knew it wasn't true. You set me up and ruined me with innuendo and half-truths. Just wait--you'll get what you deserve yet."

Loretta emerged from the gift shop and spotted her husband with his jacket flung open and hands on his hips. Hurrying across the lobby, she grabbed his arm and hauled him out of earshot. But not before he directed a deliberate sneer at the judge, getting in the last action, if not the last word.

"Wasn't winning enough for you?" she asked. "Must you taunt the man, too?"

"The way I look at it," declared Ray, "winning gives me license to gloat. It's the only fun I get these days."

"You must be doing something right," she snapped, as the elevator doors spread before them. "You have no friends left, and your enemies list grows daily." They stepped in, and the doors closed behind them.

In the lobby Judge Harry felt the joy and optimism of the day slide from his grip. He lumbered to the coffee shop entrance and leaned back against the glass until he saw Caroline coming with the Lebowitzes and LeSotos.

"What's wrong, dear?" asked Caroline. "You look awful. They turn you down for the room and concert grand?"

"No, no, on the contrary," started Harry. "We're all set. Management was thrilled and even waived the rent."

"Then why the long face, dear," she asked.

"I just had a run-in with that Symington crook, name-calling and all."

She sighed. "You of all people should know better. Come on, let's do some sightseeing."

"You go ahead without me," he said. "I don't feel much like a tourist right now. I'll go upstairs and watch some television."

"I don't like the idea of your moping around in a hotel room, dear."

"I'll be fine. I want to see Hilda, too. She's agreed to write invitations for tonight." He turned and walked away.

Caroline started toward him, but Abby took her arm and kept moving. Caroline didn't resist.

Paco's eyes took in the center city as they walked. He noted wide avenues and nondescript architecture. After five blocks, they stood before a black wrought iron gate and entered Temple Square.

They began strolling through the gardens, and Molly stopped at a larger-than-life bronze sculpture: a father hunching forward as he pulled a long-handled, two-wheeled cart. His wife and young son pushed from behind. The handcart contained their baby and all their belongings as they trekked 1,400 miles on the Mormon Trail from Illinois to Utah 150 years ago.

The Handcart Pioneer Monument took Molly's breath away. She could almost feel their struggle, but then a puzzled look crossed her face. "I always thought they rode in those Conestogie wagons."

"No, ma'am," said a friendly voice. "Mostly, the pioneers walked here. The wagons, if they could afford them, were for household goods, food, and other supplies. There wasn't any room for passengers unless they were infants, aged, or infirm." The voice belonged to a nicely groomed, handsome young man not yet twenty.

"That's most informative of you," said Paco.

"Pleasure to help you. My name's Ezekiel. I'm giving the church two years of my life, and I've been assigned to give assistance and information to the tourists."

"What's that beautiful building with the white spires," asked Caroline, pointing to the far corner of the square."

"That is our holy temple," Ezekiel replied. "Only Mormons in good standing may enter there. A wedding is performed inside every fifteen minutes, sometimes as many as forty in a day. May I suggest that you visit the Tabernacle instead. It's the building on your left."

"I thought the Mormon Tabernacle was the church," said Paco.

"Oh, no," said Ezekiel. "It is the meeting place. If you hurry, in ten minutes you can listen to an organ recital in an acoustically perfect hall."

The LeSotos and Caroline sat enrapt for a quarter hour, listening to the organ music. Like bells ringing, Molly thought.

Later they joined the entire tour to visit the Beehive House, Brigham Young's official residence.

Rheba cornered Glenn. "Did Brigham Young really have fifty-two wives?"

Glenn smiled. "More like nineteen, Reba, and some in name only. Depends on who you listen to."

Molly whispered to Paco, "How'd the guy find time to 'complish everything he did?"

"Good question, sweetie pie, I can't imagine." They looked at each other and giggled.

Several miles from Temple Square, a stooped woman with gray hair stepped down from a trolley car and entered a small suburban branch bank. She paused to adjust her granny glasses and rearrange the canvas tote on her arm, then shyly approached the manager's desk. With a tentative smile, she handed over the key to a safe deposit box. The manager led her behind a half-wall covered with planters of peace lilies and ushered her into the vault.

A middle-aged man in a tan baseball cap entered the bank. The lone teller motioned him to the counter, but he said he needed to see the manager and sat down with the local newspaper to wait his turn. Some minutes later, the elderly patron emerged from the vault area with the manager and shuffled out the front door. As she disappeared from view, her gait abruptly turned brisk.

The teller looked confused when the customer in the baseball cap tucked the newspaper under his arm and walked out. He had apparently changed his mind.

Halfway down the block, the gray-haired woman slowed down and glanced over her shoulder. The man in the baseball cap caught up with her, and the couple boarded an open-sided red trolley heading toward town.

"What happened in there?" asked LeRoy.

"When I got into the vault, the interior door at the rear was shut and locked. It was a multi-tumbler mechanism. Combination locks just aren't my shtick."

"It wasn't that way when we cased it three months ago," he said. "They always left it unlocked and ajar, at least the two days we checked. Just like in Denver."

"Yeah, convenient and careless. I didn't recognize the woman who took me back," she added. "I had to think of something in a hurry. I fished around in my bag--told her I'd made a mistake and left my jewelry at home, so she didn't have to open my box."

"Good work, Ruth. You always were fast on your feet. Oh, well, some days you just can't make a buck." He took her hand in his and winked at her.

Chapter 16
NOTEWORTHY
Same Day, Thursday, September 17, 1981

HILDA VICKERS TRIED THE LARGE BRASS HANDLE, but the polished wood doors to the ballroom had been locked from within.
Strains of muffled piano notes trickled beyond the ballroom into
the corridor--her brother Harry warming up for the recital.

She turned to her niece, fretting, "I do hope everyone
found the invitations under their doors."

"Don't worry, Auntie," Tina assured her. "I delivered every
last one of them myself."

By 6:20, more of the travelers stood around waiting for
the free concert. The sound of a bolt turning in the lock caught
their attention, and the doors swung open. Caroline, in a sequined
evening gown, beckoned with a sweeping hand. "Come in, please.
We'll begin in a few moments." Her husband, resplendent in a tuxedo, sat on the padded piano bench sipping water from a crystal
tumbler.

As the seats began to fill, Molly promenaded in on Paco's
arm. Her pink cashmere sweater gave her the look of a puffy cloud
at sunset. She peered about the room: men in blazers and ties,
women in sleek pants outfits and silk scarves. But only the judge
and his wife wore formal evening clothes. Who brings a tuxedo on
a tour bus out West? Molly wondered, as she and Paco took front
row seats. Was this impromptu concert actually programmed?

The baby grand stood proudly in front of a floor-to-ceiling
window, overlooking a formal garden bordered by a boxwood hedge.
A balcony lined the window wall, and a brace of open French doors
invited fresh air from outside.

Harry sat down and, for a long moment, stared at the keyboard while he cajoled creative messages from the muses. At last, with fingers poised above the keyboard, he retrieved the initial notes from memory. Then, the entire melody from the Liszt etude Consolation flowed from his mind to the keyboard, from the Yamaha to the entire ballroom and beyond. The piece so mesmerized the audience, they applauded and cheered him upon its completion.

Harry bowed his head in appreciation and turned to the keyboard once more, striking the first notes of Chopin's powerful Military Polonaise. Eyes closed, once more he drew the score from his head. Horn-rimmed lenses inched down the bridge of his nose as perspiration formed like dew. His passion heated, his arms leaped high above the keys. The notes flew. Finishing the final booming chords, he stood and bowed. The sounds of clapping echoed through the scantily filled ballroom once more.

Judge Sessions reached for a glass of water and noticed that the applause from Paco was particularly enthusiastic. Tears ran down Paco's animated face. "It's a powerful piece by the greatest piano composer of all time. Is that what moves you so?" the judge asked.

"I thought that honor went to Franz Liszt," said Paco.

"Actually," offered Harry, "Liszt was the greater pianist, a technician and innovator. Fredric Chopin was more the master composer."

"I see, but something else strikes me."

"And what would that be?" asked Harry.

"I had the advantage of watching you at your keyboard, and it occurred to me that no other human activity is so demanding, so exacting. I'm impressed that you play from memory. I watched your ten fingers assume thousands of configurations. Your back and arms stretch to extend your reach. One foot operates its pedal independently of the other, while your mind anticipates each move--and at such a tempo! It must be a great love to achieve this kind of perfection."

Pleasure lit up Harry's face. "Love is precisely the word. Thank you! It's been said that the brain goes through hundreds of thousands of calculations to get through a piece like that."

After dabbing his dripping brow with a folded hanky, Harry sat poised for his next opus. Then, without warning, a loud drone of machinery erupted from just below the window. Harry waited patiently for it to end, but finally lifted his fingers off the keys and shook his white head in annoyance. The droning continued.

Caroline's taffeta gown rustled as she hurried to the window. "What's going on?" she called. "I can't see a thing."

No one could. George Hurles stepped through the French doors out onto the balcony with Paco right behind him. Peering straight down, they saw a swimming pool, a kiddy pool, and a large Jacuzzi, its motor droning as it bubbled. One man sat in it. Only his head appeared above the frothy water.

"I might have known," George said. "Ray!" he shouted. "Ray!" But his boss couldn't hear him. He was too busy doing his dunking-under-the-water thing.

Molly peered over the balcony and said to no one in particular, "Mr. Ray must think that hot tub is mighty therapubic."

Loretta darted past and descended the wrought iron staircase to the pool deck. She headed straight for the Jacuzzi timer switch and turned it off. The world went silent for a short time. "How can you be so insensitive? Get out of there!"

Ray chose to ignore her by submerging himself completely. His wife sank into a lounge chair and waited for him to pop up so she could deliver a few more choice words.

In the ballroom above, Harry launched into Rachmaninoff's Variations on a Theme of Paganini, but after only a few bars, another explosion of noise burst forth. Harry threw up his hands in disgust. Caroline wailed, "Not again!"

The audience heard Loretta scream. "Ray's under water and he's not coming up--he's drowning! Somebody call 911!"

Paco ran across the balcony and down the stairs with Jake and George close behind. Paco raced to the timing switch, but found it already in the OFF position. Puzzled, he searched for a fuse box or cutoff switch box. Spotting a cable, he followed it to a wooden cabinet atop a post and flung the door open. There were three switches inside. He pulled the MAIN breaker forward. The racket stopped. The other switches, marked NORM and CLEAN, had been left in the CLEAN (High Speed) position.

When Paco turned toward the Jacuzzi itself, George and Jake, both husky men, had already hauled Ray out. Ray made some gurgling sounds, which soon turned to a coughing fit. A vile spill of water trickled from his mouth. He'd begun to come around. When he tried to speak, his words came out in a high-pitched rasp.

Soon afterward, the paramedics arrived. George and Jake stepped aside to let them do their job. As one paramedic took Ray's blood pressure and pulse, he asked, "Sir, can you tell us what happened to you?"

Ray started to shake his head no, but then it became a yes. "Something went wrong. I got sucked under--couldn't come up. It wouldn't let me out of the hole in the bottom of the tub. I couldn't breathe. I almost drowned. Then everything blacked out. Am I going to be okay?"

"Your vital signs are good," the older of the paramedics responded, "considering what happened. But you swallowed chemicals with that water, chemicals that could do a lot of damage. What were you doing on the bottom, anyway?"

"Of all the gosh-damned things. I get into the hot tub to soak my sprained ankle. I like to submerge myself all the way under the water. It's a refreshing feeling. I've done it many times in hot tubs before, but this time...I don't know."

"We probably should take you to the hospital, at least for overnight, so you can get checked out," offered the paramedic.

"And miss the bus? No way! We're leaving here at 7:30 tomorrow morning. Besides, I spent big bucks of the company's money on this trip, and I'm not going to waste it in any hospital bed." His breathing became less labored, and he waved them off. "Thanks for the offer and your help."

"If you insist, sir. But in the future, don't put your head under water in a hot tub. It's not safe--as you found out." The two paramedics checked his vital signs once more, then, after getting him to sign a release, they reluctantly packed up and left.

Toweling off, Ray asked, "Inspector, who turned the timer switch on again?"

"I don't believe anyone touched the timer switch." Paco wanted to return to the recital, but too many questions needed answering. "There's a cleaning bypass switch in that cabinet over there. Apparently, when it's in the ON mode, the circulation pump runs at many times its normal speed and force. That would account for the increased racket it made, the suction, too."

Paco also noticed a round, gridded piece of cast iron lying on the concrete deck. He picked it up gingerly, holding it as far as possible from his suede sport jacket.

"Who would do this to me?" asked Ray.

"Perhaps the same person who left this off the drain." Paco turned the heavy grate over in his hands. "The whole point of it is to prevent someone being sucked into the drain. As big a man as you are, the flow and suction pulled you into the drain hole, and your buttocks formed a near-perfect seal over it, denying you access to air above. However, we can't automatically assume someone was out to get you." The inspector knitted his black brows together. "It's possible that a maintenance worker literally screwed up and left the grate off."

Ray's eyes, bloodshot from the water, turned to angry slits. "If that's the case, I'll sue the pants off this hotel. But, somehow, I doubt it was a maintenance worker. Too much has happened to me. Inspector, you just have to do something. Where the hell's my wife, anyway?"

Loretta was nowhere to be seen. He scowled, gathered up his beach towel, and said, "I'm going upstairs to change and rest for awhile. See you later. Thanks for your help."

Molly had been watching from the balcony and clumped down the stairs in her pink leather flats. She waited until Ray had gone inside and murmured to her husband, "If he'd been a gentleman, he'd have attended Judge Sessions' recital. Everyone else in our group was there."

"It just seemed like everyone else was there," Paco replied. "Ray sure doesn't have a subtle bone in his body. He chose to indulge in a noisy activity close to the concert room. My guess is: he wanted to sabotage the judge's performance."

"Uh-huh." Molly's face lit up. "Was the drain thing an accident? Or did somebody actually remove the grate in order to do him in? But how could they have known that Ray would be in the tub?"

Paco shrugged. "Good question. Even if someone wanted to remove the grate, it's not that easy. They'd have to be strong enough to unscrew the screws that held it in place. And they'd have to be skillful enough and fast enough to take it off under water." He shook his head and frowned as he adjusted his new silk tie. "And even if they were absolutely positive that Ray was planning on getting in the hot tub, other hotel guests use it, too. It's probably more popular than the pool. How could the perp have been so sure that another guest, a complete stranger, wouldn't have gotten in the Jacuzzi first--and been drowned?"

Molly, a head shorter than her husband, tilted her face up as she listened intently. Her flushed cheeks and pink cashmere gave her a rosy glow. Paco's analysis just had to wait. "You look beautiful tonight, sweetie pie," he said tenderly.

"You too, honey bunch."

George and Jake, as well as the rest of the group, drifted back into the ballroom and settled in their chairs once more. Several minutes later, Harry pounded the keyboard in renewed fervor as he launched into a Beethoven sonata.

A disappointed Paco and Molly did not return directly to the concert, reluctantly choosing to remain at the scene to search for clues. Paco walked back to the switch cabinet and examined its contents. Just a wooden box supported by a three-inch piece of conduit pipe anchored in the concrete pool skirt. He found a complete set of plastic laminated operating instructions on the inside of the cabinet door.

Molly searched the pool skirt around the box. "Look, Paco!" She pointed to a partial shoe print leading from a puddle toward the boxwood hedge a few feet away. The imperfect print led to a more distinct one in the muddy bed. The print covered an area nearly four inches longer than Paco's shoe and at least twice as wide.

"Well, that narrows it down to one humdingous guy," declared Molly. "I'd sure hate to meet toes to toes with him."

"Big feet, anyway," admitted Paco. "Tennis court shoes, I believe. See the finer pattern of the tread? Cheaply made. Notice that line along the edge of the sole? No good shoe would use a wraparound binding."

"Unless he's wearing oversized shoes to throw us off."

"Not likely. The print depth is equally distributed, indicating the man actually filled his shoes."

"You're sure it's not a woman?" asked Molly.

"Yup, pretty sure. Sheer size, alone. From the direction of the prints, he entered the lobby through that door."

"How can you be sure this is the guy who threw the cleaning switch?" she asked.

"Neither guests nor employees would make such a beeline departure--into the muddy hedge," he replied. "Do you have the Sure Shot camera with you?"

"Never without it, honey."

"See if you can't get a close-up shot of each print."

While she snapped away, Molly commented, "Does this mean you're agreeing to protect Ray? Are we actually inquiziating a crime scene or are we merely satisfying your profectional curiosity?"

"I wish I knew how to answer that, Molly, dear," he said. "Do you mind if I let my nose take us where it will?"

"Course not, honey. It's fun to be with your nose, working this way with you. I love you, Inspector. Can I be your inspectorette?"

"As long as there's no danger to you," he replied, laughing.

"I can't understand," she said, "why Ray doesn't chicken on home and escape all this danger. If I were him, I'd get my high tail behind me and fly the coop out of here on the first plane up."

"I've wondered about that, too," said Paco. "The man is compulsive about staying with the tour. He should have the fear of death firmly planted in him by now."

Molly tucked the camera into her purse, and the two of them returned to the ballroom via the French door from the balcony. Several seats were vacant and Paco noted only a few of the group missing: the Symingtons, Thom, and Jake. Paco figured Jake had gone to check on Ray in his room.

As Harry finished the last bars of Gershwin's Concerto in C, the audience applauded wildly. He rose, turned to them, and bowed. Tina leapt from her chair and presented a dozen red roses to her uncle.

The hotel management provided the concert-goers with complimentary champagne in plastic stemware, along with a round of brie and crackers. The room blossomed into a full-scale cocktail party with a cash bar. The hotel would profit from the concert after all.

The LeSotos left the cocktail party after just a few sips of wine. Molly had had enough socializing. The phone rang in their room as she kicked off her shoes. Paco answered, listened for a few moments, then covered the mouthpiece with his hand. "Mol, it's Symington. He wants to know if I'll meet him in the bar for a drink. Says he just wants to talk. Would you mind?"

"Go 'head, honey bunch, I'll write my postagraphs."

"Thanks, presh." Actually, Paco was pleased. He really wanted a cold beer, and maybe Ray would have some useful information to offer.

Molly blew him a kiss as he left the room. She welcomed the time for writing to Dr. Avi and to his children. Even as Paco's wife, she still treasured her eight hours a day as the psychoanalyst's housekeeper and cook. As she scrawled on a jumbo postcard of the Utah state capitol, she thought about how lucky she was. All the years of working for "royalty," as she called the affluent households in Georgetown. But only after Dr. Avi hired her, did she ever feel like part of a family. Molly knew that her only sibling looked down on her for leaving school at sixteen to go to work. Her educated sister had married well and lived only half an hour away. Never once had they invited her to their big fancy house.

Molly chuckled as she wrote. "Hug Shana and give her some filly mignon and mushroons for me." She'd grown fond of Paco's two clever, colorful macaws, but no pet could replace Dr. Avi's golden retriever.

Paco's eyes took a moment to adjust to the aura of the Powder Horn Pub, a cookie-cutter hotel bar with recessed lighting and walnut paneling. He found Ray standing near the bar, shifting impatiently from one foot to the other. In a leather-covered booth at the back, they had barely placed their order before the waiter reappeared with frosted mugs, a pitcher of the local beer, and a basket of Doritos and hot salsa.

"You're doing remarkably well without your crutches," Paco observed, pouring for each of them.

"Yeah. I'm doing remarkably well period. Just being here." He fell silent and took a long draught.

Paco had switched out of his concert clothes to a turtleneck and chinos. Until he figured out what Ray had in mind, he planned to enjoy the quiet of the nearly empty bar and cold brew. Nibbling on the dipping snack, he studied the man across from him. The blue Izod shirt enhanced the wide expanse of shoulders and chest and softened the smoky gray eyes that always looked so impenetrable.

"Paco," Ray finally spoke. "Tell me...why is everyone out to get me?"

"Is everyone out to get you? If you don't mind my saying so, Ray, you invite trouble. You seem to have a talent for stirring it up."

"Don't tell me you're attacking me, too?"

"Ray, let's get something straight. I'm not attacking you. You've got a chip on your shoulder the size of a giant redwood."

"Doesn't every vice president? It's served me well so far."

"Has it? Are you saying you use intimidation as a management tool?"

"Well, yeah. Why not? I like intimidation. It works for me twelve hours a day, seven days a week, and I don't have to pay it overtime or benefits. These salesmen aren't so young any more. They're not likely to jump ship. There aren't that many jobs for guys in their forties and fifties, especially at their level of compensation. The fear factor keeps them performing. You've heard of that book *Winning Through Aggression*?"

"I've read it, but from what I've seen on this trip, your strategy may no longer be working. Even the docile tiger turns on its trainer when pushed too far."

Ray stared moodily into his empty mug. "Maybe you're right. They're more openly belligerent now. I can sense it. It's as though they know something I don't."

Paco poured a second round for each of them. He returned the drained pitcher to the table with a clunk. As if by magic, the waiter appeared with a full pitcher brimmed with foam, a fresh basket of Doritos, and a bowl of salted peanuts.

"Frankly," Ray said, "this is the only strategy I know. It's nothing new for me. I grew up with it. My father ran our house like a boardroom."

On this, his third beer, Paco's all too attentive posture had relaxed into the contours of the leather booth. He munched a fistful of peanuts and listened. Questions weren't really necessary, at least not yet. He'd keep the conversation low key and friendly--an invitation to talk, an opportunity to slip. It wasn't as though he planned to ply Ray with beer; that part was Ray's own idea. If a lifetime career as a detective had taught him anything, it was patience. An inadvertent admission or an outright confession might not be forthcoming here, but perhaps he'd learn a little more about the man.

Ray sensed the inspector's relaxed posture and took it as an invitation to talk. "Yeah, my dad was the original tyrant. I learned my lessons well. Jonathan Symington--the high-powered executive--ate, drank, and lived tyranny. Don't get me wrong. We endured rather well, a sizeable brownstone in Society Hill. That's Mainline Philadelphia, Inspector." Ray wiped the beer head from his upper lip with a cocktail napkin.

"Mother was a wuss. She let him make all the decisions and left him to discipline us boys. My brother and I could have been great friends, but our bullying father made sure that wouldn't happen. Long before our teens, he pitted us against each other. School, sports, and even board games. Would you believe Parcheesi, Othello, and Cribbage became battlegrounds? Always he'd reward the winner--but only the winner--with praise, affection, and toys. Being thirteen months younger, I usually came out the vanquished. That is, before I learned to grab the advantage, the power, quicker than the next guy."

Ray neglected to mention that he learned to cheat as well. His brother would run to the kitchen for a soda and when he returned to the playroom, he knew, but couldn't prove, that some of his Monopoly money had disappeared. Ray also learned that success breeds success. He cheated on exams at Philips Exeter, hired people to write his term papers at Wharton. His smarts and apparent successes finally won praise from his father, the praise he craved.

Ray towed a Dorito across the lumpy salsa sea and raised it to his mouth. "Why shouldn't I grab hold of the power at IMTC? I deserve to get credit for some of the hot ideas. My sales force developed the ideas while working for me, didn't they?"

"Somehow I get the impression," Paco said, "that you could have done it all on your own without the power elbow."

"Thank you, but not fast enough to impress my father."

"Is he still living?"

"No, his heart gave out five years ago in the middle of a

boardroom tirade. Look at it this way: the bastard died in the driver's seat, the way he wanted it."

"Then who's left for you to impress?" asked Paco.

"Me!" He slammed the half-drained mug down on the table. "It's hard to change a lifetime of being an SOB. Besides, I don't want to undo anything now. The whole intimidating thing is exhilarating. I should thank the old bully for showing me how."

"What about your wife?"

"Loretta? She doesn't pay any attention to me most of the time, and when she does, it's only to squabble. I like that too. It keeps me on my toes. The only drawback to being male dominant is the loneliness that goes with it. I'd probably have been better off without a father."

"I understand where you're coming from, Ray, but somehow a domineering father, any father, doesn't sound so bad to me. I never knew either of my parents. My old man ran from fatherhood as soon as he pulled his pants up, and my poor mother--bless her soul--died in childbirth."

"God, that's tough," admitted Ray in a much more sympathetic tone. "So who raised you?"

"An orphanage in Baltimore," Paco replied. "Then a few private homes, where the foster parents were more interested in the income from Child Services than in nurturing me. I'm not complaining," he added. "I managed to earn my way through Towson State University. Then after a stint in the Army as an MP, I joined the Baltimore police force. The force became my family. But...I'm telling you more than you want to know."

"You were never married before?"

"Yes, but early on, my first wife left me. She decided that being a policeman's wife sucked--the unpredictable hours, my bad moods after bad days."

"You and Molly look happy," Ray said, his voice tinged with envy.

"I never had it so good." Paco checked his watch. "Twenty to eleven. Time to go. Molly will be getting worried."

"Ah, the price for being henpecked." Ray winked at him. "She's worth it."

"Thanks for listening. Keep an eye out for me, will you?"

"Sure, but you have to do your part. Try to keep out of trouble."

They shook hands, and Paco left the bar.

Earlier, upstairs in the Grand Regency, a woman knocked on the door to room 1123. She heard a shuffling inside and then quiet again. She waited a moment before knocking a little louder.

"Who is it?" Loretta called out.

"It's Abby Lebowitz." And then she thought she heard a woman whispering and a man's voice barely mumbling back: "Can't you get rid of her?"

"I'm sorry to disturb you, Loretta," Abby said when the door opened to the end of its chain. "I did want to check in on you--make sure you're okay after Ray's ordeal."

"Abby, you're such a dear, but I've been nursing this terrible headache and I'm trying to sleep it off."

"I understand," said Abby. She walked away, and the room door closed behind her.

Loretta's slender naked form stood motionless until the footsteps receded down the hall. She listened. The elevator doors opened and closed. Silence prevailed. Then she strolled sensually across the carpet and sat down on the edge of the bed. The man reached from behind, gently cupped her bare breasts in his large hands, and pulled her to him.

"Mmm," she said lazily, "that feels good. But shouldn't we be getting dressed? Aren't you worried your wife will be looking for you?"

His fingers teased her nipples. They instantly grew hard. "She's gone shopping," he murmured. "Over at Crossroads mall, buying gifts for our grandsons. She'll be hours, yet." His lips wandered over the nape of her neck, working their way up to one ear, where he gently bit the lobe. "But aren't you worried about Ray walking in on us?"

"He's downstairs wallowing in his own muck. He'll be awhile, yet. If I know Ray, he's just beginning to feel the buzz. It takes a little more than that for him to deal with bedtime and me."

She rolled over to face her lover and kissed him passionately, her tongue seeking his. "Did anyone ever tell you your mustache tickles?"

"No one ever complained about it before."

He pulled her down on top of him, and she stretched out, relishing the feel of his hairy chest against her breasts.

And when their passion had spent itself, they lay back on the rumpled spread. Ready for a nap, his eyelids fluttered shut.

"Aren't you going to try again?" she asked.

His eyelids popped open. "What do you mean?" More than slightly alarmed, he thought she wanted to make love a third time.

"Well, you bungled the first attempt." Her purring voice suddenly took on a sharp edge. "Ray's continuing with the tour."

"Bungled? That's being a skoshe bit unfair, don't you think? I've done exactly what was expected of me--no more, no less."

"What do the others think?" she asked slyly.

"It doesn't matter what the others think. One of them will try again."

"So it is a conspiracy after all!" She bounded off the bed, dragging and wrapping the top sheet around her.

"Hey, lady...Are you implying that you didn't know anything about it?" He swung his feet over the edge of the bed and reached for his briefs.

"Maybe I did," she said. "And maybe I didn't!"

Chapter 17
BRYCE IS NICE , LYIN' IN ZION
Day Nine, Friday, September 18, 1981

"LISTEN UP, FOLKS!" Glenn began. "We're approaching one of the world's most spectacular panoramas." He waited for the cacophony of conversation to subside and those dozing to wake up. The tour had left Salt Lake City five hours ago, and now the bus rumbled through Red Canyon and beyond.

"We're entering the southwestern corner of the state, known as Utah's Dixie. It's called that because the Mormons raised cotton there. And..." Glenn paused. Eager, attentive silence filled the air-conditioned vehicle--except for the persistent buzz of two seventyish widows. Best friends since first grade, they always traveled together, and routinely preferred chatting to listening. Glenn tried again.

"We're about to enter one of the most beautiful national parks you've never heard of: Bryce Canyon. Surprising how few Americans know about it. Oddly enough, it's not a canyon at all. It's the rim of the Paunsaugunt Plateau, magnificently carved by Mother Nature. We'll be disembarking at the Bryce Amphitheater." Seeing a wave of puzzled looks, he added, "It's not an actual theater, folks. It's the section of Bryce that's shaped like one. We'll be here an hour. Don't miss the overlooks. They're all within half a mile walking distance. Oh, yes, I almost forgot. The exotic and precariously perched rock formations you're going to see are called hoodoos. Fifteen million years of erosion by wind, snow, ice, and rain have carved them into shapes that almost come alive before your very eyes. In fact, the Paiute Indians thought they were inhabited by evil spirits. They fled the area in fear. Oh, one more thing, folks.

Take it easy. We're at an altitude of 9,000 feet. Drink lots of water. Okay, everyone, door side first."

"Excuse me, Glenn," one of the widows called out. "What did you say? Where are we?" Everyone laughed. Glenn merely sighed.

Paco glanced at Ray and noted that, uncharacteristically, he didn't rush for the door ahead of everyone else.

The inspector took Molly's hand as they approached the wall. In awe they stared down into Bryce Canyon, a massive open-air temple of dazzling colored rock stretching 200 miles. They saw monolithic formations of spires, buttes, pinnacles, sails, cathedrals, and shapes never found elsewhere. Many had names like Thor's Hammer, Grand Staircase, the Queen's Garden, the Hunter, and Peekaboo Loop. Concrete walking paths zigged and zagged down among the red, electric pink, white, and yellow mineral formations. Far below, a small pine tree grew miraculously out of the ancient rock. Its healthy green needles contrasted bravely against the bleached limestone and red iron oxide.

The group fanned out to the astonishing overlooks at Sunrise, Sunset, and Inspiration Points. Loretta joined Thom and Theo.

"Coming, Ray?" she asked.

"You go on ahead. I'll catch up," he mumbled. Ray felt torn--torn by curiosity to see the seductive scenery and suspicion that another so-called accident awaited him. Suddenly, footsteps materialized behind him.

"How's it going, Ray?" He whirled about.

Gordon Whitman smiled broadly. "Joanne and I, we're taking a little hike down this path. Not far. Just enough to get a taste of this place. Join us?" They began heading for a walkway beside the wall.

"No! Uh, no thanks. I'll just enjoy the view from here."

The Whitmans disappeared, and Ray inhaled to catch his breath, but somehow his lungs seemed to be closing up. He desperately wanted to go to the canyon's rim and edged closer to the wall, determined to put up a good front. It just wouldn't do to have his sales force see him acting like a scared kid. As he edged closer, he began to shake and perspire. The armpits of his Izod polo shirt turned clammy. A tremor of nerves suddenly exploded through the length and breadth of him, and he sought the nearest park bench to recover. He needed water, but had left his bottle on the bus. His breathing felt labored, another tremor followed. More perspiration--cold chills on his brow, his upper lip, the back of his neck. He had the feeling someone was watching him, but who? From where? Then he blacked out.

He awoke to find Jake Lebowitz standing over his prone body on the bench. Jake's stethoscope hung from his neck and he waved an ammonium carbonate capsule under Ray's nose. Ray's head jerked away in reaction to the reviving fumes.

"Jake? What the hell happened?"

"You passed out. You were hyperventilating."

"What's wrong with me?" Ray pleaded, pulling himself to a sitting position.

"I suppose you had an anxiety attack. Not surprising after all you've been through. I was just getting off the bus when I saw you. I went back in and got my bag. I could give you a tranquilizer for now, but you've got to promise me you'll get a full checkup when you get home. Promise?"

"Yeah, sure, Doc," he said. "Just gimme the pills. And thanks. Again." He smiled grimly.

As Jake fished about in his little black bag for the medication, Loretta was strolling back from Inspiration Point with the Moyers. As she drew closer to the bench, she broke into a trot.

"My God, what's happened now, Doctor?"

"He's had an anxiety episode," answered Jake. "Have him take two of these with water and make sure he sees his own physician when he gets home." He handed the pills to Loretta, who nodded and tucked them into her pocket. She glanced furtively about to see who among the group had witnessed the latest near-calamity. Apparently no one had. She and Ray returned to the bus. The one-hour stop was up.

Lew drove the final eighty miles to Zion National Park over Routes 89 and 9. They entered the park through a long man-made tunnel broken only by periodic cavernous breaches that afforded a view of the central canyon. As they emerged on a winding road, a hush settled over the travelers. At Bryce, they had looked down into the amphitheater. And at Bryce the omniscient viewer felt exhilaration witnessing infinite landscapes from above. But at this moment, an unpredicted emotion took over. Here at Zion, the vast labyrinth of canyons rose up around them, instilling a feeling of insignificance--even claustrophobia, for they were surrounded and engulfed by 4,000-foot walls of sheer stone. The grandeur of Zion humbled them, this place meaning "heaven" or "utopia."

With only long dark shadows of daylight remaining, a solitary red cloud hung overhead as the harbinger of the last rays of sunshine. The bus rode a few miles farther before turning into a large motel called Canyon Lodge.

"Oh, no," Lew grumbled to Glenn, when he saw three other monster buses lined up along the side of the main building.

Glenn nodded and turned to the group. "Sorry, folks, we're the last tour to arrive tonight, so things are going to be mighty slow for us. I suggest you all go over to the restaurant and get supper while I get your room keys and the luggage sorted out. Just show the waiter your chits and you'll be served."

An apologetic maitre d' greeted them. "It will be at least an hour's wait. But we have pleasant seating on the patio outside. The first round of drinks and your desserts are on the house. Compliments of our manager."

The Miltons, Davies, and LeSotos gathered their chairs around a circular wood picnic table suitably punctured by the pole of a huge umbrella bearing the Cinzano name. Others filled up a dozen or more tables on the patio. A harried waitress took their drink orders. The Symingtons chose to sit alone, with Loretta apparently launching into a lecture and Ray scowling back.

"The Symingtons seem to be going at it hot and heavy

again," observed Paco.

"Yeah, they're always at each other's goats," said Molly. "I guess that's why they call it the marital arts."

"Molly," said Michelle, "I just love the way you capture the essence of things."

Molly giggled, "Thank you."

After five minutes, Ruth broke into the conversation. "Well, I'll be damned! Did you see that?"

"See what?" LeRoy questioned.

"The Symingtons. A waiter just took them in to be seated," she said. "I wonder how they pulled that one off?"

"My guess is he slipped the maitre d' something between a twenty and a fifty," said Monte. "I saw the transfer of some folding green a few minutes ago."

"There ought to be a law against doin' that," said Molly "It's upright inconsiderate."

Paco snickered. "It's a common practice, sweetie. I've even done it myself once or twice."

They were the last to receive their drinks and the last to be seated inside the restaurant. By then, the menu had been seriously depleted. They were all so hungry, they cheerfully gobbled up the canned chicken noodle soup, grilled cheese sandwiches, and macaroni salad.

But Ruth, usually so talkative, ate in sullen silence. LeRoy watched as she put her fork down several times to rub her left shoulder.

"What's wrong, dear?" he asked.

"Oh, nothing, really," she murmured, embarrassed that he'd noticed. "It's just aching a little. Remember when I picked up that heavy suitcase the first day? I should've waited for you."

Like an alert puppy, Molly's ears almost visibly perked up. "I've got some BenGray. Works great. Stinks to high heaven, though."

"Thanks, Molly," Ruth said, "maybe I'll take you up on it."

When a tray of desserts passed close to them, Molly declared, "I'm going to have one of those pieces of chocolate cheese-cake for my free dessert."

A round of "Me too's" followed. After removing their empty plates, the college-age waiter returned with an announcement. "I have good news and bad news about dessert. Which do you want first?"

"Only good news," said Paco. "We've had enough of the other kind."

"Well," said the waiter, "the good news is we have chocolate cheesecake for dessert, but there's only one piece left."

"What's the bad news, then?" asked Michelle.

"It's the only dessert left," he answered. "Who will be the lucky diner?"

"We'll share it," said Monte.

"I'd be happy to divide it in two for you," the waiter offered.

"Not two," said Monte. "Six!"

The waiter frowned. "That's not possible."

"Well, young man," Michelle challenged, "your manager told us if we waited patiently for dinner, we could each have a free dessert. We've kept our part of the bargain. Now you keep yours."

A helpless expression crept over his face. He knew his tip was at stake.

Molly grinned, then came to his rescue. "You bring us the cheesecake and six plates and a sharp knife, too. Heat the knife over a flame first, so it won't stick."

"Maybe," said Michelle, "we should let Dr. Jake do this surgery."

"I'll trust Molly," declared her husband. "Besides, Jake can't do it. His malpractice insurance won't let him get involved."

When the cheesecake and Molly's operating instrument arrived, a hush fell over the table as she cut six perfect slices, each one about an inch long, and laid them neatly on the plates without the loss of a crumb. The group applauded loudly. The waiter grinned with relief.

Hot Grudge Sunday

In their Canyon Lodge room, the Symingtons prepared for bed. As usual, Loretta monopolized the bathroom. Ray removed his khaki Dockers and laid them carefully across the back of the room's only upholstered chair. He brushed away the day's lint and loose dirt and sharpened the long creases between his fingers. With practiced ritual, he unzipped his tote bag and took out fresh underwear, socks, and a tan Ralph Lauren golf shirt, laying everything on the seat of the same chair. He pulled off his sweat-dried polo shirt and socks and shot a glance at the bathroom door. Deciding that Loretta would be awhile, he exchanged the ceiling light for his nightstand light and sat down on one queen-size bed to read his Ken Follett novel, Eye of the Needle.

Halfway across the room, silent movement began inside Ray's Vermilion Tours tote--movement so slight as to go undetected. It continued for some time, ceasing only when the bathroom door opened and reflooded the room in bright light.

Loretta sauntered across the carpet in a sheer black nightgown, stealing a glance at her husband to see if he was watching. Above his book, his smoke-gray eyes followed her lithe body with its pert breasts. But he didn't let on. Disappointed, she slid into her own queen bed and began leafing through The New Yorker.

Ray took his turn in the bathroom and came out wearing only his colorful boxer sleeping shorts. Still uncomfortably warm, he climbed into his bed and flipped the bedcovers to one side. He lay there in silence, depressed. The experience at Bryce Canyon had left him enervated. He had a feeling that his wife wanted to talk, and he waited, curious, until finally, she said, "Ray?"

"Yeah!"

"They are out to get you to quit or be fired."

"Who?"

"I'm not sure. Your sales force, maybe others, too."

"So what else is new? I've never been the most popular guy on the block."

"Well, what are you going to do about it?"

"Do? I'm going to sleep. That's what I'm going to do."

His light went out and hers followed suit.

In the darkness, a creature began maneuvering once more inside Ray's tote. It eased itself out, then crawled over the outer canvas, and dropped several feet to the floor. It made no sound when it landed.

"Ray?" Loretta asked softly. "You still awake?"

"Yeah," he answered with the fingers of both hands entwined behind his head.

"Ray," she asked, "do you have any interest in saving our marriage?"

"Why? Does it need rescuing?"

"Well, it certainly could use a little first-aid. In fact, CPR would be more like it."

"I'm not complaining," he declared. "I kind of like things the way they are."

"Do you love me--really love me?" she asked.

"What kind of question is that?"

"Because you never tell me you do. And we're always fighting. We never have conversations any more."

"Sure I love you. But I enjoy the scrapping," he admitted. "You're the only one who ever stands up to me. Those wimps from the office never do. They hate my guts, but only behind my back. They're all sweetness to my face. It's disgusting."

"I'm talking about us. Do you want a divorce?" she asked suddenly.

"Of course not," he responded. "Why would you ask me that? I like things this way. We've got a real marriage with real character."

"You call fighting all the time a real marriage? What about the other women?"

"What other women?" He hesitated. "So I slip once in a while. It's a game to me, doesn't mean a thing. I always come back home, don't I?"

"How do you think that makes me feel?" she asked, her voice bitter.

"How the hell should I know?" he answered. "You probably feel like going shopping to get even. At least, that's what you always wind up doing."

"Shopping is not the sum of who I am, Ray. Sometimes I do it just to get away from the war zone. Is it your job? Is that what makes you so combative?" She consciously suppressed the rest of her laundry list of what he'd become at IMTC: mean, vindictive, sour, humorless.

"Yeah, it probably is the job. When I retire, maybe I'll mellow out."

"Now there's a refreshing and pleasant thought."

"Don't count on it," he growled. "The way you spend I'll never be able to retire."

"Blaming me, as usual. Damn it, Ray, you're impossible."

He heard her pull up her covers as she turned away from him, and he started to smile. Another round won. But in the thick, unpleasant darkness, he felt another sensation--a creeping, sometimes halting and touching--along his right calf. Moving faster now across his knee, the creature felt larger, more ominous now, so he lay still, almost paralyzed, calling on his vocal chords to fight through a throat constricted from fear. "Lorr...Lorrrretta! Help! Something's on me! Get it off! Quick!!"

Loretta flipped on her light and stared in horror at the ghastly creature that resembled a pale yellow miniature lobster with a crablike set of curved pincers. A small arachnid--a scorpion--crouched on Ray's right thigh. Springing from the bed, Loretta grabbed The New Yorker and rolled it up.

"Oh, God!" he cried, his body rigid. He shut his eyes tight.

With two hands gripped around the magazine, Loretta followed through with her finest golf swing, driving the stunned creature clear across the room to land in front of the open bathroom door.

Ray gasped with a desperate inrush of air, conflicting with an equally desperate outrush of pain. Her magnificent arc had left the equivalent of a divot in his private parts.

She grabbed his shoe next to the bed, charged after the scorpion, and pounded it to a pulpy mass. Then, pulling an enormous clump of tissues, one by one, out of the box set into the front of the sink, she transported the remains to the toilet and flushed them down.

When she returned, Ray had finally found his voice. "That hurt like hell. You didn't have to hit me so hard, Loretta. You enjoyed it, didn't you?"

"Would you rather I had let the scorpion bite you?"

"A scorpion?" he gasped. "Do you think he actually bit me?" Not waiting for her answer, he slid his shorts off and carefully examined the family jewels.

"Nope!" she said calmly. "I swung a wee bit too soon for that. I'm afraid it was another one of my terrible hook shots. Oh, well," she chuckled. But her effort to make light of the incident came out forced.

She knew she'd delivered a helluva whack with the magazine, probably hitting the scorpion harder than necessary. Oh, she had no doubt Ray deserved it; his unrepentant attitude toward his womanizing had triggered her anger. But aside from that festering boil in their relationship, a new sense of dread crept over her. In truth, the scorpion had terrified her. Where had it come from? Had someone deliberately placed it in their room? And what if it was meant for her? She suddenly felt a need for the reassuring physical closeness of her husband, for the protection of his large body, no matter how neurotically he behaved.

She climbed into bed beside him, wrapped her right arm around his chest, and fitted her knees behind his, spoon fashion. Ray squeezed her hand, then immediately dropped off to sleep.

But Loretta's body lay tense, her mind restless and brooding, unable to draw a curtain on the day's events. Yesterday's experimental sexual encounter hadn't given her the emotional satisfaction she'd expected. Quite the opposite. For the first time in their marriage she'd taken outright revenge on Ray with another man. And now she felt a pang of remorse. She really didn't want affairs. She actually craved a conventional marriage filled with tenderness and laughter and hand-holding. Like Paco and Molly's. Yes, they were honeymooning, but still Loretta envied them. An hour elapsed before she fell into an uneasy sleep.

Chapter 18

A FLY ON THE WALL, ANOTHER IN THE SOUP

Day Ten, Saturday, September 19, 1981

THE BITE OF FORTY-DEGREE MORNING AIR set Paco's blood coursing through his veins. As the group boarded the mini-tram for a tour of Zion National Park, Molly cuddled close to him. Shoving her chubby fists into the pockets of her voluminous jacket, she wished she'd brought gloves like some of the other women. The tram crept along a winding path.

Theo let out a squeal. "Look, a deer!"

"A whole family," Reba cried. "But they're so little."

"Mule deer," the ranger/driver announced into his microphone.

"Maybe they'd like my blueberry muffin from breakfast. I've got it in my purse," Reba said.

The ranger's hair-trigger response startled everyone. "Friends, please don't feed the animals--ever! They get so used to it they can't forage on their own. A fed deer is a dead deer."

"Oops! Just kidding, sir," a contrite Reba replied.

As the tram wove through sagebrush and juniper, the ranger showed them all the massive stone formations that could be seen from the navigable portions of Zion. Early settlers had named many with a biblical reverence: Altar of Sacrifice, Angels Landing, and Three Patriarchs: Abraham, Isaac, and Jacob. Paco paid keen attention to the ranger's impressive knowledge and eloquent descriptions, as if the man were displaying his own personal, private treasures. The group disembarked to amble about and photograph exquisite wildflowers: golden columbine, larkspur, and the spiky red Indian paintbrush.

156

"Notice the Sego lily?" the ranger called out. "Its bulbs were a delicacy to the Indians. And here's something you won't see every day," he said, stooping to show them a plant with white funnel-shaped flowers. "It's the sacred datura--also known as jimsonweed, Devil's trumpet, or stinkweed. Those prickly fruits contain black seeds that some people have used for medicinal purposes."

"To cure what?" Joanne wanted to know.

"Oh, asthma, stomach ailments, hay fever. But the seeds contain atropine. Dangerous stuff, if it's misused. It's caused a lot of accidental poisonings. Actually, the whole plant is highly toxic." His little lecture incited a spurt of curiosity in at least one member of the tour. A gloved hand reached down to touch the plant.

Slowly, they all drifted back to the tram. As it entered a horseshoe curve, the ranger braked, gazed up, and pointed to the face of a sheer 3,000-foot cliff.

"See those two tiny dark spots about halfway up?" Everyone looked, squinting in the sunlight, but saw nothing in particular.

"That's a pair of skilled climbers, ladies and gentlemen. They started yesterday afternoon. Darkness overtook them, so they dug in for the night."

"But it's absolutely vertical," Bess chirped in her tremulous, birdlike voice. "How could anyone..."

"That can't be people up there. It's impossible," Michelle interrupted gruffly.

"Oh, it's hazardous all right," said the ranger, "but not impossible, my friends. I'll grant you there are almost no discernible crevices or ledges. What they did was, they cleated and harnessed themselves to the face of the cliff. Then they covered themselves with large blankets for warmth and protection against the elements."

"How can you tell all that from those two fly specks on the mountain?" asked Gordon.

"Don't blame you for being skeptical, sir. The serious climbers file an itinerary of sorts with us at the Ranger Station. And we keep an eye on them with our binocs. Just in case something goes wrong."

"Theo, do you remember the 'If I could be a fly-on-the-wall' expression?" asked Reba.

"Of course," Theo replied. "It's when you want to find out someone else's personal business, but the door's closed."

"I wonder who they're listening to up there," said Cookie, her arm protectively linked in Bess's.

Hilda Vickers said, "I think they must be at heaven's door--only inches from either life or death."

Ray shifted in his seat and grumbled, "I'm getting a stiff neck from all this looking up."

Loretta glared at him. "You're wrong. You don't get a stiff neck from looking up. You get it from being stubborn."

Ray pretended not to hear her.

The group fell silent, contemplating the human flies clinging to the monolithic cliff. "I can't figure out, for the life of me, why anybody would do anything so stupidious." Molly's voice rang out high-pitched and holier-than-thou.

"Some people actually believe you have to face and cheat death to fully appreciate life," Paco said. "They get a high from living on the edge. Skydivers, Mount Everest climbers."

"Life isn't always peachy pie," Molly expounded, "but I never had to climb a percypiece to get high on nature. I got me a perfect husband and a fun life now." She gave her husband a quick kiss on his bony cheek.

"Molly, not everybody is content to witness life sitting in this tram car and letting other people take all the risks," Ruth Milton challenged. "A little courage goes a long way."

LeRoy stole a sideways glance at her and scowled.

Molly cocked her head. "Like fer instance what?"

"Well, let's see..." Ruth knew she'd backed herself into a corner. People were looking at her curiously. "LeRoy and I went hang-gliding once, on the Outer Banks of North Carolina. Soaring on the updrafts...it was fabulous."

But she needn't have bothered to explain. Everyone's ears were tuned to the ranger explaining that dinosaurs had once roamed the region when the climate was much warmer and wetter, long before these canyons were formed. Now cougars prowled at night in search of mule deer for their dinner.

As the tram ended its run and deposited them at the visitors' center, a chorus of protests rippled through the group. There was so much more to see in this hypnotizing landscape.

"Consolation prize, folks," Glenn called from the last car. "You get thirty minutes in the gift shop." The magic words. Forty-seven bodies stampeded inside.

With regret, they said goodbye to the park, watching the canyons grow smaller and smaller as Lew guided the bus east toward Mount Carmel Junction and Highway 89. Soon it paralleled the Vermilion Cliffs--huge, reddish, and eerily symmetrical.

"They look like Egyptian temples," exclaimed Theo, "as if they've been carved by human hands into columns guarding the pharaohs' tombs.

Moving south now, entering Arizona on their way to Lake Powell, they stopped for lunch at a spacious roadside restaurant. "Fabulous corn chowder," Glenn recommended. The Added Ingredient sat on a barren quarter-acre of sagebrush. A chalkboard on the front porch announced: "Soups of the day: corn chowder and minestrone. Plus all-you-can eat salad and home-baked pies."

As they crowded inside, the manager met them in the foyer. "Welcome to our buffet lunch, ladies and gentlemen. If you'd be so kind as to wait right here, we'll be open in exactly ten minutes. And restrooms are off to the left."

"Oh, sir?" Loretta asked. "Do you happen to have a public phone?"

"Behind the dining room, ma'am, if you'll follow me." On his way back into the kitchen, he pointed out a phone booth. Loretta ducked in, then slowly tilted her head just enough to observe two waitresses emerging from the kitchen. Each one carried a cast iron kettle of soup, which she set at the beginning of the long buffet table. Next to the caldrons sat several enormous metal bowls of salad, with crocks of dressings set out next to them, and finally, half a dozen sumptuous pies. Then the waitresses rushed back into the kitchen. The dining room--fresh and inviting, with sparkling glassware and the aroma of hot soups--was momentarily empty.

Loretta slipped out of the phone booth, opened her purse, and pulled out a blue plastic bottle. Twisting off the cap, she padded over to the corn chowder kettle, raised the lid, and poured the liquid from her bottle into the soup. With the long-handled ladle that rested in the kettle, she swirled once, then replaced the cover. Hastily screwing the cap back on the bottle, she returned it to her purse and joined the group in the foyer.

Ray met her with a puzzled look. "So who were you calling?"

"Oh, I just wanted to check on my parents. You know how I worry about them."

The manager appeared with a big smile and waved them into the dining room. "Thank you for your patience, ladies and gentlemen."

After taking a tray, Molly dipped a ladle into the first pot and scooped up a serving to examine the contents. "This looks like a great corny chowder," she said, helping herself to a full bowl.

Retrieving the ladle from her, Paco served himself the chowder, salad, and thick slices of warm bread, and drifted off to find a table. Loretta grabbed the tongs and served herself salad. She took her time fishing out only what she liked.

"Could we step it up a little, please, we only have an hour," a sarcastic voice piped up.

"Yeah, Loretta," Ray sneered. "You're not choosing an Dior suit." She finally handed him the salad tongs and floated off for a slice of pie.

As Paco and Molly settled into a corner table, they found the Symingtons hovering over them.

"Okay if we join you?" Ray asked.

"Of course," said Molly, pushing dishes and glasses closer

together.

"Our pleasure," said Paco.

They ate in silence for a few minutes. Ray chomped away on his corned beef hero, then took up his soup spoon, not eating, just spinning the corn kernels over and over in the thick chowder.

"You're actually going to have soup after eating that humongous sandwich?" teased Loretta. She had thought to egg him on with a little negative prompting.

Ray frowned. "Lay off me, will you?" He was trying to think of a way to break the ice with Paco. "Inspector, I, uh..."

"It's Paco, Ray. Do I detect a 911 call coming in?"

"I understand, Paco," said Ray apologetically. "But I don't know where else to turn. I really don't know if I can trust anyone but you."

Paco shook his head. "Look. I know you've experienced more than your share of hard luck on this trip, but it's hardly any cause for complete paranoia."

"That's just it," said Ray. "If I were truly a gambling man, I'd have to bet against my own survival. Someone is trying to kill me. I've already told you that. I've had what appears to be an unexplained accident at least once each day since we started this trip."

"Not yesterday," Paco observed.

"No? Well, let me set you straight. Last night in our room, when we turned out the lights, something started crawling up my leg. You're not going to believe this. It was a scorpion."

Paco's right eyebrow shot up, but his voice didn't betray his concern. "We're in the desert, Ray. Things happen."

Molly's watery blue eyes grew rounder and rounder. "What did you do, Mr. Ray?"

"Loretta, thank God, clobbered the damn thing with a magazine. In the nick of time, too. I'm sure somebody planted it in our room."

"What makes you think so?" Paco asked.

"This morning I found a slit in my Vermilion tote bag. The cut in the canvas was clean and about six inches long--not torn.

Like it had been done deliberately with a sharp blade."

"Scorpion bites are rarely fatal," said Paco. "Someone could have been playing a practical joke on you--a vicious one, I'll grant you. I can also see why you're upset over the number of so-called accidents."

"But what if somebody really is trying to kill me?"

Paco thought for a while, finishing his soup before answering. "Assuming that someone did want to take your life, can you think of who and for what reason?"

Ray swirled his spoon in his soup bowl one last time and pushed it away. "Anybody want this?" he asked. "The sandwich filled me up."

"I'd love it!" Molly beamed. "Thanks!" As she drew the bowl to her and dug in, Paco caught a fleeting expression on Loretta's face. Panic? Confusion? Maybe neither. He dismissed it from his mind.

Ray began thinking aloud. "Any guy in my position has to step on a lot of people on the way up," he said bluntly. "But a little healthy competition on the corporate ladder is hardly a reason to kill a man."

"I agree," said Paco. "But if you suspect one of your colleagues at Indent Machine Tool Company, you must also suspect a motive for it."

"I do," he answered. "But I don't think I can talk about it yet. I don't have any proof."

"You might not want to wait for the proof, Mr. Ray," said Molly. "Doctor Avi, my employer, always says the proof is in the undoing. You could get killed waiting."

"You're right Molly, but it's such a terrible accusation to make," said Ray.

"You don't appear to be a screamish man to me." She finished her last spoonful of chowder and speared an artichoke heart.

"I'm not squeamish, But I do have to be careful. And I know when I need help."

"Mmm! These prickled artichuckles sure are delicious," said

Molly, changing the subject. She wished Ray would leave her Paco alone.

"You're not what you appear to be, Molly," said Ray, his troubled gaze softening. "In fact, you're quite clever. However, I desperately need your husband's help."

"It's mighty tasty of you to say so," she responded. "But we are on our honeymoon."

Paco asked, "If in some weak and crazy moment I did consent, what would you expect me to do without any concrete evidence?"

"Well, for one thing, you could watch my back," he said. "I could pay well, you know."

"We've had this conversation before, Ray. I have no jurisdiction here." Paco's piercing eyes burned with anger. "Let's get this straight. I'm not for hire, especially not as your bodyguard. My interest in your welfare is limited to that of an ordinary bystander who doesn't want to see any harm come to a fellow traveler." He pushed his plate toward the center of the table and got to his feet. "However, you may take some comfort in knowing my police instincts remain involuntarily alert."

Molly speared one last bite of strawberry pie, then set the fork back on her plate. She suddenly didn't feel so well.

Half an hour later, the designated departure time came. And went. Lew and Glenn stood outside the bus door with concerned looks on their faces. Eight members of the group were missing: the LeSotos, the Moyers, Judge and Caroline Sessions, Cookie, and Bess. Not one of the eight had ever kept the bus waiting before. Surprisingly enough, the Symingtons--even Ray--had already boarded.

Forty minutes later, a pale, sallow-looking Paco came out, walking--or, rather, shuffling--like a man ten years beyond his age. He whispered at length to Glenn, then returned to the restroom. The guide, always so steady and calm, looked shocked, then mounted the bus steps and announced:

"Folks, make yourselves comfortable. Some of our people

aren't feeling well. We'll be a few more minutes."

One by one, the eight emerged, sluggish and almost staggering. Paco helped Molly on board and the bus rumbled off at last. A buzz of anxiety flitted through the air, crackling with questions. "What's wrong? Diarrhea? A stomach bug? Are we going to get it?"

They hadn't ridden more than half a mile when Molly lurched to her feet and closeted herself in the mobile lavatory, a miserably tight fit for her rotund body. Five miles later, she still hadn't come out. Outside the door, a line formed as Paco, Caroline, Harry, Cookie, Bess, Thom, and Theo shifted from foot to foot and groaned. Lew Getz made a hasty unscheduled stop at a roadside diner.

As if roped together for a mountain descent, the eight anguished travelers ran for the bathroom. But they lined up in vain. The modest diner had only single stalls for boys and girls. Suddenly, the line broke, and the desperate and stricken headed for whatever cover they could find: a tree, a bush, even a shed behind the building itself. The owner of the Desert Delight Diner burst from the front door, bellowing four-letter words at anyone near enough to listen.

Glenn made the 911 call, and, twenty-five minutes later, an ambulance screeched to a halt before them. In the succeeding half-hour another emergency medical unit showed up; it had come from another direction, another distance.

Diarrhea, the runs, Montezuma's revenge had taken its eight victims captive. The paramedics dispensed the likes of Imodium AD. One dose, two at the most, rescued seven of the victims to a tolerable state. All except Molly. Paco knelt beside her and draped his jacket over her shoulders as she shook with chills. She had become so dehydrated that she was close to passing out. The two paramedics, with Paco's help, lifted her inside the ambulance and hooked up an IV to rapidly rehydrate her. Next they administered activated charcoal and waited for her to vomit. Now perspiring profusely, weak and pale, she soon responded.

Paco flipped open his credentials and asked one of the

paramedics, "Do you routinely sample stomach contents to find the cause of these emergencies?"

"You bet, Inspector," he replied. "We even called the Added Ingredient and told them to shut down the lunch buffet until we've had a chance to analyze everything on it. Our lab unit at the hospital is small, but it's a good one. If it's common food poisoning, we should hear some time tomorrow. With so many victims, it's not likely to be criminally induced." In a sensitive tone that suggested rather than ordered, he told the victims what they could safely eat and drink over the next twenty-four hours to prevent a recurrence.

"I'm afraid we're required to transport you to the hospital, ma'am."

"Now, don't you throw me for a loophole, young man. I'm on my honeymoon, and I don't want to miss a lick of it."

"If you insist. But we'll have to ask you to sign a waiver, an agreement to end treatment against medical advice."

"Gimme that paper." She looked over at a fretting Paco and gave him a reassuring wink.

The fire department's toxic disposal unit sprayed oceans of water and chemicals from a tanker truck all over the area, to the further consternation of the diner's owner. He proved quite adept at linking one dazzling string of expletives to another.

Nearly three hours later, the afflicted eight seemed fit enough to reboard the bus. A much weakened Molly grasped her tummy tightly as Paco assisted her to their eighth row, door-side seat. Only the apprehensive voices of Glenn and Lew broke the silence in the last miles to Lake Powell.

They arrived far too late for the supper cruise on the lake, so Glenn arranged for a Sunday morning breakfast cruise instead. For most, eating was the last thing on their minds. Only twenty-two of the forty-seven made it to the restaurant at all that night. Glenn and Lew spent most of the night with a cleaning crew from the hotel freshening up the bus.

Chapter 19
LEFT OUT IN THE COLD
Day Eleven, Sunday, September 20, 1981

LAKE POWELL STRETCHED HER LANGUID LIMBS across watery sheets, vibrating with blues and golds in the early yawning sun. Along the banks, clusters of sandstone tors were heaped like quilts tossed aside. The lake awoke with a flurry of boating activity and the promise of a three-hour cruise.

Paco and Molly encountered George and Reba on the hotel patio, sitting on lawn furniture.

"We're early," said Reba. "Wanna sit for a minute?"

"Sure," Molly agreed. "It's very pleasant out here."

"After yesterday, a little fresh air goes a long way," George remarked as he used his tiny Crescent wrench to open a bottle of ginger ale from the vending machine opposite them. He passed the bottle to Reba and opened a second one for himself.

"Clever little gadget you have there," said Paco. "May I?" He reached out for the wrench. George handed it to him.

Reba offered her bottle to Molly. "A little something to settle the stomach?"

"Oh, no, honey. I got my own anecdote right in here." She clutched her purse with affection.

"You folks feeling any better this morning?" George asked.

"Much," said Paco. "Still a little queasy and a little light-headed, but at least that's tolerable." He finished toying with George's wrench and set it on the table. George hastily stuffed it back in his pocket.

"How about you, Molly?" asked Reba.

"I never got the upchuckies at all last night. But I'm sure

glad you guys didn't get sick, too."

Paco thought for a moment. "Odd, isn't it? Only eight of us got sick. I keep wondering if it was something only we ate yesterday noon. Anything in particular on the buffet that you two avoided?"

George and Reba shook their heads slowly.

"I had to get my kishkas pumped," Molly reminded them.

Paco nodded. "Yes. She was the only one whose stomach needed pumping."

George jumped up and grabbed his ginger ale. "Hey, guys, if you don't mind, we'll go over to the boat now," he said. "I'm starved. No offense, but this isn't the best conversation to start off breakfast."

Molly shrugged. "You go on ahead. We'll follow."

Paco and Molly unsteadily descended the sloping lawn to the Wahweap dock and the waiting replica of a nineteenth century riverboat. The smartly painted vessel, white with a red sternwheel, displayed flags of a dozen countries. The LeSotos were the last of the tour to board. Soon afterward, the sternwheeler churned into action, and the craft paddled gently out onto the lake.

The Vermilion group gathered in the glass-enclosed lower deck for a continental breakfast. Molly toyed with a small dry muffin and juice. The sugared aroma of doughnuts and fruit-filled Danish actually turned her off. Paco half-heartedly nibbled a slice of toast and sipped weak tea. Then in wordless agreement, they mounted the stairs to the open upper deck and settled on a cushioned corner bench amid the fresher air. Molly dug into her purse, pulled out a small cardboard box of pills, and popped two into her bow-shaped mouth. She held out two more to her husband. "Pepto Dismal?" she offered. He accepted, and they chewed the gritty pink tablets in silence.

But Paco fretted. The recently skewed events not only puzzled, but alarmed him. What had caused eight members of the tour to suffer such violent attacks of diarrhea? Had someone doctored the food at the Added Ingredient? The irony of the restaurant's name was not lost on him. But why only eight of the group? Had they been targeted for some kind of punishment? That seemed illogical. He could think of no discernible connection--either professional or social--that bound all eight of them together. Was the poisoning a random act? A practical joke? Or a malicious design to force a few travelers to abort their tour? One significant fact kept rising to the surface: each of the victims had eaten the corn chowder. Paco knew that for sure; he'd spoken to each of them.

Paco's mind sifted through the details of that lunch. Loretta and Ray both ate salad. Ray also took the chowder. In the end, Ray chose not to eat it and gave it to Molly. Loretta didn't take soup at all. Only Molly ate two helpings, and she had gotten the sickest. Paco sighed. If only she didn't love to eat quite so much and with quite so much ardor.

A new foreboding seized him. Were he and Molly victims of a reverse conspiracy, with the other six just hapless bystanders? Had Ray and Loretta staged this event together? Paco thought back to the Powder Horn Pub, to Ray's gesture of friendship and his candor about his childhood. Could these ploys have been calculated to throw Paco off the scent of some vicious retaliation of his and Loretta's? Was he, Paco, being set up? Had the two of them conjured up the chowder plot merely to twist his arm? Surely, Ray didn't need his protection that badly.

The Pepto pills began working their magic. Paco decided that, as soon as they reached Grand Canyon Lodge, he would call the hospital pathology lab analyzing Molly's stomach contents. Maybe they'd have some answers. For now, he'd put the ugly business out of his head and enjoy the extraordinary sights of Lake Powell.

Under a cloudless sky bleached white by the blasting sun, isles with craggy peaks and sheer faces rose from the cobalt blue waters. As the sternwheeler cruised along, Glenn told them the history of the region: how Lake Powell represented one of man's best attempts at controlling and modifying nature. Construction of Glen Canyon Dam throttled back the flow of the Colorado River, bringing hydroelectric power to more than a million residents and a lake 186 miles long for recreation. The vast labyrinth of Glen Canyon took seventeen years to completely fill.

"Look to your right, folks," Glenn said. "Ten years before Lake Powell was formed, Cecil B. DeMille used that rugged peak as Mount Sinai in his production of The Ten Commandments."

"Wow!" Reba gushed. "It's hard to believe the water wasn't always here." Heads bobbed in agreement.

As the sternwheeler returned to the Wahweap dock, they all felt a bit deflated. Three hours hadn't begun to satiate their hunger for Lake Powell's seductive scenery. The cruise had taken them on an ethereal voyage through a pastel world.

Glenn coaxed them onto their bus once more for the journey south. The Symingtons had already taken their places when the LeSotos boarded.

"Well, Mr. Ray, this is a surprise," Molly observed. "You being on the bus early and all."

Ray zipped up his windbreaker, folded his arms across his chest, and grinned in self-satisfaction. "Know what, Molly? One of these days people are going to figure out that I'm not such a bad guy."

As his bass voice resonated several rows back, Michelle and Joanne traded sidelong smirks.

"Nobody said you were, Mr. Ray." Molly studied him as she buttoned up her purple cable-knit sweater.

Loretta looked up from her Ellery Queen magazine. "Molly! Paco! That was a terrible thing you all went through. How are you feeling?"

"We'll be up to stuff soon," Molly answered.

Loretta flashed them a bright, sympathetic smile. "Glad to hear it."

Lew guided the bus over a bridge on Route 89, crossing the Colorado River from Utah into Arizona just outside Page, where they stopped to visit the Glen Canyon Dam itself. An elevator lowered them into the bowels of the dam to view the astonishing construction of a wall over 600 feet high, containing 10 million tons of concrete mix.

Molly, Cookie, and Bess chose instead to acquaint themselves with a reddish slab of rock at the entrance. The sign above it said "Dinosaur Tracks."

"Look like tinysaur tracks to me," Molly said.

Bess leaned closer and lowered her glasses down her nose for a better look. "Well, they did have rather small feet compared to the rest of their bodies, didn't they?"

Cookie laughed. "If I saw those lumps in my backyard, I'd throw extra grass seed on them."

"Time's up, folks, back to the bus!" Glenn called. He stretched out his arms in a broad gesture, a border collie collecting and nudging his flock of sheep.

They crossed the Colorado River once more at Marble Canyon via the Navajo Bridge. Alternate 89 led them westward. At Jacob Lake they began the journey south through the Kaibab Plateau, surrounded by a forest of white fir, quaking aspen, and ponderosa pine. Their destination: the North Rim of the Grand Canyon.

The bus rumbled to a stop deep in the woods, where a series of single-story rustic log cabins awaited them for their one-night stay. Dry brown pine needles blanketed the ground. A crisscrossing network of paved walkways connected the log cabin village to Grand Canyon Lodge. This National Landmark, an imposing green-roofed stone and wood structure, sat nestled in a rock crevice of the high canyon wall.

No one lingered in the cabins to socialize, primp, or unpack. In the late afternoon sun, the forty-seven travelers rushed to the overlooks. Missing the views before dark would be nothing short of sacrilege.

The silent timelessness surrounded them, the oldest features dating from 1.7 billion to 250 million years ago. The canyon itself, carved out by the mighty Colorado River, along with its buttes, mesas, and spires, evolved 6 million years ago or later.

Chaotic eons of upheaval and recession, weather and erosion, ice and dust--transformations dwarfing man's life span, yet allowing him the gift of a glimpse in his own time. As each new minute of the day ticked by, sunshine's light cast an entirely different feast of color and shadows over rock and tree and tiers of limestone cliffs and precipices.

Theo laid her head on Thom's shoulder. "This is so magnificent, it's almost a religious experience," she whispered.

As darkness began to close in, they drifted unwillingly into the lodge for dinner. At the entrance to the restaurant, a life-size bronze mule sat on its haunches, as if to welcome them.

Molly extended her hand across the table to her husband, and he patted it reassuringly. They gazed out at the panoramic view as the last rays of sun licked the canyon walls in flames of red.

"It's a window to a whole new world," Paco said.

"It's kinda like I'm looking at the largest TV set ever made," said Molly. "Showing me pictures I'm not supposed to see with my own eyes."

Hilda Vickers cleared her throat, breaking the spell. "I dare say, I never thought I'd see Mr. Symington sharing a table with his underlings."

Paco adjusted the collar of his suede jacket. Can't these people ever leave anything alone? he wondered.

"Oh good grief, you're right, Hilda," said Caroline. "Maybe the man's mellowing after all."

"Not possible!" cried Harry, pounding his fist on the table like a gavel.

"I do agree it would be a miracle for that tiger to change his spots," said Molly.

"Stripes!" Tina corrected. "Tigers have stripes."

Paco shot her an angry look. Lecturing his bride was uncalled for. But Tina appeared not to notice. She blithely nibbled a celery stalk.

The shift in mood quickly curtailed further conversation, causing the diners to hurry through their meals.

"Anyone notice that beaded Indian travesty hanging over the fireplace?" asked Molly, trying to restore the exhilaration she and Paco had felt when they sat down.

"It's lovely," said a disinterested Hilda as she stood to leave the table.

"Auntie," said Tina, "why don't we have another cup of coffee out on the terrace and look at the stars?"

"Oh, no, dear, I'm sure it's chilly out there. Besides, another cup of coffee will keep me awake all night. If you don't mind, I'll get one of these good people to see me back to our cabin."

"It would be our pleasure, ma'am," assured Paco.

"But Tina, are you sure you'll be all right alone out there?"

"Oh, Auntie, of course. The path back is very well lit." Tina walked away from the group and approached a waiter.

"Can you serve me a coffee out on the terrace, please?"

"Of course, ma'am," he replied. "I'll get it now."

Tina slipped into her safari jacket and pulled it around her as she settled into a patio chair. The air was sharp but clean and pleasant. In a few minutes the waiter arrived with his tray and set down two coffee mugs with their accompaniments on the small table next to her. "But I only ordered one," she protested, holding several dollar bills out to him.

"Thank you, but the gentleman has already paid," he said, moving away.

"What gentle--? Oh, it's you." Ray had taken the chair next to her. "Why can't you take no for an answer like any sensible person?" She started to get up.

"Please don't go," he said. "I owe you an apology, Tina. I don't know what possessed me to be so bold and brazen with you. Will you forgive me?" He hung his chin on his chest in mock contrition, and she giggled at his antics.

"See? That wasn't so hard, was it?" He held out his hand for a shake. She hesitated, but decided to take it. As his large hand grasped hers, she involuntarily felt its warmth.

They sipped their strong aromatic coffee, playfully scanned

the sky for the Big and Little Dipper, spoke of places seen and people met. When the coffee dwindled to a few drops in the bottom of her mug, Tina rose from her chair.

"A perfect ending to a fabulous day," she said, stretching arms over her head. He interpreted the gesture as an invitation, quickly stood, and took a long stride toward her. She countered by stepping out of his reach. He smiled sheepishly and backed away. The game, the dance was on.

She nodded approvingly, then surprised him by taking his arm and leading him through the lodge and down the path toward her cabin.

At the bottom of the short stairway that led to her door, Tina stopped, took out her key, and turned to thank him for seeing her "home." Ray's charm and humor had caught her unawares. Her grand plan was to destroy him, but a certain ambivalence deep inside her--a wavering she didn't understand--was getting in her way. His arm encircled her shoulders and guided her firmly but gently into the shadows to one side of the cabin. She wanted to protest and push him away, but she'd waited a moment too long. His mouth, warm and insistent, found hers. She responded to his kiss and succumbed to his strong embrace, savoring the moments it lasted. She felt her breasts rise and wished she wasn't wearing such a thick jacket. He finally let go of her.

In the thin shards of moonlight that jabbed through the dense trees, it was almost too dark to see his face. But not too dark for another pair of eyes to observe their embraces and not too far off for their words to fall on tuned ears. The eavesdropper slowly backed away and took another path back to her cabin.

Tina inhaled deeply and in a hoarse whisper, said, "I know full well what you want from me, but what will I get from you in return?"

"If you're thinking marriage, wealth, and position, forget it," he said.

"One kiss gives you such delusions of grandeur? You flatter yourself. I'm not in the market to break up anyone's marriage, especially not yours. Besides, I'm already financially secure, and I happen to like my job. The question is, how important am I to you?"

"You're an exceptionally intelligent, sexy woman. We could have a very rewarding relationship, physically and intellectually. But discreet, of course."

"Since when did 'discreet' become a word in your vocabulary? You seem to go out of your way to hurt your wife."

"I'm beginning to think our negotiations are breaking down. Short of what I've already excluded, what could you possibly want of me?" asked Ray. "And by the way, a Mercedes is also out of the question."

"Let's not get ridiculous. If I wanted a Mercedes, I could buy myself one. Think hard, Ray. What would you give *pour une nuit d'amour*, for one night of love?" She slid her hands inside his jacket and let her fingers play on his chest in teasing little motions. She could feel his nipples harden under his shirt. "Would you commit murder or steal?"

"Now who's being ridiculous?" he said. "Of course not." But he began to perspire in the chill of the September night, and felt himself no longer in charge. His arousal had taken over.

"Would you give up your position at the firm—take early retirement—for one night of pleasure?"

She had to be kidding, of course, only taunting him. He'd play along. "Yeah," he said. "Sure I would." His heart pounded. Somewhere in his trousers he ached.

"Would you put that in writing?" she asked quietly. She had all she could do to keep from bursting out with laughter.

"You charming little witch. Of course not. And why in hell would you want me to resign from IMTC? What could you possibly get out of it?"

Tina sensed a note of tension and bravado in his voice. Just what she'd been hoping for. The game was over and the score was now two-zero in her favor. Without replying, she spun on her heels and whispered sweetly, "Goodnight, Ray!" She hurried up the stairs, turned the key in the lock, and disappeared inside the cabin.

Inside, Tina raised a shushing forefinger to her lips before her aunt could greet her, then leaned against the door, listening for Ray's departure outside. And when at last she heard footsteps and twigs crackling beneath shoes, she threw herself on the bed next to Hilda.

"Oh, Auntie," Tina said. "It was so perfect. I don't ever remember having so much fun. I can't wait to tell you."

"You were with Symington, I gather."

"Yes, Auntie."

"What exactly did you do, Tina? You're acting like a high school freshman home from her first date. Did you initiate this so-called meeting?"

"No, he did. That's the best part."

"And he doesn't suspect?" Hilda asked. "He doesn't know you own the paper on his mortgage?"

"He has absolutely no idea, Auntie. No idea whatsoever."

In a state of confusion and disappointment, Ray climbed the few stairs to the cabin he and Loretta shared. He slid his key in the lock, but the door wouldn't budge--the deadbolt resisted. He shook the door, but all he heard was the silence of the forest and the eerie hooting of an owl indifferent to his problem. Knocking at varying levels of urgency and finally calling Loretta's name did not advance his purpose at all. Was she asleep? Not likely, after the racket he'd made. More probably, sitting straight up in the middle of the bed with her arms crossed, biting her lower lip, venting her anger at him in silent faces. He knew the image as well as the message it sent. Had she seen him with Tina?

He had no place to go except back to the lodge. The path seemed longer and lonelier than before, and Ray shivered in the biting chill that accompanies nighttime at 8,200 feet. He turned up his short collar and quickened his pace, but when he reached the lodge, he changed his mind. His watch read 9:55 p.m. Off to the left, he heard voices. He turned to see lights there--the trading post and gift shop were still open.

Ray headed straight for the racks of warm clothes and selected a fleece-lined parka with a hood. The parka fit easy over his windbreaker. While paying with his credit card, he mulled over in his mind what his next move would be. How the hell long would Loretta keep him locked out?

"I have something that might keep you even warmer," an inviting contralto voice spoke from behind him. He turned to see not a person, but a beautiful Navajo blanket, a work of art--vibrant with earth colors and intricate patterns--held open from the top by long feminine fingers, nails painted the deepest shade of carmine.

He tugged downward on the edges of the blanket to see who the voice and fingers might belong to. The descending blanket revealed a face both familiar and friendly. She stepped closer and wrapped the blanket about him. "I'll buy it for you if you like."

"Thanks for the thought, but no need to," he said. "The clerk has my credit card already." As the young man behind the counter rang up Ray's second purchase, the woman slipped under the blanket beside him and wrapped one end around herself.

"This is crazy," he said. But he chuckled at the silliness of it, and the challenge appealed to him. They shuffled cozily together out of the store and headed into the night.

Chapter 20
A HOT GRUDGE SUNDAY
Same Day, Sunday, September 20, 1981

RUTH MILTON AWOKE TO AN OMINOUS SOUND, unsure whether it had come from a malevolent dream or from outside their cabin. Lying rigidly on her back, she listened, but heard only the whoosh of the wind in the tall pines. Her sinewy body refused to relax as it contended with the thin mattress. Eyes closing once more, Ruth rolled toward her husband, but met only blanket and more blanket.

"LeRoy?" No one answered.

Swinging her legs off the bed, Ruth pattered barefoot across the linoleum floor and flung the cabin door open. A rush of cold air flew in her face. In the sporadic moonlight her eyes scanned the little porch, walkways, and nearby cabins. Not a soul in sight. A sickening moment of aloneness and abandonment took possession of her. Shutting the door, she wiggled both feet halfway into sneakers, squashing the heels and leaving the laces flopping. From the tiny alcove that served as a closet, she grabbed a leather jacket and jammed her arms into it, wincing in pain as her sore left shoulder balked at the jerky motion. Zipping it up, Ruth stepped out onto the porch and peered through the trees. About fifty yards away, a pinpoint red glow appeared, then faded.

"LeRoy? Honey, is that you?" she called in a voice barely above a whisper, for the words simply caught in her throat. The disembodied red pinpoint glowed and ebbed once more.

"LeRoy!" she called again. This time the glow came closer and dropped lower. A man's silhouette emerged from the shadows.

"Ruth, what're you doing out here? You want to catch your

death or something?"

She descended the wooden steps and hurried to him. "Le-Roy, for God's sake, you gave me a fright. What's the matter?" When he came into view, she saw he was still in the sweat suit he always wore to bed. At least he'd thrown on a warm-up jacket. She threw her arms around him. "Is your heart acting up again? Why didn't you wake me, honey?" She nuzzled her face deep into his neck and held him tight.

"I couldn't sleep and didn't want to disturb you. I thought a walk and a cigarette might relax me."

She raised her head and looked at him in exasperation. "You know you're not supposed to smoke. The doctor said it's just making your condition worse."

"Stop nagging me. Look, it's eleven o'clock. I'm not ready to go back to bed yet. You go. I'll be fine."

"Let me get dressed and walk with you. It's not that safe out here. There are wild animals…"

"Sweetheart, " he said, "if I meet up with a humungous grizzly, I'll give him your regards. Besides, why should both of us be up all night?"

"Maybe I want to be with you, honey. Be right back."

LeRoy watched her in her comical outfit, sleep shirt flapping around her calves as she disappeared inside. He adored his wife, and somehow, just knowing she wanted to be with him helped a whole lot. He sighed. She was right, of course. He promised himself he'd cut back on the cigarettes as soon as they got home. He took one last drag, pinched off the glowing tip, and dropped it onto a cleared patch of damp ground. The toe of his oxford stubbed it out. Stripping and scattering the remainder of the butt made sure it wouldn't start a forest fire. He hoped nobody was watching from a cabin window. Glenn had lectured them on the rules of the national parks: "You never leave anything behind except your footprints." And your money in the gift shops, LeRoy thought wryly.

Only five minutes later, Ruth bounded down the steps in

jeans, feet squarely in her sneakers now with laces tied. LeRoy took her arm and led her off in the direction of the overlooks for a moonlight view of the canyon. The lodge, gift shop, and general store loomed eerily black in front of them. But LeRoy and Ruth followed a path that led around the complex. They chose a fork in the trail marked "To Bright Angel Point." The view there had been spectacular on their sundown walk just before dinner. The point had been crowded then--its popularity coming from viewing the confluence of three canyons: Roaring Springs, Transcept, and Bright Angel itself. A quarter-mile trail led them to the entrance. A denser growth of trees shrouded the trail beyond, forming a sixty-foot natural corridor to the moonlit point. He led her through the deep shadows and heavy scent of pine sap and old growth. Le-Roy spotted a fallen gambel oak and suggested they rest there and feast on the starry vastness spread above them. A chill shot through Ruth. The Miltons snuggled for both warmth and reassurance in the ghostlike silence.

A twig snapped. Ruth's body jerked to attention. A bulky shape moved down the path. "Might be an animal," she whispered, squeezing her husband's hand so hard his knuckles ached.

In the gloom of the shrubs and trees lining the path, the object seemed to LeRoy almost twice as large as a person, maybe even an elk or a bear. Having no idea what creatures stalked these regions, he shuddered. Suddenly, the dark hulk headed up the trail, and LeRoy exhaled with relief as he realized it was a human being--a male figure, probably, from the size of him. For a moment the figure hesitated on the path, blocking the view to the point, then continued awkwardly to the rocky ledge. There, bathed in moonlight, two heads now became apparent.

Ruth chuckled. "It's two people, thank God. And they're wrapped together in something."

"Maybe a blanket," LeRoy answered. "And it looks like a man and a woman. I'll take them over a bear any day." He swallowed hard and felt his heart rate thankfully slowing down.

"Isn't it a little late for that sort of thing?" she asked. "Nearly 11:30."

"Maybe they're lovers," he said.

They watched as the couple dropped the blanket and embraced in a pantomime of pleasure.

"Something funny's going on there," LeRoy whispered.

"Funny? What do you mean?"

"Well, they kissed. But now...the man steps back every time she gets closer, and she keeps coming at him. It's like she's pushing or prodding him."

More sounds, crunching dry pine needles, then footsteps. A third individual, wearing a hat, hurried past them from the lodge path. The long stride and heavy gait indicated a man. The man tripped and tumbled to the ground, losing his hat as he fell. Still on his knees, he grabbed it and jammed it back on his head. As the Miltons strained to see him get to his feet, a series of strange and chilling sounds met their ears.

"Was that gunfire?" asked Ruth.

"Sounded like it," responded LeRoy. "Whaa...?"

A bellowing yell pierced the night air. The scream trailed into the abyss beyond the canyon wall. Moments later, its tragically wailing echo returned, its decibels significantly diminished.

The silhouette of the tall, wide-shouldered figure no longer appeared at the overlook. The shorter figure, the woman, stood at the precipice alone. The Miltons continued to observe the drama with horrified fascination. The third figure, the man who had tripped, now ran toward the woman and reached for her just as she moved with certainty toward the same fateful brink. He caught her in time, grabbed her by the shoulders, and shook her violently. From their gambel oak tree cover the Miltons could just make out his frantic question to her: "Are you crazy?"

When at last the man released her, the woman uttered a pitiful anguished cry and struck him sharply across the face. He stood fixed to the spot as the woman stomped back up the path toward the trail. Had she been less preoccupied and distraught, she would have seen and recognized the Miltons just as surely as they recognized her.

The man at the overlook picked up the couple's abandoned blanket and charged after her in heavy strides. Just a few yards from where the Miltons huddled in the shadows he changed direction and disappeared without the couple ever seeing his face.

"LeRoy?" Ruth murmured when she thought it was safe to speak. "What are we going to do, honey?"

Do? You know we can't get involved."

"I understand that," Ruth said. "But this is murder. We saw her commit murder."

"I know, but somebody else saw it, too. He'll call the authorities."

"What if he doesn't?"

LeRoy rose to his feet. "Forget it, baby, we've got to protect ourselves. And right now, we'd better get away from here." Ruth reluctantly pulled herself up. On a tender impulse, LeRoy wrapped his arms around his wife of thirty-one years, held her for a moment, then led her hastily by the hand down the deserted trail and back to their cabin. Their bedside light went out at a quarter past midnight.

Chapter 21
MISSING
Day Twelve, Monday, September 21, 1981

"LORETTA, WHERE'S YOUR DASHING HUSBAND this morning?" asked Bess.

"I don't know and I don't give a hoot!" Loretta plunked her breakfast tray down on the table so hard the poached eggs trembled. She slid into the one remaining chair.

"Do I detect a nice piece of juicy gossip here?" Hilda interjected.

"Don't get to salivating yet, woman," Loretta responded. "All I did was lock him out of the room last night."

"Whatever for?" Bess asked in her innocent way. Her oatmeal bowl now empty, she took a small, flat box out of her fanny pack. Carefully opening it, she selected half a dozen pills of various colors and arranged them in a neat row.

"Let's just say he got a little too dashing," grumbled Loretta.

"Did you catch him at it?" asked Hilda.

"That's none of your damn business!"

"Oh, I love it," declared Hilda.

"Your concern and understanding are much appreciated," retorted Loretta.

Unable to decipher the verbal sparring, a puzzled Bess downed her pills with dainty sips of water.

Thirty minutes later, the bus began to load. Several in the group lingered outside to observe a clownish-looking squirrel with a bushy white tail and Mickey Mouse ears as it hugged a nearby tree.

"Folks, that's a Kaibab squirrel, a real treat," Glenn said. "I haven't seen one in four years."

"Oh, Glenn, we're onto you," Theo said. "I'll bet you tell that to all the groups." The guide just smiled.

The bus filled. No one seemed surprised that the seat next to Loretta remained empty. But soon an undercurrent of irritation, then outright grumbling began with the nonappearance of Ray Symington. After forty-five minutes of waiting, Glenn approached the empty seat of his missing passenger.

"Loretta, where is your husband?" he asked. "We have a schedule to keep."

"I know, Glenn, and I'm sorry. I have no idea where he is. Give him another five minutes. Then leave without him."

"Are you sure that's what you want?"

"Yes!" Her hard blue eyes narrowed. "It'll teach the bastard a lesson he won't forget in a hurry." And when the guide continued to look at her questioningly, she reiterated, "Leave him!" The determined set of her jaw accented her words.

Glenn's freckles jumped and shifted as his face took on a perplexed air. He strode to the front of the bus and held an elevated and agitated conversation with his driver. "Loretta says we should go on without Ray, but if it turns out he's in trouble and I didn't tell anybody, my ass is gonna be in a sling--big time. I'm going inside to call the Ranger Station and find out what the procedure is--if there is one for this absurd situation. Be right back."

Lew nodded vigorously. "Good move."

"Wait! Before you go..." called Caroline. "I saw him earlier this morning on the way to breakfast. He was with some woman I didn't recognize—not from our tour."

"I saw them too," interjected the judge. "At least it looked like him."

"That SOB," cried Loretta.

"Where did you see them?" asked Glenn.

"They came out of the lodge and got into a car and

drove off," said Caroline.

"What kind of car was it?"

"I don't know much about cars--dark blue, maybe," she answered.

"It was black," said the judge. "Yes, I'm sure it was black."

Glenn hopped off the bus and disappeared inside the lodge. Lew followed him out the door, pulled out a pack of cigarettes, and lit up.

Twenty minutes later the guide returned and motioned his driver to get the show on the road. Lew swung out of the parking area and retraced most of the previous day's trek past the monumental Vermilion Cliffs.

Glenn picked up his mike, ran his fingers through his tousled red hair, and addressed the group. "Friends, I've checked with the park ranger staff of the North Rim Unit. Normally, if somebody's missing we'd be required to remain here for questioning. But since there's evidence that Ray left voluntarily, we've been given permission to continue on our tour. The rangers do have our itinerary, phone numbers, and my emergency number to track us down if necessary."

Excited buzzing and hushed comments floated through the bus as they descended the steep weaving grade of Highway 89A and eventually leveled to a flatter roadbed. Here, four repeating features dominated the landscape of a Navajo Reservation: adobe and log hogans, looking like dark inverted bowls; shanties; mobile homes on blocks; and pickup trucks. Glenn explained the pickups were necessary to haul in huge tanks of drinking water, as this land, set aside for the Navajo Nation, lacked that precious resource.

The bus passed too briefly through the Painted Desert, where rich deposits of water-borne minerals caught the sun's glint and displayed the colors of an artist's palette. At Cameron, Lew steered west to Desert View and skirted a northern section of Kaibab National Forest.

Their reward at the end of this 200-mile leg was the Grand Canyon's South Rim. The air crackled with breathless excitement.

Entering Grand Canyon National Park, forty-seven necks craned in anticipation of an almost indescribable grandeur. But as they approached, the collective mood sank like a pricked balloon.

"Jeez!" Michelle whined.

"New Haven at rush hour," George quipped.

"Well, folks," Glenn said, facing them with his microphone, "you've seen the movie Close Encounters of the Third Kind? Here at the South Rim we call 'em close encounters of the frustrating kind. We should be out of this traffic jam in a couple of hours."

Groans erupted on all sides.

"Just kidding, folks," Glenn laughed. "Won't be too long. This is nothing. You should see it in July and August when the kids are out of school."

Molly and Paco peered out their window for their first look at the sights--straight into the windows of another behemoth luxury liner, a mirror image of themselves. Molly waved cheerfully and half a dozen travelers waved back. The buses and cars idled bumper to bumper, then slowly rumbled forward to Grand Canyon Village. They passed a huge complex of hotels, restaurants, museums, and shops.

Lew angled the bus into a large parking lot and braked to a halt in front of the historic El Tovar Hotel, their stop for the night.

The group filed off as politely as possible in their anxiety to get their first look at the glorious South Rim. The LeSotos had almost reached the nearest overlook, when suddenly, behind them, they heard foreign chattering, shouting, and running footsteps. A veritable tsunami of Japanese tourists had poured off several buses and now surged forward. Laden with cameras, the new arrivals elbowed every tourist in their path and spread their ranks to stake out claims at the overlook walls. Lighting up cigarettes, they smoked and clicked away.

Paco pulled Molly to one side and suggested they wait a bit. Too startled to reply, she tucked her arm into his and toddled along as he led her beyond the clouds of smoke.

Twenty minutes later, as abruptly as they had arrived, the Asian tourists departed. The Vermilion group gratefully moved to the overlook and gazed out as the late afternoon sun blessed the canyon walls with glowing red, purple, and gold. Paco halted a healthy margin from the wall. Despite the crowds milling around them jockeying for the best views, he felt an overwhelming sense of wonder, almost as if he were witness to the evolution of our planet.

All too soon, darkness fell and they reluctantly assembled in their hotel lobby. Loretta looked at her watch, then beelined to a bank of telephones. Despite her outward display of indifference, she could not entirely hide her anxiety over Ray's absence.

With trembling fingers, she called the Grand Canyon Lodge on the North Rim, only to learn that there were no messages from Ray. She started to ask for the number of the Law Enforcement Park Rangers, when she spotted the LeSotos, who had wandered into the gift shop. She replaced the receiver, stepped out of the booth, and approached Paco as he was paying for a glossy color booklet about the canyon.

"Paco? Could you help me?" she interrupted.

"You never know," he said. "Perhaps I can."

"I'm quite concerned over my missing husband."

"Are you?" he replied tersely. Then seeing her stricken look, he softened. "I don't blame you. However, I must admit you've been most calm and cool till now. How can I help you?"

"If you wanted to contact the police and hospitals on the North Rim, how would you go about it from here?"

Paco's bushy black eyebrows came together as he frowned in deep concentration. "I'd head for the Ranger Station here on the South Rim." He glanced about and spotted Molly, who was examining the Navajo pottery. "Honey, why don't you check in for us? I'm going to the Ranger Station with Loretta to try and locate her husband."

"Okay, sweet," Molly replied. "I understand. Don't be too long now."

Paco stopped at the El Tovar desk for directions and returned to take Loretta to the Ranger Station. They entered a two-story log structure and explained the situation to the park ranger at the desk, who asked for a picture and a full description of Ray. Loretta carried a photo of the two of them in her wallet and handed it over. The ranger immediately radioed Ray's description to the North Rim Ranger Station. Meanwhile, she and Paco were made comfortable and given coffee.

After a half-hour, Paco called Molly to reassure her. "Go ahead and eat. I'll get something later."

They waited another fifteen minutes to hear back.

"The return message says that no search has been initiated as yet," read the park ranger. "Your tour director informed the North Rim station that Mr. Symington was observed getting into a car and driving off with an unidentified female early this morning. There's been no sign of him since. The nearest hospital to the North Rim confirms that he hasn't been admitted there. However, a clerk at the North Rim trading post says he sold your husband some stuff just before closing last night. He was accompanied by a woman."

"What kind of stuff?" Paco asked.

"A Navajo blanket, but the clerk couldn't remember what else. Said they were very busy right then."

"I see," she said, scowling in annoyance.

"There's more, ma'am. Since you made a fresh inquiry here, the North Rim wants to know if there's a change in status. Did your husband just drive off with someone or is he truly lost? They want to know if you suspect endangerment or foul play."

"I hate to admit it, but if there was a woman involved, it was probably voluntary. He knows how to take care of number one, all right. You'll let me know if he turns up there, won't you?"

"Of course, ma'am," he said. "But in most missing person cases we're dealing with a visitor who's lost his way in the woods. We get a whole bunch of that sort of thing—visitors wandering off. Anyway, we have no way of returning a wayward hubby, if that's what he is. So there's no need for you to wait here any longer. We can contact you over at the hotel if we hear anything."

"Oh, thank you," she said, forcing a grateful smile.

Molly invited herself to dinner that evening with Tina, the Moyers, and the Whitmans. Hilda had gone to bed with a migraine. Molly noticed that although the conversation flourished, she herself was left out of it. Tina seemed preoccupied. The Moyers and Whitmans chatted enthusiastically among themselves.

Molly decided to take the initiative while pouring herself a glass of red wine from the carafe in the center of the table. "Tina, did you know the Moyers and Whitmans before this trip?" she asked. All conversation ceased and everyone at the table stared at her for several seconds.

"Why, yes, dear Molly," Theo interjected. "She…"

"Of course," interrupted Joanne. "We met at a wedding in Danbury, Connecticut, some years ago. We have mutual friends there."

"That's it!" stumbled Theo, as though she were finding this out for the first time.

Molly thought it mighty strange that the two women burst in to answer for Tina, who, oddly enough, chose to remain silent as she munched her Caesar salad. Molly decided that something was rotten in Danbury. She cocked her head and studied her tablemates one by one, hoping for an explanation, but none was forthcoming. From then on, the conversation seemed to her decidedly more guarded, and Tina and the Whitmans departed shortly after.

Molly was just finishing her apple pie and cheddar cheese, when Paco entered the dining room and sat down in Tina's empty chair.

"Hi, honey, where's Loretta?" Molly asked, unable to contain herself.

"She went directly to her room." As the Moyers leaned forward in unison to glean new information, Paco discreetly chose not to say that Loretta was ordering dinner from room service to avoid a lot of embarrassing questions.

Molly asked, "Any news about Mr. Ray?"

"Not really. They promised to let us know as soon as they learn anything. Apparently, he bought a blanket and some other stuff at the trading post last night when Loretta turned him out of their room."

"Sounds like he was planning to spend the night outside," she mused.

"Except the clerk said he left the post with a woman."

"Could the clerk describe the woman?" Molly asked.

"Not well. Ordinary looks, forty to fifty, dark hair."

"Boy," said Molly. "That could be just about anybody on the bus. Except me, of course." She and fluffed her taffy curls.

"Could also have been somebody not on our tour. Anybody, in fact," Paco noted.

Theo and Thom pushed their chairs back and stood up. "You'll have to excuse us," Thom said. "I've had to call a business meeting for our employees now that Ray is missing."

Molly laid her napkin down and squeezed herself out of her chair. "You go ahead and order, honey," she told her husband. "I'm going to powder my nose."

The moment she returned, Paco sensed something was up. "What's wrong, sweetheart? You've got a strange look on your face."

"I'll tell you. But first, hand me that giraffe. I'd like a little more wine. You know that meeting Thom called?" she asked as she poured herself a second glass. "They're in this little room down the hall, the Sierra Room. Their wives are in there, too. What do the wives have to do with their business? As if that wasn't enough, I saw Judge Sessions, his wife, Cookie, and Tina go in there, too. What do you suppose is going on?"

Both of Paco's eyebrows shot north. "I don't know what they have in common. Except...perhaps they all have a distinct connection to our missing man." He looked at his bride admiringly. "Sweetie pie, you're on the ball. Thanks for the intelligence."

Her chubby cheeks turned pink with the compliment. "Any time, honey. Do you think that bunch knows what's happened to

Mr. Ray?" she asked.

"Either someone in there knows something," he declared, "or Symington himself has pulled a fast one on them all." The waiter set a cheeseburger platter before him.

"I found out another tidbit, too," she said. "Before you got here, I learned that Tina knew the Moyers and Whitmans from somewhere else. They all looked embarrassed about telling me this."

"I wonder why," said Paco, squirting ketchup on his fries.

"You gonna eat all those?" asked Molly with a broad smile. She smoothly appropriated two and popped them in her mouth before he could even answer.

Chapter 22
ROCKY INTERLUDE
Day Thirteen, Tuesday, September 22, 1981

AT DAYBREAK LORETTA'S FELLOW TRAVELERS gazed for the last time into the hypnotic depths of the South Rim. But mostly, they stole sidelong glances at her, trying not to be too obvious about it. Ray's disappearance--and his wife's peculiar reaction--had cast an uneasy spell. Loretta sensed their disapproval and stood off by herself, tight-lipped and distraught.

Glenn's professionally cheery voice beckoned them to board for the trip deep into the heart of Arizona. The bus streaked past the Kaibab National Forest and San Francisco peaks. In downtown Flagstaff, Lew headed south and rumbled into the art colony of Sedona, nestled in the southern end of Oak Creek Canyon.

The bus hissed to a halt in a parking area on Sedona's main street, locally known as Highway 89A. A highway patrol cruiser pulled up beside them. The blue DPS logo painted on the door identified the car: Arizona Department of Public Safety. Glenn stepped down from the bus to greet the trooper waiting at the door. After a short exchange between the two men, Glenn re-boarded and worked his way down the aisle to Loretta.

"There's a state trooper here. He'd like to speak with you."

"Oh, my God! Does he have some news about Ray?" she asked. Her fingers clutched her Gucci purse, knuckles whitening.

"Don't know," Glenn replied. "Maybe you'd better meet with him."

Loretta pulled her Vermilion tote from the overhead rack and hurried off the bus. She saw the tall, muscular trooper and slowly approached him.

"Mrs. Symington?"

"Yes." Her voice quivered.

Under his wide-brimmed hat, his weather-beaten face looked grave. "I'm here regarding your husband's disappearance. You are the woman who filed the missing persons report on Raymond Symington at the South Rim Ranger Station yesterday, aren't you?"

"Yes! Have they found him yet?"

"Don't know anything about that, ma'am. I have instructions to hold you here in Sedona for the North Rim authorities. They'll be wanting to ask you some questions."

"What kind of questions? Can't you at least just tell me if they found him?"

"Sorry, I really don't have any information. Let's get your luggage and I'll try to make you comfortable at the station."

"Wait! How can I get back to the North Rim?"

"You can't, ma'am. The North Rim rangers are on their way down here by helicopter to question you."

Loretta's voice turned querulous. "But this is an emergency. Don't you have a helicopter that could take me to the North Rim?"

The trooper loomed over her. "No, ma'am."

"Now you're treating me like some kind of suspect."

"Well, ma'am, since you put it that way..."

Loretta caught the drift of his taciturn reply. If it was such an emergency, she would have stayed behind and wouldn't have told Glenn to leave the North Rim without Ray. Glenn must have squealed to the trooper, and this made her a suspect.

The trooper motioned to Lew and indicated that the Symington luggage had to be offloaded from the bus. With its cargo door gaping open, Lew laboriously removed bag after bag, until he came to the two bearing Loretta and Ray's tags. He dragged them out of the hold and shoved all the other bags back in.

The trooper loaded the luggage into the cruiser's trunk, then guided Loretta into the front passenger seat. She hardly noticed Harry and Caroline Sessions already seated in the rear of the cruiser.

Paco and Molly had been standing with the others in the group beside the bus, observing Loretta and the trooper. Molly itched to move close enough to eavesdrop, but Paco placed his arm around her magnanimous waist and affectionately but firmly held her in place. As the cruiser drove off, Glenn laid down the rules of the Sedona visit. Moments later, at least half the tour rushed to take the optional jeep rides into the nearby mountains.

Molly was first in line, and Paco boosted her tush up into one of the bright pink vehicles. They roared off, with the driver making stock jokes in a western twang.

"Hang on, ladies and gents, it's gonna be bumpier than a camel's back."

The jeep bounced a jarring mile or two over the ancient oxen and wagon trail between Sedona and Flagstaff. As it lurched to a stop on a small plateau, they all scrambled out.

A living desert spread before them: yucca, agave, pinon pine, and juniper. Clumps of sagebrush, prickly pear cactus, teddy bear cholla marched like a platoon of soldiers to the base of the rugged red rocks. Monoliths, buttes, and gorges changed color from moment to moment, depending on where the sun hit them and which direction one looked out.

"Ladies and gents," their driver broke in, "meet Snoopy and Lucy."

Little Bess stood on tiptoe and craned her neck. "I don't see a thing," she complained.

"I'll help you," Molly offered, sidling closer. She pointed to a massive formation of red rock horizontally striped with salt precipitation. "See the flat part? It looks like Lucy is sitting on it."

"Oh!" squealed Bess, "I see her now, her exact hair."

"You got it," Theo chimed in. "And below, on the right, there's Snoopy lying on his back."

"Goodness gracious, yes, and he looks so comfortable. The only thing missing is his doghouse." Bess giggled so infectiously that everyone joined in.

Reba stepped carefully over the small rocks on the trail and approached their driver. "Is it true that Sedona has some kind of mysterious energy?"

From under his cowboy hat, the driver peered at her in silence. George came to her rescue. "My wife means the vortexes, the electromagnetic fields that surge up from the earth here in Sedona."

"Not exactly!" Reba beamed. "I read that they are junctions of metaphysical and spiritual earth fields. They're supposed to give us a special life force and inspiration."

The driver's eyes twinkled. "Well, ma'am," he drawled, "I got two o' them vortexes in my house. You just flush the handle and there you are, privy to the magic."

Reba looked crestfallen as the rest of the group burst out laughing.

Two North Rim rangers were waiting for Loretta and the Sessions when they arrived at the Sedona police station. Loretta was asked to wait on a polished wooden bench beside the door to an interrogation room while the Sessions were directed to a table within. They informed her that someone would be with her in a few moments.

Inside, the sparsely decorated room established a down-to-business setting for the impending interrogation. Both rangers stood up from the table where they were seated and presented their commissions, identifying themselves as Law Enforcement Rangers. The taller of the two motioned them to empty chairs at the table.

"Mr. And Mrs. Sessions, I am Ranger Phil Platte and this is Ranger Samuel Long Feather. We'd like to ask a few questions about the mysterious disappearance of a Mr. Raymond Symington."

"First of all," started Harry, "it's Judge and Mrs. Harold Sessions, and since we had nothing to do with this man's disappearance, I don't see why the two of us were separated from an expensive tour which we paid good money for."

"Sorry, Judge!" Ranger Platte responded. "Sorry for the inconvenience, too, but your tour director gave your names as witnesses to the missing man's voluntary departure from the tour group. We'll have you both back with the Vermilion tour in nothing flat--just as soon as we clear up a few details. The fact is, we would like to know how certain you are of what you reported. First, how well do you know the missing man?"

"Quite well," replied Harry.

"Oh! You saw them socially?"

"Not quite, more like business--legal business. He appeared before my court several years ago. Besides, the man's singled himself out. Made a total nuisance of himself during this whole trip."

Ranger Platte looked over at Caroline.

"Don't look at me," she said. "I've hardly spoken to the man. I know him by reputation and by his abominable behavior on this trip. He's not popular with anyone on the bus."

"Ma'am," Ranger Platte addressed Caroline. "Are you sure the man you saw getting into a car this morning was Raymond Symington?"

"Of course...Well, it could very well have been Symington. You thought so, too," she said, looking at her husband.

At this time, Ranger Platte anticipated a response from Harry. "Well!"

"There's no doubt in my mind that it was him," said Harry.

"Did you recognize the woman with him?"

"No one that I knew," replied Harry.

"Me neither," his wife volunteered. "She wasn't a part of the tour."

"How were they dressed?"

"I didn't pay much attention to clothing," he answered. "My mind was fixed on his profile."

"He had on a windbreaker and slacks," she responded smugly. "Both tan. And she--a gray sweater and tan slacks."

"How far away from them were you when you spotted the

couple?"

"Oh, fifty, maybe seventy-five yards," replied Harry. "It was him all right."

"Were there any trees between you?"

"Not so many as to obstruct our view."

"Mrs. Sessions, what kind of car did they get into?"

"I don't know much about car makes, but it was navy in color."

"She means black," interrupted Harry. "Definitely black."

"I do not! It was blue, navy blue. You men don't know anything about color."

"Was it a sedan or coupe? How many doors?"

"Two," replied Caroline.

"Definitely a four-door sedan," Harry emphasized.

"No!" she argued. "I saw her tilt the driver seat forward to put something in the back."

The two rangers looked at one another. They spoke among themselves for a minute, and then Ranger Platte thanked the couple for their cooperation and told them that Ranger Long Feather would accompany them back to the Vermilion bus. As soon as they were out the front door, Loretta was led to the table where Ranger Phil Platte identified himself.

"I'd like to clear up a few details concerning your husband's disappearance," he began.

"Then you've found him?" interrupted Loretta.

"No, ma'am, although we've found some things that may have belonged to your husband."

"May have?...What things?" Her heart accelerated. "Is he all right?"

Choosing his words carefully, he said, "No, ma'am, we don't think he is okay. Early this morning one of our other visitors, exploring a trail at the bottom of a talus slope, reported some unusual findings to the Ranger Station. He'd come across a man's European walking shoe about twenty feet down. He also discovered a sizeable broken branch and some material from a fleece-lined jacket. It actually looked like a pocket torn off. From Mr. Haniford's initial report and your follow-up request from the South Rim, we put two and two together and came up with Mr. Symington."

"The shoe could be his. But a fleece-lined jacket?" Loretta's voice cracked and grew shrill. "That's not Ray's. He...he doesn't own a fleece-lined jacket."

"Ma'am, the North Rim authorities have learned that your husband purchased that jacket just last night at the lodge trading post--plus a Navajo blanket."

Loretta felt horrible. Last night she'd locked Ray out of the cabin! Good heavens! He must have been freezing. Her thoughts swirled in turmoil at the ranger's revelation. She couldn't digest it--and his attitude annoyed her. His "ma'am this" and "ma'am that" sounded so patronizing.

"The North Rim at Bright Angel Point has a precipice and talus slope."

Loretta stared blankly at him. "A what?"

"A talus slope--a steep accumulation of dirt and rocks, softer layers of rock formations, and vegetation. If your husband fell, he could have slid down that slope. The vegetation might have actually broken his fall. Farther down the talus slope, some rangers found a whole track of busted tree branches, freshly disturbed soil, and signs of blood on the cliff side of the trail. And from the looks of things, it appears he either fell or was pushed from the overlook at Bright Angel Point. That's about a quarter mile east of Grand Canyon Lodge."

Loretta's hand flew to her mouth, then dropped heavily, as if it had lost its function. The color drained from her face, deepening the creases around her eyes and mouth, intensifying the garish blue of her eye shadow and fuchsia lip gloss. She felt suddenly older.

"He's dead, then?"

Ranger Platte slowly adjusted the set of his rimless glasses before he replied. "Without a body, they can't be sure. Or, for that matter, if it's even him. By the way, they found something else at the overlook: a locket with a broken chain. It has the name Constance engraved inside. Ma'am, do you ever use that name?"

"Constance? No, of course not," snapped Loretta. "And I never wear anything as corny as a locket." Noting the ranger's questioning gaze, she realized how inappropriate and trivial she must have sounded and softened her tone. "Is there any chance for him?"

Platte shrugged. "People have survived such a fall. However, it may be days before one of the search and rescue teams is able to find anything. SAR teams. They're the qualified emergency response rangers on the South Rim. The terrain is terribly difficult and there's so much ground to cover." He paused, placed his elbows on the table, and leaned toward her. "Mrs. Symington, you chose to continue on the tour even though your husband was missing?"

His question threw her off balance. She lowered the sunglasses perched atop her teased hairdo, and fitted them over her eyes, a shield against his sudden attack. "Well, yes."

"May I ask why?"

Loretta found it easier to answer behind the dark glasses. "This is terribly personal, Officer...We haven't been getting along very well on this trip. I thought he was spending the night with another woman and I was angry." She began drumming her painted nails on the table. The diamonds in her wedding band danced in the glaring overhead light.

The woman's got something to hide. "So you took his suitcase with you?"

She shrugged. "Yes."

"But not his tote bag."

Her body stiffened.

The ranger crossed his khakied legs and continued. "A maid found it in your room after the tour bus left--a Vermilion Tours carry-on bag with Mr. Symington's luggage tag."

"It had his toilet articles and medications in it. I expected he'd be going back to the room...I thought he'd need them."

"Okay, ma'am." The ranger stood up. "Under the circumstances I think it best that you return to the North Rim while we continue the search for your husband."

Her face brightened with visible relief. "That's what I've wanted to do all along!"

"We'll have more questions for you later. Meanwhile, I'll make some arrangements to get you there."

Back in the center of Sedona, the remainder of the tour scattered up and down the art colony's main drag to be gobbled up by the abundance of its galleries and working studios. Once again, the Native American art, lore, and trinkets proved a formidable force in separating the tourist from his wampum.

At 1:45 Paco took Molly by the hand and they ambled back toward the parked tour bus. The two observed the Sessions getting out of an unmarked car parked directly in the bus's path. Coming even closer, they noticed a Law Enforcement Ranger sitting in the driver's seat. Paco approached the ranger and tried to strike up a conversation. Although he was reluctant at first, Ranger Long Feather loosened up a bit when Paco identified himself with his own county police badge and commission.

"I assume this is about our missing passenger, Ray Symington," Paco asked casually.

Long Feather didn't answer for a minute or so and then, trading procedural precautions for some possible insights, he nodded.

"Can I be of some assistance to your investigation?" Paco tried again.

"A list of passengers would be an excellent start."

"I'll get the list from Glenn Haniford, our tour director," said Paco. "He's right over there talking to Lew Getz, our driver."

"It's imperative that we keep all of the bus passengers together until we reach your Scottsdale hotel. I understand it's the last scheduled overnight for the tour. Sedona doesn't have adequate facilities for us to conduct a preliminary sunquiry, so a team of criminal investigators will meet the bus in Scottsdale."

"But we're making another stop this afternoon--at Montezuma Castle," said Paco.

"Yes, I'm aware of that," said the ranger. "I don't like the idea, but I'll be following you in my car to make sure no one wanders off."

"Maybe I can help keep an eye on everyone for you," offered Paco.

"I can't ask you to do this, but then again I can't stop you either. However, if even one member of the tour walks, I've told Mr. Haniford he will be held personally responsible. His company, too. "

"Understood," said Paco.

"Maybe you can tell me--is there anyone on the tour by the name of Constance? Does the name mean anything to you?"

"No, sir," said Paco, "although I must admit it does sound somewhat familiar. Why?"

"A locket inscribed with that name has turned up," said the ranger. "Let me know if anyone comes to mind."

"Turned up? Where?"

"Perhaps I've said too much already."

Chapter 23
UNRAVELING
Same Day, Tuesday, September 22, 1981

LEW SHIFTED INTO GEAR, AND THE COACH RUMBLED out of Sedona. Glenn grabbed his microphone.

"Friends, I'm speaking to you in an unofficial capacity. A North Rim Law Enforcement Ranger is following our bus. He's in the gray Chevy behind us. There'll be an inquiry when we get to our hotel tonight. The rangers will want to speak to each of us. I've been informed that I am being personally held responsible for keeping you all together. They have been gracious enough to let us make our comfort stop at Montezuma Castle, so please, everyone cooperate and stay together. I'll be counting heads, and the ranger has requested a roll call as you re-enter the bus."

"You mean we're not going to see everything at the castle," complained Reba.

"Don't worry. You'll see all there is to see. We'll assemble at one of the best vantage points and I'll give you all the facts."

"Why is that ranger following us?" asked Theo. "Is this about Ray Symington?"

"Have they changed their mind about Ray running off with some babe?" asked Gordon. "Do they suspect foul play now?"

"Does that mean he's some kind of detective?" asked Joanne.

"Please, everyone," Glenn pleaded. "I don't know much more than you do. The ranger following us is a lawman, so I suspect they're not buying Symington's voluntary separation from the tour. Probably they're thinking accident or foul play."

"In Ray's case they should be thinking homicide," offered

Tina.

"Hey, Paco!" taunted Joanne. "Maybe if you'd agreed to protect him, Ray'd be alive right now."

"That's harshly fair, Miss Joanne," protested Molly from her driver-side seat in the twelfth row. "It's leaping to convulsions. You have no right to be making such a crazen accusation. Paco is on our honeymoon and, besides, he has no official effluence in this state. If Ray's been bumped off, I think at least one of you on this bus is a purpletrator and a whole bunch of you are guilty of something else, and my husband's going to prove it. Aren't you, Paco, honey?"

"Pipe down, woman!" Joanne shouted. "You have no idea what you're talking about."

"Ah, but she does know and she's also right about me," Paco said. "I don't have jurisdiction here and maybe I've already said too much. However, since you've chosen to challenge both my wife and me, I will present my conspiracy theory to you."

Judge Sessions blurted out, "That's preposterous!"

"Let me begin by telling you I do have some proof of a conspiracy," replied Paco. "Perhaps insufficient for a trial judge and a legally constituted jury, but certainly enough to satisfy a policeman's knowledge of criminal wrongdoing. Attempts to harm Ray Symington have been made at almost every stop on this trip. These episodes have varied from petty annoyances to possibly attempted murder. I believe I can also establish that the numerous attempts to harm Ray were not perpetrated by the same person. They were, in fact, planned in advance in a well-thought-out scheme."

"What do you mean by that?" demanded Joanne, while everyone watched Paco flip the pages of his spiral notepad.

"Ah, Joanne Whitman. Perhaps you don't remember that charming little row you caused in Denver the first night of the tour."

As she shook her head furiously, her disheveled, dirty-blond hair flopped from side to side. "I don't know what the hell you're talking about."

"The Mile-High Sportsmen's Inn? We all saw you try to slap your husband's boss in the Tailgate Restaurant."

Joanne sprang from her seat. "That's not fair! I had a little too much to drink, that's all."

"So be it then," Paco said. He turned to face the Whitmans. "Let's go back to that Friday night in Rock Springs, Wyoming--the Jackalope Cabins when Ray was scalded in the shower. That night I checked the hot and cold water valves outside at the back of the Symingtons' cabin. The cold water valve had been shut off. Naturally, that would force only hot water into the shower. I discovered a tangle of blue thread stuck to the cold water valve. The texture and color of the blue thread are consistent with the weave on your blue New York Giants cap, Gordon."

"That's ridiculous!" exclaimed Gordon. "There must be millions of Giant football fans with identical caps--maybe even more with caps that are similar."

"True. But you'll have to admit we're pretty far from the Giants' Meadowlands Stadium."

"Like Giant fans don't travel? You're really reaching, Paco, and I don't like it."

Paco's eyes, dark and penetrating as a crow's, remained fixed on his prey. He pulled a color photograph out of a manila envelope and held it up for Gordon and everyone else to see. "This is your cap, Gordon. It has a red ring of rust inside from that cold water valve handle. You placed your cap over the valve before you shut it off to avoid leaving fingerprints. I also managed to collect rust samples from both your hat and the faucet."

"You're a small-town cop, Paco. A nice guy, but no way are you a forensics expert," Gordon countered. "And without finger-prints you're nowhere."

"I have another fascinating bit of evidence that belongs to you," Paco continued. "A blue slip of paper that dropped out of your handkerchief in Jackson Park. Two things are written on it: 'Friday, 9/11' and 'Flaming Gorge.' A strange coincidence--the exact date and location of Ray's scalding. And by the way, the blue slip just happens to have the IMTC logo at the top." He paused to let this information sink in.

"But..." Paco said, "just so you won't feel I'm picking on you, Gordon, let's go to Saturday, the 12th. That seemed to have been a banner day for you people. Let's start with the ice water incident on the bus." He enjoyed the thick silence that permeated the air. Not a soul dared speak for fear of being accused. He turned toward the Moyers.

"Theo, you were the last one off the bus Saturday morning. And that afternoon, after we rotated seats, you sat directly across the aisle from Ray in row five. You seemed to enjoy his discomfort more than anyone else. You could easily have tucked the ice cubes into his seat."

Theo's gray eyes flickered with amusement. "You can't prove it, Paco, and besides, it was a harmless practical joke, no matter who did it. Ray's pants got soaked. So what?"

Paco parried the question with a new tack. "Okay, Theo. That same day we went to the Buffalo Bill Historical Center in Cody. Don't tell me you've already forgotten that you were nearly robbed. A blue slip of paper with the date 9/12 on it fell out of your purse during the robbery attempt. And surprise, surprise. The paper also has the IMTC logo on it."

Theo merely grinned with satisfaction.

Paco's eyes scanned the rows of seats. "We spent the rest of the day in Yellowstone. Our last stop was the Lower Falls. Joanne claims she saw LeRoy Milton try to push Ray off the scenic overlook."

"That's right!" Joanne cried out jubilantly. "I recognized him from that weird spider tattoo on his arm."

"She's a crazy bitch, that one," shouted LeRoy. "I was trying to save Ray's butt, and that's the thanks I get for it. Besides, I don't have any tattoos. See!" He bounded to his feet, rolled up the sleeves of his polo shirt, and extended his arms for all to see.

"Thank you," said Paco. "I think Joanne might have meant Monte's tattoo and mistaken him for you, LeRoy."

LeRoy nodded smugly and sat down. Monte tried to cover up the red scorpion splayed across his left bicep.

"Now," Paco continued, "let's proceed to Sunday morning at the Sagebrush Inn. When most of us were at breakfast, the stair banister just happened to collapse. Oddly enough, Thom, not Ray, fell down from the mezzanine onto a sofa."

"See, Paco?" Monte sneered. "There goes your conspiracy theory."

"Not quite, Monte. My wife discovered another one of those curious blue slips on her seat cushion in the bus. It had only two things written on it: 'Sunday, 9/13' and 'Yellowstone.' Now... George and Reba always precede us in the bus seating arrangements. Therefore, I can only assume that the note belonged to them."

"That's a mighty flimsy assumption," challenged George.

"Is it?" Paco asked. "Then hear this: All the bolts in that banister were loosened by your wrench, George—the one you carry on your key chain."

"Hey, Inspector LeSoto, you know damn well that all of us sales managers at IMTC carry one just like it."

"I understand that, George. But yours left its own signature. Some rather unique scoring marks on each bolt. Markings made by a practice of continually opening pop bottles with your wrench. You also left some doubt as to your intended victim. I think Thom's unscheduled visit to his room rescued Ray from that one." Paco shifted his gaze from George to the entire group. "Shall I go on, ladies and gentlemen?"

A tension-filled buzz lasting several minutes ended in abrupt silence. Paco took it as a cue to proceed. "Later the same day, at Old Faithful, Ray narrowly escaped a charging bison incited by Michelle's paper bag popping. So many witnesses to that incident."

"I was just having a little fun," said Michelle petulantly. "I wouldn't try to murder the guy in public, would I?" No one answered her as each one considered the matter. "Oh, so I'm still the ex-con. Just because I did three months' time for shoplifting when

I was twenty-five, you'll always think the worst of me. I'm not a murderer!" She shrank back into her seat.

"No one said you were," responded Paco.

Molly could hear his voice beginning to crack from all the talking. She handed him a water bottle. He took a swig and pressed on.

"Things got worse on Monday, September 14th, in Jackson. Symington's crutches were stolen in the men's room. Ray told me he thought the thief wore fancy boots. Monte, I should think those fine-tooled Wellingtons of yours would qualify. The Jackson Hole police found Ray's wallet on the men's room floor the same day and returned it, cash and credit cards intact. So, if the motive wasn't robbery, what was it?"

"You're saying I'm the only person in the world wearing Wellington boots? That's another load of your bullshit," Monte retorted.

Paco paused to take another long gulp of water while he surveyed the group, his eyes darting up and down the rows. "Tina, let's talk about you. Specifically, about you and Ray at the Mountain King Resort that evening. The rest of us were at the Covered Wagon Cookout and Wild West Show. But Ray seemed to have recovered enough from his mugging to have dinner with you. Gossip travels fast on this bus, Tina. I heard that the two of you got in the Jacuzzi after dinner and you roughed up Ray's family jewels--a price he paid dearly for exploring in all the wrong worlds."

With a graceful hand, Tina flipped her shoulder-length hair. "That crud had absolutely no scruples," she said. "He didn't know the meaning of no. He got what he deserved."

Paco shot back: "If he's dead, did he deserve that, too?"

Tina colored, then looked indignant. "No, of course not."

Her aunt, seated beside her, had at first smiled in total agreement. But now Hilda's heavily lined forehead creased in anxiety, as if her niece had talked too much.

"Let's move on to Tuesday, the 15th, the Snake River trip," Paco said. "Reba, I'm sure you remember when Ray almost fell overboard."

"How could I forget? I held his leg so he wouldn't fall in."

"Yes. Well, others who were in the raft thought you were doing something else: holding his leg up so high that it kept his head down in the river. Maybe a trifle too long, Reba?" Paco glanced up one side of the bus and down the other. Every ear, like a satellite dish, seemed tuned to what he had to say. "Another thing. Later you were using a certain piece of blue memo paper as a bookmark that bore the date and place of that so-called accident."

"Oh, yeah?" Reba lashed out. "Maybe that's because your angel-faced wife stole it from me! And then she bought me a new bookmark to pretend she didn't."

Molly's face turned pinker. "I can't imagine what you mean, Reba. The paper was lying on the lobby floor, and I just swooshed it up. It didn't have your name on it."

Paco smoothed the collar on his Western-style shirt and fingered the silver buckle of his new tooled-leather belt. He felt a spasm of discomfort at Reba's accusation, but decided to protect his wife by ignoring it.

"Let's proceed to Thursday's madness in Salt Lake City at the Grand Regency," he said. "Ray got sucked into the bottom of the hot tub."

"If he had been a gentleman and come to Harry's concert like everybody else, it wouldn't have happened," Caroline Sessions replied hotly.

"True, Caroline, but let's talk about the incident itself." Paco's eyes searched and found Moyer. "Thom, you removed the grating from the drain at the bottom of the hot tub. Then you turned the pump on to its super-high velocity, the cleaning position. Had I not gotten there in time, Ray surely would have drowned."

"Whoa!" Thom's mustache twitched as he replied. "You're not gonna hang that one on me. I wasn't anywhere near that switch."

"No?" asked Paco. "We've documented your 13-5E footprints in the boxwood garden at the base of the switch box."

A low-level din churned through the bus. No one bothered to watch the passing scenery: rust-colored and gray mountains; patchworks of red and yellow soil; round-eared succulents armed with green quills; and occasional reminders of humanity as they passed the towns of Rimrock, population 25, and Cottonwood, population 1,300. A hush returned when they realized Paco hadn't said a word in several minutes.

"Friday night Ray had a visit from a scorpion," Paco went on. "Only Loretta's quick thinking and her thorough disgust for those creatures foiled that attempt. I would have thought the arachnid a chance visitor, had it not been for the long, thin razor slit in Ray's tote bag. He pointed it out to me the next day. I can only guess at this one. It would take someone who didn't panic at the sight of a scorpion. Maybe that would be you, Michelle. I watched you toy with that spider on the bench at Old Faithful."

"Oh, no," Michelle gasped. "You're wrong. You're still picking on the ex-con."

"Am I?"

"Leave her alone," Monte demanded. "She couldn't do anything like that."

"And who could forget this past Saturday at the Added Ingredient?" asked Paco. "Eight of us got food poisoning. Symington, always the unpredictable one, chose not to eat his corn chowder and gave his portion to Molly. Unfortunately, it was her second bowlful, a double dose."

Tina tossed her head and interjected: "That could have been the restaurant's fault, Paco. Perhaps the kitchen used unclean equipment or the cream in the chowder was spoiled."

"I doubt it," he said. "I called the lab that analyzed the contents of Molly's stomach. They informed me that the corn chowder had been laced with a laxative, most probably magnesium hydroxide--better known as milk of magnesia."

Cries of "Oh, no!" sputtered through the group.

"And who do you plan to blame for that one?" asked Theo.

"It's been said that poison is a woman's weapon," Paco suggested.

LeRoy interrupted. "You've been reading too many mystery novels, Inspector."

Paco ignored him. "Because Loretta was first in line for the buffet, I can only conclude that Ray's own wife spiked the chowder."

"Shame on you. The woman's not here to defend herself," reminded Hilda.

"True enough," responded Paco. "But she was certainly the one with the best opportunity. She went through the dining room to make a phone call before the manager let the rest of us in. It turned out that only those who took chowder at the start of the line were affected."

"But why would Loretta save Ray from the scorpion the night before," asked Judge Harry, "and try to poison him the next day?"

"That's hard to say," replied Paco. "Maybe she reacted impulsively to a repulsive situation, and then again, maybe their relationship had undergone an emotional rift. We know they fought all the time."

"Paco, honey," Molly interrupted. "It looks like you got more criminals on this bus than the local whatsgow."

"Hoosegow?" he questioned.

"Uh-huh!"

"That's exactly the point I'm making, Molly. Ray may have been somewhat accident prone and altogether disliked for a long list of reasons, but the number of malicious acts perpetrated against him hardly suggests random occurrences."

"What are you suggesting, then?" demanded Judge Harry.

"It's more than a suggestion, Judge," responded Paco. "We have a widespread conspiracy here, although, for the life of me, I can't figure out how some of you are connected to each other."

"This theory of yours is ridiculous," sneered Thom.

"Is it now? You held a meeting last night, a select group

that included the four IMTC sales managers, an ex-circuit court judge, two college professors, and a widow from Rhode Island. Not to mention an assortment of spouses. Your stated purpose was business. Would you deny this, Mr. Moyer?"

"I don't suppose it would do any good," Thom said softly.

"That's enough, Thom," warned George. "Don't say another word. He doesn't have enough of anything to connect everyone."

"But I do, sir," corrected Paco. He held up four folded pieces of blue paper arranged as a playing hand.

Several of the listeners, with worried faces, rummaged through wallets and purses, then returned their attention to Paco. He slowly opened the first one and held it up for all to see. The IMTC logo at the top stood out prominently.

Paco read it aloud. "Friday, 9/11, Flaming Gorge." He gave the first slip to Molly and opened the second one in plain view. "Saturday, 9/12, Cody." He unfolded the next slip. "Sunday, 9/13, Yellowstone," Molly took the third slip from him while he unfolded the fourth one.

"Circumstantial, at best," cried George.

"Perhaps, but maybe it's a family affair. Oddly enough, they're all in what appears to be the same handwriting." Paco read on: "Monday, 9/14, Jackson."

"So what?" interrupted George. "Who cares whose handwriting it is? They're just dates and places. There isn't a single word on those memos that talks about criminal intent."

Paco continued. "I've deduced that these blue slips are a mere sampling of many more that were used in a blind lottery to harass Symington. But I keep asking myself why. What could the motive--or motives--possibly be? Why should so many of you band together to accomplish that end? Most, if not all, of these incidents were designed not to be fatal. My guess is that the more zealous of the group got carried away." Paco held up his notepad for everyone to see. "I see it as my duty to turn these facts over to the police at the inquiry."

Judge Sessions pulled himself stiffly to his feet and cleared his throat. The jowly sad-eyed bloodhound was about to hold court. "Paco, you seem to present an excellent case for conspiracy. But conspiracy to do what? Pranks and that kind of harassment are hardly more than misdemeanors. In my experience, the sheer number of participants and the totally unsubstantiated hearsay would not go very far toward building a prima facie case. Despite your elaborately constructed conclusions, I fail to see any connection to Symington's present whereabouts or his ultimate fate. That's what this inquiry is all about, isn't it?"

"I believe there is a connection to the missing man--and she's right on this bus," Paco declared. "George, what's your sister's name?"

"Huh? Cookie! But you already know that."

"I do, but I seem to recall that you've called her by her given name as well. It took a while for me to remember where I'd heard it before." Paco began working his way down the aisle, grasping each seat handle in its turn. He stopped at Cookie and Bess's row. "Your given name is Constance, isn't it?"

Cookie merely blinked in astonishment.

"Where are you going with this?" George demanded.

"Constance Adams? Cookie? Where's the locket you normally wear around your neck?"

Cookie's hand flew to her throat. Large tears oozed from her downcast eyes. "I don't know," she whimpered. "I seem to have lost it somewhere."

"Don't say any more, Constance," George bellowed.

"Okay," shrugged Paco, "have it your way, but wait until the rangers get wind of this." He returned to his seat.

As Lew guided the coach onto Arizona highway 17 south, a pall spread through the vehicle, row by row, like an infectious disease. Cookie stared out the window to avoid meeting the anxious eyes of her brother. Paco had generated a sense of fear among the passengers, making them all feel vulnerable and violated. The trip of a lifetime had taken a disastrous turn.

And just when morale had reached its lowest point, Jake

spoke up. "Inspector, you've accused almost everyone else on the bus of something. Should I feel slighted? Should I notify the Anti-Defamation League of your prejudice?"

Abby jabbed him in the ribs with her elbow. "That's not funny, Jake."

"See, you're against me, too," he grinned.

No one shared the humor. Glenn could feel their anxiety, and he was prepared for it. Years of leading these tours had taught him that each busload was a microcosm of a real-life community, and his leadership depended on more than just pointing out the hoodoos in Bryce Canyon. Dealing with emergencies required the skill of a psychologist. He grasped his microphone and began to speak.

"Folks, I realize all of this has been very traumatic for you. It is for Lew and me, too. So let's all try to relax as best we can and enjoy the last legs of our tour. Let's remember that being here, viewing these wondrous sights, is a gift we've all given ourselves.

"Now...we're approaching Montezuma Castle. The Sinagua farmers began building it in the twelfth century: a five-story, twenty-room dwelling set in a cliff a hundred feet above the valley. There's another structure nearby that's only a ruin now. It was once a six-story apartment with forty-five rooms. Close to 150 Sinagua lived in these villages for almost 300 years, but we'll only be here one hour."

Lew took the bus onto a narrow stretch of paved road and pulled up to the Montezuma Castle National Monument. He didn't release the pneumatic door until Ranger Long Feather had positioned himself beside it, checking off each person's name as he or she got off. However, not all the passengers debarked.

Paco and Molly sat down on a low wall to read the National Park Service pamphlet. Montezuma had never been anywhere near the monument. Early Native Americans, the Sinagua and Hohokam, created these adobe shelters set high into the cliffs to elude their enemies. They were farmers, making full use of the fertile soils along one tributary of the East Verde River. Early Spanish settlers mistakenly named it for the last Aztec emperor of Mexico.

Those who had remained aboard the bus requested that Lew and Glenn leave them alone for the duration of the stop. And so a meeting of conspirators took place and a compromise offering was prepared.

Forty-five minutes later, aboard a full moving bus, a spokesperson came forward. Thom picked up the mike. This vigorous, athletic man, who flashed his warm smile often and with ease, now looked somber and rather stiff.

"Inspector LeSoto," he began, "we beg your indulgence. As far as we know, Ray's alive and well, enjoying another one of his extramarital flings. We never intended any kind of harm. However, just to convince you, we're willing to take you into our confidence. We mapped out a two-pronged strategy. First, to get Symington to step down from his position as vice president at Indent Machine Tool Company. We had a plan for making this happen. We tried to get Ray to leave the tour midway through. Our CEO, Maynard Larchmont, had warned him that this was supposed to be a confidence-building, fence-mending trip, and Ray had to complete it successfully or his job would be in jeopardy."

"How did you know that?" Paco challenged. "Certainly, that would be a confidential matter between the CEO and Ray."

"Well...yes," Thom admitted reluctantly. He cleared his throat. "We obtained a copy of the memo Maynard sent Ray spelling it all out."

Paco scowled. "I'll bet you did."

Thom pretended not to hear the sarcasm and continued his defense. "Our second strategy was to force Ray to relinquish his stock interest in the company."

"The usual procedure is to offer an executive money for his stock--not physically strong-arm him," said Paco. "Is it not?"

"True enough," replied Thom. "But if he were unwilling to surrender the perks he enjoys as the sales vice president--the power, the money, the prestige--what then?"

"Why is it necessary that he step down?" Paco asked. "I assume he earned both the stock and position honestly."

"Your assumption is debatable," Thom declared. "Ray has stifled revenue and growth for years. His stupidity and criminal neglect have led to costly lawsuits, accidents, and even one death. At best, Ray is a difficult man to deal with. Plant morale is at its lowest point in years, and long-term customers are deserting us every month. You've called us a conspiracy. We prefer the term coalition, a coalition for the survival of IMTC. I grant you there might be a tiny fringe among us that desires a tad more justice or even a touch of vengeance."

"How can I condone the fact that your course has taken a violent path?" Paco interjected.

"The coalition shares one goal: Ray's early retirement. But I can assure you it's the only thing we've agree upon. Individuals, not the coalition, are responsible for each of the incidents you've described. We had hoped the incidents would frighten or mildly disable Ray into leaving the tour and coming to terms with us."

"This still doesn't whitewash the violence," Paco reiterated.

"I admit that not all of us are entirely business motivated," Thom said. "Some have personal axes to grind. Perhaps some of the others have gone a step too far."

Paco shook his head. "Thom, you still haven't shown me any reason why I shouldn't turn over what I've learned to the police investigative team at our hotel in Scottsdale."

Thom shot him an angry look, laid down the microphone, and dragged his size 13 feet to the seat next to Theo.

They still had ninety miles to go before reaching Scottsdale, their last stop.

Chapter 24
THE BANQUET
Same Day, Tuesday, September 22, 1981

ANXIETIES MOUNT AT THE END OF ANY GROUP JOURNEY—camaraderie about to be severed all too soon, shared experiences dissolved, excitement's rush braked. The thrill's pitch turns to a downer at the prospect of returning home to laundry, grocery lists, a job. But the last day of this tour loomed with a more unpleasant, even sinister anxiety for all of them: the police inquiry.

The tour bus sped through the rugged Sonoran desert. From her window Molly snapped the final shot on her last roll--Camelback Mountain, a massive brown lump in the desert landscape. As the camera rewound, she fretted. Had she taken enough pictures? Would she and Paco be able to identify every shot when they got home? Should she have savored the sights more, knowing they'd probably never be back? Were all the necessary gifts and souvenirs acquired? Not quite. She'd found a chew toy for Dr. Avi's golden, but nothing yet for Paco's macaws. Bird treats just didn't seem to figure in these shops.

When their bus finally parked and contritely knelt before Scottsdale's Cactus Garden Inn, Lew did not open the doors immediately. He waited for Ranger Long Feather to appear and board, as prearranged. Long Feather introduced himself and explained the procedures he expected them to follow. First, they would not be allowed to check into their rooms just yet. A groan of annoyance rippled through the rows.

"However," he said, "you will be allowed to have your farewell banquet, and that's where you're going right now." He led them into the Armadillo Dining Room.

"Let's enjoy our dinner, folks," Glenn encouraged. "You can order drinks from the Rattlesnake Bar and use the restroom facilities. But the remainder of the hotel is off limits, at least until the rangers complete the preliminary inquiry. It'll be held in the meeting room across the hall. They'll escort each of you there, in your turn."

"Some party that's gonna be," George snarled, his face beefy with anger. "And..." he added in a near-shout, "don't think I'm going to let my sister go in there alone!"

Snow-covered Mount Moran had displayed more warmth than their banquet room as they grudgingly took seats at round tables for eight. At first, even the crisp linens and crystal goblets, the baskets of fresh hot rolls and sweet butter failed to shake the gloom. But when it came time to take their beer, wine, and mixed drink orders, the white-jacketed waiters could hardly write fast enough. And by the time shrimp cocktail and salads had been consumed, all kinds of spirits had been lifted. That is, with two exceptions.

Bess Izaks shivered over a cup of weak tea, nearly nauseated with worry for her friend. And Paco, much as he longed for a cold Bud, downed a Coke instead. He wanted to keep a clear head.

Molly sipped her White Zinfandel, and her cheeks grew rosier, her mind lighter as her blue eyes darted from face to face, searching for something more among her fellow travelers. Her gaze settled on the Miltons. Ruth had just whispered something to Glenn. He nodded, and in turn, spoke to Ranger Long Feather, standing next to him.

Paco felt Molly nudging him, and together they watched the ranger lead the Miltons across the hall. Paco's right eyebrow shot up. Why were they being interrogated first? Was it voluntary? Ruth appeared so supremely confident.

The fluorescent lighting cast a sallow complexion over the meeting room. The Miltons encountered a second ranger seated across the table from them. Long Feather took a seat beside him. The second ranger rose from his chair.

"I'm Ranger Phil Platte, and you are...?"

"Ruth and LeRoy Milton." Ruth slid her lean body easily into a chair and reached to pull out the one beside her for LeRoy. She stopped suddenly. The motion had caused a stabbing pain in her left shoulder, and she winced as it traveled down her arm. Avoiding Platte's scrutinizing gaze, she poker-faced her angular features and arranged herself erect and alert.

LeRoy managed a pleasant smile, dimpling his chin. But under his bushy gray hair, the sharp lines at the outer corners of his eyes projected like arrows. "We have information for you, sir," LeRoy said. "But before we give it to you, we want your guarantee that you'll keep our names out of the investigation."

"Why should I do that?" Platte's index finger hovered above the PLAY button of a tape recorder in the center of the table.

Ruth's eyes fixed on the small machine. "Must you?" she asked, a hint of sarcasm in her voice.

"Yes, ma'am," Platte answered. "It's routine. For your protection as well as ours."

"But," she protested, "we're afraid of recriminations from others in the group."

"No promises. We'll try to keep your names out. But if there's a trial, all bets are off. Now...what do you know about Sunday night, September 20th?" He held his freshly sharpened pencil poised above a yellow legal pad.

The Miltons explained that around 11:30 they'd trekked to the lookout at Bright Angel Point.

"Oh?" Long Feather asked. "What were you doing out there so late? Were you dressed for it? It gets into the forties at that hour."

"Yeah, it was cold," LeRoy admitted. "But I couldn't sleep. We thought we'd get a look at the canyon in the moonlight."

"And did you?" Platte asked.

"Not exactly...We found the going on the trail a bit precarious. Narrow, with steep drop-offs on both sides. So we retreated into the woods behind a grove of pinon pine and sat down on a fallen oak. Never got any time to look at the scenery. We saw a woman and a man together at the overlook. First they were kissing. Then she shot him."

Platte's body jerked in reflex as if he himself had been hit. "Shot him? The woman had a gun?" He wrote furiously on his pad, while Long Feather stared at LeRoy in disbelief.

"Oh, yes," Ruth said smugly.

LeRoy elaborated. "They were having quite a shoving match. He was doing most of the pushing. The woman had something in her hand. It was strange. There were three clicks, loud cracking sounds that must have been gunfire, and flashes of light, too."

"Then what happened?" Platte asked.

"The man fell over the edge screaming. It was ghastly," Ruth said with an involuntary shudder. "You could hear the echoes in the canyon."

"What did you do then?" Platte asked.

"Uh...well, nothing," LeRoy said. "Right after the guy fell, we saw another man. He was running toward the woman. I think he had a fishing hat on. He tripped over some roots, it looked like. His hat fell off and he got down on his knees to find it and then he got up. He grabbed the woman, and we heard him yell at her, something about 'You crazy? You're not going to kill yourself if I can help it.' "

Ruth couldn't resist adding: "Would you believe she wasn't even grateful? She smacked him across the face!"

"Oh?" interjected Long Feather. "What happened next?"

Under the rangers' steady gazes, LeRoy began breathing heavily. "Then the woman left. She ran up the trail toward the lodge--back to her cabin, I would guess."

"Did you see her face? Did you recognize her?" Platte challenged.

"We did, sir," Ruth said triumphantly. "It was Cookie Adams. She didn't see us, though."

Platte scribbled an occasional note on his pad to link the voices with the tape. Looking up, he asked, "What about the guy in the hat?"

"He stayed at the overlook for a minute and picked up what looked like a blanket the woman left behind and some kind of a stick, maybe a walking stick," LeRoy said. "He took a path around the far side of the ledge so we didn't get to see who he was."

Platte nodded as he wrote. "So...You saw a man fall into the canyon." His eyes darted from Ruth to LeRoy and back. "Did you notify the authorities?"

LeRoy licked his dry lips. "No."

"Did you tell anyone?"

"No."

"Why not?"

"We were afraid to get involved," Ruth interjected smoothly. "It...it was so dark, just moonlight. We didn't want to falsely accuse anyone."

Platte tried to conceal his disgust. "Anything else?"

They shook their heads.

Long Feather stood. "I'll escort you back to the banquet now."

LeRoy's heart tom-tommed in his chest. The Miltons rose and left the room. They moved out into raucous laughter and the clinking of silverware on plates in the banquet room.

Long Feather selected Cookie Adams as the next person to be questioned. Cookie lowered herself into a straight-backed chair at the long wood table across from the two rangers. She sat with her full lips pressed stubbornly into a thin line as she glanced at her new surroundings. Framed prints by Georgia O'Keeffe, Rosa Bonheur, and other Southwest artists studded the walls, but even their brilliant colors didn't alter her grim mood.

"I want my brother here," she demanded.

Platte pressed the STOP button on the recorder and sent Long Feather to fetch George.

Emboldened by scotch and soda, Hurles bulled through the door. He pulled up a chair as close to his sister as he could and whispered in her ear, behind a cupped hand. "Only tell them the bare minimum, Sis."

Cookie nodded and waited for the questions to come.

"Ms. Adams, is your given name Constance?" asked Long Feather.

"Yes," she whispered.

Platte spread a gold locket and broken chain on the table before her. "Is this yours?" When she hesitated, he popped the clasp on the locket to reveal the inscription inside.

"Yes," she admitted as her right hand flew to her collarbone.

"Then I suppose you remember where you lost it," plied Long Feather.

"I suppose so." Cookie's voice trembled through the words. She began to shake uncontrollably.

"Would that have been somewhere on the rim of the lookout at Bright Angel Point?" Platte leaned over Cookie, his eyes drilling into hers. "Could you have lost it during a scuffle with Ray Symington? A scuffle that ended with you pushing him over the edge to his death?"

"It didn't happen that way!" she cried. Then, abruptly, her demeanor changed to defiance. She squared her shoulders and met Platte's stern gaze with a why-are-you-doing-this-to-me stare.

"Then, Ms. Adams, I think it would be best for all concerned if you would tell us exactly what did happen out there on Bright Angel Point Sunday night."

"You don't have to tell them anything, Sis," George bellowed at her protectively. "The recorder is running, you idiot! You could incriminate yourself. They don't have a thing on you."

"That's enough, George," she wailed. "It was all a horrible mistake. None of it should have happened."

Platte broke in. "You're not under arrest as yet. But perhaps your brother is right, Ms. Adams. An attorney might be appropriate at this time if you think there's a chance you might incriminate yourself. Do you understand?"

"Damn it, Sis. He's giving you a break!"

"I can't take this any longer. I want to make a clean breast of things."

Her exasperated brother covered his flushed face with his hands.

Cookie meted out the meager details of her rendezvous with Ray as if she were handing out Halloween candy--a few hoarse words at a time. She and Ray had met unexpectedly late at night in the North Rim general store...Loretta had locked him out of their cabin...Cookie had been sympathetic...they'd talked and walked some. She had let Ray kiss her at the overlook, and when he pressed for more, she pushed him away. She'd only meant to frighten him. His falling had been a horrible accident.

Long Feather turned to Cookie. "Ms. Adams, why did you want to frighten Ray Symington? What did you hope to accomplish by scaring him?"

Suddenly, Cookie broke into anguished sobs. Her body seemed to shrink into her turtleneck sweater.

"Ranger Long Feather," George said grimly, "I can explain this for my sister."

Platte held up one hand. "Mr. Hurles, I should also remind you of your rights. You have the right to remain silent. Anything you say can and will be used against you in a court of law. You also have the right to an attorney..."

"Yeah," George agreed gruffly, "I know, but I'm volunteering to tell you this. It might help Cookie's case."

"Your choice," Long Feather replied. "Go on."

"I introduced Constance to Skip. They got married, and worked together for a time at Indent Tool. Then, when Skip left to go out on his own, she went to work for him in his shop. She continued to work for him until he was murdered."

"Did you say murdered?"

"Yes, murdered," George replied. "But the courts didn't see it that way. Skip bought an automatic punch machine from IMTC. Ray Symington--that power-hungry, incompetent moneygrubber--claimed he knew how to assemble it. Ray was nothing more than a two-bit salesman then. In an effort to save the installer's fee and get his commission faster, he did the job himself. The bastard forgot his wrench and left it inserted on the back side of the rotator platform, where it couldn't be seen. Well, when Skip turned on the machine for the first time, the rotator automatically swung around to the initial operating position. As it did, Symington's wrench flew off and struck Skip in the temple. My brother-in-law died two days later." George's voice broke. "He wasn't just my sister's husband. He was my buddy."

"I'm sorry," said Long Feather. "It's a terrible way to lose a husband and friend. What did the courts say?"

"They denied our claim for criminal negligence. That weasel Symington convinced the jury that Skip did the installation himself. Testified that Skip was impatient and couldn't wait for the company installer. Even went so far as to say he warned Skip against going ahead with it. This was a total lie. But Ray's a very persuasive guy. He committed perjury and got away with it." George swallowed hard. "Cookie and her lawyer read chapter and verse from the company's policy manuals, specifying that the machine was to be professionally installed. No way would Skip have done it himself--he knew it would invalidate the machine's warranty. He wasn't even in a hurry for the machine. It wasn't a rush order. He had no need to be his own installer."

"So there was no award, then?" Platte asked.

George shook his head. "IMTC offered to pick up court costs and made a token $5,000 good will gesture. She was forced to take both. It was that or nothing."

Ranger Platte probed. "Wasn't Symington your boss?"

"Yeah."

"Mr. Hurles, why would you continue to work for a man you have so much anger toward? Why didn't you switch jobs?"

George shook his head. "Sometimes I wonder about that myself. I've looked, but we're in a specialized business. The right opportunity just hasn't come up."

Long Feather resumed the interrogation. "You led Ray to

the overlook to kill him, didn't you, Ms. Adams? So you could control him, drive him to the edge to his death."

"Not true! Our meeting in the general store was happenstance. The thought actually crossed my mind," Cookie admitted in a plaintive voice. "But I just couldn't do it. We had wrapped ourselves in the blanket we'd bought at the general store. He kissed me and I tried to back away from him, but he lost his balance and grabbed my locket chain. It broke. Then he slipped and fell over the edge. I can still hear him scream--that awful scream."

George rose from his seat and leaned over his sister. "Sorry, Sis, I just couldn't find the locket in the dark. Maybe if I'd gotten there a little sooner or looked a little harder...I'm so very sorry, sweetheart." Cookie squeezed his hand and allowed it to slip free. She understood. He moved back out of the way.

Platte nodded in mock sympathy. "What did you do with the gun, Ms. Adams?"

Anger flashed lightning bolts from Cookie's wet eyes. "What gun? I've never owned a gun in my life. I'd be afraid to even touch one."

George barked a sardonic laugh. "My little sister with a gun? That's the most ridiculous thing I've ever heard."

Ranger Platte looked Cookie squarely in her doe-like brown eyes. "Two witnesses say they saw you there with a gun."

"That's impossible. What two witnesses?"

"I'm not free to say right now," Platte replied.

"We want a lawyer," George boomed, pounding the table with his fist. "She's innocent. You can't hold her and treat her like this!"

"Of course we can hold her. For murder or manslaughter. She had motive and opportunity. At the very least, she was a material witness in an accidental death. I'm running the investigation here. I suggest you get her a lawyer now if you're so inclined. I intend to read her her rights now." Platte leaned forward to emphasize his authority.

"I will, damn it, as soon as you let me get to a phone. Then

I intend to post bail!" George rose and leaned his burly frame across the table and thrust his face, now the color of his red flannel shirt, within an inch of Platte's.

Platte lowered his chin to his chest to avoid the boozy breath. He stood up to disengage from the ongoing tango of confrontation. "Calm down, Mr. Hurles, take your seat. We're just following procedure here, just trying to find out what happened."

George sank reluctantly back into his chair as Platte droned through the Miranda cautions.

Cookie had stopped crying by now. Abruptly, her tragic expression switched. "Gentlemen, I need to talk to Bess Izaks. We're traveling together. May I have some time alone with her?"

Platte and Long Feather exchanged uncertain looks. "Unless Ms. Izaks is an attorney," Platte replied, "I don't think we can allow complete privacy. But I don't see any reason why the two of you shouldn't have a brief consultation. We'll stand just inside the door where we can keep an eye on the two of you."

"George," Cookie said, "you've been a doll, you can go have your dinner now." She hugged him tearfully.

At the LeSotos' table in the banquet room, the waiter arrived with their dinner plates balanced up his left forearm. He looked about to see who ordered what.

Molly couldn't wait to help him out. "Mine's the 'talian special, chicken pam and john."

Paco grinned. Damn, he still couldn't tell if she was serious or fooling around with her words.

George took his place at their table. "Bess," he said curtly. "You're up. Cookie's across the hall and wants to see you. The rangers said they'll allow it."

"Oh, dear, really? I guess I'd better go then." Bess's skinny knees knocked together as she stood, and her trembling hands brushed against her water goblet, splashing a few drops onto her half-eaten roll. Befuddled, she took several steps, then returned for her purse. She eventually made it to the door, where Long Feather assisted her across the hall.

"Ms. Izaks, let me check your purse," Long Feather said. "Turn completely around once for me, then you can join your friend."

"Oh, dear," Bess trilled. "Oooooo, am I being frisked, young man? How exciting!"

"Not exactly, ma'am," Ranger Long Feather said, suppressing a smile. He left them together.

A disheveled Cookie rose. "Oh, Bess, they think Ray Symington's dead and they're blaming me. But it was an accident."

Bess cringed. "What? That's outrageous. You a murderer?"

Cookie raled a major sob, and the tears streamed forth. A confused and sorrowful Bess had no alternative but to embrace her close friend of fifteen years. She cried, too.

Cookie pleaded. "Oh Bess, please believe me. I didn't kill him. It was an accident. He fell from the overlook at Bright Angel Point on his own. It's important to me that you, of all people, believe in me."

Bess looked miserable. "I guess I do, Cookie, I believe you. But how can I help you?"

"The rangers say they have two witnesses claiming they saw me shoot Ray. But I didn't! I don't have gun. You know I don't. I just wanted to tease him to the brink of the canyon and make him suffer, too. I had no idea he'd go over the edge. Maybe he'd had a few drinks." She emitted a sigh of hopelessness. "But I suppose it's my fault anyway. I wish I knew who the witnesses were."

"It's not too hard to guess," said Bess. "The only couple I've seen leave the farewell party to be questioned were the Miltons. Must be them."

"The Miltons! I never saw them out at the overlook. I wonder where they were hiding. And why squeal on me, of all people?"

"Maybe...just maybe the Miltons want you out of the way for that little hassle I got into with them in Denver," Bess suggested.

"You think so?"

"And just maybe we can mess with their game," declared Bess with a new set to her chin.

Cookie called over to the rangers. "We're done now, gentlemen."

Platte turned a straight-backed chair around and straddled it.

"So what gives, ladies?"

"Ranger Platte," Cookie began, "I've cooperated with you completely in the hopes that you can find a way to show me some leniency. What if I told you I can help you solve another crime--one I'm not involved in. Would it help my cause?"

"Possibly. Please note, I'm turning the recorder back on. What's the nature of this crime?"

A light seemed to turn on in Cookie's head. "You know what? I'd like Inspector Paco and Molly to be here to hear this. Maybe it'll put them on my side."

Platte scowled at the stalling, but ordered Long Feather to call the LeSotos in. A moment later they appeared, Molly's cherub face a bit sulky. She hadn't finished her dinner yet. She took a seat at the long table, but Paco ambled over to Ranger Platte and murmured to him, "I'm not sure why Cookie wants Molly and me here. Maybe just for moral support—Molly's, anyway."

"No problem," Platte replied. Then he turned to Cookie. "Let's have it, Ms. Adams. What've you got for us?"

"This has nothing to do with the murder investigation," Cookie replied. "But Bess and I have information about a crime committed by a couple on this tour. A bank robbery--maybe even more than one. Bess, why don't you tell them? You actually saw the money."

"I'd love to," said Bess, flushing with the excitement of being center stage. "They put it in their suitcase."

"Pardon me for interrupting," Paco said. "But who are 'they' and what is 'it'?"

Bess trilled, "The Miltons robbed a bank in Denver. All the money they stole is in their luggage."

Molly's eyes widened. Her pam and john could wait.

"The Miltons," Platte repeated flatly. "How do you know?"

"I saw it in one of their bags. Packets of big bills. New ones, too, all fifties and twenties. Looked pretty strange to me. Most people have credit cards and, um, traveler's checks when they go on a trip. The bills were in those little mailing boxes, the kind you get at the post office. Only they said Flite-Ex or something like that on them."

Paco's right eyebrow shot north. But he said nothing. He and Platte exchanged glances, then Platte asked, "Just how and when did you have the opportunity to see all this money, Miss Izaks?"

Bess pressed her lips together, then continued in a rush of importance. "It was the first morning, sir. Of the tour, I mean. After breakfast I went back to our room to brush my teeth like I always do. I brush after every meal, I do. Floss, too. Our bags were still out in the hall, waiting to be put on the bus. I'd tucked my cosmetic kit in my big suitcase, in the outside pocket. So I unlocked it, unzipped it." Bess took a deep breath, then twittered, "But I got mixed up. I undid the wrong bag. My key fit it. This other one, it was just like mine--black with a Vermilion tag, only it was next door. And when I stuck my hand in, feeling around for my cosmetics bag, I felt these boxes instead. So I got curious and I opened one--just the end flaps, you know, and I saw all that money. I opened a second one, too. It had even more. I saw thousands."

Platte looked quizzically at Cookie, who explained that all this had happened at the Mile-High Sportsmen's Inn in Denver.

"What did you do then?" Platte asked Bess.

"I zipped and locked everything back up and went to my own bag next door."

"Did you tell anyone?" he asked.

"Only Cookie. She didn't seem to think it so strange until we read about it in the Denver paper."

"Read about what?" Ranger Platte looked annoyed.

Bess began wringing her small gnarled hands and glanced

at her friend for help.

Cookie came to her rescue. "A robbery at Alpine State Bank, one of the suburban branches."

"Why didn't you report it to the police?" Platte asked.

"It was just a suspicion," Cookie protested. "Didn't have any proof, didn't want to get involved 'cause it might have interfered with the tour."

"How did you find out it was the Miltons?" he asked. "Did you see their name on the luggage label?"

"No, I...I don't remember," Bess piped up. "When I finished brushing, Mrs. Milton, she knocked on our room door. LeRoy, he was standing behind her. Anyway, Mrs. Milton was holding a purse. She asked me if it was mine. It was! I was so embarrassed! I did a dumb thing. I'd dropped it on the floor next to their suitcase. It had my whole life in it, my wallet, everything. Well, the Miltons, they returned it to me, with my wallet and all, and I thanked them. Actually, they were quite pleasant."

"Was that the end of it?" Paco pushed.

"Oh, yes," Bess replied. "At first, I was so scared, terrified even, but then Cookie and I got to thinking, why would somebody rob a bank and then return a purse with a lot of money in it?"

Platte pursued the questioning until he was satisfied with all the details. Then, turning to his colleague, he said, "I believe this is a matter for the FBI." He thanked Bess and the LeSotos and motioned for Long Feather to escort them back to the banquet room.

But Paco stayed behind as Bess and Molly left with the ranger. Cookie sat silently on the opposite side of the table, periodically dabbing at her damp eyes while Platte phoned the local FBI office. He was still on the phone when the second ranger returned to the room.

Long Feather was surprised to see that Paco had emptied his pockets onto the table. A second tape recorder, two cassettes, two pocket-sized spiral pads filled with scribbled notes, and several photographs had caught his attention, but he waited for Platte to finish his call first.

Platte hung up the phone and turned to Long Feather. "Agent Emilio Martinez from the FBI is on his way over to cover the bank robbery aspect."

"What's all of this stuff," Long Feather asked.

Paco showed the rangers his gold detective's shield and accompanying identification. "It's information that might have a bearing on the Ray Symington case. It'll make more sense if you listen to the tapes first."

Platte nodded and depressed the PLAY button. The four people in the room listened intently to the revelations on the bus for the next twenty-five minutes. At the tapes' end Platte depressed the STOP button and began studying Paco's notes and photos.

"Now that I've had the opportunity to scan your stuff and listen to the cassettes, they seem to document all the suspicious events you and your wife encountered along the way leading up to the murder--that is, the alleged murder. Plus the photos you indexed in the notes. Obviously, you suspected foul play all along."

"That's what led me to begin the note-taking."

"And you did nothing to try to stop it?" asked Platte, his look stony. "You could have brought the police in earlier."

Paco's neck began to feel clammy under his collar. "Ray Symington insisted that we leave the police out of it. He did solicit my protection, but I had to turn him down."

"You refused to help him?"

"It's not like that," replied Paco. "He wanted a bodyguard. I'm a semi-retired, off-duty detective. No jurisdiction here, no backup. I even suggested to Ray that he leave the tour, but he refused that, too. Besides, I told him I'm on my honeymoon with a first duty to my bride."

"Take it easy, Inspector. I'm not accusing you of dereliction of duty."

The two men glared at each other, with Paco feeling very much on the defensive. "There were many incidents directed only at Ray, where the rather sketchy clues either led nowhere or pointed at an increasing number of suspects. Some of the incidents seemed more like practical jokes. My notes contain the conclusions I've drawn from them."

"I see, Inspector. And the audio cassettes?"

"I used the recorder to tape a running dialogue of the trip between Sedona and here. I questioned everybody on the bus. That is, everybody I felt was relevant to this case. I hope you don't think I've overstepped my bounds. The cassettes establish that a conspiracy existed to remove Symington from his position at Indent Machine Tool Company. Of course, I did manage to establish the owner of the locket. And there you have it, sir."

"Not quite, Inspector. It would appear that we have eye and ear witnesses to the killing. However, there are some major discrepancies in their stories."

"Who are the witnesses?" asked Paco. "And what's the difficulty?"

"I'm not at liberty to say who and what. For one thing, two witnesses are claiming that Ms. Adams here shot the victim. But she insists she didn't have a gun."

Paco looked stunned. He'd been thrown a curve. As precisely as he'd taken his notes, as carefully as he had observed, nothing about a gun had come up. He shook his head in embarrassment. "If she had a gun, I know nothing about it."

"Could she have used your piece?"

"My piece? I don't carry. Rarely ever have. Platte, I don't know where you're going with this."

"You own a piece, don't you?"

"Actually, I own a whole lot of guns. My service revolver, of course, but it's locked up at home. Along with my antique gun collection."

"You're saying you don't have a piece with you?"

"Not exactly. As I said before, I don't carry, but I did purchase a Colt Peacemaker from an antique dealer in Jackson Hole. I don't suppose that's what you're referring to."

"It might be. Is it in working order?"

"I really don't know. The dealer said it was, but I hadn't planned on test-firing it until I got home and cleaned and inspected it myself. I can show it to you if you like. It's still in the dealer's wrappings."

"I'd appreciate your bringing it by."

"Of course. You'll see that it hasn't been fired recently. In fact, it's still covered in Cosmoline."

"Okay, Inspector," said Platte. "I'll restudy this stuff of yours. I'd like to lock up every last one of your alleged conspirators, but I'm afraid most of what you have is circumstantial. Collectively, you've managed to put together quite a conspiracy theory, but there's little substance to prosecute with." He gathered up the notes, then held the cassettes between his thumb and forefinger. "I'll have to hang onto your notes and these tapes as potential evidence, though it's debatable whether they would be admissible in court, because the tour group didn't know they were being recorded. In fact, Paco, I consider your actions aboard the bus reprehensible. You may have jeopardized any opportunity to prosecute that bunch. I'll be in touch if I have any more questions. Meanwhile, I now have two crimes to solve, so if you'll excuse me."

Paco, humiliated and upset, left the room.

Long Feather handcuffed Cookie and led her away into custody.

Ranger Platte continued to question members of the Vermilion tour for the next hour and a half and by the time the last person had been interviewed, the waiters had already begun serving eclairs, napoleons, and coffee. The desserts set the stage for speeches, toasts, tour company pitches, address exchanges, and farewells. The mood had grown festive and sentimental, despite the circumstances.

Finally, the preliminary inquiry over, Ranger Platte entered the banquet room and gave a short speech, cautioning the group not to discuss the case with anyone, even among themselves. He told them they would be receiving formal interrogatories in the mail and he saw no reason why they shouldn't resume their tour schedule. Glenn handed out their room keys, allowing them to retire for the night.

Shortly after Special Agent Emilio Martinez arrived at the hotel, Ranger Platte advised him of Bess Izaks' statement. Martinez interviewed her personally and then decided to seek a bench warrant to search the Miltons' room and luggage. It was almost midnight when a second agent returned from the U.S. Magistrate's house with the warrant. Emilio reluctantly decided to wait till morning to conduct the search, but to be on the safe side, he posted the second agent outside the Miltons' hotel room door throughout the night.

Paco, Molly, and Bess rose early Wednesday morning and waited with the rangers in the little meeting room used for the inquiry the previous night. The two FBI agents knocked on the Miltons' door and confronted LeRoy with the warrant.

LeRoy studied the document with a puzzled look on his face. "Aren't you guys investigating a murder? I don't understand this. What's this search all about?"

Nobody answered him. Veins pulsed in LeRoy's forehead as he and Ruth were told to sit on the bed and wait.

The FBI agents each opened a suitcase and began picking meticulously through the Miltons' belongings. Minutes went by. The only sounds in the room were zippers being opened and closed, plastic bags of underwear and socks dismantled, and LeRoy's anxious breathing. Ruth sat with her arms crossed defiantly and a look of contempt in her expression. Fifteen minutes later...nothing. Not a single small packet containing bills, not even a stray fifty or twenty. The two agents exchanged sheepish looks.

Emilio frowned. "Start with the dressers and search the entire room. The stuff's got to be here somewhere."

After forty-five minutes, LeRoy's tone turned from confused to indignant. "Either you tell me what the hell this is all about or get out of here and leave us alone."

Emilio motioned for the other agent to leave. "I'm terribly sorry for the intrusion. We were given good reason to believe you were carrying the proceeds of a major felony. We won't disturb you any longer. Thank you for you cooperation." He closed the door behind him and quick-stepped to catch up with his colleague down the hall.

The moment the meeting room door opened, Paco could see frustration written on Martinez's face. Emilio pulled up a chair and confronted Bess once more. "Miss Izaks, are you positive you saw those mailers full of money?"

"I did, I did," she fluttered. "I opened at least two--all fifties and twenties and the like."

Paco faced her squarely. "You're sure the bag belong to the Miltons? Think hard, Bess. How did you find out it was their bag?"

"Well, I...I assumed it was theirs when they knocked on the door to return my purse. They said their room was next to ours." Tears rolled down her crinkly cheeks. "How was I supposed to know it was somebody else's?"

Molly gently patted Bess on the back and whispered, "We all make mistakes."

"But I accused them," Bess whined.

"Do you remember which room the bag was in front of?" asked Paco.

"It was next door to us on the same side of the sixth floor."

"Closer to the elevator or farther away?" Agent Emilio asked.

"Closer, I think," replied Bess.

"I see," said Emilio, making a few notes. "Do you remember your own room number?"

"I think it was 627," replied Bess. She wished Cookie were here.

"But you're not sure," he posed.

"We've been in a lot of rooms since then."

"I understand that," reassured Emilio.

"Can I go now, sir?" asked Bess.

"Yes, we're done, for now, anyway." Molly put her arms

around Bess and led her away to her room.

"Sorry, Emilio," said Paco. "But I suppose it was just too good a lead to pass up."

"We might be able to make something of the robbery yet. A phone call to the Mile-High Sportsmen's Inn should tell us whose room was next to Bess's." He curtly waved Paco off and began dialing the phone on the table.

The door opened, and Molly entered. She sensed the chilly atmosphere. Noting that her normally confident husband looked deflated, she shrewdly decided not to press him.

He steered her out of the room. "Come on, Mol," he said grimly. "Wasn't there some serious souvenir shopping you wanted to do?"

"Yes, for Bobble and Fumble. They'll squawk like crazy if we don't bring them a present. But first there's something I've always wanted to do."

"What's that, sweetheart?"

"I'd like to sit in the lobby of this fancy-shmancy hotel and watch the hoity toity go by--just for a half-hour or so. Do you mind, honey?"

"Of course not, dear. I'll join you." Paco had nothing else to do.

Chapter 25
STOLEN DREAMS
Day Fourteen, Wednesday, September 23, 1981

INSIDE THE VAULT OF THE SCOTTSDALE PIONEER BANK, the sweet smell of a chloroform derivative lingered. A woman in a business suit lay unconscious on the floor. Duct tape covered her mouth and bound her wrists and ankles. Only moments before, the assistant manager had cheerfully opened a customer's safe deposit box. It stood empty now, leaning halfway out of its niche. At the back of the vault, a woman in a shapeless dress and support hose feverishly opened cash boxes usually reserved for the bank's own use. She wore white cotton gloves, and within minutes, transferred almost $80,000 into a roomy University of Arizona tote bag. With great care, she arranged two skeins of beige yarn and a pair of steel knitting needles over the packets of bills, then knelt down to place a ring of keys in the assistant manager's bound hands. Before departing, she checked her reflection in the stainless steel door, using it as a mirror to smooth her tightly bunned blue-white hair.

"Thank you, dearie," Alice said aloud to the figure on the floor. "You have a real nice day now, y' hear?" She left the vault and shuffled out the front door, nodding pleasantly over her granny glasses to the lone teller.

Only one other patron remained in the bank, a man in jeans and straw sun hat. The teller watched him at the counter on the far wall as he hunched over a deposit slip--or was it a withdrawal slip? He replaced the chained ballpoint pen in its holder, pocketed his paperwork, and departed without conducting business.

Turning left just outside the door, then left again at the

corner, the man in the straw hat spotted the white-haired lady. He quickened his pace to catch up with her, and the two disappeared into the clusters of tourists in Old Town Scottsdale. They mingled with the shoppers ambling along the picturesque streets, studded with art galleries and expensive crafts. Three blocks later, the couple sauntered into a small shaded park and wound their way through its cypress trees and succulent shrubs covered with purple blossoms. Passing behind a huge bronze sculpture of three rearing horses, the duo emerged from the park on the opposite side. Walking briskly for another three blocks, they crossed the street and entered the Cactus Garden Inn.

At the concierge desk the couple retrieved two large shopping bags, then traversed the vast carpeted lobby. They never noticed the LeSotos seated nearby on a sofa between two stucco columns.

"Paco!" Molly whispered, nudging him with her elbow. "See that couple going into the bathrooms?"

"Yeah. So?"

"There's something familiar about them, but I can't put my thumb in it."

He shook his head. "I think you're mistaken. They look like a lot of old people." He chuckled. "Older than us, anyway."

Ten minutes passed. Ruth Milton came out of the ladies' room carrying a shopping bag. Looking stylish in a pastel pants suit, she drifted over to the men's room door and stopped.

Molly started to wave and call hello, but Paco covered her hand and shushed her into silence. "Wait, hon! Let's see what's happening here."

The men's room door slowly opened, but only partway. Nobody came out. Instead, Ruth moved to the door and passed her shopping bag to an outstretched hand inside. Casually, she stepped aside and waited for several more minutes. The door swung open, and LeRoy emerged in khakis and T-shirt. He carried two sizeble cardboard boxes bearing mailing labels. LeRoy joined his wife, and they crossed the lobby.

To Paco the cartons looked freshly assembled. When Molly shot him a triumphant look, he murmured, "You were right, hon, that's why they looked so familiar. Now...do me favor, babe. Go into the ladies' room and tell me if anyone is still in there. Hurry!"

Molly entered the ladies' room, then almost immediately reappeared. She motioned to Paco with chubby thumbs down. He darted into the men's room, looked around quickly, and came out. "It was them," he whispered. "Let's go." He hooked her arm in his and led her around the perimeter of the lobby, scanning the lounge chairs and sofas, looking for the Miltons. He spotted them at the concierge desk.

Paco guided Molly to the reception counter ten feet away, and was about to ask the clerk to ring Agent Martinez's room, but he didn't have time. Watching the Miltons in his peripheral vision, he saw the cartons sitting on the concierge desk as LeRoy talked with a bellhop. Hastily, Ruth and LeRoy each picked up a box and walked toward the revolving door that led to the street.

Paco made an instant decision. "I'm going to follow them, hon. See if you can reach Martinez. Explain everything. I think our friends are headed for the nearest post office or mailing service."

"Be careful, sweetiekins," she whispered. "Lots of traffic out there. It's ferocious crossing the street. And what if they're armored?"

Paco suppressed a smile. "I doubt that they're carrying guns." He squeezed her shoulder and left.

Ruth and LeRoy pushed the revolving door around and stepped onto the sidewalk. As soon as Paco saw them turn left, he exited via an automatic glass door to the side street. Keeping a discreet distance, he tailed them.

In the Cactus Garden lobby, Molly tried to figure out her next move. Where were the Miltons going? Then she had an idea that took her to the bellhop at the concierge desk.

"Excuse me, but do you remember the couple with the two boxes? They were here about five minutes ago."

"Yes, ma'am, they were looking for a mail service."

"Oh. They're my friends and we're supposed to have dinner together. Do you know if they're coming back here?" asked Molly.

The young bellhop nodded. "Yes, ma'am. They left their luggage with us. Said they'd be back in a half-hour. They went to Mail Station Ltd. Three blocks down on your left at the corner."

Happily armed with this new intelligence, Molly returned to the reception desk and asked the clerk to ring Agent Martinez's room. Shifting from foot to foot, she checked her watch, grateful when the clerk motioned for her to pick up the house phone.

His response was brusque. "Got something for me?"

"Yessiree." Molly drew in a long breath, preparing to give him the details, but Martinez told her to "hang tight," he'd be right down. He was on his way to assist the local police in investigating a new bank robbery.

Molly bristled with excitement as she met Martinez at the elevator doors. "We think the Miltons might've made another bank hoist. Paco's following them now." She told him how they had emerged from the restrooms where only an elderly couple had entered minutes before. How they left the hotel with two large boxes. And, finally, where they were headed.

"Maybe I shouldn't adventure an opinion," she added, "but I betcha Bess actually saw the money from the first robbery, and they've been using the mails to send it home. I betcha they're your bank robbers in this case, too."

"Thank you, Mrs. LeSoto. I've got to go now. Another agent's waiting for me out front."

"I'll join you," she said.

"Sorry, I can't allow it. You might get hurt."

Her face fell.

"You've been a real help," he added hastily, and disappeared through the revolving door.

As the Miltons entered Mail Station Ltd., two women browsed through the greeting cards. Along the right-side wall, a man fingered through letters he'd just removed from his rented postal box. Ruth and LeRoy headed for the service counter at the rear, making their way down a narrow aisle between overloaded modular shelving units.

In five minutes the Miltons completed the transactions for their two packages. But the clerk proved overly talkative as he adhered the postage to each wrapping. Ruth watched, impatient and agitated. Equally antsy, LeRoy helped himself to a drink from the bottled water cooler that sat in the corner beside the service counter.

From inside a trinket shop next door, Paco waited and watched for the police. When he saw an unmarked cruiser pull up diagonally to the curb, he realized Molly had made contact with Martinez. Emilio and another FBI agent leaped out, and Paco greeted them on the sidewalk: "The Miltons are inside."

Emilio nodded. "Wait out here," he ordered. They entered the store just as the man left with his mail. The second agent ushered the only two browsers from the store, then he and Emilio approached the counter. They arrived just after the clerk had placed the two packages in a bin on the floor behind him.

"Well, well," Emilio said in a pleasant tone, "if it isn't Mr. and Mrs. Milton."

LeRoy wheeled around. Ruth's mouth gaped open.

Emilio's voice turned cold. "The search warrant presented to you this morning is still in effect, so if you'll empty your pockets, please, and put everything on the counter in front of you."

Too stunned to even reply, they submitted to a pat-down until he was satisfied that no weapons were in their possession.

Then LeRoy let loose. "Martinez," he shouted, "this is outright harassment. I'll sue the shirt off your back. You already searched everything we own this morning."

Emilio ignored LeRoy's threat, flipped open his ID and badge holder, and asked the nervous clerk, "Would you be so kind as to retrieve the two packages these lovely people left with you?"

The clerk nearly fell over himself getting to the boxes. He lifted them to the counter and set them side by side. Emilio asked him for a blade to open them up.

LeRoy yelled, "You're destroying private property. It's against the law."

Emilio made the first cut. "Private property--against the law, is it? Then you freely admit these packages are yours?"

LeRoy and Ruth refused to answer. Emilio examined the address labels: one made out to the Miltons' Washington, D.C. address and the other to Mr. and Mrs. R.A. Smith in Nome, Alaska. The packages bore no return addresses.

"Let's see what the Smiths are getting for their anniversary this year." Emilio's sarcasm sliced through the air as sharply as his knife cut through tape. Tackling the first carton, he made four surgical slices at the taped flaps and peered inside. A smile traveled across his face as he lifted out the contents, one by one, and held each item up for all to view. The Miltons winced to see the wig, granny glasses, flowered house dress, support hose, U. of Arizona tote, and faded men's jeans.

Emilio carefully placed the items back in the carton and set it aside. The Miltons stood by in sullen silence. Emilio made the necessary slits with the blade in the second box and began to pull out a brown department store shopping bag. Scrawled across it in black marker was the message "Happy Halloween!" Emilio leered. "Are we ready to see what the Miltons are sending themselves for Halloween this year?" But the shopping bag had been wedged so tightly into the box that he had trouble lifting it out. As a last resort, he upended the box over the counter and after several severe shakes, the shopping bag dropped out and tore open. Paper bands binding the packets separated, and the bills spewed forth on the counter and floor.

Ruth could stand it no longer. She screamed, "Leave that alone!" Plunging both hands into the pile on the counter, she scooped up fistfuls of fifties, tossing them high into the air like so much confetti.

Before Emilio could recover, Ruth grabbed two more handfuls and jammed them into the pockets of her jacket. Agent Martinez lunged at her, but she pulled the spring water bottle from its roost to fall in his path. The heavy plastic bottle crashed to the floor, gurgling out water in a wide arc as it spun. He lunged a second time, but the sloppy flooring wouldn't allow him the necessary traction. She lurched sideways to dodge his second try and slid behind the second agent, placing him between her and Emilio.

Reacting with practiced speed, the agent shoved LeRoy up against the counter. He twisted and gripped one of LeRoy's arms behind him with one hand as he brought out a pair of handcuffs with the other. He began the Mirandizing procedure. But with both his hands occupied, the agent became an easy target for Ruth. She head-butted him directly into Emilio's path. The cuffs meant for LeRoy clunked to the floor, and the agent crashed into the nearest shelf, causing stacks of unfolded cartons to collapse onto both law enforcement officers.

LeRoy seized the moment to exploit the chaos. Pivoting away, he knocked the feet out from under the agent trying to stand up, then grabbed Ruth's hand and yanked her toward the mailbox side of the store. She instinctively understood his next move. Together they ran behind the shelving unit opposite the mailboxes. Placing their backs against the unit, they shoved with all their collective strength. The unit teetered dangerously. With a resounding crash, it toppled onto succeeding shelves like dominoes until the one closest to the opposite wall hit the floor. The flimsy shelves separated from their metal frames. Office supplies, stationery, bubble wrap, and Styrofoam peanuts littered the floor, blocking the way out for Martinez and his colleague.

Oblivious to the ruckus inside, Paco paced the sidewalk in front of Mail Station Ltd. That is, until the crash of the shelves. Suddenly on full alert, he was about to go inside, when LeRoy and Ruth burst through the doorway.

Ruth darted down the street like a broken field runner with LeRoy close behind. Barreling into a dense crowd of lunchtime pedestrians, the Miltons pushed, shoved, knocked down, and otherwise intimidated anyone who had the nerve to be strolling in their path. Angry shouts, shrieks, and curses followed them, but they heard nothing. At a corner souvenir stand, LeRoy intentionally upended two carousels of paperbacks. The vendor bellowed in frustration.

LeRoy caught up to his wife, then led the way through the crosswalk, but Ruth looked over her shoulder and saw that the two FBI agents were gaining on them. In a frantic ploy to buy time and distance, she dug into her jacket pockets for her second stash of bills. As she ran, she scattered them behind her. Pedestrians squealed with delight and dove to recover the loose money-- even one fifty was worth the trouble. The two men in pursuit lost ground in the tangle of pedestrians fighting over the bills. A block behind, Paco joined the chase, but he knew his days of outrunning criminals were over.

LeRoy rushed forward. But in the middle of the next cross street, Ruth hesitated. Muscle spasms shot between her shoulder blades. Pain radiated down her left arm. She bent over to catch her breath.

LeRoy, with his own chest heaving and temples pounding, yelled to her from the opposite curb: "Ruth! Don't stop now--we're almost there. Just two more blocks, then we can blend in."

A horn blared as a driver slammed on brakes, a motorcycle skidded to a halt. LeRoy watched in horror as Ruth's right hand clutched her heart, her face contorting, eyes rolling. She slowly collapsed onto the hot macadam street, her angular body folding in on itself, toppling like a tower of blocks under a two-year-old's fist.

LeRoy hovered on the curb, torn between escape and turning back to protect the only person he had ever loved in this world. "Ruth!" he screamed. "Don't die!"

More cars screeched to a halt. Others maneuvered their vehicles around the limp figure. LeRoy stepped off the curb and started toward his wife, then hesitated when he saw the agents closing in. LeRoy retreated toward the curb he'd just left and allowed a slowing tractor-trailer to squeeze down the constricted street between them. In a burst of adrenaline and remarkable physical strength, he sprang toward the big rig. Luck was with him. He found both a handhold and foothold on the broad side of the trailer and clung for his life, hanging on as the truck resumed its speed.

Emilio's colleague reached Ruth first. Kneeling beside her, he radioed for an ambulance. Emilio continued the chase and searched a few of the nearby stores, but soon realized that LeRoy had eluded them. The agent scowled in disgust, mostly at himself, and growled, "We lost him."

Chapter 26
DROP IN, DROP OUT
Same Day, Wednesday, September 23, 1981

WITH TREMBLING HANDS, Bess packed her nightie, the last of her clothes, then zipped up her suitcase. Things were going badly. She'd tried so hard to help Cookie by revealing what she knew about the Miltons and their packets of cash. But Agent Whatsisname didn't believe her. This morning he'd informed her that he had searched the couple's room and found nothing. For Bess, the whole trip was ruined.

A sharp knock at the door startled her. Straining on tiptoe, Bess tried to look through the peephole, but she came up short. Timidly, she opened the door a crack.

"Cookie there?" the visitor asked.

Bess fainted.

Theo Moyer stormed out of the hotel's Pueblo Cafe and Grille, leaving her veggie burger half eaten, and fled to the elevators. "Damn," she murmured when the car failed to respond to her first press of the button. The bell sounded as the car arrived at last. She stomped into the mirrored cubicle. A conversation she had overheard at lunch still burned in her ears. "Does she know?".... "I doubt it."

At first Theo paced like a tigress in the confines of its cage. Then, as the second floor rolled by, she caught sight of herself, and the image unnerved her: a half-crazed look that negated her cultivated bearing. Struggling for self-control, she rearranged loose strands of hair, then slathered her hands with a squirt of lotion from a tube in her purse.

When the elevator doors opened on the seventh floor, a

244

composed woman emerged, resolved not to destroy her eighteen-year marriage. Thom is still a catch worth keeping. He has great potential to head the company someday. And we love each other. As best friends, we finish each other's sentences, for heaven's sake.

Theo strode purposefully down the hall. Absorbed in her own thoughts, she didn't hear footsteps, muffled by the thick carpeting. At the Moyer suite she slid her key card into the slot. The green light flashed, and the door handle yielded to her grip and push. Stepping inside, she kicked the door shut with her heel, but never heard its final click. Thom wasn't in the sitting room, so Theo dropped her purse on a wing chair and continued on into the spacious bedroom.

Seconds later, a silent figure entered from the hall through the still-open door and stole across the sitting room to where the Moyers could be observed indirectly via their reflection in the mirrored bathroom door.

Theo found her husband lying on his back on the bed, fully dressed, hands clasped behind his head, stocking feet crossed. Although Theo intended to suppress her anger, her first order of business was to take control of their conversation. But Thom stole the momentum and spoke first.

"Hi, Theo. Did you ever get rid of the memo like I told you to?"

"What memo is that?" She wanted to annoy him.

"You know damned well what memo--Maynard's memo to Ray. Where is it? We don't want the police finding it in our possession, do we?"

"Don't worry" she replied. "It's safe in my purse in the other room."

"For crissake, Theo, I told you at the beginning of the trip to hide it someplace else."

The eavesdropper's eyes immediately fell on the leather handbag lying on the chair in front of him. Slowly, fingers unsnapped the clasp and plied through the clutter: a small notebook, map of Arizona, pen, sunglasses, and cosmetics case. The only part left to search was the center pocket. A pull on the zipper, quarter-inch by quarter-inch so the unzip wouldn't be heard, opened the pocket, revealing only one item: a white trifolded sheet of stationery. The eavesdropper unfolded the corporate memo, began reading it, and silently cursed.

Sharp voices rose from the bedroom.

"Burn it, flush it down the toilet, do whatever you have to. Get rid of it," Thom's voice barked. "Damn it, woman, you look like a distressed old hen ready to hatch an oversized egg. What's wrong?"

"Since when do you talk to me like that? In our entire marriage I've never heard you take that tone with me. You've spent too much time around the Symingtons--it's beginning to rub off."

"Sorry, Theo. It's just that we're in big trouble. This whole thing has degenerated so fast."

"Hasn't it, though?" Her lovely gray eyes locked onto his. "You don't have enough to worry about, you have to go cheating on me?"

"Cheating on you?"

"As if you didn't know," she said. "I was never so embarrassed in my life. I was peacefully having lunch downstairs when I heard them over the top of the booth."

"What are you talking about?"

"I'm talking about Abby Lebowitz asking Reba about us. To quote: 'Whether Theo knows that Thom is having an affair with Loretta.' Apparently, she heard you two messing around in the room in Salt Lake City after the recital."

"It was only one night. Not even a night--only a couple hours. Less! And a big mistake. I never--"

Thom stopped midsentence. Wild-eyed, he stared past her. Theo spun around to face what disturbed him. She screamed.

Ray Symington stood in the bedroom doorway. The fire of near-insanity leapt from his bloodshot eyes. His haggard, stubbled face was scarred with ugly red marks on both cheeks and another on his neck. A long cut flecked with dried blood slanted from his forehead down across the left brow. He moved in slow motion toward the bed. A whimpering Theo backed into the bathroom.

"R-R-Ray!" Thom stuttered. The name stuck in his throat as he struggled to sit up. "Thank God you're alive! What a relief! We thought you were dead."

"Thank God I'm alive? You mean, too bad I'm alive, don't you?"

A knot of fear took shape in Thom's belly. His boss's deep voice, so controlled, exuded more menace than if he'd shouted, as he had so often in sales meetings. And there was something skewed and strange about his clothes--a black Harley-Davidson T-shirt, black chinos, and sneakers--that somehow made him look even more threatening.

Thom rose to lean on one elbow. "Hey, Ray," he said, his manner calm and beguiling, "why don't we go in the other room so you can sit down. Theo's got our travel medical kit. She'll fix you up. And we can get you something to eat from room service. Tell us what happened."

Symington remained rooted to the carpet just a few steps from the bed. "You really care? Shrubbery and tree branches broke my fall. I slid a helluva way down that slope. Thought I'd broken every bone in my body. I must have lain there half the night. It took me the rest of the night to climb back up. Surprised myself, actually. I'm in better shape than I thought. Unfortunately, the bus had already left by the time I got back to the cabins."

The knot in Thom's stomach spread, amoeba-like, digging into his gut wall. He tried not to show his fear. "That's a real miracle. But how'd you get all the way here?"

Symington peered at him with bloodshot eyes. "I still had my wallet. I hired a private tour van at the lodge. Cost me 400 bucks. Fortunately, he accepted my credit card. Don't you like my outfit, Thom? We stopped for it along the way. It's my new image."

Ray stood over him now. His hulking frame threw a shadow on the bed. "You son-of-a-bitch," he said. "I came here because

I thought you were my friend. Some friend! You plot to kill me and then you diddle my wife."

"Hey!" Thom protested. "I don't know what you're talking about?"

"Haven't you played enough games?" Ray's hand shook as he pulled the memo out of his pants pocket, unfolded it, and waved it over Thom's head. "I got this out of your wife's purse. You people really should learn to lock your door. Now it's all clear. The conspiracy to force me off the tour and screw me out of my job. And then you screw Loretta in Salt Lake City, right under my nose. You move fast, don't you?"

Thom tried to swing his legs over the edge of the bed and stand up. But Ray, even in battered condition, was waiting for him. He leaned down, grabbed Thom's shirt at the throat with his left hand, and jerked up hard. With his right fist he jabbed twice at Thom's jaw.

Ray roared, "What was she, Thom? The spoils of victory? Rape and pillage--the company next?" He slammed his fist again into Thom's face.

Thom's jaw throbbed, he tasted blood, but as Ray pulled his arm back to strike again, Thom rolled toward him, struggled to his feet, and tackled his boss about the waist. The two of them crashed to the floor. They struggled, rolling over and over, neither finding an opening for a clean swing. Thom kicked and missed his target. His foot got tangled in a cord, bringing a floor lamp down. The shade rolled away, distracting Symington, and Thom realized that his boss was now more bravado than strength. Nobody could survive a fall into the canyon and not emerge weakened and in pain.

Thom jumped on Ray's body, sat astride his chest, and began to pound the scarred face. Blood spewed from Ray's nose and mouth. Suddenly, a terrified Theo burst out of the bathroom, where she'd been watching. When the sight of the beating became too much, she let out a horrified scream.

Her anguish traveled through the sitting room and--with

the still-unlatched door ajar--out into the hall. Within moments, the suite filled with spectators to the struggle in the bedroom. George and Monte arrived first. Neither chose to intervene. They were too shocked by the sight of their "dead" boss returned.

Thom had underestimated the adrenaline, fueled by revenge, pumping through Symington. Ray slammed his fist into Thom's left temple. Another strike broke Thom's nose. These stunning blows gave Ray the upper hand. He shoved Thom off his chest, rolled over, and straddled him. Ray knew it was now or never: he went for a choke hold on Thom's throat. Thom tried desperately to pry Ray's hands apart. Ray hung on, pressing and pressing. A moment later, Thom's arms dropped helplessly to the floor.

Theo shrieked, "For God's sake! George! Monte! Somebody stop Ray! He's killing Thom!"

This cry for help reached Paco and Molly, who were on their way to check out, rolling their luggage behind them. Paco dropped his suitcase and hurried into the sitting room. He called out, "Is everything all right in there?" Then he heard his answer, a thud mixed with the prolonged sound of shattering glass. Paco raced into the bedroom and pushed his way past George and Monte to the two men on the floor. "Get a doctor! Call an ambulance!" he shouted. George sprang to the phone on the desk.

Ray shuddered violently and collapsed on Thom's chest, then slid off, flopping onto his back. His eyes were wide and blood red as he looked, first at Monte, then at George. In a barely audible voice, he mumbled, "So you're here to finish the job." With one ghastly shudder, he exhaled his last breath.

Paco knelt and placed two fingers at the carotid artery on Ray's neck. After a few seconds, he shook his head. Theo ran to the bathroom, sank to her knees, and vomited into the toilet. Molly, peeking in from the sitting room, turned away. Paco, now the detective, not the honeymooner, studied with curiosity the tiny burn marks on Ray's neck and cheeks. The detective also realized that he was kneeling amid shards and chunks of glass. Among them he discovered horse's heads, legs, tails.

"Hon? I betcha I know what that fractioned thing is." Molly's voice quivered as she stood in the doorway, gripping the frame for support.

He looked at her over his shoulder. "You do?"

"Yessiree. They had glass sculptings at the Buffalo Bill place."

"Ah." Her description clicked in Paco's head. The museum shop in Cody. Perhaps a glass replica of a Remington. Pulling a handkerchief from his jacket pocket, he gingerly picked up one of the larger pieces and saw fingerprints, some smudged, but at least one that might be usable. Bringing it to his nose, he sniffed and was rewarded with a fragrance of some sort. Hand lotion? He couldn't quite identify it.

A near-hysterical Theo stood sobbing. "George! Did you call 911? Did you call the hotel doctor?"

"Nine-one-one, but not the house doctor," George answered. "The police are coming."

"Well, call the house doctor!" she screeched. Then her voice broke. "Thom's dead. It's too late."

"No, it's not too late," Paco said, turning his head to one side and laying his ear on Thom's chest. "He's still breathing, only it doesn't sound too good right now."

Just then, Thom's eyes flickered open. His lips moved, shaping words, but none came out. Blood ran from his nostrils across his bruised cheeks. He began to cry. Theo, her face contorted with tears and despair, sat down on the floor and held a washcloth compress to his nose.

A uniformed police officer was the first to arrive. He had already notified the Scottsdale Fire Department, which showed up quickly with its Emergency Medical Technicians. By then, Paco had told the officer that a murder--or accidental death--had been committed, and the officer officially announced the suite to be a crime scene.

Realizing that Ray was beyond help, the two EMTs turned their attention to Thom and, after stabilizing and packaging him, transported him off to the nearest hospital.

Chapter 27
WHO'S TO BLAME?
Same Day, Wednesday, September 23, 1981

THE POLICE SERGEANT, FIRST ON THE SCENE, analyzed the situation and called in Detective Sergeant Langston, who headed one of the city's crime scene investigative units. The crime scene, now blocked off with yellow tape, buzzed with official activity, including the collection of fingerprints, photos, glass, blood, and fibers. The coroner pronounced Ray dead and sent the body on to the morgue. While the forensic team conducted its grisly investigation in the Moyer suite, Langston interviewed witnesses in the same meeting room that had served for interviews and interrogations the night before. Langston arrested Theo immediately after she admitted to the deed. Hours later at the arraignment, a sympathetic judge granted her bail to be at Thom's bedside.

By 4:30 that afternoon most of the principals and witnesses to Ray's second demise had begrudgingly delayed their airline departures. None of them would be leaving for the airport until the next day except for the LeSotos. They could still make their 10:30 p.m. red-eye because Paco had prepared a detailed written report for the local police. Seeing that the LeSotos had the clearest grasp of what had transpired, Langston decided to interview them second.

Afterward, Paco intercepted Ranger Platte in the hall next to the interview room. "I'm curious," he said. "Where was Symington all that time between his fall into the canyon and his showing up here?"

"Ranger Long Feather got a telephone report half an hour ago from the North Rim rangers," said Platte. "The so-called body they were searching for turned out to be the new jacket Ray had bought at the North Rim. One of the pockets got hung up on a large branch high in a tree as he fell, and Ray had to slip out of the jacket to reach the ground. When he let go of it, the branch catapulted the torn remnants over a second precipice. Apparently, the jacket had broken his fall and saved his life. We can only piece together the rest. Sheer strength and guts enabled the man to claw his way back up that steep muddy talus slope without assistance. And wearing only one shoe and a windbreaker in a nighttime temperature of 40 degrees."

Platte flipped through his own sheaf of notes. "The rangers located the driver of the tour van that Symington hired to get to Scottsdale. The driver said that when he pulled up to the lodge, Symington came out from behind a clump of bushes, like a man hiding from someone. And he looked so disreputable that the driver almost turned around and left on the spot without him. Thought he was going to get mugged--or worse. But when Symington offered him $400 and showed him his driver's license and Visa card, the van driver decided to take a chance."

Paco frowned. "But what about that business with him being seen getting into a car with another woman?"

"That turned out to be a lot of hooey. The judge and his wife apparently saw what they wanted to see," Platte said wryly.

"But what do you think happened when Ray got back here?"

"Langston told me that Symington used the house phone to call the florist shop in the lobby. He ordered flowers for Cookie Adams. He waited in view of the florist shop and then discreetly followed the delivery boy to her door. He must have remained partially hidden until the flowers were delivered. Then he went to Cookie's room--with revenge in his heart. Of course, he didn't know that we had Ms. Adams is in custody, and that Ms. Izaks had accepted the delivery. When he knocked on their hotel door and Ms. Izaks answered, the old gal fainted at the sight of his ghost."

"Poor little woman," Molly piped up. Standing next to

Paco, she clutched the fringes of her Navajo shawl. "She's been through a lot."

"You're so right," Platte agreed. "As for Symington...Failing to find Ms. Adams in her room, he went back down the hall, spotted Theo getting off the elevator, and followed her back to her suite. God knows how he avoided being seen by her. Mrs. Moyer gave us a statement. It seems that Symington's visit wasn't all that malicious--at least, not until he discovered the memo from their CEO and the gossip that Moyer had been messing with his wife. He learned all this while eavesdropping on Thom and Theo from the sitting room of their suite. At that point I assume he flew into his rage, and I understand you witnessed the rest...some of it, anyway."

"When you add those two elements to the conspiracy, I'm not surprised. Sounds about right," said Paco. "What's going to happen to Theo?"

"Hurles and Davies claim they saw her bash Ray with the glass statue. And thanks to your careful handling of that large hunk of glass, Langston's pretty sure Forensics will be able to lift her prints."

"But considering that she saved her husband's life, wouldn't you call it justifiable homicide--or involuntary manslaughter?"

"I suppose a good defense attorney could make one of those cases. Symington would have killed Moyer if she hadn't clobbered him. She insists that she wanted to stop the man, not kill him. On the other hand, a prosecutor could argue that Theo willingly participated in the conspiracy against Symington and that she had motive--and finally, opportunity--to kill him."

"There's no doubt," Paco said, "that her husband had the most to gain if Ray was forced out of the company. Thom was next in line for the vice presidency of sales. Frankly, one thing in particular bothered me when I entered the bedroom and saw the fight going on. Neither George nor Monte was making any attempt to stop it."

Platte scowled. "You have to wonder about their own agendas. It's not a pretty picture. Anyway, conspiracy or not, it's not our case any more. Langston will have his hands full sorting this one out."

"By the way, where is Loretta?"

"She's on her way here from the North Rim. Our people escorted her there from Sedona to wait for news of her husband. She's been staying at the lodge, and since learning of Symington's death, she's been quite distraught. Of course, she's no longer a suspect. The autopsy's going to take a few days. Then we'll release the body to her and she'll be able to take him home."

Molly could restrain herself no longer. "Ray wasn't a nice man, but he sure didn't reserve to get hisself killed."

The door to the interview room opened and Special Agent Martinez stepped into the hall carrying a brown leather briefcase. He looked annoyed at encountering the group so near the door and quickened his steps to get around them.

"Hey, Agent Emilio?" Molly called to him. "What about Mr. LeRoy?"

The embarrassed FBI agent reluctantly stopped and turned back. Running his fingers through his thick black hair, he admitted, "LeRoy got away from us when Ruth collapsed in the street. We'll catch up with him, I can assure you. He'll do hard time for his part in four bank robberies. Just how much time will depend on how much of the money is recovered and how well he can convince a jury of his remorse. If he has any, which I seriously doubt. We recovered the cash from Mail Station Ltd., of course. A good defense lawyer will argue that no lethal force was employed. But that's not quite true. Ruth assaulted her victims and chloroformed them. According to the police reports, they all recovered, but that won't sit well with a jury. And LeRoy was more than just her accomplice; actually, a second degree principal. They planned every move together."

Molly's pale blue eyes filled with tears. "Poor Ruth. But what did she die of?"

Agent Emilio replied, "The paramedics said she probably had a heart attack. When they got to her she was already in cardiac arrest."

Large tears pooled on Molly's cheeks. "I feel real bad. Sure, she was a bank robber, but I didn't expect her to wind down dead. Ruth was nice to me. She was a hairdressing beautytician, you know."

Paco shook his head. "I didn't know."

"Oh, yes. She showed me how to comb my curls to make 'em more bouncy."

Paco looked puzzled. "When did she do that?"

"Oh, in the ladies room at one of our comfy stops."

"I'm sorry, baby," Paco said tenderly. Seeing Agent Martinez glance away uncomfortably, he hastily held out his hand. "Good luck, Agent," he said. Martinez shook it, nodded, and sprinted down the hall.

Paco addressed Ranger Platte. "What's the outlook for Cookie Adams?"

"I'm not sure. The court can hardly convict her of murder or manslaughter when the corpus delicti reappeared after the fact. Then again, can she be tried for attempted murder, disfigurement, or accidental injury when there's no plaintiff? Of course, Loretta might press charges in a civil suit against her for attempted murder or, at the very least, reckless endangerment, claiming that if it hadn't been for Ms. Adams, Ray would still be alive. Hurles is hiring a lawyer to push for extenuating circumstances. She'll be tried for something--a prosecutor will see to that."

"Did you ever determine what happened to the gun that Cookie fired at Symington?" asked Paco.

"There wasn't one. In fact, there wasn't any sign of a gunshot wound anywhere on Symington."

"So I didn't have to bring my gun to you after all."

"Right! Much too big for her to have handled and too cruddy to have been fired recently."

"I agree," said a relieved Paco.

"She was telling us the truth. But when we sent for her complete credit card records, we discovered that she had purchased a cattle prod, of all things, at one of the stops in Wyoming. That's what caused the snapping noises that the Miltons thought were gunshots. And the flashes they described...Well, if you press one prong against the skin and hold the other one away, it can cause an arc of light. She pumped and discharged the prod on Ray's perspiring skin."

Good God, thought Paco. He recalled the dinner with Cookie, George, and Reba at the Wooden Nickel early in the tour: Cookie's interest in 'that strange stick thing on the wall.' She'd never seen a cattle prod before. "Well, I guess that accounts for the burn marks on Ray's cheek and neck. Did you find the prod?"

"Yes. It's a common type. A twenty-two-inch shaft, takes four C-sized batteries. Odd, isn't it? The bank robbers led us to Ms. Adams's weapon. LeRoy and Ruth described a man sneaking away from the North Rim with what they thought was a walking stick. Seeing that brother George was so close to sister Cookie, I put the pressure on him. Told him I would arrest him as an accessory if he didn't cooperate and hand over whatever he'd been concealing. He did. He pulled it out of his luggage."

Paco checked his watch. "Sorry, sir, time for the shuttle to take us to the airport. There are still so many unanswered questions, many of them depending on who is indicted in which jurisdiction."

Chapter 28
JUDGMENTS
Eight Months Later

A SHAFT OF PUNISHING SUNLIGHT penetrated the tall windows of the Superior Court in Phoenix, spotlighting the wooden bench where Loretta sat. But the 105 degrees outdoors couldn't compare to a different kind of heat inside the room. The grieving widow remained ramrod erect in a somber suit, a sale number she'd picked off the rack at a local department store. On her lawyer's advice, no conspicuous designer outfits and only the sparest makeup. Not that the IMTC bunch noticed or even cared. Clowns one and all, Loretta thought bitterly.

A grand jury had ordered that Theo be tried for second-degree murder. Her trial had erupted into a virtual Cirque de Soleil for the performing conspirators. During their testimony, George and Reba, Monte and Michelle, and Joanne and Gordon studiously avoided meeting Loretta's accusing eyes. Each of them, with peculiar self-righteousness, had resented the intrusive return to Arizona.

Loretta listened uneasily to the rehash of each bizarre event, the parade of assaults and pranks the conspirators had inflicted upon her husband. She asked herself: these people she'd known for so long, these salesmen and their wives with whom she'd socialized at company parties--were they as mean-spirited as the evidence professed them to be? Or had Ray actually brought their wild revenge upon himself? Had she been completely naive during the trip, warning him over and over that he was accident prone, blaming him? Somehow, he had seemed to enjoy placing himself in harm's way. But, then again, she knew for sure he didn't deserve to die.

Loretta had loved her husband deeply and thought she knew the kind of man she'd married: sharp, ambitious, good-looking, and well-versed--yet pompous egotistical, domineering, and snobbish. She knew there was more, but had never admitted it before, even to herself. It took this day of testimony for her to acknowledge the ruthless, vindictive, evil side of Ray. As ambivalent as she felt, how would she be able to mourn this husband of conflicting attributes?

Her throat tightened as she listened to Thom painfully whisper his testimony. Ray's stranglehold grip on his neck had severely and permanently damaged Thom's vocal cords. What would have happened if Theo hadn't smashed the glass sculpture on Ray's head? Would Thom be dead and her husband charged with murder?

Theo's participation in the conspiracy had raised doubt as to her professed motive in hitting Ray. But a compassionate jury found her guilty of a lesser, involuntary manslaughter charge, and a benevolent judge gave her a three-year suspended sentence. Both judge and jury had concluded that Ray's ultimate death was not a product of a harassment conspiracy.

Before the proceedings actually adjourned, the district attorney summoned the eight offenders and their lawyers to appear before the judge. They received a tongue lashing about the seriousness of their deliberate plot to harass the deceased. But the intent to actually harm him had not been proven. The judge reasoned that--because their plot had been conceived prior to the trip out West--Connecticut law should have jurisdiction. Therefore, he intended to forward the transcripts of these proceedings to the judiciary there with a recommendation to prosecute.

Some weeks later, a stern judge in New Haven offered them a tough choice: plead guilty to a variety of misdemeanor harassment charges or he would instruct the district attorney's office there to bind them over for trial. All of them chose to plead. The judge deemed that Thom had suffered enough punishment and suspended his sentence. The other three sales managers and their wives received sentences to serve several hundred hours each of community service.

Two months had passed since Theo's trial. Today, under a cloudy Connecticut sky, Loretta stood at Ray's grave, cradling a bouquet of yellow roses.

Conflicting emotions throbbed in her head. Although she had no use now for her husband's former colleagues, she somehow understood their cowardly attacks. A nagging voice of conscience forced her to wonder whether she had been too much of an enabler at home. Had she encouraged her husband's worst instincts every time he started an argument--by taking the bait, warming to the fight? If they hadn't had such a hostile marriage, would Ray have been less combative at IMTC? But she rejected that thought. Ray had come come into her life as an obsessive competitor. It made him seem sexy, macho, and slightly dangerous. Early in their marriage, she found that side of him exciting, along with his tall physique and broad, hairy chest. She shook her head. No way could she have changed him. He had thrived on pitting his regional managers against one another. He couldn't stand the thought of one of them showing him up by earning a patent or capturing a new district with millions in sales--a more accomplished salesman than he'd ever been.

No, she thought stubbornly, it wasn't her fault. And no matter how nasty a boss Ray had been, his sales gang always had another option: they could have found other jobs. Nobody had held a gun to their heads to stay at IMTC. A bitter taste filled her mouth as she thought about the leniency of the punishments. They got off easy. They still had their jobs and healthy incomes.

Loretta laid the bouquet down at the base of Ray's headstone and marched back to her BMW. She'd received a call from her lawyer this morning. At her insistence, he'd filed a civil suit against the four sales managers for committing a conspiracy that led to Ray's death and for his future loss of income. Yes! She saw herself as the victim here, and she wanted financial relief, damn it, especially in her present dire straits.

Ray had left his widow with a huge financial burden and no foreseeable income to pay it off. What was left of a quarter million in life insurance wouldn't go far in her scheme of living--Ray had already borrowed on it. Her car sailed past a mall and she resisted the temptation to pull in just to browse a little. She knew she always spent too much money. Did her extravagance force her husband to the wall? The vacation house in the Hamptons had seemed like such a good idea when she pressed him to buy it. She'd argued that it would enhance their social standing and be good for his business. Of course, Loretta had assumed that Ray's earning power would continue for at least ten years. Ray had always referred to it sarcastically as "the palace" and she wasn't sure why. Now she knew. He'd been too proud to confess that the vacation house put them in a financial bind. The down payment had cost them most of their savings and stock portfolio.

Also, her accountant had informed her that, in addition to the second mortgage, Ray had taken out a separate personal loan to swing the deal. For this loan, his shares of stock in IMTC were being held as collateral--along with the power of attorney to vote them. And just yesterday, her accountant had phoned her to dish out another helping of nightmarish news. While on the Vermilion tour, Tina Barton had purchased the loan, hoping that Ray would default on the house payments. Tina would then get her hands on his company stock, along with his voting power on the board at IMTC.

While the accountant was spelling out the details of this revelation, Loretta could barely listen. Painful heartburn--an everyday visitor now--had filled her chest. Tina Barton! That cocky bitch, Miss Professor at American U, Miss big shot consultant. Tina and Ray had been fooling around together in the hot tub at the Mountain King Resort in Jackson. A flash of recollection hit Loretta. Tina's uncle was Judge Harry Sessions, whom Ray had forced to step down from the bench. Why, of course! Tina's revenge was personal.

Loretta clenched the steering wheel as she guided the BMW into her driveway. The financial and emotional turmoil were destroying her. She hadn't slept more than four hours a night in weeks. Tossing her keys on the marble console in the foyer, she decided to take immediate steps to bail herself out. Funny, Ray had almost always made the decisions in the family. Now, completely alone, she had to take control--with three major decisions. She'd already made the first one: the civil lawsuit to recover damages. Second, she would put the house in the Hamptons up for sale.

Decision three was harder: she needed to consult a therapist. Nothing long term, mind you. In fact, the very idea of spilling her private thoughts and confessions caused a fresh surge of heartburn. Maybe she could persuade him to just give her prescriptions for sleeping pills and stronger antacids. Neither she nor Ray had been the soul-searching types. In fact, they'd looked down on the whole business of introspection and analysis as socially unacceptable, and certainly suicidal in the world of business leadership.

Loretta uttered a deep sigh as she slipped into a sagging warm-up suit. She'd dropped ten pounds since Ray's death. Much as she hated to admit defeat, she knew she needed professional help to get her emotional life under control. But the therapist would have to be someone outside her social circle. Even better, in another city. Then she remembered Molly LeSoto's Dr. Avi, and all the affection and confidence Molly felt for him. Loretta sat down at her desk and dialed Information for the number of Dr. Avram Kepple in Black Rain Corners, Maryland. She made the appointment for two weeks from that day.

Chapter 29
CATCHING UP--OR NOT

DR. KEPPLE PROVED TO BE ALL THAT MOLLY HAD PROMISED and certainly the best medicine for Loretta. He assured her she didn't have to sign on for several years of intense psychoanalysis; he also did short-term therapy. She found the white-haired analyst a pillar of kindness, understanding, and knowledge. The patient came away with a measure of solace and hope, knowing that she would see him once every two weeks until they both agreed he could do no more for her. No sleeping pills, though.

Loretta felt so buoyed up by her first visit, so relieved by Dr. Avi's unintimidating demeanor that she yearned to thank Molly for recommending him. Avi directed her to the LeSoto home on Willow Way, only a block from Locust Lane, where he lived and practiced. Loretta eased her BMW down the hill and over one road to Willow. At the white brick cottage, she rang the bell and waited.

Molly filled the open doorway with hands on broad hips, a gravy-speckled apron sweeping her girth. "Ms. Loretta," she shrieked. "Whatever brings you to our neck of the trees?"

"Actually, you're responsible, Molly. You recommended Dr. Kepple, and I just had my first appointment. I'm ever so grateful, and I just wanted to thank you."

"Come in and make yourself comfy." Over her shoulder, she called, "Paco! Paco, honey! Come on out to the living room and see who's here."

Paco appeared behind her. "Well, well, Mrs. Symington--Loretta," he said. "What a surprise."

"Come join us in the dining room and make yourself a seat," said Molly. "I was just winding up the tail on dinner."

Loretta shook her head and took a step backward. "I didn't realize I'd be interrupting your dinner hour. I should have known. I just wanted to..."

"Nonsense, Loretta, of course you'll stay," Paco said.

"But I'm spending the night at the inn and I can catch a bite there."

"No trouble at all," Molly insisted. "I got enough to feed a navy here. That way I can send a nice care bag over to the good doctor. I worry about his not eating right when I'm not around."

"Well, if you're sure. I wasn't looking forward to eating alone. I've been doing far too much of that lately."

Paco led her into the tiny dining room and held a chair for her. The detective's practiced eye took in a woman who was smartly dressed, but somehow more subdued, less arrogant than he remembered her. The garish eye shadow and black eyeliner were missing. The hard blue eyes looked dull, some redness there, too-- she'd been crying.

"What brings you down from Connecticut, Loretta?"

"I..." Loretta stumbled. It was easy to tell Molly, but not quite so easy to confide in the detective. "I...took Molly's advice... and went to see Dr. Kepple. I'll be going every couple of weeks for awhile. My life's been such a mess..."

"You don't mind the drive?"

"It's about six hours, not too bad. Frankly, Paco, it's more comfortable to come down here than worry about bumping into someone I know near home."
Paco nodded. "Of course."

As Molly retreated to the kitchen, she said, "It must be awful lonely without Mr. Ray."

"It sure is," Loretta called into the empty kitchen doorway.

"It sure is!" squawked a voice from the living room.

A bewildered Loretta spun around.

Paco laughed and pointed to a cage in front of a living room window. "Don't be alarmed, please. Those are my feathered friends, Bobble and Fumble. They love to mimic everything anybody says in this house. They've developed quite a repertoire."

Loretta rose to get a better look. "But there's nothing in the cage," she said. Then she spotted a four-foot pole with a long wooden crossbar. Two large macaws with brilliant red, green, and blue feathers sat on the perch. The one on the left kept swaying from side to side, lifting one clawed foot and then the other.

Loretta flinched. "They're allowed to run around? I mean, fly around?"

"Oh, yes, they have the freedom of the house."

Loretta grew braver. "Oh, I'd love to hear them talk some more." She started toward the perch, but stopped short. "Do they bite?"

"Sometimes. Well, rarely, but I don't recommend getting any closer." Paco nimbly approached the perch and clipped a light-weight plastic leash to one foot on each of the birds. "Third down and two," Paco prompted.

"Quarterback sneak!" squawked Bobble.

"Pass over center, you dummy!" croaked Fumble.

Loretta giggled, then crowed with laughter. The happy skit was too much for her. It was the first time she'd actually laughed in months. Paco understood and led her back to the table just in time for Molly's entrance with their first course.

Molly set a wooden tray down and handed out three small plates. Loretta was taken aback by what she saw. Looking up at her was a round face made of chopped liver and decorated with sliced olive eyes, celeried nose, and a carrot curl mouth. A semicircle of Wheat Thins finished off the creation. "Do the LeSotos eat this elegantly every night?"

"As a matter of fact, yes," answered Paco. "Molly has been doing it for so many years for the Kepple family that it just comes naturally. It's what she does best. Only problem is, I've already gained three pounds and we're not even married a year."

"You can afford it, honey bun," Molly grinned.

As his wife cleared away the plates, Paco seized the moment and fetched a letter from a triangular desk in a corner of the dining room.

"I received this from your lawyer," he said, handing the sheet to Loretta. "He wants me to appear as a witness in a civil lawsuit. I'm surprised that you've chosen to sue the whole corporate bunch. I hope you're not tackling too much."

"Let me explain," Loretta said hastily. "A lot has happened since that letter went out. We've found a way to settle out of court."

Paco frowned. "Nice of them to inform me. I don't understand."

"You see, Ray's death left me with a pile of debts and very little cash. His life insurance didn't begin to cover it. I asked my lawyer to sue."

"So what changed your mind?"

"About two weeks after the letters went out, Judge Harry Sessions contacted me through my lawyer. Judge Sessions is back in private practice now, and he's representing the IMTC salesmen. At first I didn't want to have anything to do with them, but my lawyer convinced me it was in my best interest to listen to their offer."

"They offered you a substantial settlement check, I presume."

"More than that. IMTC bought our vacation house in the Hamptons. We bought it two years ago and it's already appreciated. IMTC returned all of our equity. They also bought back my husband's shares in the company from a third party and even paid me a little more than their market value. The judge indicated that many of them had to go into hock to meet their settlement obligation--sizeable loans, too. When I heard that, I knew I'd gotten my pound of flesh.

"But!...Paco, you'll never believe this: Tina Barton held those IMTC shares, plus the paper on a personal loan Ray took out to buy the house in the Hamptons. When I found out, I nearly went through the roof." Loretta's fingers toyed with the stem of her water goblet. Her momentary pleasure over the macaws had evaporated.

"All during the tour," she continued, "Tina was playing footsie with my husband. I saw them together outside her cabin the evening he disappeared. Yeah, I was spying on the two of them."

Paco squinted at her. "I thought he was with Cookie Adams that night."

"He was--later on," Loretta said grimly. "But listen to this. It turns out that Tina was having an affair with Maynard Larchmont, IMTC's CEO. He had no idea she'd bought the loan on our vacation house."

"And she also owned Ray's stock?" Paco asked.

"Yes. Maynard was furious when he found out. He broke off their romance and aborted her scheme to wangle a seat on the IMTC board. I feel a little better now. The settlement that Judge Sessions negotiated means I can get out of debt. But I'll have to get a job, too. Surely, I won't be able to continue living in my customary manner."

As Molly placed a china tureen on the table, she thought to herself, Yessiree, Ms. Loretta, your customized spoiled bratty manner. A job will do you good. Aloud she said, "That's some story. They musta been afraid of you." She uncovered the tureen and sweet-smelling steam escaped from rolls of stuffed cabbage in rich broth.

"They were afraid of me. But Theo's trial really made me mad. All the conspirators rallied to her defense."

"Yes, I know," said Paco.

"She got a three-year suspendered sentence," added Molly.

Loretta looked startled. "You heard?"

"Platte brought me up to date," Paco said. "He also told me the salesmen and their wives got community service."

"Yes," Loretta said. "Except for Thom. He's going to need a mechanically vibrated voice box for the rest of his life. His windpipe and larynx were damaged during their fight." A shadow of sadness fell over her face. "I actually feel sorry for Thom. I really liked him and Theo. They were the classiest ones in the bunch. But I can't say I feel bad for Cookie, after what she did to Ray. Maybe she had her reasons, maybe she didn't. Anyway, I was just wondering what happened to her."

"Platte told me she pleaded out and is serving an eighteen-month sentence."

Molly sat down after ladling out the stuffed cabbage. With one cheek filled, she said, "It don't seem right. Theo Moyer kills your husband and walks, while Cookie winds up in the whosecow. I just don't believe she purposely pushed him. No way, not pre-medicated murder."

Loretta ignored the remark and chewed delicately. "Mmm, this is delicious."

Molly's curls bobbed as she tilted her head. "Maybe justice is like a recipe," she mused. "You can vary the intergredients to taste, but not everyone likes the outcome."

Paco smiled. They'd finished eating, but Molly wasn't quite ready to clear the dinner plates. She laced her short fingers together and faced their guest. "Ms. Loretta, I got a question for you."

Loretta shifted warily in her chair. "I think I know what it is, Molly, but ask it anyway."

"Did you put the milky magnesia in the corn chowder?"

Paco gazed at his wife with astonishment and admiration.

A deep flush suffused Loretta's face. She nodded. "That's another reason I'm here. I was hoping to get up the courage to confess. Frankly, I'm not sure I'd have had the guts to say anything to you if you hadn't brought it up. But I wanted to, Molly, I really did. It's one of the reasons I went to see Dr. Kepple."

Molly interjected, "You mean it's been noshing away at you?"

"Has it ever! I cringe when I think of how sick you all got. I didn't mean to hurt any of you, I swear! I just wanted to get to Ray. I had this crazy notion that maybe it would be the last straw, and he'd stop hitting on other women and acting like such a jerk. I'm so very, very sorry."

Paco scowled, but said nothing.

A sharp squawk pierced the silence. "Crack in the back!

Fifteen-yard penalty!"

The three of them broke into laughter.

Still chuckling, Paco walked into the living room and picked up the newspaper from the coffee table. "Speaking of major infractions, have either of you seen the article in this morning's paper? The one about the old lady in Louisiana?" He passed it to Loretta for her to read.

"You mean the one about grandma's eyes?" asked Molly. "Sure, I read it. I just think it's a mighty troublesome way for him to make a tributary to his wife."

Chapter 30
IN MEMORIAM
[The following article appeared in the
Annapolis Journal-Gazette on July 20, 1982.]

Oh, Grandma, What Big Eyes You Have!

Baton Rouge, La. - An elderly woman shuffled into a sub-urban branch of the Pelican State Bank yesterday and made off with nearly $80,000 of the bank's own money. Pretending to be a safe deposit box holder, the woman used chloroform to subdue a branch manager and gain access to her keys within the vault. The thief then helped herself to the bank's ready cash reserves and strolled leisurely out of the building.

The manager was treated at a nearby hospital and released. She described her assailant as "seventyish, the kindly grandmother type...granny glasses and gray hair in a bun." Police said the suspect, about 5 feet 8 inches tall and 180 pounds, wore a pink and white flowered dress. Another bank employee noted that the suspect carried a large embroidered bag topped with pink skeins of wool and two knitting needles.

Local police are cooperating with the FBI in the investigation. The special agent in charge, Emilio Martinez, said this hold-up was patterned after other bank heists in several Western and Midwest states over the past two years.

Authorities are "optimistic" about an early arrest.

Also by Rosemary & Larry Mild

Daniel and Rivka Sherman give up successful professional careers as engineer and editor to become booksellers at The Olde Victorian bookstore in Annapolis, Maryland. They also become unwilling sleuths

Rare fifteenth century typesetting artifacts journey through time to the present, leaving behind not only their original innovation, but a horrifying imprint of murder, robbery, kidnapping, and mugging in their wake. Professor Abner Fraume gives his life to protect their whereabouts.

Available on Amazon.com, Kindle, and Nook.

PRAISE FOR *Cry Ohana*

"Cry Ohana is certainly a page-turner, and the authors seem to have a good take on the evolving concept of "ohana" and fractured families in modern Hawaii, and the action proceeds in a logical and gripping pace....The characters in this large novel are all drawn well...." **—Burl Burlingame, *Honolulu Star Advertiser***

"Cry Ohana captures the essence of Hawaii while providing a suspenseful adventure about family, redemption, hope, and justice.... The use of Hawaiian slang and references to historical landmarks adds to the authenticity and flow of the story. A thrilling Hawaiian journey." **—Kathryn Franklin, *San Francisco Book Review***

"Shame can tear families apart, and murder can obliterate them....A story of family and reunion for the betterment of it all, and dedicated to Hawaiian culture. A choice pick, highly recommended." **—Margaret Lane, *Midwest Book Review***

"I was hooked from the very first page. There is plenty of suspense, intrigue, blackmail, and betrayal. The characters are very easy to connect with. The descriptions of Hawaii are excellent. A book you won't want to miss." **—2011 Gold Seal *Reader's Favorite* Award**

"Rosemary and Larry Mild bring us a struggle that makes *Cry Ohana* such a compelling story....Chase scenes and plot twists abound. We are given murder and blackmail as well as human pathos and drama in abundance. *Cry Ohana* is an exciting and poignant story rating a 9 of 10 on the Weaver meter." **—Sid Weaver, *Mainly Mysteries***

"This book was very endearing....My heart went out to Kekoa. I was able to relate to his struggle of survival....Even the patience and tenacity Leilani had, never wanting to give up on finding her family, was inspiring....I recommend this book and these authors." **—Nikkea Smithers, Pres., Romance Writers of America Book Club**

Also by Rosemary & Larry Mild

The Paco and Molly Mystery Series

Locks and Cream Cheese—set in an old Chesapeake Bay mansion full of hidden rooms, locked doors, and secrets out of the past. A million-dollar painting and a jeweled key are the prizes, but are murder and trickery worth it? The wily police detective and housekeeper/cook are on the case.

Hot Grudge Sunday—Paco and Molly, finding love and marriage, go on a honeymoon bus tour out West. Bank robbers, conspirators, and murderers interrupt their bliss and once more they are called upon to uncover spine-chilling schemes as spectacular as Zion, the Grand Canyon, and Yellowstone.

Boston Scream Pie—A young girl's persisting nightmare leads Paco and Molly to the Boston family household, where the children churn up vicious undercurrents that threaten two families. Four deceased husbands lie in Mom's past. When another family member dies under mysterious circumstances, the clues point to murder. Paco and Molly see through the sinister connections and set things right.

Available on Amazon.com, Kindle, and Nook.

"....I was fascinated by a tale that had a little dab of V.C. Andrews mixed with a bit of Leeann Sweeney. But, believe it or not, the Milds pulled it off and *voilá*, it was a winner. I loved it!....This mystery sparkles 'n shines and if there is such a thing as a V.C. Andrews 'cozy' you'll love it!"   **—*Feathered Quill Book Reviews***

"*Boston Scream Pie* is a page-turning novel of suspense that will hold the reader's attention from beginning to end."   **—*TCM Reviews***

"*Boston Scream Pie* was heartwarming, but suspenseful. It has a surprise ending that will shock you....one of the best novels I have read in quite a long time! It shows a very familiar part of life; true things that can really happen to people, and was just so delightful!"
—Gina Holland, *Rebecca's Read*

"This mystery provides page-turning excitement without the inordinately graphic gore to make it unpalatable. Full of injuries, illnesses, and attacks, the book shares murders and mayhem in a lower key than that sung by Hannibal Lecter. This well-researched theme causes one to wonder which individuals in the story are related—or are they at all?"
—Patty Inglish, MS., *Armchair Interviews*

"The Milds have whipped up another pleasing concoction in this charming series with their likeable protagonists, clever plotting, and generous dashes of humor. Paco and Molly are astute detectives and Molly's malaprops are as tasty as her kugel. *Boston Scream Pie* is a thoroughly enjoyable treasure."
—Anne White, Author of the *Lake George Mystery Series*

"....the plot and outcome were all carefully drawn with a resolution that I am sure will satisfy most readers. I should also note that there is a bit of sexual content as well, though nothing very graphic or gratuitous—I felt that it was pertinent to the storyline. My rating: 4.5 out of 5 stars. I recommend *Boston Scream Pie*."
—Melissa, *Mystery Mondays*

"A fast, charming read."   **—*Futures Mystery Anthology magazine***

"*Hot Grudge Sunday* takes us on a delightful action packed ride. The story is full of surprises and kept me riveted. I'm already looking forward to Molly's next adventure."
  —Mary Ellen Hughes, Author of the Craft Corner Mysteries

"Working in tandem, the authors created scenic vistas, lively characters, and enough plot twists and tension to carry the reader swiftly to the finish."   **—Edie Dykeman, Amazon review**

"The Wild West is a lot wilder whenever the Milds' tour bus arrives in *Hot Grudge Sunday*. Rosemary and Larry had me hanging by my fingernails throughout the trip. They also gave me an enticing glimpse of a part of America I've never seen. A great read."
  —Robin Hathaway, Agatha Award-winning Author of the Dr. Andrew Fenimore Mystery Series

"I had not read any of Paco and Molly's adventures before *Hot Grudge Sunday*. That will be changing. I really enjoyed them and their adventurous spirit. I can't wait to read more! I highly recommend this book!"   **—Dawn Dowdle, *Mystery Lovers Corner***

<u>*Boston Scream Pie*</u>

"We have added *Boston Scream Pie* to our recommended reading list....It is worth picking up. There is a little of something down there for everyone."   **—John Raab, *Suspense Magazine***

"...In Chapter One I met a woman who I decided I hated immediately. And she was sleeping! The case twists and turns...and kept me glued to the pages until the end."
  —Kaye Barley, *Meanderings and Muses*

"If you want a light and funny mystery to read, I would definitely recommend *Boston Scream Pie*."   **—*Mystery Reader***

"If you enjoy cliff-hanging, crisis-to-crisis mysteries filled with suspense, then you are going to enjoy *Boston Scream Pie*....Deftly written and highly recommended...plays fair with the reader...."
  —*Mystery Bookshelf*

Photograph by Craig Herndon

Rosemary and Larry Mild coauthor mysteries and thrillers. Eight of their "soft-boiled detective" short stories have appeared on line in *Mysterical-E*. Regular panelists at the Malice Domestic and Left Coast Crime conventions, the Milds divide the rest of the writing year between serene Severna Park, Maryland, and addictive Honolulu, Hawaii, where they cherish time with their children and grandchildren.

Rosemary is also the author of ***Miriam's World—and Mine,*** her second memoir of their beloved daughter Miriam Luby Wolfe, whom they lost on Pan Am 103 over Lockerbie, Scotland. Available from Rosemary, on Amazon.com, Kindle, and Nook.

E-mail the Milds at: <u>roselarry@magicile.com</u>

Visit them at: <u>www.magicile.com</u>